W9-CPZ-266

A WALTZ OF SIN AND FIRE SERIES: BOOK ONE

ΕΛΠΑΞ

THE
CROSSING
GATE

ASIEL R. LAVIE

Absolute Author
Publishing House

Absolute Author
Publishing House

THE CROSSING GATE

Copyright © 2021 by Asiel R. Lavie

Printed in the United States of America.

Edited by Shalini Gopal, Ellie Firestone
Cover Design by Sara Oliver
Map Illustrations by Alaa' Al-Hazaimeh

Library of Congress Cataloging-in-Publication Data
Lavie, R., Asiel, author.

The Crossing Gate / Asiel R. Lavie—First edition.
pages cm
Summary: "In the kingdom of Elpax, juveniles must walk through the mysterious Crossing Gate to become adults—and seventeen-year-old Lenora is determined that her third attempt at crossing to adulthood will be successful"
—Provided by publisher.
ISBN (paperback) : 978-1-64953-264-0
ISBN (ebook) : 978-1-64953-265-7
ISBN (hardback) : 978-1-64953-266-4
[1. Women's fiction. 2. General fiction. 3. Fiction by a female author.]
First Edition: January 2022

Published by Absolute Author Publishing House

For all the half adults who faced injustice and struggled to survive.
For Lynn & Ryan

Please be aware that this book contains scenes of violence and sexual assault.

Alphatoli

Betis

Inferos Prison

Própodas village

Orakros town

Theia Glass Factory

Ourea Southern Mountains

The Royal Palace

Mount Gaia

Theirna
"The Capital City"

Poseidone Lake

Vitoli

Gamotos

The Ionian Sea

Malum Forests

Apollo river

Delvoris

Hera Falls

Mount Maroon

Zetikas

Roses Hills

Zoiterra

The Crossing Gate

Elpax International Port

PART I

"THE INNOCENT"

All you need to live a normal life is a full third line . . .

PART I

CHAPTER 1

IF I CROSSED TO ADULTHOOD today, sin-spots would start appearing on my body whenever I committed a sin. Not that I was planning to become a sinner, but I wished I could learn more about them beforehand. Such a fateful decision would change my life forever.

"Curiosity is a sin," was my teachers' usual answer whenever I attempted to learn more about sins. It was Mom's response, too. If inquiring about them was considered a sin as well, then how could I avoid them in the first place?

The sound of the Ológramma—the holographic television in the living room—rose a bit, pulling me out of my dark thoughts, and the sweet aroma of Mom's herbal tea filled the air. She must have woken up. Soon, she would come to check if I had finished getting dressed. I turned to my closet and picked up the Crossing Day formal dress—a floor-length gown with short puffy sleeves, dazzling in its whiteness.

"Hurry, Lenora," Mom snapped as she shoved my bedroom door open. "It's almost eight. You can't be late for your Crossing Day."

Lenora ... she knew I never responded to that name, but the appellation wasn't my biggest problem at the moment. Crossing Day was.

"At your command." My fast words came out sharp. Yet, I couldn't help staring at her slim, pale face. It showed the remnants of her faded beauty, hidden by the hardships borne over her forty-two years. I gazed at her retreating shoulders and pondered the woes that had befallen her since her own Crossing Day.

Unsettling thoughts rushed through my mind. When had Mom's problems started? Was it when she fled with us from Betis to the Zetikas province? Or when the government revoked her medical license and changed our caste to the working-class?

I looked around at the bare essentials. The great sun of June's rays glittered over my single bed, ornate cabinet, and small desk. All of these structures were made of white steel. That was all the furniture I had in my room, and they weren't even really mine. Our half-furnished glasshouse was the only option we could rent from the island of Elpax—the Ionic Sea's only Greek kingdom, the place I called my homeland.

I grabbed the dress and wandered into the bathroom. After a quick cold bath, I rubbed my teeth with salty baking soda and brushed my long, silver-mint hair. I was one of the many Elpaxians with this hair color. As we learned in school, some families—including the royals—developed a genetic defect after World War III, which caused the color to appear.

Standing before the tall mirror, I scrutinized my dress from all angles, and misery drowned me. The dress looked like an elaborate wedding gown. White wasn't my color; I looked pale and washed out in it. With my hazel eyes and pale complexion, I needed darker colors to make myself stand out. I wanted to wear my normal jeans and a black T-shirt, but the rules forbade it. Our kingdom had rules for everything, from the random sin-spot checks performed by the Law Corps on adults to the regulation of knowledge for children and juveniles.

I took a deep breath and stepped into our living room, wearing the atrocious dress. Mom got up from the lone couch, her brown eyes scanning

2

me. "You look pretty."

A faint smile crossed my face at her compliment, especially since I wasn't wearing the slightest bit of makeup, but I knew her words were just a preface to the crux.

"Don't come back without a third line."

Ah! That was the one.

Mom fixed her gaze on my face for a while, her eyes stern enough for me to lower mine. She took a step closer and lifted my chin with her long fingers. "Lenora, I am expecting you to do the right thing today."

Despite Mom's stiff face, I discerned a hint of anxiety in her voice. I couldn't fault her fears. She wasn't sure if I would traverse the Crossing Gate today. I didn't know how to reassure her when I wasn't even sure what I would choose. I just wanted this day to be over.

I looked up at her eyes. We stared at each other for a long time. Long enough for me to realize that her words weren't just a simple request, but an order.

"At your command," I murmured. I glimpsed my left wrist's reflection in the mirror and sighed. Those two parallel black ID lines announced my phase of life to the world. When I was born—like every other child in the kingdom—a nurse put me in an automatic trolley that drove me through the Crossing Gate, and the first line appeared on my wrist as a sign of my childhood phase. At age eleven, I walked through the Crossing Gate into the adolescence phase, and the second line appeared alongside the first. We didn't have the choice to cross to adolescence, as we weren't mature enough to decide what was best for ourselves. We just did as the government commanded.

And now, at seventeen, for the first time, I had to make a decision that would affect my entire life.

Mom sat on the couch, following the live broadcast of the preparations for the Crossing Day ceremony. Hermes, the news broadcaster, was talking about how important crossing was for juveniles, as well as relating other news about the royal family that didn't concern me.

3

"Where are the twins?" I asked Mom, not having seen my sisters since I woke up.

"Still sleeping." She peeked at me. "Have you finished your portraits?"

"Yes, Mom. They're on my desk."

"How much will you earn?"

"*We*, Mom. *We* will earn around a hundred paxin."

"Still, not enough." She sighed.

I bit my lip, looking at her with sorrowful eyes. The government wouldn't allow young people to work until after their third crossing. *I mean, actual work*. But they made an exception for working-class juveniles. We could help our parents with light jobs—like housekeeping and babysitting—as long as there was an adult relative physically present in the same house while the juvenile performed their chores. With Mom's two jobs, my only option to help her with the housing expenses was painting portraits for the wealthy. The government considered art to be enough of a light pastime that working-class juveniles were allowed to create and sell creative work, even without their parents' home.

It wasn't enough, though.

A car horn honked several times outside. We turned to the floor-to-ceiling windows of the living room, where Mom had pulled aside the heavy white curtains earlier. Mary was out front in her fancy, bright copper car—a color her mom had chosen against Mary's wishes. I ran to the kitchen and poured some fresh orange juice for her.

"Bye, Mom." I stepped out of the main door and rushed through the small garden toward Mary's car. The wing door slid open as I approached.

"Glory, Mary." I handed her the cup.

"Nothing beats fresh orange juice on a warm June day." Her giggles were the brightest part of my morning. She took a big sip and gave the smart driving system the appropriate instructions. "Drive to the Crossing Gate."

"At your command, Lady Harisbryg," said a monotonous female voice. The car moved at once, cutting between the working-class's glasshouses,

4

which reflected the sunlight brilliantly. Most people were heading to work in the cork stopper factory, and tension filled the crowded streets. The Law Corps soldiers stood on the uneven, dusty roadside, wearing their distinctive silver uniforms and stiff faces, holding laser guns and other weapons. Many of their armored tanks rumbled along the roads, too. As usual.

"Leen, you don't look fine," said Mary.

At least my best friend called me by the nickname I'd chosen for myself, not the name my absentminded father had selected. Someone I never wanted to think about.

I turned to her and took in her appearance. Her shiny hair flowed down her back like a black waterfall, with a few strands falling on her pretty brown face. We'd met in the childhood school years ago. The orders of the late King Islabour Vasilas were explicit concerning the dilemma created by class differences. All students in the kingdom had to attend the same school, sit in the same classroom, and wear the same pale teal cotton uniform. The kingdom couldn't afford another civil war.

"Mary, would you close the car roof?" I asked, trying to hold my hair in place.

"Sure," Mary said with a sweet smile, and pressed the button. She turned on the *Zorba* music that comforted me. "Jason said he called you several times to wish you a successful crossing."

I narrowed my eyes and took my Iméfono out of my pocket to check. The translucent device looked like a foldable, flat pencil. It allowed me to call, text, and play music. Alas, it wasn't like the adults' version, which had a camera and a private web browser. I focused on the screen. Indeed, Jason had called. I switched off the silent mode and rested my head on the seat cushion.

"I can't understand Jason!" I said. "He's one year older and doesn't want to cross, yet he wants me to cross and even wishes me good luck with it?"

Mary's lips curved upward. I couldn't read her facial expression under her oversized dark sunglasses. "Leen, if my mother hadn't forced me to cross, I would have stayed in adolescence until my twentieth birthday."

She understood! But she didn't know everything. I couldn't tell her what had happened to me the past two years. People assumed I didn't want to cross, that I was scared of growing up, but none of them knew that I had good reason to be wary of going through the Crossing Gate. I had tried to cross twice in two years, but couldn't seem to step inside the gate. A frightful, unusual vertigo always forced my limbs to stop moving. Each time, I moved away quietly, without anyone knowing about my near blackout. And who would believe me if I told them?

Mary turned the music down. "Adulthood is great with—"

"All of its responsibilities."

We both laughed. Of course I knew how that line ended. We all did. The government burned it into our brains from childhood.

"Are you planning to attend college?" she asked.

"I want to, but I can hardly cope with school right now. I'm not as smart as you, studying . . . what's your major again?"

She giggled. "Sustainable energy." Her nose wrinkled a little. "But you draw very well. After your crossing, I suppose you can work in the factories and carve pottery statuettes—you'll earn much more doing that than painting portraits."

"I might do that, but I need to know more about what will happen if I cross." I closed my eyes, struggling to wipe the memory of my *sinner* father, and what he had done to Mom . . . to me.

"Well, you're about to find out everything. Just walk through the Crossing Gate."

I sighed, clutching my dress with nervous fingers. "What's the big secret? Everyone seems to hide something. I need an actual and concrete incentive that would be guaranteed to help with this stage's burdens. You know . . . the only thing I'm sure about is that Mom will force me to marry, and I can't avoid that fate for long."

Mary's face fell with a wry acceptance; there were few choices for the working-class girls. We sat in silence for a while, deep in our own thoughts. I looked up at the word-catcher that floated over our heads—a tiny but sensitive device that picked up any banned word spoken by an adult and attempted to explain the things prohibited to children and juveniles.

Mary pointed at it and whispered from the corner of her mouth, "I wish I could tell you more about adulthood, but I don't want to get in trouble. You know that saying even one word about it will send us to Inferos prison at once."

I nodded with understanding. She had told me once that she could dance around the words and write some answers, but what about the sin-spots that would appear on her body if the Law Corps investigated her?

It was a double-edged sword.

After half an hour, the road ahead widened, and oak trees appeared on the sidewalks leading to the Crossing Gate. Mary slowed the car; she wanted me to pull myself together before we arrived. The crossing guides' governmental vehicles, free working-class buses, and the Brazilian-made cars of the middle-class bypassed us, one after another.

"You know, Mary, I wish I could cross on my own without the loud noise and cameras everywhere, just like you did."

"Oh, but you can! That isn't an exceptional case just for the wealthy. The kingdom gives that right to the other classes. But . . . you know . . . It comes with a lot of conditions."

My eyes widened. I had never heard about a person from the working or middle-class crossing alone before! I wanted to ask her to return home so I could try to cross on a quiet day, but we had already approached the yard of the Crossing Gate.

I gulped.

It was an enormous square with a well-maintained lawn. To the right stood a shaded amphitheater for the friends of those who wanted to cross, with a special section for the wealthy. On the left was the royal family cabin. And in the middle were the shaded seats lined up for those who wished to cross. There was no fence of any kind around the area. I guessed the mounted security cameras on the Crossing Gate were enough to guard it.

Take a deep breath, Leen, I told myself. *Stop shaking, for God's sake.*

We drove between the groups of enthusiastic juveniles. Their eyes glittered with joy at the knowledge that they would soon grow up and learn everything about adulthood.

Mary parked in one of the wealthy's private spots. "Here we are," she said, getting out and turning to my door.

I crossed my arms, not wanting to get out yet. My heartbeat raced, and a million thoughts flooded my mind. I still didn't feel ready. I didn't want to face that condition ever again. I'd always heard that *facing your fears is the first step to healing.* It didn't sound true in my case, though. I tried to face that abnormal vertigo last year, thinking that I was exaggerating the first time I stopped in front of the Crossing Gate—but when the world spun around me for a second time, I knew I wasn't making it up.

"Come on, Leen. Time for you to leave adolescence and grow up." Mary tilted her head and extended her palm, waiting.

I stared at her face for a while. My loyal friend, who had always been there for me since that day in school when she fell into the mud during gym class. She'd been crying, and I suggested exchanging uniforms so she could avoid her mother's brutal punishment.

She wouldn't encourage me to do something harmful . . .

I closed my eyes to gather my strength, then squeezed Mary's hand and got out, standing beside her. She was tall as a branch of moringa, but not as thick. We were the opposites of each other. Her tall and curvy body clashed with my slim and . . . not so tall one.

Mary waved her hand toward the path leading to the Crossing Gate yard. "After you, Lady Evgenís."

I poked her side, and we giggled while walking between the kingdom's flags, which waved in the wind.

"The land of peace and hope, ladies and gentlemen," Mary said, pointing at the flags. "Look at you. A true citizen, matching the kingdom's colors!"

8

I laughed at her joke, looking at the tricolored flags marked with the kingdom's official shades. A white background and a silver metallic peacock whose feathers were spread behind it with pride, surrounded by an arch representing the Crossing Gate. Below the image, written in shiny teal Greek letters, was the kingdom's name: ΕΛΠΑΞ.

As we walked farther down the path, I saw the Crossing Gate behind the crowd in the middle of the square, and my heart skipped a beat. There it stood in solemn dignity, waiting for me.

It was a three-meter-high passageway through a path of tangled flowers which stretched longer than our living room. I still didn't get why it took an entire minute to cross it.

The passageway's history had always been shrouded with secrets. Some said the government had built it with advanced technology. Grandma told me it had magical powers. No one knew for sure how complex it was. Or how much energy emanated from it. Or how it affected our bodies and perception.

Was it just a symbol for getting older, or did it really control our maturity? It was a mystery.

The royal guards in their teal uniforms were stationed every few meters along the path to the gate. The incomprehensible static sounds coming from their wireless devices didn't stop for a moment. Mary pointed at the tables kept in front of the gate for identification and registration. I turned to her and fidgeted with my skirt.

"I'll be here the whole time," she assured me with a gentle touch on my hand.

I looked around at the vast, crowded place. Gathering my courage, I walked toward the table, which was festooned with the words *The Third Crossing*.

I stood in the lengthy line designated for females. My feet shuffled forward as my thoughts turned to the past. I remembered my Crossing Day from childhood to adolescence. How I'd jumped with joy because the crossing meant I could move to a school where I'd be allowed to choose some of my courses. But my pleasure had dimmed when I took the introductory adolescence courses and learned about things like lying, racism, execution, and deception. That was a world I never wanted to live in.

"Next!" yelled a stern-looking brunette employee, and I jumped a step backward. "What are you waiting for?"

I walked closer to her with a deep breath, and she scanned my identity lines with a small device. All my information appeared on a transparent smartboard in front of her. "Lenora Santos Evgenís, daughter of Yorra Karakas, your guide is Otis Barros." She pointed to a chunky man with black-framed glasses sitting on the opposite side of the table.

I nodded and stepped out of the line, heading toward him.

In front of Mr. Barros were a few juveniles, chatting with each other. I recognized some girls from my town, but the rest were strangers. My neighbor Danira smiled and broke from the group. As she headed over, her warm voice reached me.

"Aren't you excited?" Her green eyes shimmered.

I nodded. Not a single word escaped my lips.

Danira held my hand and walked me over to the group. Her eyes turned to the holographic image that stretched across the sky, recounting the live broadcast for the ceremony. "Looks like Prince Thaddeus will attend today's ritual, as always," said Danira, her focus still on the program. "He looks creepy."

I looked up to where Hermes was showing a picture of Prince Thaddeus II. He was the kingdom's prime minister—a tall and foreboding figure with a thin, angular face and silver-mint hair slicked back. His sharp cheekbones and black eyes stood out, and his lips appeared forever compressed in annoyance. Danira was right. He looked evil and imposing from most angles.

"I guess so," I mumbled.

Each of the six provinces of the kingdom had their own scheduled day for crossing to the next phase, regardless of the class of the people crossing. While some of the wealthy, like Mary, could opt to cross another time, the vast majority of people crossed on the predetermined date. The royal family attended all the Crossing Days of Vitoli province, because most of the wealthy lived there in the capital, Theirna. They never showed up for Crossing Days in other provinces. Except ours.

"Their decrees make little sense." I shrugged, thinking about how unusual it was that Prince Thaddeus had never missed a Crossing Day in Zetikas. I always wondered why our province was so important to him.

"You know, Mom told me that things were better during King Stavros's rule," Danira hissed, looking around her. "Power has corrupted everyone since he died."

I narrowed my eyes and wanted to ask more about it, but the guide called her name. She let go of my hand and hurried to answer. I was next in line. Sweat dripped down my body, and the idea that the dizziness would hit me again in front of the gate terrified me.

The guide called my name as Danira was finishing her registration. Mr. Barros looked at the transparent smartboard in front of him as I walked closer. His eyebrows went up, and his face turned thoughtful. I knew what was on his mind.

"Lenora Evgenís, this is your third attempt, right?"

I bit my lower lip and hesitated to answer. The single question felt like the start of an interrogation.

He looked at me inquisitively.

"Yes." A drop of sweat ran down my neck.

"My duty is to make sure you feel mature enough and want to cross over. So, are you sure this time? Do you want to cross to the adult phase today?"

Sure wasn't the right word. Part of me wanted to cross, but the other part refused. I knew that damn vertigo would force me to fall right before I could step inside the Crossing Gate. It was a frightening experience that I wished I would never go through again. Maybe it wouldn't happen this time, but could I take that chance? What was the correct answer?

My eyes turned around to the Law Corps, to the cameras broadcasting the ceremony, to the Crossing Gate. My breath quickened. It felt like everyone was staring at me . . . as if I was walking around without clothes.

"I'm ready," I mumbled with uncertainty, afraid of what would come of a path I knew so little about. But I had to say that, since I was sure Mom was watching the ceremony at home like everyone else.

How nerve-wracking!

Mr. Barros stared at me from above his eyeglasses. "If you don't want to cross today, you can postpone it till next year."

I bit my lip again and glanced away, wishing I had the power to become invisible and escape from this place.

"Miss, don't force yourself. You can postpone it until your twentieth birthday. The royal orders are explicit in this matter."

"But—"

"The cameras aren't able to broadcast our conversation. If one of your parents is forcing you to cross over, they won't know what we're talking about. That's the whole point of preventing them from attending the ceremony."

My heartbeat sped up. I wanted to go back home, but Mom would welcome me with loud, violent screaming or icy coldness. I didn't want to face either. She'd never hit me before, but I guessed backing out yet again might break her control.

"I have one question," I said.

He waved for me to continue.

"Sins, Sir. What counts as a sin?"

"Ah." He took off his eyeglasses. "They are the same things you already learned after your second crossing."

I knew that. Killing was a sin. Greed was a sin. But I was asking about the other things that no one talked about. The ones that would land me up in Inferos. My eyes told him what I was thinking.

"Don't worry about sin-spots," he said, leaning his elbow on the table. "After you cross, you'll receive a list with all the sins that would scatter sin-spots on your body. Most of them you would never commit." He put on his eyeglasses again. "Make up your mind and come back again when you're ready. Next!"

I was clouded in an abyss of turmoil. At that moment, I wanted to leave. But a wise voice inside me hissed, *if you back out now, who will help your mom with her onerous duties?*

True . . . who would? Father wasn't around, and the burdens of life caused most of the working-class to marry after their third crossing just to share the living expenses. Mom didn't want to remarry, so she went about working two jobs and looking after the family. I was her only current hope of helping with the financials. Now, having been reassured about the sin-spots by Mr. Barros, there was only one problem: the damn abnormal dizziness.

But Mom wouldn't understand. She would think I was pretending to be dizzy. She would tell me I wasn't being responsible, and the last thing I wanted was to disappoint her. She was the one who had looked after me ever since I could remember.

The girl behind me came closer and started passing me. With a sweep of my arm, I stopped her.

"I want to cross," I said to Mr. Barros before I realized how rude I was. I peeked at the girl and whispered, "Sorry." She nodded with understanding and stepped behind me.

"As you wish." He shook his head in contemplation. His fingers tapped on the smartboard, and he added without looking at me, "I wrote your name. Once you have a successful crossing, you must take bus number eight to attend the introductory courses for the adult phase."

I acquiesced and glanced at the large buses behind the Crossing Gate. My name appeared on the display of bus number eight, which doubled my tension. I forgot to thank Mr. Barros, and I rushed to the chairs where the rest of the girls sat. I took the seat behind Danira, and I looked around, searching for Mary in the wealthy section. She waved at me and I waved back. Her bright smile relieved my tension a bit.

Soon after the last guide finished recording the final crosser's name, the identification and guiding tables moved away automatically, and the five guides lined up to the right of the Crossing Gate. Journalists remained ready with their cameras, and the military music cranked up.

"All rise," a voice announced. Everyone stood at once when the queen mother—Arianna—appeared in the royal cabin, accompanied by her retinue. She was followed by Queen Olympia, the king's wife.

That was weird! I thought Prince Thaddeus would attend. It was unusual for either of the queens to show up, let alone both of them.

The conceited broadcaster, Hermes, descended in the elevator from the high cabin, wearing a teal suit adorned with white peacock feathers. He strutted along with a puffed chest until he arrived in front of the Crossing Gate. He looked around, taking in all the people, then approached the microphone and spoke through his smug smile. "Glory to Elpax and Queen Arianna Vasilas. To Queen Olympia Vasilas. To Elpax and its brave citizens. Glory to a kingdom that even the 'Modern Roman Empire' couldn't conquer, despite its relentless endeavors. To every martyr who defended his homeland. Glory to you, juveniles. Let your crossing today be successful and blessed." Hermes lifted his left arm, extending his fist to show his ID wrist lines. Then, he exclaimed in a firm voice, "Glory to Elpax and its brave citizens."

I raised my arm like everyone else, and the crowd shouted, "Glory, glory!"

I didn't make any sound as I moved my lips. No one would hear my voice in this crowd, anyway. Everyone fell into silence until the national anthem finished playing.

"Well," said Hermes, "let's start with our first guide, Mr. Otis Barros."

Mr. Barros approached the electronic box on the left side of the Crossing Gate. He extended his wrist to the flashing red light to get his own identity scanned. After a soft beep, I heard a monotonous female voice.

14

"Identify yourself."

"The guide, Otis Barros. Zetikas province. Third crossing."

"Identification successful."

The interwoven branches of the passageway spread to the sides, and even their gentle movement increased my heart rate. The distinctive smell of wet wood fed the atmosphere and overshadowed the scent of grass and flowers. The branches unveiled a long passageway with wooden floors and light flooding in from the other end.

Mr. Barros looked at his smartboard for a while, waiting until the program picked a random name for the first crosser. Silence prevailed, but if anyone was listening carefully, they could have heard my galloping heartbeat. *It's okay*, I told myself, trying to calm down. This time, I would try not to remember what my father had done to us, and I would focus on one thing only: my mom. I wanted her to be proud of me. If I kept my mind clear, then I would cross normally, and I wouldn't feel the dizziness that stopped me cold the past two times I tried to cross. With all these boys and girls, this crossing process would take at least a few hours, and by the time they called my name, I would be rea—

"Lenora Santos Evgenís."

The name shot into my heart like a lightning bolt, and my throat dried at once. My eyes widened, looking at Mr. Barros. He looked back at me, waiting. Everyone followed his gaze and turned to me. My paled face was projected across the sky.

The entire kingdom was watching me now.

"Come on," Hermes said with a smirk. "Don't be shy."

Danira smiled and waved at me to go forward. I got up and dragged my feet toward the gate with the light gleaming at its other end. One of the word-catcher floated above my head, its noise increasing my fear. With a rising trepidation, I stood in front of the entrance. I peeked at one of the cameras as the guide next to me spoke. "Your journey starts now. You are on your own. Good luck."

I could hear the sensor's beep as a red line flashed on the ground a

15

few centimeters away from the Crossing Gate's entrance. My raging breaths sped up, and the halo of light in the passageway widened, becoming brighter with each second, as if it was seeking me out to swallow me whole.

That's it. There's no going back to my safe zone.

I took a deep, shaky breath. My feet moved to step inside the gate, but a wave of terrible dizziness knocked me to the ground. Oh, God, not again! Why was this happening? My limbs spasmed, and something in me whispered, *don't cross.*

I closed my eyes to fight the darkness, and the murmured words escaped under my breath as I forced myself to my feet. "I don't want to cross."

"What was that, Miss Evgenís?"

I turned around. My panic rose and threatened to seize my throat. Everyone was staring at me, their eyes carrying an open challenge, the unspoken accusations mocking me. Numbness took over my body, and the universe spun. I knew I was shoving myself into untold trouble when the tremulous words escaped me. My body became disjointed as I screamed on national television for millions to witness.

"I don't want to cross. I said, I don't want to CROSS!"

16

CHAPTER 2

COMPLETE SILENCE REIGNED ACROSS THE yard as I stood there crying with faint sobs, head bent.

Mr. Barros grasped my shoulder, his fingers covering the tiny microphone on his suit. "It is fine. Don't cry," he whispered, looking at the approaching medics. "Do you want a wheelchair to drive you in?"

I shook my head. I didn't have a medical insurance for this luxury, and besides, I was so shaky and scared that I didn't want anything related to the crossing. I might pass out if they tried to wheel me in there. I just needed to vanish. To stop existing, or to leave . . . leave to any place on the planet.

"Don't worry. You can try again next year." He gave an encouraging smile.

I nodded several times, enough to make me feel dizzier.

Mr. Barros patted my shoulder and yelled into his mic, "Let's resume!"

I breathed a sigh, so glad that he didn't comment on my behavior any further. I turned around to leave the square. All the girls and boys were up on their feet, their scornful stares scanning me. The sneers made my fingers tremble again. Some were laughing and shaking their heads at the spectacle I'd caused. Even Danira wore a look of disapproval. *Why has Mr. Barros not prepared a statement to soften the blow in cases like this? I can't be the only one who's ever had this problem.*

I cast my eyes to the royal box. Among the curious nobles, Queen Arianna's sharp green eyes scrutinized me, and a weird speculative expression appeared on her pretty face. Queen Olympia was on her feet, her hand covering her mouth. I didn't want to decipher what all that meant; I just wanted to escape.

Three men from the ruthless Law Corps approached and enclosed me in a loose circle. My heart skipped a beat, as I thought they would arrest me, but they didn't touch me. One of them waved me ahead without a word. I walked with them, skulking my way through the crowd, and kept my head down to avoid the petty, ridiculing stares. The whispers soon filled the air. "A stupid, fragile girl!" was what I heard and chose to ignore. But my heart didn't, and tears filled my eyes. How frustrating and painful it was that people who hadn't lived my life were judging me. They didn't understand the suffering I was going through. My inability to cross wasn't a weakness or an excuse.

At that very moment, I made my decision. I wouldn't let anyone or anything decide how I should live my life. Not Mom, not Mary or Danira, and certainly not Danira's mother, who used to make fun of me whenever I climbed the oak tree in our garden.

That was it. Here, I would draw the line. I'd work around the clock to make ends meet, but there would be no crossing until I felt ready. Absolutely ready.

At the edge of the grounds, the Law Corps soldiers allowed me to go, and I ran to the nearest bus station. In my anxiety to escape, I heard Mary calling my name from behind. I didn't want to see the censure in her eyes, so I ignored her too. Her steps soon closed in on me, and she grabbed my arm. "Wait!"

I turned to her, waiting for her next words.

The air turned cold between us. I looked up at the clouds that had gathered, which blocked most of the sun's rays.

An ironic smile spread on my face. *Even you, the glorious sun of June, couldn't impose your power on a handful of evaporated water!*

"It's your third attempt!" Mary's harsh tone brought my gaze back to her face. She rolled her eyes skyward, sounding exasperated. "When, Leen?"

I jutted my chin out. "When I wish." I shook off her hand and ran far away from the gate of my nightmares.

As I walked away from the crossing yard, my Iméfono rang over and over. Mom called, and so did Jason. I switched it off, wanting to escape Mom's harsh words. My plan hadn't included disappointing her, but I appeared to have done so anyway. It was just too difficult to deal with all her accusations at the moment. I needed time to think. I'd wanted to take the bus home, but missing the free bus ride by just one minute overwhelmed me even more. The day was turning worse by the second. As if it had been waiting for me to think that, thunder cracked, followed by lightning, and the sky started pouring water down on me.

Oh no!

I wasn't a *rain* person. It seemed that whenever a drop of it touched my skin, my entire body became weaker. Only the sun's rays gave my bones strength and brought peace to my mind. The same sun that had let me down today.

With two puffs from my bronchodilator, I was ready to run. I lifted the silly dress up, and my feet flew over the grass and stones as my lungs strained. If there was anything special about me, it was my speed. When I ran against the boys in my childhood school, I always beat them. But blessings always came with a price. Mine was asthma and nosebleeds.

It took me ten minutes to arrive at the station, and by then I was completely drenched. My feet were burning up, and my soaked dress stuck

20

to my body. I climbed down the stairs and made my way to the nearest cash deposit machines scattered inside the crowded hall. Trying to ignore all the people staring at my appearance, I extended my left wrist to the ID scanner and deposited my money. A red light flashed over my wrist lines, and the low iron barriers twisted to allow me in. With quick steps, I reached the train on time.

I entered the train's automated doors and sat in the first empty seat in the juvenile section, hoping no one would sit next to me. As the train traveled from the underground station toward Zoiterra city, I opened my Iméfono and leaned my head on the window, pondering everything that had happened today.

It was a day of emotions. I felt like I had gone through a wringer and been left to dry. I had nothing else to give. Crossing Day was always especially difficult for me.

The train's display was broadcasting the Crossing Day ceremony. It was Danira's turn by now, and everyone in the yard clapped at her successful crossing. I sighed, staring at the Crossing Gate on the screen. Why should we cross? Did all the people from other lands have to cross to become an adult? I mean . . . how did this gate come to Elpax in the first place?

My family couldn't afford to travel. And even if we could, the government only allowed adults to travel out of the kingdom—just for a short time. But who would want to leave the land of peace and hope anyway? Elpax was the only region that survived the Modern Roman Empire's invasion.

As we had learned in school, our island was around 50,000 kilometers in area, incredibly high above sea level, and surrounded by steep cliffs with sharp rocks that formed a natural barrier around the whole kingdom—except for the far north side near the Malum forest. The kingdom's five million people were scattered across six different provinces. Most of us were Greek, with a few foreign tribes living in the Alphatoli desert.

"Glory to Elpax and its honorable citizens. The next stop is the Victory Station."

The Victory Station reminded me of the war it was erected in remembrance of—The Brazen War, World War III. It started in Gaul—which used to be France—in 2026, around 120 years ago. It was ruthless, wiping countries and civilizations off the map. The human race barely survived, along with some technology they had back then, and people from other countries in Europe and the Middle East came here to seek asylum.

From the start of the war, Elpax was a neutral kingdom, and King Giannis Vasilas welcomed all refugees. He died a few months after the war started, and his sixteen-year-old son, King Proximo, came into power.

Realizing that the resources necessary for a pleasant quality of life were diminishing, King Proximo closed the borders to all, except the wealthy who brought trade and finance to the kingdom. The rich came from all over the world—Russia, Asia, North America—and most of them stayed in Theirna, the capital in Vitoli's province.

After the war ended, the Modern Roman Empire arose from the devastation, seizing hold of Asia's organic energy resources. The Empire brought many countries under their direct control, making Latin their national language and changing the cities' names back to the old ones—except for Rome, their capital. They discovered a high level of technology that they only used within their borders.

During the rule of the late King Islabour, son of King Proximo, the Roman Empire, true to its old ways, started eyeing Elpax. The attack started from the lowest point of the kingdom in the Malum Forests. The history lessons in school stated that the citizens fought alongside the army without fearing death, and Caesar of the Modern Roman Empire had to sign a peace treaty with Elpax after he lost thousands of his men.

I was wondering why the Law Corps became so ubiquitous after the war had ended when the beep of an incoming text from Mary roused me.

Girl, where are you? Come on. I'll drive you home.

I was at once ashamed of how rude I'd been to her; she was my best friend, and we always took care of each other, no matter what. I looked out the window. It was still raining, and the train was just about to reach the next station. We'd arrived at the largest city in Zetikas province, Zoiterra, where most of the middle class lived in organized towers.

Outside of the Victory Station. I'm not sure what the name of the street is. It's a new place for me. I'll text you again when I find out.

I disembarked and waited outside the station, away from the rain. I looked at the bustling markets on every corner of the broad, clean road. The people gleamed in their formal suits, and the air had the same luxurious odor as Mary's car, mixed with the refreshing smell of earth after rain. All of this made for a radical contrast with my small town, Roses Hill.

The billboard screens were still broadcasting the Crossing Gate yard, and Hermes's voice filled the city's streets. I walked for a few steps to explore the area before I huffed, realizing where I was. How ironic was that? To escape crossing into adulthood just to find myself on the adult street?

The street name was Icarus 69. The major adult street in every city and town was named Icarus. Number six referred to Zetikas province, and number nine to Zoiterra city. Juveniles and children could walk around, but could not enter the shops with an "Adults Only" signboard. All the buildings here had a security camera with an ID reader on their front doors.

I never understood what adults could buy that we juveniles couldn't. Like all other houses, our house had a small windowless room inside my parents' room, where they kept the adult stuff. It could only be opened with a parent's ID. One day, Mom accidentally left its door ajar, and I sneaked a glimpse into it. It contained a single bed, an oldOlógramma, and a closet. I had no time to search the drawers before she came back.

I texted Mary the street's name and looked at the shops, trying to guess what they contained. A pink storefront with a lace ribbon seemed to be for women. Then the blue must be for men. The sign showing a bottle with a glass indicated a shop that sold the "adult drink"—the one my father used to buy and become dazed after drinking.

I hadn't yet figured out some symbols, such as harem pants, an apple with a chiffon tie around it, a pink arrow, and a rainbow flag. What did they symbolize? What would happen if I looked inside one of those shops?

23

Perhaps getting a peek at adult life would help me fight the dizziness during my next crossing, to show my stupid brain that crossing wasn't so scary after all.

I walked to the store with a pink apple on it. All I needed was a peek—just one. As I approached, I noticed the flashing writing on the door. "Curiosity is a sin." I rolled my eyes and put my ear to the door. There was the sound of music and men's voices. They were yelling numbers as if they were fighting to buy something. I could hear one woman laughing, and another moaning.

What the hell was going on in there?

"Juvenile!" yelled a man's voice from inside, and I jumped a step backward. "Go away before I call the Corps."

For sure, my crossing dress told him who I was with no further investigation required. I sighed. I wished Mary could answer my queries about these shops. If only the pesky word-catchers would allow her to.

What if we had a code that she could use to tell me? Why had I never thought about that before? A code was an excellent idea. How would the government ever find out?

Oh, right, the sin-spots investigation would tell them.

I turned around, searching for Mary, and soon her car pulled up beside me. We both looked at each other and burst out laughing.

"Mary!" I exclaimed as I sat in her car, my eyes scanning her dripping hair that soaked her green shirt. "How did you get so wet?"

"How do you think? Running after you, trying to make my voice heard in the thunder and lightning," she quipped.

"I'm sorry for ignoring you, Mary. It felt like everyone's sarcastic words were following me." I touched her hand in apology.

She squeezed my fingers. "Don't worry about it. In fact, I owe you an apology. You weren't ready, and I pushed you to cross." She started the engine. "Now, are you ready for the big day tomorrow?"

"What day?"

"My wedding, silly! Have you forgotten already?"

"Of course not." My heart sank in shame. I hadn't even remembered Mary's wedding with all my worries about my crossing. My hand reached my eyes, rubbing them. "I still don't know what drives a sensible person to marry. You don't need his money!"

"Leen, we cannot limit the purpose of marriage to money, and I can't talk more about it." She smiled. "All I can say is he's a kind man."

"I'm happy for you, my friend. But for me? I will never cross for that reason."

Mary was about to take off, but the Law Corps' armored cars showed up out of nowhere, blocking our way. I gulped. Did the man from inside the adult shop call them already?

Apparently, I wasn't the target. The cars stopped across the street, followed by a ground mobility vehicle, its weapon pointed at a group of women. Soldiers rushed out of the car. They held riot shields and long metal bars.

"Selene Dukasi. You are under arrest."

Her picture showed on some of the tower's billboard screens. The rest of the women stepped aside at once, leaving their friend shaking with fear. She ran as fast as possible, but the soldiers followed and knocked her down.

"I did nothing, I said I did nothing!" she yelled, resisting the soldiers, who started beating her up with their bars. My eyes widened with horror—yet, people in the street ignored what was happening and continued walking on. I stepped out of the car right away.

"What are you doing?" Mary shouted from inside. "Get in the car!"

But I did the exact opposite. My feet bolted across the street toward the woman, who curled up on the ground, bleeding. The soldiers were beating her while other female soldiers surrounded them, forming a human barrier, preventing anyone from coming closer.

"Juvenile, do not interfere!" a blonde soldier cried out. Her solemn face burned with anger, and all the female soldiers raised their bars at once to stop me.

"They're killing her!" I said, my feet pacing continuously as I tried to

25

reach the woman on the floor. "Stop it . . . please . . . stop it!"

"Juvenile, this is your last warning!" she yelled, and all the soldiers hit the ground hard with their heavy boots, ready to beat me up too. Although their orders didn't allow them to touch juveniles, their solemn faces showed the determination to do so. I fought my eagerness to kick them, but this was a fight I couldn't possibly win; they might arrest me too if a high ranked soldier ordered them to. My helpless eyes turned to the woman. She was moaning with anguish, and blood splattered on the ground and soaked her clothes. It was a scene that would haunt my dreams for the rest of my life.

How long would women keep suffering at the hands of the ruthless Law Corps? They never bothered to arrest men this way, as far as I knew.

Amid this chaos, one of the male soldiers stepped out of the armored car. My heart sank into my legs as I noticed his teal uniform replete with silver military medals attached to its lapel. He was a high ranked general.

The general approached me with measured steps, holding a small device and pointing at my ID lines.

He wanted to know who I was.

CHAPTER 3

"ARE YOU CRAZY?" YELLED MARY, grabbing my shoulder from behind. "Come with me."

"Miss!" exclaimed the general, his solid face twisted in rage as he reached for me.

Mary snapped, "She's with me." She pointed at her car.

The general apologized at once and backed away. He shot me one last glare before he turned around toward the woman, tightening his lips.

Ah, the power of the wealthy!

Mary practically dragged me to her car. I walked with shaky limbs—my brain couldn't comprehend how to act. That was the first time I had seen the arresting process. *I mean, ever.* As I sat in Mary's car, my eyes turned to the woman on the ground.

"Leen, you know that we can't, under any circumstances, interfere in the governmental business. That's the number one rule. Your mom has been teaching you that since you uttered your first word, right?"

"Why this brutality?" They were the only words that escaped my dry lips. My arms wrapped around my body, trying to stop it from trembling. My eyes still turned back to the Law Corps, who were carrying the woman to their armored car.

"One of two possible reasons," said Mary, her face strained. "Either she messed with the royal family, or she said something about the adult's world to a child or a juvenile. Regardless of the reason, we should *not* get in their damn way." With that, she started driving toward my home.

Both of us stayed quiet for the rest of our journey. We had seen a harsh truth about the reality of our lives. The kingdom was brutal in its laws and their execution.

Had it always been like this? Danira said things used to be different. What made the kingdom change? The Brazen War? Or the civil war? Were women's lives like this before the war?

A change needed to come, but who would bring that about?

It was around 2:00 p.m. when I arrived home. Flowers and colored ribbons decorated the entrances of many houses in the neighborhood to greet the juveniles who had crossed today. But not mine. I didn't know if Mom decorated ours and took it off before my arrival to avoid the neighbors' cynical comments about my breakdown. Or perhaps she didn't bother with the unnecessary luxury. At the moment, I didn't care. I was still disturbed by what had happened an hour ago.

I took a deep breath to fortify myself for Mom's mood. My ID lines touched the control sensor, causing the main door to slide aside, and a short, distinctive melody sounded. I sighed. These doors announced my entry to our neighbors—quite impossible to escape from. What a pity!

Clearly having waited for this moment, Danira's mother looked over from her garden, her narrow brown eyes gazing at me. "Well, well. It looks like the princess backed out again." She smirked, enjoying teasing me.

This woman always kept prying into my business. During her short, snappy visits, I'd heard her whispering to Mom that I would never grow up as polite as the other girls, and no one would marry me. Unfortunately, Mom never stopped her or placed boundaries on her. And Mom was strict about my manners, preventing me from responding with even a single word. But I couldn't handle it anymore.

"Glad I didn't disappoint you," I replied, and shut the door behind me. That was my best answer at the moment. After crossing into the adult phase, I would have had the right to tell her it was none of her business and that she shouldn't stick her nose into my affairs. I smiled at that thought. Perhaps that was the bright side of the crossing.

"Lenora, is that you?" My mother's voice came from the kitchen. I looked around our simple living room; Sarah and Moria weren't there. I swallowed. Did she send the girls somewhere so she could yell at me, or worse, hit me?

"Yes." I rushed to my room, closed the door behind me, and sat on the floor, praying that Mom would forget all about me. My eyes stared at the floor-to-ceiling windows. There were no curtains; Mom couldn't find the extra money for them. Or maybe it was her way of avoiding the morning battle of waking me up for school. The sun never bothered me. In fact, watching the shaft of light illuminating the dancing motes of dust was relaxing.

Alas, just when I was thinking Mom would go with the "icy coldness" attitude, her footsteps approached my room. She knocked not on the door but on my heart, scarier than my darkest nightmares.

"Lenora." Her voice filtered through the closed door.

"Please, Mom," I beseeched her. "I need to sleep."

She paused for a moment. "How about a warm bath?"

Her words jolted me. This wasn't Mom's usual way. Throughout the return journey, I had been dreading Mom's response in the back of my mind. I thought she would scream in my face and deliver a stern speech about me being an irresponsible girl, asking me to grow up. But this kindness was most unexpected. After a deep breath, I got up and opened the door.

"Oh, my sweet lord!" she said, looking at my soaked dress. "Do you want to get pneumonia?" An expression akin to worry flitted across her face, just for an instant, before her practical nature took over. "I don't have enough money for IV medicines if you get sick. Just relax in the warm bath until lunch."

I nodded, and she left my room.

The sound of shuffling outside my door reached my ears. A blond head tilted in, and blue eyes found me. I gestured for the shadow to come closer. Her lips curved into a smile at my grin.

"Hi, Sarah."

My sister's smile spread wide enough to fill her beautiful face, giving it a glow of happiness—yet, she didn't respond. She didn't talk much, unlike her twin, Moria, who never ceased to talk, even during her sleep. Sometimes, when Moria's dreams got too vocal, Sarah would sneak into my room to sleep on the other side of my bed—not too close, though. Because the government always told us that we would get a fatal disease if we got too close to each other. We always limited physical contact to handshakes or squeezes. Even when Mom wanted to lift up my sisters when they were children, she always kept a fair distance between them.

"Where were you?" I asked.

"At Karya's, playing." Sarah glimpsed the tattoo above my wrist and smiled at me again before she left the room. I sighed, knowing what she had in mind. Two ID lines. And a third wouldn't accompany them for a long time now.

Half an hour later, Mom raised her voice, calling us for lunch. I got out of the bath and rushed to put on my pink pajamas before she started screaming our names. Loud voices still startled me. They took me back to the unfortunate childhood days when my parents quarreled for the

29

slightest of reasons.

At the kitchen's circular dining table, I sat without a sound, while Sarah and Moria scrambled into their chairs with plenty of fuss to sit next to me.

"Electricity and water prices have both gone up," Mom announced, pouring the red lentil soup into our bowls. "Bathing is now allowed only twice a week."

"At your command," we all replied, and sipped the soup. I didn't lift my eyes off my plate for the next few minutes until a single question pierced the silence at the table.

"Leen, why didn't you cross today?"

My throat dried up at Moria's words. She was the more inquisitive of the twins, and she matched Sarah in every way except when it came to thinking before she spoke.

"Hush! It isn't the right time to ask that," explained my clever Sarah.

"When is, then?"

My cheeks burned from resentment. There was a direct path from Moria's thought to her tongue, and she never stopped to analyze. I cast a glance at Mom, who turned to the window, avoiding my stare.

"Not today." A familiar dread rose in my body, knowing that my words might be the spark that would ignite Mom's fuse. I didn't want to quarrel, but I needed to reaffirm that I was not going to cross until I was ready. What surprised me was that she didn't comment.

"Why? I pity Karya, because she was forced to cross after her twentieth birthday, and everyone is still bullying her for that reason."

Moria had a point. Karya suffered from a furious blast of propaganda against her because she missed her last chance to cross, and the government assumed she was starting a rebellion against crossing. The citizens agreed out of fear that Karya had to be punished. Even after the authorities made her cross, our community never treated her the same.

"Oh, I can't believe that I've got to wait two years until I cross into adolescence," added Moria.

I looked at her bright nine-year-old features—so enthusiastic about growing up—and a bittersweet smile stretched across my face. I almost asked her why she wanted to cross. I didn't know much about adulthood yet, but it was enough that it had many trials. There was no play, only responsibilities. No innocence, only experience. No peace of mind, only an uproar in one's world.

My doubts came from Mom's past. She used to live in the capital with her parents, enjoying the middle-class's exclusive benefits until she met my father at a party. He was a working-class musician from the Própodas village. I never understood why Mom insisted on marrying him. A middle-class woman marrying a worker was rare, and it caused a furor in her family. Despite the complicated governmental marriage decree, which prevented people from marrying outside their class with only a few exceptions, she went through with it and moved to his village in the Betis province. But Father soon changed and started beating her up.

I recalled Mom's categorical decision to end that farce of marriage when the abuse had begun to affect us children. She rushed to the court at the Palace of Justice, the only way a woman could hope to get a divorce in Elpax. Even though she had no special immunity like the wealthy, she ran straight into the courtroom. The Law Corps held her, preventing her from approaching the judge without permission.

"Look at her bruises." Mom pointed at me. "He keeps hitting my child. I don't want a paxin of his money. If you don't divorce me from him, I will rid the earth of his soul by any means!" She yelled the words from her spot with determination born out of years of abuse. I was nine years old, and at that moment, I didn't understand how she planned to get rid of my father's soul.

Her frozen palm held my little hand, and she walked out of the hall. The tapping of her simple shoes still echoed in my mind whenever I thought of that day. My heart had been beating so fast. As a child, I was aware of the "contempt of court" term, and I couldn't help fearing they would arrest her for that reason—or worse, because she brought a child to the adult court with her.

I didn't want to marry a man like my father. I didn't want my children to face the same fate.

But I wanted to help Mom support our family.

Yet, all the unfamiliar terms I had learned in adolescence about killing and treason and other terrible things made me wonder . . . were there more of these things in the adult world? Maybe that was why seeing the Crossing Gate made me feel so dizzy.

But Mary seemed happy after her crossing—and other girls did too. It seemed that I was the only one in the kingdom who got dizzy and couldn't cross. Or maybe I wasn't mature enough, not yet. But I didn't know how to grow up, how to feel ready. Simultaneously, even if I wanted to cross, something was preventing me from stepping inside the Crossing Gate.

I needed to find out more about adulthood. I needed to know if anything in this world made it worth leaving my safe zone so early. I needed to start searching for answers, but how could I do that when nobody was saying a word about adulthood?

The sound of a car stopping in front of our home interrupted my thoughts. We looked at the floor-to-ceiling windows, and my face blanched.

"In my room, both of you," said Mom to the twins, who hurried out of the kitchen. I swallowed, looking at the Law Corps soldiers stepping out of their armored car.

"I'll call Jason for help," I whispered, and Mom hurried to open the door for the soldiers.

"Glory to Elpax, Mrs. Karakas," a blond solid-faced man said, his green eyes checking me.

"Glory, sir." She swiped her hands on her dress. "Please come in."

I held my Iméfono, trying to remember how to use it, as the man looked right into my eyes and stepped inside our humble living room, followed by another five soldiers.

32

CHAPTER 4

"MAY I SPEAK TO YOUR daughter, Mrs. Karakas?"

Mom nodded. She looked at me as I dragged my trembling feet closer to where the Law Corps soldier was standing.

He gestured for me to sit on the couch. His solemn green eyes turned to Mom. "Alone."

My heartbeat sped up as I sat, and I exchanged a tense look with Mom, sending her a silent message not to leave me alone with these monsters.

"Can I get you something to drink, sir?" Mom asked, rubbing her hands together, while I texted Jason fast.

"No," he replied. Mom had no choice but to follow the order and walk to her room. The man waited until the door clicked shut behind her.

"So, Miss Evgenís. My name is Kosmos, and I am a crossing consultant." He came closer. "Your public fear of crossing today caused a problem."

I cleared my throat. "What kind of problem?"

"A big one." Mr. Kosmos sat up and opened our Ológramma. My eyes widened; the news report was all about me and my failed crossing. I stared at my holographic image without understanding. Why had they made such an enormous deal of it?

"You see, Miss Evgenís, you scared some other juveniles out of crossing today. The kingdom has had to schedule another Crossing Day for the Zetikas provenance. His Royal Highness Prince Thaddeus is not happy about it."

"I didn't mean to!"

"Of course, Miss Evgenís, but your behavior says the opposite. You don't want the term *rebellion* to be linked to you, do you?"

I clasped my hands against my chest. "No!"

"I didn't think so." His face tightened. "Did your mother force you to cross?"

"No! I just . . . hesitated."

"It's easy to detect if you're lying. Should we investigate your mother to make sure that she didn't force you?"

"Please don't!" my shrill words pleaded, because I knew how humiliating the sin-spots investigation could be.

He smirked as he stood tall, tightening his uniform. "To prevent this from happening again, you must attend the government-sponsored psychological evaluation sessions, starting in September. Next time, you will cross without breaking down, or the results will be devastating." He walked toward the door before turning to give me one last look that froze the blood in my veins. "By the way, don't interfere in the governmental arresting process again. We see, we hear, and we *know* everything. Have a pleasurable day!"

He walked out of the house while the soldiers followed. I swept my hands across my forehead, wiping away the sweat drops. Mom rushed out of her room to close the main door.

"Did they hurt you?" Her eyebrows rose a bit as she approached me.

"No." I couldn't tell her about how he had threatened to investigate her. A tear ran down my cheek just at that thought. As if it wasn't enough that she had to go through the random sin-spots investigations that the

Law Corps imposed on adult women, now I would give them a reason to run it again.

"Is it about the crossing?"

I nodded and peeked at the Ológramma. My holographic image still hung there in the void, a witness to my stupid action. Oh, God! What kind of trouble did I get myself into?

Mom sighed. She picked up the remote and changed the channel.

"Mom, I tried. I'm sorry." My hand reached for her clammy one.

She paused for a moment. "My child, I need to know what is wrong if I'm going to help you. Why don't you want to cross?"

I shifted my eyes, looking at my feet. "I can't explain. But I promise to find a solution soon."

She nodded with understanding, and I got up to do the dishes.

Half an hour later, the doorbell rang—two short notes followed by a long one.

"That's Jason." I turned to Mom, who nodded approvingly.

Jason's blue eyes greeted me as I opened the door. He was a handsome boy. Between the whiteness of his complexion and the redness of his cheeks rested a cherubic homogeneity.

"Leen, I came as soon as possible," said Jason with his sweet husky voice. "Is everything all right?"

The smell of his expensive cologne enveloped me at once. He'd never changed this perfume since I met him years ago in childhood school— the day when Mary fell into the mud during gym class. Jason was sitting with his friends quite a distance away, but his eyes settled on us. He got up and waved for me. He asked why Mary was crying, and when I explained, he handed her a handkerchief to wipe her tears. Ever since that day, we'd been the best of friends. The three of us used to ride our bikes for hours, exploring the province and hanging out downtown until we crossed to adolescence. Since then, he'd moved to the boy's school and kept busy with his studies, but even though we didn't hang out on a daily basis anymore, our friendship stayed strong.

With a tense smile, I waved him in. He stepped inside the house to shake Mom's hand. She grinned, checking his elegant white shirt and gray trousers. She welcomed our relationship, often hinting that he would make a suitable husband. I had to remind her every time she mentioned it that a worker and wealthy's marriage was impossible in Elpax, so she had to stop dreaming.

I led Jason to my room and left the door ajar. He sat on my bed. "So?" he asked, smiling, although his eyes were worried.

"A man just came . . . a crossing consultant or something like that. It was . . . creepy."

Jason waved with his hand. "Oh, don't worry. He probably just wanted to make sure you aren't starting a rebellion." He giggled, trying to defuse the tension.

Nothing could disturb this boy's ever-joyful spirit! I wished I was like him. He wasn't careless, but . . . practical.

"You're not doing that, are you?" he teased, and I rolled my eyes. "Of course you aren't. But be careful. You never want to get the royal family's attention for the wrong reasons." His mood turned dark for a second. "Now that's a family that never jokes." His words sounded casual, but his voice was cautious, carrying a wisp of lingering fear.

"Did Mary tell you about the woman we saw today?"

His fingers ran into his black hair, his eyes squeezed tight. The skin appeared taut over his face in worry. That was what scared me the most. If Jason was acting this way, then there must have been something awful he knew about. It took him a moment to control his expression and start talking. "Look, nothing is as it appears in this kingdom, Leen. You know my father has a lot of business with the royal family, right? I heard him talking to Mom about them. They aren't who they pretend to be—one big happy family. They cover their ambitions and greed with civility when they move around in public. But they're ruthless in their private dealings. Nothing stops any of them from getting what they want, no matter the cost."

"What do you mean?" I swallowed, scared of Jason's next words.

"The blood of the innocent is on their hands, and traces of it cover their walls. They're on the prowl. Something is cooking, Leen, and it smells rotten!"

On Mary's wedding day, I wore Mom's navy-blue dress. It had a simple fitted bodice with a high neck, and it followed the lines of my body, fastened at my waist with an elaborate gold belt. I wore light makeup and wove jasmine in my hair. My problem was with the high heels. I was sure I would trip, even though I'd practiced wearing them for days.

The doorbell announced Jason's arrival. I unlocked the door, and there he was, wearing a coal-black suit with a white shirt, carrying a flower in his hand.

"Hey, Jason. Come on in."

Jason's mouth dropped. I waved a hand in his face to make him focus. "Jaaassssoooon!"

"Leen, look at you." His eyes were all over me. "You look beautiful."

"You clean up well too. What's with the flowers?"

"Oh, this is a wrist wreath. It would go with the one in your hair."

Interesting! What the wealthy did with flowers surprised me. I shoved my right hand into the wreath, and it fitted well on my wrist.

Jason had come to pick me up in his family's luxurious car, driven by his chauffeur, Nicholas. He opened the door for me, and I slid right in. The seats were luxurious, made of leather, and very comfortable. The windows were tinted too. Nobody could see us, and yet I could see everything outside clearly. I took in the sights as the car cruised through the workers' area of the town with its cluster of people moving about their jobs, and headed off the main road to a unique world. The panoramic view that greeted me was something I had never seen in seventeen years of my life. A wide, smooth road was lined with giant trees that provided shade as we drove along. Jason slid down the car window with the press of a button, and the first thing that hit me was the quiet. The entire area was so peaceful, with only the sounds of nature and the humming of the car to punctuate the silence. I turned out the rear window to look at the ground we'd covered, and only a white sedan car was on the road behind us. I thought it must be filled with other guests heading to Mary's reception.

Jason's car turned down a side road, following a thick wall on the right side. It was reinforced by sharp spikes on the top, and ended in a gate flanked by cameras and operated by security personnel.

Upon our arrival, we got out of the car and walked to the nearby gate's door. The guard looked between my name on the guest list and my modest dress several times. He didn't even give a second glance to Jason. After a great deal of visible hesitation, Jason was hopping mad. I thought he might punch the guard when he shouted, "Moron! She's on the list. Just let us in!"

The guard apologized and allowed me to enter. I grabbed Jason's arm and forced a weak smile as we walked on. "Let's not make a scene. It's Mary's wedding day." Although I'd expected the guard's behavior, it still disturbed me.

Jason held my cold palm, and we stepped through the gate into the garden surrounding Mary's home. I halted. It was *huge*. I couldn't even see the boundaries of the land. Now I knew why Mary never invited me over. Her mother would never allow me to step into such a lap of luxury. *Well, the arrogant woman doesn't deserve immortality on paper—at least, not in my life story.*

Thinking back to my childhood, I remembered when she came to check on Mary at school and saw me sitting next to her daughter. The next day, the principal moved me to another class. That was only the start of an even stronger friendship.

I'd wanted to see Mary's room and her toys, which she avoided talking about in front of me so I didn't feel inferior. But I'd always asked.

"How do you spend your time? Do you play the piano? You must have a

big one in the middle of your mansion lobby."

"Never took to it. My fingers aren't long enough to chase the keys. I prefer to spend my time with you."

I smiled, as her lines pleased my ego. Not to mention that her fingers were plenty long enough to play the piano if she'd wanted to.

Now, I couldn't seem to take it all in. I was pulled in all directions by the lushness of Mary's home.

The mansion was so tall that I got a crick in my neck when I looked up. The doors stood a story tall. Today, strings of lights dropped from the circular terrace. A film of Mary and her husband was broadcasting on the walls. On either side of the palatial entrance, the tall cypress trees, too, were lit up with colorful electric lights. Flowers of all hues and shapes filled the garden. Staircases went up and up. Dancing fountains bubbled everywhere . . . when I couldn't even afford to bathe.

Guests moved around in groups and scattered over every half-meter of the garden. Men were dressed in formal suits of all colors except the forbidden red, which was the symbol of the Modern Roman Empire. The women wore gold, along with shiny gems which seemed to sparkle and reflect in the light. Most of the guests' suits, long dresses, and bouffant gowns had peacock feathers featured prominently.

I knew the wearing of feathers was limited to the princes and official social ceremonies of the wealthy. As I learned in school, the first person to popularize such a marvelous accessory was the late King Islabour. The feathers symbolized the peacock's pride and uniqueness, just as Elpax was unique in its struggle with the Empire. Some people said that each feather represented one of the different nationalities that found peace in Elpax.

Even though Mary hinted earlier that I should wear jewelry, I couldn't tell her that we didn't have any. My confidence took a dip. I realized that I stood out with my moderate dress and lack of adornment. No wonder the security guard at the gate had hesitated to let me in. Soon, all eyes would censure me. Nevertheless, I was delighted that Jason didn't overstate his own outfit by donning feathers. His only accessory was a white buckle on his black suit.

A well-dressed server guided us to our round table near the dancing floor. Seated to our right was a dignified gentleman, his long white mustache curved upward. On his left sat a redheaded woman wearing a huge crimson dress, with yellow gemstones and feathers affixed to her head.

"Bonum vesperum. Glory to Elpax, sir, milady," Jason intoned with a gorgeous smile. He pulled the heavy chair out for me. I smiled and greeted them in Latin, too. The wealthy preferred to speak it with an air of false sophistication. We learned Latin in school on the principle of knowing your enemy's language, but I couldn't use it anywhere else in the kingdom. Except here, at this high society gathering.

The woman's eyes scrutinized my outfit. Obviously, she found me lacking—a derisive expression crossed her face, as though she was wondering what miracle allowed me to come to this occasion and share her table. The man nodded at us and shook hands with Jason.

"Jason Valemont."

"Glory." The man nodded while lighting his *electronic* pipe. "I think I know your father. We were on the same business trip to Brazil."

He looked at me with sharp hazel eyes and greeted me with a genuine smile. He opened his mouth to say something, when the lady remarked in a scathing tone, "Feathers don't seem to concern you."

Here we go again. The wealthy version of Danira's mother!

I simpered. "I don't see what kind of desired aesthetic value is achieved by plucking a wonderful live bird."

The man roared with laughter, and the woman threw a disgusted look at all of us. I turned my gaze to the man and refused to look at her again, a direct barb at her for trying to make me feel inferior. I could practically feel the daggers her eyes were shooting into me. She tossed her serviette on the table, and with short, huffy steps, she hurried away as fast as her heels would allow. It seemed that she couldn't wait to escape us.

I stared at her back in awe. How come my reply insulted her so much that she left? Surely she shouldn't care about my opinion. I almost

40

apologized to the man, when he complimented, "Well said." He stretched his hand out across the table to shake mine. "Maximus Dorgalous."

"Lenora Evgenís."

"You've got a pleasant name, Lenora. Tell me, are you . . . ?" He left the rest of the question unspoken.

"A worker." I lifted my chin up, refusing to bow down to the superior air of those wealthy who didn't seem to respect anyone.

He nodded as if he already knew, and he puffed on his pipe, chugging out smoke. "You guys are the best. Without you, we would die of starvation."

Well, if we're so valuable to you then maybe you should pay us better.

My mouth curved into a joyous grin. I pointed at the woman, who by now was flouncing into a new seat. Before I could speak, he said, "Oh, don't worry, I keep telling her the same thing about the feathers. But it always falls on deaf ears. Hearing it from you probably made her feel as if we had a prior agreement; that I trained you to say the words." He guffawed at his own joke, and we tittered with him.

Mr. Dorgalous blew his pipe smoke and leaned toward me. "Your observation is smart, but it's wise not to mention it to strangers," he warned with a courteous smile. My eyes widened. He looked around himself to check whether anyone was listening. "I guess you don't know the age-old lore about peacock feathers?"

He paused, waiting for my response. My eyes narrowed as I tried to remember the related mythology. I turned to Jason, who shook his head, and we both looked at Mr. Dorgalous with curiosity.

Mr. Dorgalous leaned toward us with his elbow on the table and lowered his booming voice. "The myth states that the Greek goddess Hera wanted to keep her husband, Zeus, in check. So she sent Argus Panoptes —her faithful companion with hundred eyes—to snoop on . . . you know . . . her husband's adventures with women. And I can't explain further, because you're still in the second phase." He pointed to my wrist before pressing on. "In general, Zeus came to know about the spy who reported

41

the news to Hera, lay in wait for the one with the hundred eyes, and killed him."

My mouth fell open, and I peeked at Jason's frozen face.

"When Hera found her faithful companion dead, she cried and mourned for him. At that moment, a bird flew overhead. Hera caught the bird and transferred the hundred eyes from her friend's body to that living bird's tail, so that his eyes would live on forever in . . ."

"The peacock," Jason whispered in astonishment.

Mr. Dorgalous nodded, and a huge smile exploded on his face as he enjoyed our fascination. He returned to smoking his pipe for a few seconds, then cast his thoughtful gaze at me and lowered his voice again. "The peacock isn't just a symbol of resistance, but also of the monarchy—it's a symbol of their moles that follow us everywhere." He pointed at the word-catcher, which had flown close to our table, and to the security cameras near us. "There are eyes and ears everywhere, Lenora. It would do you good to heed caution before speaking radical words. The government wouldn't hesitate to label you a traitor."

I gulped.

He leaned in and whispered, "I know who you are. I saw your refusal to cross yesterday. Miss, be careful. You may not be aware of the consequences of your actions, so let me tell you. You've created chaos because of your hesitation, and they may come after you. Inferos isn't a place for a young girl like you. Pardons are no longer available in the kingdom. Change is afoot, and wealth and power have changed hands. You aren't safe in Elpax anymore."

CHAPTER 5

HEARING THESE OMINOUS WORDS, I turned to Jason, and we both exchanged tense looks. Everyone was warning me not to cross the lines of the laws. What was the problem? It was my right to choose when to cross over. I did nothing wrong.

Maybe the government needed to find someone to pin a high-profile crime on to distract everyone. Perhaps it was trying to plant fear in our hearts so we wouldn't find out what it was up to.

I tried to stay calm, and silence reigned at our table while the voices of the nearby ones filled it. To break the awkward mood, Jason began conversing with Mr. Dorgalous about their common associates, but my thoughts turned inwards. The wealthy got immunity, and the worker-class was threatened penalties for almost everything. What did the middle-class get?

I remembered what I'd learned in school about the class system. During the Brazen War, when the wealthy came to Elpax and opened their companies, they paid better salaries than the governing bodies. People asked the government to raise their salaries, but late King Islabour couldn't afford to do so, as the royal funds were depleted from the war. The bullying and the name-calling started then, and grew into something much worse.

The citizens who worked for the government treated those who worked for the wealthy horribly, and smashed their cars and houses. As these terrorist attacks began to affect the wealthy citizens' companies as a whole, the civil war began.

When Elpax was about to fall to the Roman Empire, however, the citizens together stood up for their homeland until King Islabour signed the peace treaty with Caesar. At that point, the king had the chance to manage civil tensions. The ones that were working for the wealthy split from the rest. They were the educated people who formed the middle class; they did their work and didn't interfere with politics, preferring to remain aloof. The ones who didn't have a degree or a diploma became the worker class, and they had to settle for careers in fishing, farming jobs or factories. Before his death, King Islabour stated that a worker could attend college and become middle class if he passed the acceptance exams. That announcement was the most shameful thing ever. The unspoken truth behind it was clear: *if you aren't educated or smart enough, then you don't deserve to live with dignity.*

Jason touched my hand to direct my attention to a glass of orange drink with sparkles that popped out from the table itself, along with a plate filled with round cakes.

"The table has an inner mechanism that was prepared with your preferred juice and cakes," explained Jason. "Yesterday, you were too stressed to fill out the form ahead of time, so I did it for you. Did I get it right?"

I smiled. "Yes, you did." I peered at Mr. Dorgalous's red drink.

"Looks like he prefers the adults' sour grape drink," Jason hissed. "With the company of that woman, soon we will need one too."

I chuckled while sipping my juice. "Jason, do you know the other guests?"

"Some . . . not all. Most have come from Theirna, as Mary's father has business dealings with the capital. The fair gentleman you see there with the black hair, Mr. Po, is originally from the Diocese of Asia in the Roman Empire." He tilted his head toward the opposite table, where a woman with a fair complexion and blond hair was seated. "She's my mother's friend, Madam Koptevo. She's from what used to be Russia before the war destroyed it. She's a kind woman who pays a lot of charity. And the one sitting next to her, dressed in the beautiful cloth with tanned skin, is Miss Surat from the District of India. That style of draping is called a sari."

"It's so pretty!"

A voice announcing the beginning of the ceremony interrupted us. The lights dimmed at once, and two men opened the mansion's heavy golden doors. Twenty beautiful dancers came out of the mansion in single file. Their long gowns of light and dark blue tightened along the curves of their body. A vibration of loud, slow drums pulsated for a while before the horns blew their melody, and music launched from the loudspeakers.

The dancers swayed to the beat, one after the other. They were many, yet they were one in dance. They moved sensuously on both sides of the stairs, ten on the left and ten on the right. On each of their heads was a gold candelabra, with battery-operated candles glowing on them. The dancers soon approached the marble dance floor, which gleamed in shining colors, reflecting the candlelight. The women became dancing lights, moving synchronously as one. I was awestruck. I had never seen anything like this before . . . ever.

Jason leaned in to whisper, "They aren't human." My worried eyes turned to him as he clarified. "They are robots. Look at their eyes; they're gleaming."

Oh, my goodness! I had heard about robots, but I'd never met one of them, as they were exclusively manufactured in the Roman Empire.

"Mary's mother paid a fortune to rent them from Rome," said Jason, rolling his eyes. "She wanted to choose something different from the regular Elpaxian wedding theme."

45

"I notice the music is strange, too."

"It's the Pharaoh's music. From the ancient civilization of Aegyptus." He held my hand. "Now this is the best part. Watch carefully."

Twenty well-built men with a stern attitude, wearing only white harem pants and blue turbans around their shaved heads, walked out of the entrance and stood on the stairs. All at once, they blew a stream of reddish-yellow fiery color from their mouths.

"Wow! What is that?" I whispered, staring at the fascinating scene.

Jason turned to me. "Don't panic. It's just a three-dimensional simulation."

"Of?"

His eyes lit up with amusement. "The *Forbidden Fire!*"

My jaw dropped open. This was the first time in my life I'd seen fire. It was both a fabulous and terrifying thing, dancing in the air—a breathtaking blend of colors.

I leaned to Jason. "Are the wealthy allowed to set fires?"

He shook his head. "No one can start a fire. That is the only absolute law in the kingdom that's valid for all."

Yes, I knew that. The lifetime curse that accompanied adulthood. We learned that during the Crossing Gate's construction, there was a defect in its design. After crossing to the adult phase, shiny round teal spots—bigger than moles—would appear on the body of anyone who had sinned. That wasn't the only problem. These damn sin-spots were sensitive to fire. Hence, it was taboo to start a fire in the kingdom, as all nearby sinners would spontaneously burn to ash.

As the music reached a crescendo and slowed down, Mary came out of the mansion draped in her long white gown, adorned with white ostrich feathers and blue jewels, almost blinding in their breathtaking luster. Tears filled my eyes as I looked at her. She was a vision to behold, smiling while grasping her husband's arm.

Mary and her husband, Peter, walked forward together and sat at their table. The music softened, eventually stopping, and the lights dimmed.

46

In the silence, an elderly woman, withered and wise, walked in, accompanied by personal guards and several well-built men. She wore a long black dress and a scarf around her head. She had silver tattoos with an elaborate design on her chin and neckline. The woman's slow steps headed straight toward the new couple, and she bent down to hold Mary's palm.

"Jason, who is that?"

"She is a diviner from Alphatoli province. The princes and the wealthy often call one of them to read chiromancy at their celebrations."

My eyes widened in astonishment. The woman's voice resonated with a monotonous rhythm while she read Mary's palm, foretelling a joyful life with Peter. The grin didn't leave Mary's face. She raised her eyes toward our table and winked at me. I smiled for her happiness.

The crowd clapped cheerfully when the diviner finished with her prophecy. She turned around and walked toward a little blue tent in the corner that was kept ready for her.

A voice announced that it was time for dinner, and our table's glass top turned into a screen, featuring pictures of an array of exotic cuisines. I blinked several times, trying to figure out their names. All of them were things known by the wealthy, imported from the Roman Empire. I couldn't tell Jason that I had no idea what chocolate was . . . or the white pearl albino caviar!

"Jason. If you were to choose a vegetarian meal, what would it be?"

He smiled and pointed to several pictures. I didn't focus enough as I tapped on their icons; I just wanted to be done with it. The plates popped out of the table's inside. As Jason explained, the kitchen itself was underground, with a kind of elevator that would push our choice upward.

Interesting!

I looked at the dish that appeared in front of me. Some kind of weird blue round things wobbled in the soup. I stared at it for a while till Jason leaned toward me.

"Don't worry. They're vegetables." He rolled his eyes. "Colored with stupid blue dye."

I giggled and was about to pick up a big spoon . . . or a small one? Two silver spoons and three forks around the dish put me in a dilemma. They were daring me to pick up the wrong one.

My hand trembled over them until Jason kicked me lightly under the table. I turned to him, wondering. He picked up the first left spoon in front of him and shook it with a graceful move, winking at me. I understood it was the one. I picked up mine and tasted this strange-looking delicacy. It was fantastic! I decided I should learn the recipe—without the dye, because Moria would make fun of it.

After the exotic dinner, the new couple and their guests danced to music with a different rhythm than the previous performances. As I watched them, I wished there were lyrics in the songs—but those were mostly available only for the adults, and they could only hear them alone in the windowless room.

Those who hadn't yet reached maturity could only hear lyrics if they were in lullabies and military marches. This rule felt strange to me. How could words be banned and forbidden to be heard?

"Why do you look so miserable, Leen? Come, let's dance together."

I forced a smile. "Jason, I don't know how to dance like this!"

He held my hand. "It's the traditional Elpaxian waltz. I'll teach you."

Jason pulled me to the edge of the dance floor, grabbed my hand, and put it on his shoulder, keeping a distance between us. He placed his other arm behind his back.

"Follow my feet! If I step back, you step forward, and so on."

At first, it was hard; I stepped on his shoes countless times, and floundered among the surrounding dancers before getting the hang of it.

"Look at you!" Jason grinned at me once I started doing it properly.

All at once, I had a feeling that I would fall. My head felt as heavy as a rock, and dizziness overwhelmed me.

"I'm tired," I said to Jason. "Let me sit down for a minute." I let go of his hand and turned around, only to dash into someone. I tripped over my long dress, and one thought popped in my brain as I fell to the ground: *I shouldn't have worn high-heeled shoes.* My brain soon stopped working as my head hit the marble floor, and everything went black.

The darkness soon evaporated a bit, and I found myself standing alone in a rainforest, holding a glass stick.

My stomach twisted in horror. *What is this place?*

I turned around, trying to find a way out of the trees, and my heart shivered. An enormous golden temple stood behind me, flashing in the darkness. The loud sound of drums arose out of nowhere, and the chanting of an old man's voice became clear. It was a language I had never heard before.

Before my brain could comprehend what was going on, or even ponder how I got here, a man with a pale complexion and long silver-mint hair appeared right before me.

"Who are you?" I screamed, my feet moving a few steps backward. "What the hell do you want?"

He didn't answer. Instead, his gaze shifted momentarily from me to the stick in my hand, which started to glow red, illuminating the surrounding darkness. The light showed his long, simple white robe and his bare feet.

His silver eyes glittered as he whispered, "Run, *OukSali*. Run!"

CHAPTER 6

"LEEN, ARE YOU OKAY?" JASON'S panicking voice covered the old man's chanting, erasing the entire scene of the forest and the silver-haired man, bringing me back to reality.

My head was pounding, and I could hardly open my eyes. People's blurry faces stared down at me. Putting my hands on my head, I touched something sticky and groaned in pain. "My head hurts."

"You hit it hard. Come on, I'll help you." Jason held my hand and helped me sit up straight. I could feel the dizziness coming up on me like a wave.

"Leen . . . Leen, are you okay?" Mary's voice echoed as she took hold of my other hand. I looked at her, and soon her face became clear. I was in the blue tent, and Jason, Mary, the diviner, and another beautiful lady were looking at me. My eyes took in the lady's gown, which was made entirely of peacock feathers. I jerked with the realization. She was Queen Olympia, King Alexei's wife!

"Please accept my sincere apology," said the queen gently. "I ran into you."

My mouth fell open. I never knew that royals attended marriages of the wealthy! Given my foolish behavior, not to mention everyone's previous warnings about the royals, I couldn't seem to find the right words. "It . . . happens," was my dumb reply, or I thought it was dumb. But her mouth curved into a smile.

"Madam Oshina offered to help. She's a healer too," said the queen, pointing to the diviner. "If you need anything, kindly ask."

I mumbled a thank you, and Queen Olympia got up, dragging her long dress behind her. She bent down and walked out of the tent. I breathed, glad that she didn't order her men to arrest me. Perhaps Jason and Mr. Dorgalous were exaggerating when they warned me about the royal family. The queen seemed really nice, and she handled the situation professionally. Or maybe she had to act that way to maintain a certain image in front of the public. Either way, I was glad that the situation ended peacefully.

I turned to Mary. "I'm sorry. I didn't mean to spoil your wedding."

"Don't worry." She squeezed my hands with a gentle touch. "I have to attend to my guests. I'll be right back."

Mary smiled and left. I looked at the old diviner who sat on the floor, and I sensed a strange aura around her. She seemed as old as time, born from the sands of the desert that she lived in. She looked at me with her green eyes. "I applied a mixture of herbs to the wound. You can wash it tomorrow."

"Thank you," I responded. "How much do I owe you?"

"It's on the house. Still, each guest gets a complimentary reading. Do you want me to read your fortune?"

I turned to Jason, and he forced a tense smile. "Do you think you're up to it?"

I stared at him for a while. Should I tell him about what I saw when I passed out? I shook my head. Maybe it was nothing, and my brain was playing me.

"Leen?" said Jason, waiting for my answer.

51

I nodded. I had never seen a diviner, much less had my future read by one. It would be interesting, and I needed to distract myself from that strange vision.

Oshina took my tiny palm, enclosed it in her rough, calloused ones, and stared at the lines for a long time. She swung her gaze between my face and palm. There was pity and worry in her eyes as she gazed at me. A vein popped out of my neck in trepidation, and my heart started beating fast.

"There are five letters in a man's name," she whispered. "In its folds lies your misery or happiness, and an interminable journey that almost ends at its beginning."

I strained to understand what she said. She lifted her steady gaze and looked straight into my eyes. I froze in place, and my limbs quivered.

"Mark my words, you might carry a red color that will generate a lost peace."

My eyes widened with astonishment, and before I could ask her what she meant, she looked at Jason and beckoned him.

"A good boy. One who finds him becomes delighted. If you lose him, he will come back to you, even when no symbols exist between you."

"What do you mean?" I hissed; my throat dry.

She didn't answer. Instead, her wrinkled face smiled. She released my hand and pointed toward the opening as a clear sign that our time was over.

"But I don't understand!"

"You will," she responded casually.

I had no other option. I got up, and I was about to leave with Jason when she spoke from behind. "Remember, when you see the torch in your dream, it will all start. I'll be waiting for you."

What?

I exchanged a tense look with Jason. We walked out of the tent and stood at its entrance, astonished. Was she referring to the glass stick I saw when I passed out a few minutes ago? Should I go back and tell her that I had already seen it? Or was she talking about another torch? The stick didn't look like a torch to me, but it glowed with a red color. And what about that freaky man in the forest? Was he the one with the five letters in his name?

I turned to Jason. "Did you understand anything? Anything at all?"

He blinked several times. "Yes. You will stick with me forever," he teased with a grin.

My arms curved on my hips like sugar bowl handles. "Are you complaining, Mr. Jason?" I pursed my lips, pretending to be annoyed.

"I'm joking." He giggled. "Don't worry about prophecies. They're like lines etched in the sand, gone forever with a little breeze."

I forced a pale smile and walked out—out of Mary's house with her family and guests, out of the sights of the royalty, and out of the realm of the diviner. But my mind was churning. There had to be more to it than what the diviner showed me. A strange feeling of foreboding came over my mind, and I couldn't help but shudder.

I turned to the window of the agriculture classroom, which overlooked the front yard of the school. Scattered fall leaves filled the streets, swirling in the gentle breeze. It was the fifth of September, the first day of school. A beautiful morning crammed with promises. Yet, my teachers seemed to have lots of questions to ask me about the day I failed to cross three months ago. The principal wanted me to get psychoanalyzed to find out why I didn't cross. Queen Arianna had established that program a few years ago. If a juvenile's teachers made them participate, they had to answer questions to assess their maturity and work out whether they could cross the following year. That was a totally different assessment than the one the creepy consultant offered.

The class was lonely without Mary. I felt lost, and my fingers rubbed my forehead in defeat. I needed her at the moment to discuss the dream that had plagued me since her wedding.

It was an icy night as I stood in our living room, shivering. Sadness permeated the air in my house. Mom walked in, wearing a black shawl. Her eyes were red and puffy, as though she had been crying. A storm started when a man knocked on the door. Mom hurried to answer, and the visitor yelled that he needed to talk to me. I ran to hide under the little table in the living room while Mom denied him with a forceful "NEVER!" and slammed the door shut. Thunder and lightning raged around us. I shuffled back to my room and stood by the floor-to-ceiling windows, overlooking an unfamiliar rainforest instead of our house's front garden. The man approached my window. His clothes weren't wet despite the heavy rain.

I wasn't scared anymore. Looking into his gray eyes filled me with the tranquility that had so far escaped me. We stared at each other for a long moment. Time moved back and forth between us, but the moment remained timeless. He put his hand on the glass, and I lifted mine as if to touch his. Our eyes bespoke a thousand answers to a thousand questions.

Every time, when our hands were about to meet, I woke up. It felt like I was being choked. My body was exhausted, like I'd been battered black and blue, though not a single mark was on me. The dream wasn't scary, but not being able to understand its significance had been bothering me for months.

Mary and Peter had been on their honeymoon to Theirna since June, so I couldn't discuss it with her on the Iméfono. Jason was a boy, and it wasn't comfortable to talk about such matters with him. All of this left me alone with questions in my mind and no options to find my answers.

I sighed and looked around. The other girls had gathered in their circles, chatting amongst themselves about things that didn't concern me. I didn't know most of them. Not only were they two years younger, but my school, which was halfway to Zoiterra, catered to many nearby towns and villages.

Miss Cassia entered the classroom, and all the students returned to their seats.

"Glory, girls," said Miss Cassia as she stood behind her desk. "I have good news for those who didn't cross over this year." She glanced at me.

"The government changed the curriculums, so you'll not study the same subjects as last year. Now, let's—"

The young, plump student supervisor interrupted Miss Cassia with a few cautious knocks on the open door. "Oh, Glory, Miss. I apologize for interrupting, but we have a fresh student. Go ahead, Francine Mellas."

A small, beautiful girl with carrot-red corkscrew curls and eyeglasses ambled into the classroom. Some wealthy and middle-class girls laughed at her, and my eyes widened at their cruel mirth. Miss Cassia knocked on her desk. That was all she could do to discipline them. But if a worker did the same, Miss Cassia would send her to the principal at once.

"Come in, Francine. Please take a seat."

Francine's face flushed with mortification. Her cheeks turned red like the hue of pomegranate seeds. With her red hair, she looked like a radioactive mass awaiting eruption. She stood near the door. Her eyes scurried all over the class in a panic, trying to find an empty seat to escape the curious gazes. I pointed at the one next to me, and she sank down into it with a sigh. My lips curved into an encouraging smile, and she responded with a faint one.

I understood her situation. The "new girl" title would precede her everywhere until another one joined the school. I knew that stifling feeling of not belonging and the curious glances that surrounded her today. I'd faced them eight years ago.

Miss Cassia took a deep breath and pushed back her short black hair. She pressed a button, shutting off the lights and closing the curtains, then turned the Ológramma over. The same old film started—the one I knew by heart. There he was again, the conceited broadcaster Hermes, with a large feather covering his head.

"Glory to Elpax and its brave citizens. Our good juveniles, you must cross the Crossing Gate once you are fifteen years old if you feel ready. You are then welcome to join the Law Corps to defend your land so that its glory endures now and forever."

I couldn't help but roll my eyes. His holographic image walked closer and stood before me.

"Juveniles, the adult phase allows you to work, to marry, to have children, to drive cars, and much more. Juveniles, Elpax is your homeland, and it would not grow without you. Glory to Elpax and its brave juveniles."

The lights switched on automatically. "So," said Miss Cassia, "open your smartboards to the first chapter."

I glanced at Francine, trying to guess her caste. In our school, one could often tell the differences between the castes, despite everyone wearing the same uniform. The wealthy girls carried nice silk bags and wore expensive shoes with feathers attached to them. The middle class often wore silver or golden chains. And as for the workers? Nothing.

My mom's wedding ring was silver, and even when we were a middle-class, she didn't buy gold. According to her, it was an *unnecessary luxury*.

Francine's bag was simple, and her shoes had no feathers on them. I couldn't see if there was a golden chain around her neck, but most likely she was from the working class, just like me.

She stared at her smartboard with confusion.

"What's the matter?" I whispered, leaning in.

She turned to me and spoke in a hushed tone. "I joined in late."

Oh. She didn't have time to download the material in the principal's office.

I brought my device closer. "Let's share." She looked at me with gratitude and extended her delicate fingers to hold the board with me. "My name is Lenora. Call me Leen."

I showed Francine around the school and escorted her to her next class. Then, I ran to public health class. Before I opened the door, the student supervisor called my name. "Hold on, Miss Evgenís. The principal needs you in his office."

"Regarding what?"

"It's for your psychological evaluation."

My jaw tightened at her words. "I thought the royal orders were clear in this matter. I can cross whenever I want until my twentieth birthday." My tone came out sarcastic. I was no longer able to contain myself. The truth was, I wasn't ready to answer why I couldn't cross, because I myself didn't know the answer. If I said that I felt dizzy, would the government force me to cross like they did with Karya? They drugged her and put her on an automatic hospital trolley bed that transported her across the Crossing Gate. Afterwards, they launched furious propaganda against her, as her punishment for not following the orders and a lesson for all those who thought of swimming against the tide.

The supervisor's pupils dilated with suppressed fury. "And helping you to settle your mind and rethink your decision is an order, too! Miss Evgenís, I don't have to warn you about your attitude."

I sighed aloud and rushed to the principal's office. A few minutes later, I backed out of his door, trying not to trip over my own feet. The creepy crossing consultant was in his office. He wanted me to sign an electronic pledge, which stated that since I had already given up many chances to cross, it was my last chance to redeem myself and act according to the kingdom's laws. And if I failed to do so, the principal would take action against me. The school frowned on such behavior as repeatedly refusing to cross. While the principal wasn't allowed to expel me, the pledge gave him the power to call upon the staff and students to shun me!

I refused to sign any deed that gave the principal this power over me. Only I would decide when to cross. I didn't even care if he sent my report to the Queen Mother Arianna. It was so upsetting that he had taken advantage of Mary's absence. He could never be bothered with the wealthy and their friends.

My studies that day felt long and tormenting. I rushed out of class when the bell rang announcing the end of the school day. Hiding behind a group of girls, I walked down the glass corridor, surrounded by the cacophony of my fellow students rushing to reach the primary gate.

I stood in front of the gate for a second, searching for my bike key, when a loud bang detonated from above my head. The girls screamed. I rushed away from the door and looked up, quivering. Some sparks emanated from the lights around the school's name board, which automatically switched off at once. I put a hand on my chest to calm my pounding heart. We were very fortunate that, being juveniles, our bodies all lacked sin-spots. Even one spark could lead to combustion, and we would have been ashes.

"Lenora," said Francine while walking toward me. "Sorry, I mean Leen."

I forced a smile, my heart still pumping fast. "No worries. Are you waiting for the school bus?"

She shook her head.

"Then we can ride our bikes together. Where is your home?"

"I don't have a bike. I live in Zoiterra."

Zoiterra! Oh, so she was middle-class. I thought it might not be all bad, though. Only time would tell if she concerned herself with classist thoughts.

She looked at my bike keys. "Where's your home? My brother can drop you."

"On the outskirts of Roses Hill near the orchards, but I don't want to bother you."

"Not at all."

It was surprising how nice she was. It might be her way of thanking me for sharing my smartboard with her. Accepting the offer, I stood with her, waiting for her brother.

"So why did you leave your school in the city?" I asked.

"Oh! I'm from Gamotos, but my father got a job in Zoiterra, and we moved recently. The government transferred me here because there was no vacancy in the city's schools."

"I see."

Out of nowhere, a line of armored cars drove down the road. The Law Corps got out and started checking the IDs of random men in the street—the law prohibited adult men from standing anywhere close to the juveniles' school. Only those who were there to pick up their kids were allowed to wait inside the school's border.

"Do Law Corps always come to this school?"

"No, Francine. Never." I wet my lips with a sudden nervousness. "This is the first time that I've seen them around. I wonder what's different today."

"It's probably not a big deal. I could ask Erick about it."

"Your brother? Is he a soldier?"

"No, he's a lawyer in the legal department of the state. I think he might have some answers."

"Miss Evgenís!"

I turned around to see who had called my name. It was the same student supervisor again, coming for me. I needed to run away, fast!

"Sorry!" I mumbled to Francine and ran into the crowd, hiding from the student supervisor. While my feet were racing, I glanced back for a split second to check that she'd lost me, and I bumped hard into someone. My smartboard fell out of my hand, hitting the floor hard.

"Damn!" I cried out, and a young man bent down to grab my smartboard. My face flushed with embarrassment. "I am sorry . . . I didn't mean to curse you. I mean . . . not you . . ." My ears were getting hotter by the second, so I just waved for him to give me back the device.

He smiled while standing tall, checking my smartboard for damage. "Don't worry."

I felt that I had heard his voice before, but I couldn't figure out who he was due to the sunglasses that covered his eyes.

"Here you go—it's as good as new." He handed me the device and took off his sunglasses, looking at me with his golden-gray eyes.

At that first glimpse, electricity ran through my body, piercing the deepest parts of my soul. My heartbeat stopped for a second, announcing its rebellion against the normal rhythm. My heart quivered, annoyed by this bizarre imbalance, and pumped wildly with an intensity that I could feel pulsating in my ears. A frigid chill swept down my body like a wave, in cadence with my heart's violent revolution.

It was *him*—the man in my dreams. I could never forget his gray eyes, which followed me day and night.

Francine's voice echoed somewhere near me. "I see you met my brother."

My body shuddered like a dry leaf carried by fall winds to an unknown place. What I felt wasn't just fear or curiosity. Perhaps it was a mixture of both, or something else I knew nothing about. It seemed like my life had ended while starting anew, and the journey I was about to go on had begun without my will or permission.

Who was he?

CHAPTER 7

"MISS, WHAT'S WRONG?" HIS DEEP voice tugged at my consciousness, filtering through the darkness like a ray of light, bringing me out of the stupor I had fallen into.

The student supervisor, the crossing consultant, and some of the Law Corps team, partially hidden by a pillar, were discussing something amongst themselves while casting glances at me. The supervisor soon came to where I was standing. Her loud voice dragged the attention of the other girls nearby. "Miss Evgenís, you must sign the—"

"I will tomorrow," I snapped, and walked off to end the conversation. It wasn't possible for me to deal with the electronic pledge and the analysis anymore. All I needed at the moment was to go home.

"Wait up, Leen." Francine pulled my shoulder. "You don't look fine. Let's drop you home. Erick insists."

"Thank you, Francine. But my bike—"

"We'll drop your bike too," Erick interrupted, smiling at me.

My poor heart began to shake again. I took a few deep breaths and coughed several times. *That's what Mom had taught me to do whenever I felt my heart had lost its rhythm.* I didn't want to get in the same car with him. But refusing this invitation would be rude, especially when he hadn't done anything wrong to me. Besides, I wanted to know who he was and why he was haunting my dreams.

"All right," I said, walking to the bikes' parking spot. Erick followed me while my trembling fingers unlocked my bike. He carried it to his car's trunk and opened the back door for me.

I got in, struck by the day's events, wondering if I had landed in some parallel universe. After I gave my address to Erick, I sat in silence, listening to the thudding of my heart, glimpsing his deep-set eyes in the rear-view mirror. I took in his appearance: a delicate nose and a generous mouth, a lightly tanned face with sharp planes, and a well-defined jaw ending in a small cleft chin. He'd styled his overlong hazelnut hair back, and there wasn't a single strand out of place.

Erick caught me looking at him, and I shifted my gaze to my bag. I tried to peek at him again, and his eyes settled on me. The more our eyes met, the tenser I became—yet the knot in my chest loosened up, one breath at a time. Something was swirling about inside me, and it didn't feel like fear.

Something else. Something new.

Soon, the car turned onto my narrow street and stopped in front of my house.

"Thank you, Francine. I'll see you tomorrow." I stepped out of the car, and so did Erick. He walked to the back and opened the trunk for me. I extended my hand to pick up my bike at the same moment as him. Our fingers touched, and I winced, pulling away fast. He looked curiously at me. His gray eyes shone, and their golden flecks sparkled as he placed the bike on the ground.

"Thank you," I mumbled, and threw my bike in the garden as soon as he left. I rushed to my room and lay down on the bed in my school uniform, still wearing my shoes and clutching my bag. A delicious riot of thoughts churned inside my head. The details of fact and fiction overlapped and brought me into another world filled with questions. How could worry and comfort both be gathered in my heart? How could an unknown man force me into such a state of shock?

"Don't you hear me calling you?" Mom's voice pulled me out of my thoughts. She was standing at the bedroom door, staring at me.

I looked at Mom, searching for an answer to give her.

"Lenora, what's wrong?"

I shifted on the bed. "Not sure," I said, shaking my head. "My hands feel numb, and my heart is racing along with my breath." I wondered how to explain something I didn't understand myself.

Mom came closer, put her hand on my sweaty forehead, and felt my hands. "Your hands are cold, and your forehead is burning up! Are you coming down with something?"

"Oh, don't worry. I'm fine. I'll come right out to help you with lunch."

She stared at me for another long while. "All right, then. Hurry up, or I'll be late for my night shift."

Mom walked out of the room, and I turned to the floor-to-ceiling window with unseeing eyes and a mind spaced out. It was as if someone had hit me on the head, stopping all my thoughts. My concentration seemed shot, and I couldn't focus on anything except for the name Erick. My mind was a kaleidoscope filled with his distorted image.

All of this annoyed me a bit. I wanted my serenity and peace of mind to come back. I hated this strange restlessness, a tempest of feelings I could hardly understand. This wasn't me!

"Lenora! Why haven't you changed your clothes yet? It's been half an hour. What were you doing?"

I raised my eyebrows in astonishment and turned to the clock. I almost accused Mom of exaggerating, but she was right; thirty-five minutes had been stolen from my life, non-refundable.

"Lenora!"

I raised my eyes upon hearing my name. Miss Cassia was staring at me, waiting for an answer to a question I hadn't heard her ask. The girls turned to look at me too. I sighed. It was obvious that I wasn't following the lesson.

Miss Cassia didn't wait for my answer. She walked over to the classroom door and opened it. "I'm done scolding you for not paying attention. Go to the principal's office." She crossed her arms, waiting for me to move. The girls chuckled while I silently walked out in a daze.

That had been my life for the past two months now. My nights were sleepless; sleepless were my nights! It was hard to close my eyelids for more than a few minutes at a time. A progressive, unpleasant headache encircled my head, and question marks jumped in my mind, demanding a reason for the whole mess. I didn't know how long I could go on like that without having a breakdown. I couldn't find any explanation for my condition in the school's library. The doctor said I was exhausted, and she suggested that drinking anise tea would help. It didn't.

The principal didn't seem to care when I arrived at his office. "Pay attention to your teachers." Then, he reminded me to sign the pledge. I nodded, promising that I would do it soon, and dragged myself to the school's main gate. I stood there in a state of suspense, waiting for one glimpse of Erick, as usual. I'd exchange a few simple words with him each time he picked up Francine from school. I politely refused their generous invitation to drop me home many times, because Zoiterra was in the opposite direction from my hometown.

When the brown-haired security officer bypassed me, I looked away before he could make another joke about my behavior. He was sure there was something wrong with me because I was the first to arrive at school most days. Today, I got there when it was still dark.

"I can give you the key to open the school tomorrow," he remarked in a sarcastic tone, as if I was after his job.

Even the working staff didn't know what to make of me. I was a student eager to start the school day, yet I skipped doing most of my homework.

Erick's brownish-black car had arrived, and I approached him to say hello. Most times, the conversation went like this: Hello—How do you do—Fine—See you tomorrow. Sometimes I asked about his work, and other times he asked about my family.

Weird . . . I know. But those few words were enough to make my day. And that was even weirder. Why did they?

After saying goodbye to Erick, I rode my bike home. It was another interminable day. It felt as if there was a barrier between my family and me.

I cooked lunch with an almost absent mind, and forgot to add vegetables to the soup, serving salty boiling water.

Sarah, the gregarious one who could usually pull me out of my funky moods, had to throw up her hands in defeat. "Leen, you seem lost! What happened to you?"

I sighed, wishing I could answer her question. Mom and Moria gave me puzzled looks.

After Mom came back from her night shift, I made sandwiches with only bread and nothing in between. Mom threw a fit when I put salt instead of sugar in her tea.

"Lenora, shape up! I don't have the money to keep wasting food." Her eyes blazed with fury.

I couldn't agree more. On both counts.

Eventually, I went to bed . . . or so it seemed. I sat on the floor, leaning my head on the glass wall of my bedroom, hoping that the moonlight would break through my mind and show me a solution. I succumbed to my turbulent thoughts until the moon disappeared and darkness faded under the pink sunrise shadows. I thought I'd imagined it, but it was dawn, for real!

How did I sit on the ground for eight hours?

I got up to prepare for school. On my way to the bathroom, I found

Mom in the kitchen, making orange juice.

"For the past two months, you've been getting up early," Mom remarked, keeping her eyes on the oranges.

"It's the heat." I picked up an orange for her.

She turned to me with stern eyes. "It's only fourteen degrees! Do you have a fever?"

I didn't feel the cold she was talking about. *Is it really fourteen Celsius? But how? I was sweating a river!*

"No, I'm fine," I said, squeezing the orange.

Mom grabbed the orange from me and put her palm on my forehead. "Your face has lost its shine and become paler than your canvas. What's going on? Do you want to skip school today?"

I breathed a sigh. In the past, she had always forced me to attend school; I never skipped a day even during sickness. But now, school had become my life. Well, not school per se—rather the tall man who always came there. "Mom, I'm fine."

I finished the dishes and went to the bathroom. I locked the door behind me and sat on the edge of the bathtub with my head bent down. I sank into my thoughts again. Why was it so hard to get Erick out of my mind? I really didn't know . . . .

For a moment, I forgot what I was in the bathroom to do. I washed my face several times confusedly, awakened by Mom's firm knocking on the door. She was still in the kitchen when I got out. The twins had woken up. I smiled at Sarah and Moria on my way to join her again, but then the doorbell rang.

The twins paled, and I exchanged a tense look with Mom. It was seven in the morning, and we knew only one reason someone would be ringing at this hour.

"Is there anything to worry about?" I whispered to Mom.

"Open the door," she said sharply. I gazed at her with unease for a second and headed toward the door to open it.

Through the light fog, I could see a Law Corps car in front of our small house, its teal and orange lights repeatedly flashing. Five women and two men, all soldiers, lined up outside. I gulped. It was the sin-spots searching team, here for their random checks.

"Glory to Elpax and its honorable citizens," shouted the tall Ms. Iris, and a smug fake smile spread across her wicked face.

"Glory, Ms. Iris," I mumbled, tension tightening my chest.

She ignored me and entered our house with the rest of the female Corps. The tread of their heavy boots on our clean floor caused my heart to quake in fear. Some of the neighbors had come out now, whispering amongst themselves. The first one pointing toward our house was Danira's mom. A malicious grin spread across her face, her superior attitude making its presence known. I closed the door behind me and walked back into the living room.

Ms. Iris looked at Mom with her intense black eyes. "Yorra Karakas, let's begin."

The female soldiers stood at attention, and Mom nodded, accepting the situation for what it was. She sent me a silent message with her eyes that I was quite familiar with. *Take your sisters to my room.*

Anger lit a mutinous fire in me, but I had to obey her. I rushed the twins to Mom's room and kept the door ajar to see what would happen. The color left Sarah's face, while Moria bit back sobs.

I clasped their hands. "Hush. Don't worry—our mother is a respectable woman." I forced a smile and looked out of the narrow gap, although I wasn't supposed to. If any of the soldiers noticed me, I would be arrested, but I had to check on Mom. Ms. Iris swiped Mom's ID lines with the infrared reader, then nodded to her. All expression drained from Mom's face, and she took off her articles of clothing one by one until she stood naked in front of the five strangers.

"Have you written any banned word to your daughters?" Ms. Iris asked Mom.

"No. I haven't written any banned words or actions to my girls."

Ms. Iris held out a small device with a blue light and coursed it all over my mother's body. She gestured for Mom to turn around and did the same for the back. She walked around her for a few seconds before her smile shone forth.

"Impressive, Mrs. Karakas," Ms. Iris commended. She nodded to the Law Corps, and they went out of the house while Mom started putting her clothes back on. I hurried out of the room with the twins once she was fully dressed.

"What audacity is this? It's just seven in the morning!"

"Lenora," Mom said while tying her robe around her waist. "You know very well that the sin-spots searching is random. The important thing is that it went peacefully."

"Mama, I'm very proud of you," Sarah said. "Your name has never appeared on the news among the sinners."

"Well, Sarah, we have to adhere to good morals, right? Come on, get ready for school. I don't want to be late for work."

Anger overwhelmed me. There was no choice for women in this stupid kingdom. It was a ridiculous law. These random searches only included adult women. I always thought it was a curse to be born here. In fact, if they were going to search anyone, they should search the bodies of adult men—they caused the actual calamities worldwide.

I went to my room, got dressed, and rode my bike to school as fast as I could, driven by anger. A single thought penetrated my mind like a lance, slicing it wide open. If even one sin-spot had appeared on Mom's body, they would publicize her name on the news, followed by an extensive investigation into the reasons behind the sin-spots. And in all likelihood, the penalty would be imprisonment in Inferos—if she was lucky.

My soul shuddered at the thought of such a thing happening to Mom. What would happen to us if she were imprisoned? The twins were in their childhood. The kingdom would send them away as properties of the state and do with them as they wanted. I would never allow anything to happen to the twins. I would protect them and Mom, even if it would cost me my life.

PART II

"THE DISCOVERY"

All you need to live a normal life is a full third line . . . not two.

CHAPTER 8

THE NEXT DAY WAS JASON'S Crossing Day . . . and maybe mine, too.

He chose to cross on a quiet day, just like Mary had done. I was supposed to meet him at the Crossing Gate yard after school. The sun appeared bright and shining in the cloudless sky, although the air was a little bit cold, like most November days. Not only did I get Mom's permission to go out with Jason, but she welcomed it. She hoped Jason's crossing would be a beneficial influence on me, and that I might follow him.

I knew right away that taking a taxi was a stupid decision. The car was decrepit, and its constant bouncing over bumps on the uneven roads made my bones groan in pain. The sullen attitude of the driver made it worse. I had to bite my tongue many times to stop myself from screaming.

I should have taken the subway or a bus, but I thought the taxi was a faster option. It turned out to be the dumbest one; the taxi drivers' rude habits in Roses Hill seemed impossible to curb, and no one bothered to check their sin-spots. Only the women had to go through that humiliation. Alas, the law gave men free rein to do anything. Wasn't my father one of them?

A sudden noise from the engine interrupted my thoughts and made the taxi jump and stop. The driver tried many times, but couldn't get the car to start again.

"Miss, get out here. I can go no further."

"Call for another taxi, please."

"I can't. You'll have to manage on your own."

That was downright cruel, as all taxis were connected by live cameras, broadcasting the ride to the transportation center. He could have called another one easily enough.

I got out and slammed the door. "Thanks for your help!" I yelled, and stood on the roadside in a huff. After a long time of waiting for another taxi with no luck, I called Jason, and he came to pick me up.

We reached the Crossing Gate shortly. Jason's guide wasn't the same as mine, but he was tactful and didn't comment on my failure to cross a few months ago.

For the first time, I waited for someone on the opposite side of the Crossing Gate—Mary's mother didn't want me to come when her daughter crossed. A bright light emitted from the passageway's exit, but I could still see Jason when he came midway down the pathway. He seemed quite comfortable, and even waved to me. He walked with quiet, confident steps, giving an enormous smile as the third line got tattooed on his wrist. His eyes met my fearful ones with a quiet understanding, and a tear fell down my cheek. Jason was the only one who would never tell me what to do or when to cross. I was happy that, like me, he didn't believe in forcing someone to do something only because everyone else was doing it. It was one of the reasons that we had become best friends.

Jason ended his crossing with a cheerful jump. "I've finally become an adult!" he shouted, and pointed to his third line. I touched it. Still warm and shiny.

"Congratulations!" My words were heartfelt as I looked up at him.

He smiled. "I'll never forget that you stood by me. You're the best."

"Please! I wish I could do more."

"Your wonderful friendship is all that I need." His smile widened. "So, do you want to cross?"

My breath sped up.

"No pressure. If you prefer to cross alone today without all those silly cameras, my father can issue an approval for you right now. The government doesn't limit the VIP crossing permission to the wealthy, as you know."

"What a brilliant idea!" I wet my lip. "Did you feel anything weird? Like . . . dizzy?"

"No, why?"

I shook my head. "Never mind. Oh, I almost forgot." I took a gift from my bag that I'd made for his Crossing Day: a picture of him which I'd drawn and framed.

"Leen! This is incredible!" He exclaimed, taking hold of my hand.

"It's nothing. Thank you for your idea about letting me cross alone. I don't feel ready to cross today, but I'll think about it."

His guide approached us, interrupting our conversation. "Excuse me, Mr. Valemont," he said in a firm tone. "Before you do anything else, you must come with me to attend the courses pertaining to the adult phase. I don't need to remind you that the authorities forbid you from telling the juvenile," he pointed to me, "about anything you'll learn."

I turned to Jason, my stomach churning with anxiety. He gave a calm smile, reassuring me without words, and rushed with the guide toward the government-issued car. Sighing with sorrow, I got into his family car so Nicholas could drive me home. On the way, one thought increasingly concerned me. I knew change was constant; I felt it when Mary and now Jason crossed. Everyone thought I was immature and spoiled. I wasn't. I needed to know why I couldn't cross. Why did I get dizzy when others could cross so easily?

Where should I start searching?

I held my umbrella and walked out of the school gate, lost in contemplation after my meeting with the creepy consultant.

Today, he finally forced me to sign the electronic pledge before we started the session. It was our . . . I'd stopped counting the sessions after the twentieth one. These meetings took place in the principal's office every Thursday at the end of the school day, and consisted of nonsense chatting that always led to an impasse. I thought the crossing consultant would at least help me pinpoint what was scaring me the most about crossing, or prescribe some medications to soothe my anxiety. Alas, we spent our sessions talking about my father's family, who I didn't know much about. His parents were living in Betis, but his sisters died before I was born.

Eventually, I found myself standing in front of Erick's car. I blinked. Francine skipped school today, so why was his car parked there?

I approached the empty car in confusion, staring at it for a while, wondering where he was. I wanted to wait for him, yet standing next to his car would be suspicious. After a few moments of hesitation, I turned around and was startled to find Erick walking toward me with a big smile on his face.

"Nice to see you, Leen." He extended his hand to me.

His deep voice increased my heartbeat. The "nice to see you" wasn't a familiar line in our conversational catalog. The unexpected offer of a handshake brought my tension to a peak. My mouth went dry, and I knew right away that I would stutter if I spoke.

"Me . . . me too." I held out a trembling hand. His strong, warm grasp caught my smaller one.

"Your hand is icy! Are you all right?" A worried expression passed over his face. I didn't reply, but I looked away. He squeezed my hand with a gentle touch to direct my attention. My face flushed, and I looked again into his pretty eyes.

"Where's Francine?" I asked, trying to skip over the awkward moment.

He let go of my hand. "She's sick, and the principal called me in to discuss some issues."

"I hope it's nothing serious."

"Oh no, it's a simple cold."

I nodded. "I'm glad she's okay. Well, see you later." I almost walked away when he called out.

"Leen, would you allow me to drive you home?"

My heart pounded. Did I hear that right? Did he want to drop me off at home? Alone? In his car? I wanted to jump with elation until a sensible voice in my head, which sounded like Mom, brought me back to reality.

"We can't do that, Erick," I said. "You know that only a wealthy adult can hang out with a juvenile without a relative present."

He pointed at the balanced scales logo stuck to his car's window. "This symbol is for people who work in legal affairs. The authorities allow us to be alone with juveniles." He extended his hand to me again. I hesitated for a few seconds, but I could feel that he was genuine in his intentions.

I gave him my bike lock. His left wrist touched the ID sensor on the car, and he opened the door for me. "Please wait in the car."

I nodded and shook my umbrella, tension roiling through my body.

The car was super clean, just like it had been the first time I was in here. My eyes moved all around, examining every corner. It intimidated me. A man with a meticulous car like this wouldn't care for anything random, and I was random—very random. This particular thought made my chin tremble.

Is it possible that there are imperfections at his core that will allow him to accept my own? Or should I feign perfection in his presence?

A golden chain hung from the rear-view mirror with a pendant of Gamotos's flag and the Eiffel tower. I turned to look at Erick through the dark window. He had finished putting my bike in the trunk and, with undeniable grace, climbed into the car. His perfume spread through the closed air and caused my limbs to quiver. It was that potent.

I pointed to the chain. "It . . . it's pretty," I mumbled, trying hard to forget my awkward feelings before he could notice.

75

"That's kind of you. It was a gift from my mother."

His last name is Greek, I thought. *Judging by the Eiffel Tower pendant, his mom's ancestors must be from Gaul.*

He glanced at me. "She's not well. She's in the hospital due to a chronic illness."

"Oh, I'm sorry."

Erick nodded with sorrow, and silence reigned in the car until he asked a random question. "So, what are your hobbies?"

At least he didn't start talking about the weather! "Climbing trees."

"Me too! The serenity that you get when you sit on the branch of a tree, surrounded by green leaves, is impossible to describe in words."

"You said the exact thing I had in mind!" I exclaimed. A wide smile showed on my face.

He nodded, smiling too. "I guess we share something in common, then!"

My face turned crimson. "Erick, when did you cross?" My words came out as if it were an earnest inquiry, not a casual question.

"Six years ago, at the first possible opportunity."

So, if he crossed right after his fifteenth birthday, he must be twenty-one years old by now. That's cool!

"Aren't you going to ask me why I didn't cross?" I mumbled.

"Leen, it's your own business. If you ever want to share your reasons, I'm ready to listen. But I believe everyone should decide for themselves."

I turned my face, looking out the window, and welcomed the warm feeling inside me. He understood.

We were close to the Roses Hill security checkpoint, and the Law Corps soldiers motioned Erick to stop the car. My face paled. I knew that we weren't breaking any laws here, as Erick had assured me, but one could never trust the Law Corps. They had the right to arrest a worker for any reason.

"Don't be afraid," Erick reassured me before opening his window.

The soldier walked closer, his rifle on his shoulder. "Glory to Elpax,

76

sir. May I see your ID?"

"Sure," said Erick with confidence, and extended his left wrist to him.

The soldier checked his ID with a small reader and looked at me, sending my stomach sinking down to my toes. "You too."

CHAPTER 9

I STRETCHED MY ARM OUT to him, and he scanned my ID. "Have a pleasant day, sir." He gestured to Erick to move ahead.

I heaved a sigh of relief. Erick drove in silence for a while before he turned to me.

"Why did you get so pale?"

Surely, as a lawyer, he knew the dangers the working class faced for the slightest violation of the rules. But I didn't want to show my weakness in front of him—I had already embarrassed myself enough by making a scene on my Crossing Day, and I had to prove to him that I was mature, strong.

Except I was terrible at lying to people. I remembered when Danira told me *it's okay to tell a "white" lie and save yourself from embarrassing situations.* I searched for a suitable lie to utter, but only a corny one came to my mind at the moment. "I have a headache."

"I'm sorry if I caused it by any chance."

"Oh, no. I'm having fun now." I rushed to explain, "But my meeting with the crossing consultant today is still disturbing me."

Erick narrowed his eyes. "May I ask what annoyed you?"

How could I tell him about it? He was a stranger, regardless of how much my heart pounded in his presence. I couldn't tell him that the creepy consultant had asked about my father, insisting on finding out about the family tragedy. That would bring more questions that I wasn't ready to answer.

I turned to him after a while. "He asked about my goal in life."

"And what did you say?"

I took in a sharp breath. "To stay exactly where I am." I peeked at him. His face tightened, and I couldn't figure out if my answer was palatable to him.

"If that's your choice, so be it."

My smile widened at his diplomacy. For the first time, I felt there was someone other than Jason who understood me. "I wish I could work without crossing, though. Do you need an undercover investigator? I swear I won't tell anyone," I joked.

He laughed. "I wish." His sweet reply made me blush. "Do you have a light job?"

"Yes. I paint portraits."

His eyebrows went upward. "Interesting. Can you draw me?"

"You can't afford it," I joked, and he laughed.

We'd almost reached my house when I recognized the short silver-mint hair of our neighbor Karya. She was walking on the roadside, struggling with a pair of heavy fabric bags. One of them tore, and oranges scattered on the ground. Karya bent down to pick them up when a boy approached her and kicked the oranges away. Anger seeped into my blood, and I was about to tell Erick to stop the car, but he did it without me saying a word.

He resolutely stepped out onto the road, shoving the door shut behind him. The boy yelled at Erick to mind his own business. I rushed out to Karya, who rolled her arms around her slim body.

"Let me help you."

She looked at me with nervous gratitude, and we bent over together to

79

pick the oranges off the ground. I sneaked a peek at the boy's ID lines, and surprise flooded through me. There were three on his wrist. What a pity for an adult to behave this way. I thought if he had been a juvenile, Erick would have had a better chance of disciplining him.

Erick's voice rose in fury, and the neighborhood men gathered around, trying hard to end the quarrel, which felt like it would escalate to physical hands-on fighting.

"Your companion shouldn't do that," Karya mumbled. "I'm used to it."

"Karya! Are you insane? Your late crossing should give no one a reason to bully you."

She sighed with sorrow and took the last orange from me. "I can understand you, but . . . don't do what I did. Just use the wheelchair next time and don't get the royals' attention."

I understood why she cared. After all, the government had forced her to cross and spread awful propaganda about her. The government kept telling us we had the choice of when to cross. But that wasn't the reality.

I always believed that this was absurd—to bully a girl because she chose a different path. We were the only family in the entirety of Roses Hill who spoke to her.

Karya didn't give me a chance to express any of my thoughts. Instead, she took her bags and turned to walk away, but hesitated. "One more thing," she whispered, turning back again. "If you want to know more about the crossing troubles, ask Isaac."

"Silver-haired Isaac? Our neighbor from the childhood school?"

She nodded. "The one you beat in the running competition. You remember that he tried to cross at age fifteen, right? He backed out once he stood in front of the Crossing Gate. He didn't say a word at the time. Next year, he used a wheelchair."

"So, he felt dizzy, too? In front of the gate?"

She didn't answer. I understood that she didn't want to put herself in more trouble. At least she gave me a hint of where to start my investigation—a thread of hope that I wasn't an odd case.

I looked at Erick. He approached us after the young man left with the others.

"Miss," Erick said to Karya, "I'm a lawyer, and I'm offering my services to help you sue that man, free of charge."

"There's no need for that."

Erick took the bags from Karya. "With your permission, I'll drive you home."

She looked at me with uncertainty, and I smiled to reassure her of his good intentions. As Erick placed the heavy shopping bags in the trunk, Karya leaned over and whispered, "He's a principled man, and will be a suitable husband."

I wanted to explain that he was just my friend's brother, but Erick opened the car door for her. We sank into silence until we reached her house. He accompanied Karya right up to her doorstep, carrying the heavy bags. Then, he drove around the corner and stopped the car in front of my house.

"Thank you for what you did for Karya. It was noble."

"Please tell her that my offer was sincere."

I was about to tell him he'd have to sue the entire town, for almost everyone bullied Karya and her family, but I heard the door music that indicated someone was coming outside. I turned to see my mother standing right there in the entryway. In her eyes was a clear look of worry, along with anger at my late arrival from school. I wet my lips in sudden anxiety as both of us stepped out of the car. Mom approached us with a clenched jaw, taking in the sight.

"Mama," I hurried to explain, "Mr. Erick is a lawyer. He's my friend's brother." I looked at him. "My mom, Yorra Karakas."

Mom shook hands with him, and her sullen facial features transformed into a wholehearted smile. I had hardly ever seen her grin so widely.

"My apologies, Mrs. Karakas, for the lateness of the hour."

Mom glanced at me from the corner of her eye. It was hard to figure out what she was thinking. *Am I in trouble now?*

"Where do you work, Mr. . . . ?" Her words were calm, so I took a deep breath, trying to reassure my racing heart.

"Erick Mellas. I work at the Union Company in Zoiterra." His beatific smile stretched out.

"Thank you," she said in a firm tone, and pointed me toward the house. I nodded to Erick and put my bike away.

Mom and I entered the house. She picked up her handbag from the table near the door and waited until Erick drove away. I hurried into my room to avoid any further discussion. Before I could shut the door, she called to me, "He's handsome!"

What? That was unusual!

"For real, Mom?" My eyes widened at her. She nodded with a smile. I couldn't believe her! I exhaled sharply. "He's middle-class."

"Study at the university, and you'll become a middle!" She stepped out of the house and closed the door behind her while I was still staring. She approved!

I tried hard to take a nap, but it wasn't possible. Rest seemed to have disappeared from my life forever. I called Mary, and it was a delightful surprise that she was back in town—and she wanted to visit me in two hours. I checked on the twins, washed the dishes, and finished the laundry. When the doorbell rang, I ran over and slid the door open happily.

"Come on in, Mary. How are you? How was Theirna?" I grabbed her umbrella to hang it on the rack.

"Hold on, Leen. Let me get in first, and then I'll answer your questions."

We walked to my room, where she sat next to me on the bed and unbuttoned her elegant beige coat.

"It was great!" Her eyes narrowed. "But forget about me. What's wrong with you? Why do you have black circles around your eyes? Aren't you sleeping?"

I wet my lips. "Well, not really. I haven't slept well for two months

82

now. I'm dizzy most of the time, and thinking clearly has become so hard. I don't feel hungry or thirsty. It's like I'm floating in another world which I can neither escape nor gain full access to."

Her eyes popped out. "Since when?"

I was silent for a few moments. My eyes began to swim with tears. "It started with a dream after your wedding."

Our eyes met for a moment, and she became quiet, scrutinizing me thoughtfully.

"Every night, I have the same dream." I started telling her everything about Erick, and her face grew more and more astonished as I kept narrating all that had happened to me. I thought that her eyes might pop out of their sockets. My heartbeat accelerated as I gauged her reaction, and my instincts cautioned me that it was an enormous deal—perhaps more than I thought it to be.

"What is it, Mary? Tell me."

Her forehead furrowed in deep thought, and she threaded her fingers through her hair several times. I watched her hesitation with a jumping pulse. She had to say something.

"How did this happen?" she hissed at last. "Do you remember being ill?"

My brows snapped together. *What is she talking* about? Yes, I got sick a lot. Chronic asthma, nosebleeds, and anemia were all to blame for various illnesses throughout my life. Which one had caused me to become delirious? I couldn't say for sure, because such an incident had never happened to me before.

"Oh, I think I've figured it out," said Mary, snapping her fingers. "Maybe bumping your head at my wedding caused a chemical reaction in your brain that has made you experience the symptoms you mentioned, and you blamed the first unfamiliar person you encountered."

"You can't be serious!"

She shrugged.

"Mary, it's too wonderful—not like an illness. Even if it is one, it's as beautiful as a dream. Look, for the first time, the symptoms of my illness have drawn me into a foggy, magical world where my heart seems to beat out of joy rather than routine. And for the first time, my throat's gotten dry in anticipation. Not the way I feel parched on summery days."

"It isn't possible," she blurted out, shaking her head.

That sentence held my attention right away. "What is it, Mary? What isn't possible?" My face fell in misery. "Tell me what's wrong with me."

She stared at me for a while, then got up and grabbed my notebook from my desk. She sighed and sat next to me again, holding the charcoal pencil between her fingers. "What you're asking of me will get us into endless trouble if anyone ever finds out. But damn it! I can't leave you so worried." She handed me the pencil. "Write out the entire alphabet."

My eyes narrowed at her in confusion.

"In the sin-spots investigation, I can safely say I didn't *write* or *say* anything about it," she said.

"You mean . . ." My jaw dropped open. She nodded approvingly. Oh my! She was about to tell me something about the adult world!

Intelligent Mary, as always. I wrote what she asked with a smile I couldn't hide. At last, she would tell me something new, and it seemed important.

"Never utter this word," she warned. "What you are going through is the start of this thing." She pointed to the letters with her finger one by one. I wrote the word as her finger moved, and my eyes expanded in curiosity.

A D M I R A T I O N!

Mary sighed and took a few deep breaths, but didn't explain further. She looked disturbed, and my smile vanished. Her pale face scared me. Her serious reaction toward all of this caused my breaths to speed up while my stomach twisted with an unknown tension.

"Will it kill me?" I practically screamed the words.

"No, it won't!" she huffed. After a few moments, she started talking again. "It's not a disease. It's a feeling. It's a kind of emotion that you should only realize when you have crossed and become an adult. Never before that. Never. Ever."

My skin tingled, and I reached up a hand to my slightly blocked throat.

How did I get an adult feeling? How?

"Mary, what will happen to me now?"

CHAPTER 10

I SPENT THE NIGHT TWISTING and turning in bed. Visions of Erick imploded my mind. He was my sun, and I was a sunflower, blossoming in his rays. My heart craved to beat next to his. I wanted to feel his breath on my skin. Recognizing the emotion and giving it a name made me feel it more intensely. I wanted to be alive and to live with him. His hand reached out, calling me to him. My soul answered, making me run down unseen cobbled paths in search of him. Nothing would stop me now. It was only him that I wanted.

The world turned ancient, filled with strange people and even stranger creatures. The swirling mist obscured my vision, and I could hear him imploring, making a desperate appeal. There was sadness in his voice. Its echo haunted me, and I was lost. I was alone. The very air was suffocating me, and a scream penetrated the silent otherworld. I ran to answer it.

Erick . . .

I woke up with a start, his name on my lips, my body drenched in sweat. I looked at the windows, trying to calm my racing heart. The sun was about to rise. A cold, beautiful morning heralded a new weekend. When I made my way out of my room, Mom was standing in front of the main door, ready to leave to buy groceries. I stopped her. "Mom, can Jason and Mary come over?"

She stared at me for a while, balancing things in her head. "Jason has grown up, so his visits should be less frequent from now on."

I gave a quick bark of laughter. I thought she was joking with me, but her stern eyes didn't budge. I didn't understand why. Jason was one of the wealthy, and he was the same boy as the one he'd been yesterday. Wasn't he?

She took a deep breath and agreed. "But follow the law, Lenora. Keep the visit short and the curtains pulled aside." She closed the main door behind her, leaving me in a state of astonishment.

"Ew, it looks like you got into trouble again," observed the ever-watchful Moria. I turned to the twins, who were sitting in the living room.

"Let's see your homework." I texted Jason and Mary and helped the twins with their studies for an hour, then I decided I should see Isaac. Maybe he could tell me something about why I couldn't cross.

I walked out of the house. "I'll be right back," I said to my sisters, shutting the main door behind me. I walked to Isaac's place with a determination to find something, anything.

I looked around before my hand reached toward Isaac's bell. The street was almost empty, and there was no sound but the birds chirping. I waited for a few seconds before I rang the bell again.

A dark-skinned woman inside the house pulled the curtains aside, her black eyes gazing at me. "What do you want?"

"Glory ma'am. I am sorry for the inconvenience," I said to her. "I need to talk to Isaac."

She let the curtain fall without a word.

I sighed with sadness. She used to welcome me, and even send us some pastries occasionally. What happened to her? Was she avoiding me because I couldn't cross?

I walked out of the garden, ready to return to my nearby house when

87

I heard a whistle from behind. Turning around, I saw Isaac waving for me from his room's window, pointing at the kitchen.

I checked the house windows, making sure that his mom wasn't looking, and rushed to the kitchen side. He opened the window for me.

"Where is your mom?" I asked.

"In the adult room." He glanced around. "What do you want?"

I scanned the street before I hissed, "I want to know if you felt dizzy when you went through the Crossing Gate."

"Who told you?" he snapped.

"Does it matter?"

Isaac looked back into the house again, then whispered, "You are crossing a line here."

I rolled my eyes. "Is that because I won the school's running competition? We were children!"

"No, silly girl," he breathed. "Look, do you know what curiosity did to the cat? Curiosity is a sin, Lenora. A fatal one."

"I am not a cat." I kept my eyes on him, showing my absolute determination to find what he was hiding.

He sighed. "All right, if you need to know, then yes, I did. But I didn't make a scene like you! I don't know why it happened to me. But don't mention this in front of anyone."

"I wasn't going to. I just needed to know the truth."

"The truth is, if you refuse to cross again, the government will definitely accuse you of rebelling. That's a sin, Lenora. Or if they find out about your dizziness, they may arrest you and begin experimenting on your brain. Just be careful."

"I will. Thank you."

"And remember, we didn't have this conversation."

I saw Mary's car approaching my home further down the street. I nodded, heading back to my house. At least he confirmed I wasn't an odd case here. Now, I had two principal problems. Why was I experiencing adult feelings? And why I couldn't cross?

I knew that my sinner father and my childhood agony were part of the problem. The sin-spots searching team, too; I could never agree to expose my body to strangers. It felt like my dilemma had many sides to be solved. I would start with why I was feeling something for Erick, then why I couldn't cross physically.

I let my friends in and made tea for the three of us. We sat in my room, keeping the door ajar. Mary went to use the bathroom, while I stayed with Jason. I looked at him from the corner of my eye. He didn't look different since becoming an adult. The only change was that he'd started helping with his father's business.

"How is it becoming an adult? Any different?"

He held the teacup. "Lots. But I can't talk about it. You know, the word-catcher . . ."

"Oh, got it. But you can surely read."

"Huh? Where are you going with this, Leen? Should that scare me?" He snickered while I grabbed my notebook and opened it.

"What is this, Jason?" I pointed to the "admiration" word. As soon as he saw it, he spat out the tea, staining his clothes and mine.

"Oh my God! How do you know this word? You're a juvenile!" he whispered in panic, turning his head toward the floor-to-ceiling windows, searching for word-catchers.

"Relax, Jason. They aren't cameras!" I grabbed a towel to clean up the mess he'd caused. "Here, scrub your shirt."

Jason asked in a serious tone, "Who is the crazy one who told you about this? This is serious! Did you forget that nearly every Saturday the government punishes those who break the law? Damn it, Leen. The process of judgment happens almost every week. Whoever told you about that word could be next, and you could end up in Inferos. What's wrong with you?"

"I told her," revealed Mary as she walked in. "But I didn't explain any further."

He shook his head. "You shouldn't have. Have you lost your mind?"

89

Jason rubbed his shirt with rough, angry strokes, while Mary sat beside him. "No, I haven't. She already *feels* it."

He turned to me, his eyebrows snapping together. "What did she just say?"

"I felt it when I saw a man," I clarified, kneeling on the floor to clean it. "And he hasn't left my mind ever since. I almost see him in your face."

For a few seconds, he froze like a block of ice. He glanced at Mary, and a weird vibe wavered between us. I didn't understand the reason. Was he angry with me? I felt sad—I didn't want to lose him. He and Mary had been my only friends since I moved to Zetikas. They were part of my family.

I shook myself to get rid of those melancholy thoughts and sat on my chair. "I thought about it for a long time. Do you remember what the diviner said about the five letters in a man's name? I think she meant him."

"And now what? You'll think about every man with five letters in his name? That's insane!"

"Not every man, Jason! Him! I saw him in a dream even before I met him."

"Then why am I the last to know about this?" His eyes were blazing by now.

"Why are you so mad?" I yelled, and Mary started laughing.

Jason crossed his arms and screamed back at Mary, "Why are you laughing? He might be a rebel!"

Now it was my turn to burst out laughing, unable to contain myself. Jason watched us giggling, and a wave of crimson covered his face.

"Are you done?" he mumbled.

"Well, I can assure you he isn't a rebel," I answered in between my chuckles.

"So, are we expecting a crossing soon?" Mary winked at me.

I gulped nervously. "About that . . . I didn't tell you everything."

Both of them looked at me with curious eyes.

"About what, Leen?" asked Mary with a kind voice, as if she was talking to a child.

90

"Hmm . . . you know . . ."

"Spill it, Leen."

I threw up my hands in defeat. "I can't cross."

"We know that!"

"No, I mean . . . I physically cannot cross. The moment I take a step toward the Crossing Gate, I get headaches, dizziness, and shaky limbs. I want to cross . . . well, most of the time I do. But I can't cross because of some external force, even beyond my fear and anxiety. I'm not doing it on purpose like everyone seems to think."

Jason and Mary looked at each other. I knew they, too, had thought I was refusing to cross on purpose. But they were my best friends, so I forgave them.

"So, you are afraid of adulthood, but you also feel that something else is holding you back from crossing?" asked Mary.

"Exactly! And this adult feeling has left me exhausted. I need to know more so I can deal with it. Guys, you have to help me."

"Wait a second," Jason snapped, his face tensing up.

"What?" we both asked him.

"If . . . if . . ." he gulped. "Leen, if you have this adult feeling, will you get the adult sin-spots too?"

The color drained from my face.

CHAPTER II

I JUMPED FROM MY CHAIR, shocked by the realization. My heart fluttered like a baby bird's wings, trying to survive a ruthless hawk's hegemony. I gasped several times, struggling to remember how to breathe.

Jason held my sweaty palm at once, his other hand on my back. "Look at me, Leen. Just breathe."

Mary rushed to the kitchen. She soon came back with a glass of water and handed it to me. I couldn't hold it, or even take a sip. My chest tightened, and it felt like I was choking to death. I pointed to my inhaler on the desk and Mary hurried to pick it up for me. One puff, two, and I could finally feel the air inside my lungs, bringing me back to life again.

"Look at me, Leen," snapped Jason. My worried eyes met his, and he gathered his hands in front of his mouth as if he was about to pray. "Have you lied to anyone recently?"

I couldn't remember, so I shook-nodded my head.

"All right. Tell me a lie right now . . . just say anything that isn't true."

"What if that makes a sin-spot appear?" Mary whispered in a disturbed voice.

"It's okay," Jason assured her. "She can redeem this sin."

"I can't afford it, Jason," I hissed.

"But we can, Leen. I have the time and money for it. I'll pay the required money for the government right now if it comes down to it." He looked at me, waiting for an answer.

I wasn't comfortable about taking a thousand paxin from my dear friend, even if he'd willingly offered. I narrowed my eyes, trying to find another solution. I recalled that I had lied to Erick, telling him I had a headache instead of answering his question, and no sin-spots had appeared on my body since then—as far as I knew.

"When you lie, does the sin-spot appear on your back?" I asked them.

Jason shook his head, and pointed at his face, arms and chest. I rushed to the bathroom to double-check, lifting up my shirt and peering under my arms. Fortunately, I had no sin-spots.

Going back to my room, I told them about what had happened earlier with Erick. They dropped on the bed with slumping shoulders. Their breathing returned to normal.

I sat on the chair and looked at them. "I want to know more. I know lying is a sin, but what are the others?"

"That, we *can't* answer," said Jason. He glanced at Mary, who agreed. Jason took a deep breath and whispered the next few words, as if speaking to himself. "Leen, I understand your concerns. But what you want to know is too dangerous. It might create more problems for you and your family."

"We can't tell you things outright, but you need to know what's happening to you. We need to know too," Mary said. "So here's what we'll do. I'll tell you what I can about certain feelings, and maybe you'll recognize some of them. Then, I'll teach you a cool cipher I learned about recently. It's called the Vigenère cipher. We can use it to text about whatever you want."

Jason tried to argue, but she shushed him. I picked up my notebook, and Mary started pointing to the various letters, one by one, while I wrote them. Mary spent around an hour using this method to explain various words. Love, longing, jealousy, nostalgia, romance and flirting. These were the words the word-catchers could recognize if we spoke them. Mary wrote a side note that there were other adult feelings, but I didn't need to learn about them at the moment.

Love is a progressed version of admiration, and it could lead to babies being born. I finished writing this last line and blinked at it in surprise. Although Mary didn't explain further, I wondered how a feeling could produce whole people.

Mom had told me once, when I asked her where children came from, that after two people got married, Eros threw his arrow toward a bird that fell in front of a couple's house. When the woman ate the bird, it would turn into a child growing inside her body. Nine months later, her belly button widened, and the baby came out. I never could imagine how my skinny mother ate two similar birds at the same time that later became Moria and Sarah!

Perhaps, for that reason, I never ate meat. Although I knew that the bird usually only turned into a child after being eaten by a married adult, I'd heard that some juveniles in other provinces had given birth to children without marriage, and they'd disappear. No one knew where they ended up.

I always thought the accident of birth allowed contradictory people to gather under one roof, and now I had new words and emotions to contend with. Words that were banned in the juvenile phase. And I was the odd one who felt at least one of those emotions but couldn't work out why.

"So, what do you think?" I asked, pointing at the page where I was trying to come up with a symbolic code to say "I love you." Using my own coding. That Vigenère cipher was too difficult for me to write in by myself. Σε αγαπώ (7 letters, 2 words, 1 meaning) = 721

"Interesting." Jason shook his head. "You aren't planning to text him this, are you?"

"I don't think I'm there yet!" I poked his shoulder. "It's for you guys."

"Oh, you are so sweet!" exclaimed Mary. "Well, 721 too." She winked at Jason. "I suppose it's your turn to say 721 to Leen."

He narrowed his eyes as his face turned crimson. "Leen, I still don't understand how you felt something for that guy."

I understood that he wanted to change the subject, so I picked up on his line of inquiry. I told him the explanation Mary had suggested earlier, and he roared with laughter, telling her that hitting my head wasn't a scientific explanation and she should stick to studying sustainable energy.

I buried my head in my hands, thinking, and suddenly it hit me. "It all started with the diviner. She put something sticky on my head."

"Those were only herbs, Leen. I was there," Jason assured me. Yet, his eyes were worried.

"But there must be a connection. I need to call her."

Mary's forehead creased. "That diviner was a wedding gift from the Queen Mother Arianna. But I'll ask my mother for the diviner's name and contact information."

I thanked her. But in the meantime, I suggested searching in the only place that might have an explanation for my case. It was too risky to search the private web browser for answers, even with my friends' secured Iméfonos. Mary and Jason refused to let me go alone, and they insisted on coming with me.

It took a lot of careful strategizing to carve out a plan that would get us to our destination, where we hoped we'd find some answers. It was risky, and we knew we would be charged with treason if the Law Corps caught us.

The next week, after Jason came back from a business trip in Theirna, Mary came over to my house with a big bag that contained the necessary props. Mom had gone to work, and the twins were being babysat at Karya's place.

"Leen, stop wriggling so much."

"It tickles."

95

"Get used to it."

I had to stand still while Mary arranged the blond wig on my head and applied heavy makeup to my face. I refused to wear the dress she'd brought. I had never worn such a gauzy material, and I'd break my ankle in her high heels. She gave in when I said that I could never run in those shoes if we had to escape. I perched huge round eyeglasses on my nose. By the time I looked in the mirror, I couldn't recognize myself.

I didn't want to think about our destination until we got into Jason's new car. No one spoke for the entire car ride. The tension started escalating, and I could imagine how fast my friends' heartbeats were rising. My heart was pounding as if it wanted to leap out of my chest. But I had no choice—I had to do this. It was unsafe not knowing. If sin-spots started appearing on my body before I crossed and the government found out about my case, they might arrest me and send me to a place where they'd run tests on my brain as they pleased. No one could rescue me then—not even my wealthy friends or a lawyer like Erick.

Jason turned to Mary. "Keep your Iméfono switched on so I can hear you." He drove onto Bolina Street in Zoiterra and stopped a few meters away from our destination.

The National Library.

The government collected books from all over the world to preserve humanity's heritage in the national library, despite the electronic versions adults could access on their Iméfonos. It was a noble thing the kingdom had done for the public, as usually the kingdom imported nothing but basics from the other great power in the world, the Republic of Latina—Union of Latin America. We weren't like the wealthy, who would import air from the Modern Roman Empire if they could.

Mary and I got out of the car. She confidently crossed the street, while my feet were trembling, and I almost fell midway. I tried my best to keep the tension off my face when we entered the majestic place. The very air inside called for stillness, inviting us to take a tour and imbibe all the great works of literature the stones were a silent witness to. High arched ceilings,

96

huge pillars, and black-and-white marble flooring all reflected the light cast by the enormous chandelier.

The security men searched Mary's bag and checked that our Iméfonos had no cameras. Mary had to bring her old juvenile Iméfono, so that she wouldn't be able to take pictures of the adults' books and show them later to a child or a juvenile.

I walked into the quiet library with false confidence, the silence broken only by Mary's high heels tapping the solid ground. The sound reminded me of another day, when the stride of my mother's shoes broke the stillness of the court, and my life changed forever. We had fled my father's abuse and escaped with our lives intact.

A circular desk sat in the center of the vestibule, manned by a young brunette. As I stood at the reception, waiting for the girl to notice us, I looked up at the way they'd built the place. I strained my neck, but couldn't see the far end of the library. The architecture gave the impression of an arena, with circular glass floors widening away from the center. Chairs spread out in a semicircle on alternating sides of each floor, which made the arrangement look like a steep maze when I peered upwards. Only the first floor was straightforward, with the children's bookshelves to the right and the ones for adolescents to the left.

"Glory to Elpax, Miss," Mary greeted the receptionist. "I want to access the third floor."

"Glory. May I see your ID?" the girl said in a bored tone, without bothering to look up. Mary extended her wrist. My feet were tapping on the floor, my eyes glancing around, looking for Jason. He was late! Damn, he was late.

"I need your Iméfono," said the receptionist to Mary. Then she looked at me, holding the ID reader in her hand. "You too."

Mary arched her eyebrow and tilted her head, asking me to come forward. I had drawn the third line earlier with my liquid eyeliner. Because the shades between the fake and real lines were different, I had also painted the other two, hoping that the girl wouldn't notice they were somehow

97

darker.

As I held out my wrist, unease slithered down my spine. *Where the hell is Jason?*

98

CHAPTER 12

BEFORE SHE COULD PLACE THE device on my wrist, a voice interrupted the whole proceeding.

"Glory to Elpax, Miss!" Carrying a huge bouquet of white lilies that almost covered his face, Jason hurried through the foyer, making his footsteps as loud as possible. "One of your staff won a bouquet from my flower shop in a random draw contest, and I want to deliver it personally. Would you call for him?"

I breathed easier. It was true that Jason owned a flower shop. He and Mary had spent hours searching for the staff names online, and I wrote their names on the random name picker application. That way, the staff member technically *had* been selected by a random draw, so Jason wouldn't get sin-spots for saying so.

"Glory, sir. Please wait while I give these two girls an access card, and then I'll do that for you."

The girl moved the device toward my wrist, and my fear reached its zenith. I kept it hidden in my chest with the strength of my will power. My face looked still and nonchalant, but my heart pounded like drums beating in a rising crescendo.

Jason threw the flower bouquet on the desk in front of the employee, hitting my wrist and thrusting it aside. "Come on, beautiful. I'm in a hurry," Jason urged the girl, whose eyes widened with suffused joy. "I'm glad that I had to deliver the flowers and got to see your beautiful face. It made my day."

The wide smile stretching right up to her eyes stunned me. "Oh, get out!" she said, blushing while looking at him through her lashes. Her voice, which had been brusque with us, changed to something akin to softness. I almost laughed. This was a crazy world.

"What's your name?"

"Carlota."

"What a wonderful name, Carlota. What would you say if I invited you to dinner with me tonight?"

"Well, I'd agree," Carlota replied, throwing the magnetic elevator card on the table without paying attention to us.

"And what kind of food do you prefer? Let me guess—seafood? I know a great restaurant close to this place and . . ."

I was curious to find out where that conversation would end. Mary was right. When we were planning this endeavor, she had said that no woman could ignore Jason's charms and sultry voice. When he laughed at something Carlota said, I glanced back to observe him. He was very handsome.

Before I recognized the feeling of admiration, I used to simply prefer things. For example, I preferred orange juice over apple juice, or talking to Sarah over Moria. Still, I couldn't figure out how I was supposed to feel about guys flirting with me. I guessed there was something in the adult world that prevented women from ignoring a husky voice!

Mary pulled my arm toward the glass elevator, rushing me away before Carlota came out of her trance, and placed the thin magnetic card in a special slot next to the elevator. I had never stepped inside one in my entire

100

life, and it scared me that I'd get stuck in it. I wasn't so concerned that the elevator might fall. In fact, falling in an elevator would be better than being found in one if the authorities discovered my counterfeit line.

Mary looked at me with a tense smile and pushed me right in. I was aware that there was no time to hesitate, and I was glad she took charge. We'd already succeeded in the first stage of our plan, and the authorities were none the wiser. My troubled heart calmed down, but the urge to get out fast didn't subside. The elevator reached the third floor in seconds, and I burst out at once, scared of getting caught between its doors.

The entire floor was so huge that reaching the other end would take me half an hour. The semicircular seating area had glass tables, each with wooden and steel brackets and a small lamp at the edge. Black steel bookshelves were placed in between the seats, which gave a hint of privacy.

"Mary, how do you know we're on the third floor?"

"From the elevator's number. But it's a misnomer. The entire place is like a labyrinth. Once you've spent some time here, you'll know where to go. The bookshelves give a bit of an idea, too. Look to your left; that's the electronic screen. You can tap on it and put in the book's name, and it'll give you directions to the bookshelf it's on."

We walked further to a secluded area, and Mary placed her bag on a table. I sat on a comfortable steel chair with cushions and propped my elbow on the table, accidentally touching a peacock feather logo, which turned the glass top into a screen. Mary smiled when my eyes popped out. It was the private web browser—the network forbidden to juveniles. She nudged me and tilted her head toward the tiny cameras on the edges of each bookshelf.

"Don't use it. I'll be right back." She walked to get the books we needed, and I looked down through the glass partition. Jason was still chatting with Carlota, feeding her lines about her beauty and dinner outings, making sure to keep her busy so she'd forget all about us.

Beads of sweat popped up on my forehead. My friends were taking so many risks to help me. Mary had just gotten married. What would Peter think if she got caught? Her mother would blame me for everything. I shuddered when I thought of the repercussions our quest could have.

Mary came back with a pile of books as tall as her head, and I rushed to help her. One by one, we sorted through them. The books had a special feel to them. It felt like I was touching the past—words written by the ancients from all over the world. Even the turn of the pages seemed to whisper to me. It was the sound of knowledge I longed to obtain.

"Here it is," said Mary, opening the ancient tome she'd found yesterday when she came alone to check for the necessary books. "I couldn't read this ancient Greek language. I think you still remember some of it from school."

I nodded, looking at the page. "I'm glad that I never skipped a class like you guys did."

Mary couldn't copy these pages. Only children and juveniles could do that with their allowed books. My eyes hurried to scan the facts in the papers, which sent a bolt of shock through my body.

After the peace treaty with the Modern Roman Empire, the rich settled in the Kingdom of Elpax, and a civil war started due to financial discrimination. His Majesty King Islabour Vasilas was in a fix. He was convinced that love was the key reason for all the tragedy and war in the world. A desire to possess either money or power divided people, but it all started with love. Love was the father of the fundamental problem, and intolerance and jealousy were its illegitimate sons. They were the heralded trio that had plunged the world into bloody wars and darkness from the beginning of time.

His Majesty King Islabour took drastic steps to prevent another war from breaking out in Elpax. He placed strict constraints that would codify knowledge at specific phases and ages. He wanted to create a generation of juveniles *(Anílikoi)* that were completely free of noble emotions until they passed the advanced phase to become adults *(Enílikos)*, at which point they would have the maturity to deal with them wisely. Sympathy toward each other and loyalty to the kingdom were the only two emotions ingratiated in all since childhood.

Thus came about the Crossing Gate, a feature unique to the Kingdom of Elpax, the land of peace and hope.

My skin sizzled with this knowledge. I realized that the Crossing Gate had to have some kind of magic or powers to divide knowledge between the stages of life. But who gave King Islabour this technology in the first place? The page said nothing further.

I nodded to Mary, and we walked to the bathroom, away from the cameras. Once we shut the door behind us, Mary gave me her secured Iméfono, the one that only the wealthy could use and wasn't monitored by the government. I wrote out the translation of the passage for her.

"Mary, has your grandma ever said anything about that when she talks about her life before Elpax?" I asked when she finished reading.

She frowned. "I asked her once, and she said she remembers nothing before the Crossing Gate."

"Nothing?"

"Well, she remembers escaping from North America, but it's like a black gap between her arrival in Elpax and her crossing into childhood. Maybe because she was only five years old."

We exchanged a tense look, then got back to our table. I opened another old book. Most of it was written in a script that had more symbols than words. The page had some words we could decipher—*Gate . . . Army . . . Guatemala*—and a picture of a translucent creature, like a gigantic dog, standing between the trees with a Roman soldier dead in front of it. We read further and could make out the words *Lord . . . Apple . . . midnight . . . Pine forest . . .* but nothing else.

I sat back in my chair, stunned. What had we really learned? Now we had more questions than answers.

"Mary, the pine forest—what is it? We only have the Malum forest."

She stared at me for a while before her eyes popped out with sudden understanding. "Malum is a Latin word meaning *evil*. Look at the dead Roman soldier—we all know that the Roman army disappeared in the forest. They might call it Malum for that reason."

"But Mary, it also means *apple*. Look at the apple in the picture; are there any apple trees in the forest?"

She shook her head and opened a romance book she'd brought so I could learn more about love. I read the lone page that Mary allowed me to see, and it made me understand my feelings for Erick even more.

I opened another old book. One word kept popping up—Takasha. Who or what was it? At the back of the book, there were two half-torn pages with the words erased by time. I flipped the page and gasped, looking at a black and beige picture.

"Mary?" I gulped, hardly able to catch my breath. "I know this man!"

She leaned over to look at the group of ancient men with different skin colors, long fair hair, and glowing eyes staring back at us. I pointed to the one that stood in the middle. "I saw him at your wedding . . ."

"My wedding?"

"No . . . I mean, when I passed out. I saw a vision . . . he told me to run."

"From what?"

"Mary Jane Harisbryg, is that you?"

Both of us turned toward the voice addressing her. All the color drained from Mary's face, and she closed her eyes slightly. The voice belonged to an arrogant woman, fair of skin and tall in stature. She was wearing an ivory dress and a white hat embellished with turquoise feathers.

Mary stood. "Oh, Lady Mabel. I haven't seen you since my wedding."

The woman smiled and came toward us. "I was busy." She looked at my modest clothes, and her pleasant expression faded. "Who is that girl with you?"

I stared at the rude woman, and my breath hitched in fear.

Mary stumbled over her words. "My . . . my friend."

Lady Mabel scanned me from head to toe. I gazed at her in defiance. Her eyes shifted toward my wrists, and she cried, "Oh, merciful God, what is this?"

I followed Lady Mabel's line of sight . . . to my left wrist.

104

My blood ran cold. The eyeliner on my wrist had smudged, and the lines were chaotic and blurred!

Mary acted within a split second. She moved in front of me to obscure Lady Mabel's view. "Ah, my Lady, is this a new hat?" she exclaimed. "Exquisite. Who is your stylist?" She waved her hand at me behind her back.

The woman glanced at me again, but Mary kept her busy. As quietly as possible, I got up and started moving back toward the elevator, sliding behind a bookshelf. Fear coursed through my veins, and my weak legs could barely carry my trembling body.

When I was close to the elevator, I heard Mary say, "Ah, look at the time. I'm late for an appointment, Lady Mabel. It was nice seeing you." I could hear the trepidation in her words, but I didn't turn around. Moving quickly, she passed me and whispered, "Run away!"

There was a group of people waiting for the elevator, and Mary had our card. My veins were drained with adrenaline, and I couldn't stand to wait with her, so I moved toward the emergency stairs. Before I pushed the door open, I turned back to see what was happening. Lady Mabel had leaned over to check what we'd been reading.

I knew there wasn't time to escape. She would, no doubt, raise the alarm; she certainly looked the sort. My trembling feet moved double-time, slipping on the stairs, missing a few, flying down them to the foyer. In the meantime, Mary got out of the elevator, and we both walked fast to the main doors. Jason followed us, and before my hand could push the door, Mabel's hysterical screaming echoed from above.

"That's a juvenile . . . CATCH HER!"

CHAPTER 13

THINKING TWICE WASN'T AN OPTION. I pushed my way out the doors, dragging Mary with me. The security guard caught my arm. Without thinking, my nails went for his eyes, and I scratched down his face. I twisted my arm from his firm grip and hurried into the street as fast as my unsteady feet could run, floundering among the surrounding people while security guards followed us.

We fled for three whole blocks. I glanced behind while trying to catch my breath. The guards were closing in on us. If they caught us . . . me . . . there would be no hope. I knew they'd take me right away to Inferos. I could hear their pounding footsteps. They were running with focused determination, as if they had taken an oath that they'd never let us escape.

The word-catchers floated over our heads, and the trumpet of a Law Corps' armored car sounded around the corner. My heart fell somewhere between my running feet. The cars moved aside, allowing the ground mobility vehicle to drive unhindered down the street, coming for me.

"Mary!" I pointed to the right. "The restaurant . . . hurry!"

We rushed into the restaurant and cut our way through the tables to reach the kitchen, looking for a back door. I knocked a waiter down, along with the tray he was carrying. The chef yelled as we jogged out the back door to a small alley, then stepped through the first open door and into the building's primary entrance. We got out on the road and kept on running until we reached another alley.

As we rested our backs against the wall of a building, I looked both ways. I could only see a white sedan car moving down the road. It looked like the same one that had followed Jason's car when we attended Mary's wedding. I waited until it was out of sight, plus a few more moments to make sure it didn't come back.

"I think . . . we . . . lost them," I gasped, panting violently. Mary was no better; she could hardly speak. I guessed running with those heels made her feet scream in pain. We hid behind a garbage can until the whistle of the Law Corps' car faded.

"Leen . . . your nose . . . is bleeding," said Mary, giving me a handcrafted piece of fabric to wipe it. I took off my wig and the fake eyeglasses and handed them to her. She dumped both in the can and crouched down, waiting for Jason in silence after texting him the address.

When we heard two short honks—the chosen signal—we stepped into Jason's car. With a pale face, he started driving as fast as he could.

"You are crazy, both of you!" he yelled. "You have to be more careful! God, I don't want to think about what will happen if they arrest you."

I pressed my lips tight, and my eyes met Mary's.

Jason looked through the rear-view mirror at me. "Especially you. The royal family has no mercy on workers."

"What the hell were you doing on the third floor of the library?"

I had barely taken my first step inside the house when Mom's words burst through in a wave of fury. She didn't even wait for me to shut the

107

door. My heart stopped for a second in soul-binding fear of repercussions. I closed my eyes in defeat, knowing I had nowhere to escape. Perhaps I could brave it out. After all, I had been in disguise. "What floor?"

"Lenora Santos Evgenís, don't you dare lie to me!" She walked toward me with short, measured steps, the color heightened on her face and her eyes blazing with restrained anger. I wanted to hide in my room until she calmed down, but she grabbed my arm, preventing my hasty escape.

"Do you have any idea what kind of insults I've had to endure from Mary's mom about my daughter's shenanigans? Don't even try to explain it, Lenora. I'll hear none of your usual excuses. They won't work. I have only one question. Why?"

I fidgeted, but refused to speak.

"I need to know. Why would you do something against the law?"

I pursed my lips, trying to stop them from trembling, and refused to look at Mom.

"Look at me and answer my question!"

I kept my gaze averted, hoping that her anger would subside after her initial yelling. I kept a tight rein on my emotions. Fear had frozen my face in a blank expression, when I heard a WHACK, and a stinging pain burned its way across my cheek. My head reared back, and my neck cracked.

Mom had slapped me!

For the first time!

"What the h—"

"Don't you dare use that tone with me. Not today. Not any day. Mary's mother said it all. She called me names, sneered at my upbringing, and threatened to call the Law Corps on us if they interrogate Mary. Do you want to shame this family? Do you have any idea what could happen to us? How could you?"

Mom started crying, and her body shuddered in abject misery. The slap didn't hurt me as much as Mom's sobs. Each tear was like a barb in my heart. I kept silent and stood there, taking in the sound of her agony. Tears rolled down my cheeks. I never thought I could cause her so much anguish.

Mom calmed herself down and ran to the bathroom. My need to get to the truth had stirred up a storm that affected everyone. Lady Mabel's one Iméfono call had started it. I wished she had kept her mouth shut and not interfered. But when had anything stopped the wealthy from doing whatever they wanted?

Poor Mary. Her mother wouldn't have spared her either. She would force Mary to tell the truth. Could her mother coerce her to speak about the ancient tome?

I shuddered at the thought. Would Mary lie about it? Would she get sin-spots? So many thoughts were swirling in my head, each scarier than the one before it. My head felt as if it would explode. The government wouldn't spare me if it came to know the truth.

Blood rushed down to my feet, and I had to sit with my head between my knees. Mom walked back into the room and sat next to me.

"I'm sorry, Mom. Please don't cry." I said, keeping my head down.

"I can't understand you, Lenora." She slammed her palms into her knees. "Didn't you think beyond your actions to the consequences for all of us?"

I met her smoldering stare.

"What was on the third floor that was worth risking your life for?"

Oh no! I'm not ready to answer this question.

I sat there, waiting for something or someone to rescue me. How I wished my life was a book whose pages I could rapidly turn, pretending their contents never existed.

Mom gazed at me, waiting for an answer, but I uttered none. She took a sharp breath, trying to soften the blow. "Don't you remember Icarus? He flew too close to the sun, and his wax wings melted in his enthusiasm to escape the Labyrinth. He plunged to his death because he didn't listen to his father's advice. We, too, need to get out of our labyrinth of difficulties, but with caution. Knowledge at the wrong time can be dangerous."

"But I want to know more about the adult knowledge—"

"You're not mature enough to handle it. Today, you took a colossal risk, not only with yourself but with us too. You broke the law."

I shrugged. "The laws are stupid. They don't help women or protect us from abuse."

"So be it. But you're still living in Elpax, and you have to follow the laws. You're seventeen, and you haven't crossed over, yet you want the information reserved for the adult phase! How long will you be so irresponsible?"

I remained quiet. What could I say to that?

"Answer the damn question!" Mom yelled, unable to calm down. "Do you plan to cross next year?"

"Not sure." I swallowed, knowing that her anger would annihilate me.

"How long can you continue like this? You can't be so reckless. Damn it, Lenora, for God's sake, grow up! Or else . . ."

I looked up at her.

"Or else I'll make you grow up. I'll see that you cross next year. At any cost."

She walked out of the room, leaving a chill of fear in my bones. I couldn't tell her the truth; she wouldn't believe that I was suffering from a forceful dizziness, because I'd crossed into my adolescence phase without any incident. But now, I was losing my freedom to choose when to cross to adulthood.

I shuffled to my room. Every part of me was in pain, so it seemed. I closed the door, slid down to the floor, and called Mary many times, but there was no answer.

My heart throbbed, and I wept inconsolably. Half an hour later, my Iméfono buzzed with a brief message from her.

I'm so sorry for what my mother did. Don't worry, no one knew about . . . you know. Mom forbade calls to you, or else she will tell. 721.

I typed a quick reply. **I'm sorry, too. 721.**

Unforgiving stillness left long shadows in the house. The twins were subdued, their natural enthusiasm stilted, and soon they left for their childhood school. Mom left for work, and I took a day off from my routine and spent it at home. Her anger had left me with lingering guilt and a longing for my childhood friends.

After cleaning the house and making lunch as an apology to Mom, I wrote all that had happened in the past weeks in my diary. I needed to sort out the strange feelings I had for Erick. Feelings that didn't seem to be reciprocated.

Mom got back from work and entered my room with a perfunctory knock. Her eyes darkened with sorrow. She sat at the edge of my bed, touching my hand in a muted apology.

"Lenora, I'm sorry. I shouldn't have slapped you. I lost control when I heard Lady Harisbryg besmirching our family name."

I closed my notebook and leaned over to hold her hand, accepting her genuine regret. We were stuck in our roles, led by the wheels of fate. The only option was to move forward on our respective paths. Stopping wasn't an option. "No, Mom, I'm the one who should apologize. I promise, I'll make it up to you."

She took a deep breath. "All right, my child. Mary came to the factory today and explained what happened. She wants to meet you at Jason's place. Karya will take care of the twins."

I nodded and rode my bike to Jason's. There was hardly any traffic on the roads—just a white sedan car with black windows, which passed me slowly and receded into the distance. As I approached Jason's house, I heard a car from behind. Turning around, I almost fell from my bike. It was the same sedan car as before.

My stomach roiled over itself. Someone was following me!

CHAPTER 14

WHO ARE THESE PEOPLE, AND what do they want from me? I called Jason right away, asking him to inform the guards that I was at the gate. My bike cut through the gate as it started opening, and my legs pumped furiously, trying to reach the house as fast as possible before the car followed me.

I dropped the bike on the ground and waited until my breathing returned to its normal rhythm. Maybe they were following me because Mabel told the government about me. But wait—*I saw the same car when I went to Mary's wedding. I swear it's the same car. What do they want?*

I looked at the gate again; the car wasn't there. Maybe I imagined the whole thing, and it was a total coincidence.

I took a deep breath and walked to the entrance. Jason's home was gorgeous and just as inviting as Mary's. The magnificent foyer's ceiling seemed to go on forever. Beige marble flooring gleamed as I walked in, reflecting the lights of the huge cut-glass chandelier. It looked like diamonds swaying from the ceiling.

Jason's mother, Lady Margaret, welcomed me as if I were her best friend. She was a beautiful, dignified woman with well-styled blond hair that gave her the royal air of a princess. A light green form-fitting jacket and short skirt completed her outfit.

"Glory to Elpax, Lenora."

"Glory, Lady Margaret."

She walked with me across the foyer. "How are you? How are your family and your twin sisters?"

"They're good, Lady."

"I've always wanted to have daughters—to hear the laughter of girls in this empty house."

I smiled without commenting. I knew Jason was her only child; I didn't know why Eros hadn't stopped by her place again. She was a delicate woman. Maybe she didn't love her husband enough to produce another baby.

"I wish to meet your sisters one day."

The sentence struck me as odd. Why would she want to meet the twins? "I'm afraid if they see your place, they won't come back home!" I joked.

"We'll see if I can do something about that."

I forced a tense smile onto my face, pondering her strange words.

"I'm sure your mother has explained to you the necessity of reducing your private meetings with Jason. Of course, you are always welcome in my home. What I'm trying to say is that it's different after your third crossing."

My eyes widened at the warning. I gave a slight nod and kept silent. I didn't want to discuss my crossing or non-crossing.

Lady Valemont pointed toward the living room. "Make yourself at home. I'll call Jason."

I looked around the huge living room—it was triple the size of ours! In fact, our entire house would fit in this space. Lady Margaret had placed tables with a flower vase at each window to catch the sun's rays. Statues and couches gave the room a comfortable yet stately look.

A huge painting hung on the wall above the electronic fireplace, flanked by olive green and golden columns. The canvas captured the light brilliantly. It was a portrait of Jason's family. They were well dressed in traditional Irish clothing from their original homeland. His father appeared stern and his mother detached. The artist had mixed the colors well to produce a strong yet soft tone. I moved toward the picture and stood staring at it for a few minutes, until I heard Jason's footsteps coming from somewhere behind me.

"Leen, you came!"

The delight in his voice brought a smile to my face right away. He gestured for me to sit on the couch and lowered himself down close to me. I moved away a bit. He looked askance at me.

"You won't get a disease, Jason, but I will if you sit any closer."

"Leen . . . no . . ." He was about to say something, but closed his mouth, not allowing the words to escape.

"Have you changed your perfume, Jason? It seems so familiar."

For a moment, I thought he hadn't heard my question. His face took on a slight pinkish tinge.

"Would there be a problem in telling the name of the fragrance to a juvenile?"

Jason laughed; his face became redder, as if I'd embarrassed him with my question. "Cold mint."

"And what's wrong with cold mint?"

"Nothing Leen, it's just . . ."

"It's just what?" My inquiring gaze stayed locked on his face.

He looked up and gave me a shy smile. "It's how your hair smells."

"My hair . . . ?" My forehead puckered in thought before I realized he had complimented me. Was he flirting? I didn't know how to react. This was Jason, my oldest friend from childhood. Thinking of the moments we'd shared and the pranks he'd pulled on me over the years, I punched his shoulder. "You're teasing me. Stop fooling around."

For a second, a strange expression appeared on his face. Was it regret?

Or something else? Ever since he had crossed to adulthood, I found it increasingly difficult to gauge his mood.

He smirked, trying to drive away the awkward moment. "Well, it was worth a try!"

The conversation died down, as if there was a barrier between us. Jason looked at me twice, opened his mouth to say something, but closed it again.

"What is it, Jason?"

He shook his head and kept mum. The silence had turned claustrophobic, and I wished Mary would hurry up and get here.

"Is he worth it?" he said at last.

I froze. I knew who he was talking about. What could I say? Was Erick worth it? Yes! But I didn't want my friends or family to get into trouble with the kingdom because of him and me. "Well, I didn't expect the trip to the library would end this way."

"That wasn't my question, Leen."

"That's the only answer I have now. I can't answer it any other way."

"Can't, or won't?"

I knew Jason's mood had darkened. I couldn't stand it when he became angry. His face took on a gray hue when he was about to reproach me. I refused to answer his question. He was free to think about whatever he wanted. I slid down from the couch and sat on the floor.

"If my parent forbade me from meeting you, instead of Mary, would you have still gone ahead with this dangerous adventure?"

"Well, that's not the case."

"You know," he whispered, "I thought a lot about what happened yesterday. All I'm asking is for you to be careful and not take risks. That was too close." He sat on the floor close to me. I shuffled a few centimeters away. His hand found mine, and his warmth transferred to my fingers. "I can't lose you to the kingdom. Or to anyone else."

A chill coursed through my body at his words. I looked away and shifted my hand out of his grasp.

115

"For sure, I'll be careful," I declared, trying to gather myself.

The surrounding air was turning vague, and the conversation had become too heavy and filled with subtexts I didn't know how to decipher. Our easygoing friendship seemed to have weakened.

Soon, a maid came in with a golden tray of teacups and cakes. She placed it on a low table, curtsied, and walked away. The main door opened, and I heard the sharp tapping sound of heels on the marble floor, walking at a brisk pace. That could only be Mary.

I jumped up and headed toward her as she entered the room. She held my hand and squeezed. There were no words between us—just tears.

"Please stop crying, both of you." Jason was exasperated. "I hate tears."

"Oh, shut up, Jason," Mary said. "You can join in if you're feeling excluded."

He rolled his eyes, showing us what he thought about Mary's suggestion. We sat on the couch with Mary between us.

"I'm sorry, Leen," she said. "I couldn't bear the thought of you being punished by your mom, all because Mabel noticed your ID and started screeching."

"I'm sorry to cause you trouble. But what did you tell our mothers?"

"That you were looking for a book that would create an urge for you to cross. I didn't specify much and left it all vague, telling them that I was monitoring what you were reading."

"Did they buy it?"

"Yes. Must have, as none of them questioned me further on it. You're still a juvenile. They wouldn't expect us to be researching feelings and the secrets of the Crossing Gate."

"But Mabel saw what we were reading! Didn't she say anything about it to your mother?"

"That's where my part comes in," said Jason. "I took care of it."

He didn't explain any further, but the meaning was clear. He threatened her with something.

For the next hour, we discussed all that we had learned, which was barely anything, until Mom called and I had to go back home.

"I'll see you around. Try not to worry," reassured Mary. She squeezed my hand when I got into Jason's car. Nicholas had already placed my bike in the trunk, and Jason was ready to drive.

We were halfway to my house when an alarm echoed through the entire kingdom. A short, loud blast that preceded a governmental text message.

Royal Order. All children and juveniles must travel to the nearest Safe Cell in the area within twenty minutes. The process of judgment will start soon.

What was happening? It was a weekday, not a Saturday afternoon as usual! What was the need for the processing siren now? Jason and I exchanged tense looks. We couldn't figure out why the rules had changed all of a sudden.

"There's a Safe Cell in front of us. Hold on." Jason sped up the car. Mom called, and I assured her that Jason was driving, and that we were a couple of blocks away from the nearest Safe Cell.

"That's good. Karya is taking the twins to the Children's Safe Cell. I'm at work. Come back once it ends. I should be home by then."

An inexplicable sensation gripped me. Life had changed since I became a juvenile. I remembered going to the Children's Safe Cell before I crossed to the adolescence phase. That hall was bright with white walls and many colorful pictures, most of them showing peacocks. The entire atmosphere was cheerful. They allowed us to watch cartoons until Mom came to pick me up.

Life was so innocent as a child. I crossed at eleven. And then I came to know about the processes of judgment—Elimination, Exclusion, and Purgation. Nothing was told to us in detail, but we knew that they punished sinners, and that death was possible.

Who will they punish today? I shivered at the thought.

Jason stopped the car with a jerk in front of a Safe Cell for female juveniles. "I'll be waiting here."

I hurried to the Safe Cell. The Law Corps soldier scanned my ID and allowed me in.

The hall was a wide room with gray, windowless walls and no furniture. It was filled with groups of girls chatting amongst themselves in whispers. Some sat alone on the ground or against the walls, faces ashen and eyes closed. It was a gloomy atmosphere, where fear permeated the very air. A sense of impending doom arose in me; I knew this was something different. Sending us to a Safe Cell on a weekday was almost unheard of. It had to be something catastrophic.

"What's wrong?" I asked the brunette standing next to me.

"No idea. But it has to be one of the three processes. They wouldn't send us here otherwise." She shrugged and looked away. I glanced around, weighing her words. She was probably right.

Usually, these affairs occurred on a Saturday, in the capital's public square under the Arch of Victory. None of the juveniles or children got to see the process. It was why the government built the Safe Cells in each neighborhood. Children were told that the gathering was for their entertainment, but as juveniles, we knew better. We knew that while they gathered us here, someone was being punished in Theirna.

The lights muted, and the sound of the national anthem floated from the external mics. Once it stopped, we all sat, and the holographic image of our kingdom's flag started waving. In front of it, as usual, was the loudmouth broadcaster, Hermes. He started the announcement, telling us that the crimes both of today's culprits had committed were too ugly for the juveniles' innocent ears.

"If they're that ugly, it means they'll eliminate the sinner and their entire family will be shamed," whispered the girl, her lips trembling in fear.

If someone's punishment was Elimination or Exclusion, then they could never return home. They'd only persist as a name in the pages of history. But the Purgation was different.

Karya had told me that once. She pointed out a family in my neighborhood, where the father was walking strangely as if one of his legs

118

didn't work as well as the other. There were also odd marks on his body—not a tattoo, but something else. He'd been through Purgation. Nobody spoke to the members of that family. Everyone shunned them.

My heart pounded, and a thought struck me. Changes were happening in this kingdom. So far, juveniles had never been punished; the government might imprison some of them in Inferos, but they had only done so in rare cases. We were practically safe. Would that change soon? Would the kingdom begin to punish its juveniles? *Sentence them to death?* If they did, then it could have very well been me standing there, awaiting my judgment. Good luck or God's care had saved me. I sighed, putting my hand on my chest to calm my rapid heart rate. We were safe; I was safe.

The hall darkened, and Hermes disappeared. When the picture of the two sinners showed up on the void, my heart sunk, and an ear-splitting scream came from a girl sitting in the other corner.

"My brother! No!" she cried. I put my hand on my mouth, trying to bury my own scream.

The other sinner was Carlota, the receptionist from the National Library.

119

CHAPTER 15

THE LAW CORPS SOLDIERS RUSHED to carry the girl who had screamed—she'd collapsed, and was barely able to struggle upright. They held her arms and dragged her out of the hall. I couldn't hear what Hermes was blathering about. All I could see was Carlota's innocent eyes, staring at me, seeming to blame me for her punishment. The room spun around me, and I started choking. It seemed that I couldn't take a single breath.

The girl next to me patted my back. "Look at me. Just breathe." I turned and focused on her face; a breath of air rushed into my lungs. "Did you know any of them?"

"Carlota . . . What is . . . ?"

She looked at me with sympathy. "Hermes just said her punishment is Purgation. They'll do it to her after that poor girl's brother has been eliminated."

Tears rolled down my cheeks throughout Hermes's announcement. Up to this point in my life, I hadn't realized how one second could destroy an entire family. I was the one responsible for the torture and punishment of an innocent person. I couldn't help feeling that they should have punished me, not her. She didn't deserve it; she had done nothing wrong. I wanted to get up and confess. Only the fear of what would happen to my family stopped my legs from moving forward to the soldiers. Silent tears continued to fall down my cheeks right through the ethics film they showed every time this happened.

It was the longest thirty minutes of my life. My body ached to its core; I had aged years over the half-hour. The excitement I had felt, thinking I was doing the right thing by trying to find out the meaning of adult emotions and the kingdom's history, was vanquished the second that Carlota's picture appeared on the screen.

Soldiers switched on the lights and opened the hall's doors. I barged through the crowd, looking for Jason, who was waiting in his car. He was pale, as if his blood had pooled at his feet, never reaching his heart.

I got into the car fast, before the Corps could notice my tears. Jason drove me toward my home while another alarm echoed. It was the first alarm to notify the citizens about the Curfew, which usually followed the process of judgments, and it would start in half an hour.

"Did you see it?"

Jason blinked several times. "They broadcasted it across the sky as usual, Leen. They wanted to make sure that the adult who tricked Carlota would watch it, no matter where they are. I couldn't escape it even if I wanted to. It was hideous. What they did to that innocent girl . . ." A tear fell from his eye and he brushed it aside. Silence reigned in the car; the guilt was killing us.

I balled my fingers into a fist. "It was my fault."

"It was Mabel's," Jason said, attempting to console me.

"No, Jason," I replied with a shaky voice. "Mabel followed the law."

"Look at me, Leen." His face became redder than usual. "Don't mention it to anyone. Never ever utter a word about it to anyone. Don't worry. She's alive. She won't be able to use her hands for a while. But I promise you, I'll try to help her."

121

My eyes popped out. "What did they do to her hands?"

"I can't tell you."

I turned sideways in my seat. "I . . . I don't understand. It happened so fast. They never hold judgment on a working day, so why now? Shouldn't they have investigated further? Like checking her body for sin-spots to see if she was lying. If they checked her, they would know that she had no idea I was a juvenile, so she wouldn't have any sin-spots. I don't get it."

"Look," said Jason under his breath. "She allowed a juvenile into the adult section. That is deceit, according to the kingdom. There was no reason to investigate further. I don't know why they didn't come after you." He slowed the car a bit. "Perhaps because you were with Mary, and she is wealthy . . . I don't know, Leen. I only know that you're safe for now."

"SAFE? Is anyone safe in this kingdom?" A vein throbbed in my neck.

"Calm down. Screaming will only attract unwanted attention."

I sighed, resting my head on the seat cushion.

"Dad told me that something was brewing in the kingdom. I knew a change in the rules was coming, but I didn't know that they would punish adults without a proper investigation. I suppose they had to punish someone for neglect, since Mabel raised the alarm."

We mired in silence.

"Then I'll confess."

"Hell no! You will not." Jason snapped. "Look, you can't change anything about this. It's over."

My teeth clenched at his words. What he asked of me was impossible. I could see Carlota's face when I closed my eyes.

"You have to be very careful. The government now knows about a juvenile walking around the kingdom knowing her phase's forbidden history and emotions. Wipe your tears. We're almost home."

I looked out the window at the street, which was filled with people rushing to get home before the second alarm of the Curfew sounded. The Law Corps would soon start checking our IDs at home. I couldn't breathe, and my heart got heavy, overwhelmed by what had just happened. My life

122

had changed so much in one hour.

I'm sorry, Carlota, I whispered in my mind. *I'm so damn sorry.*

Carlota was connected to me forever. What happened to her and what was happening to women all over the kingdom became harder to ignore. It made me mull over the women's situation and our rights. I wanted to do something for them. My guilt from having a hand in Carlota's punishment annihilated me, and from its ashes came a burning desire, which grew overnight.

What if there was a female lawyer who defended women? What if that lawyer was me?

I knew it was a dangerous idea, but it had burrowed into my soul. The only person who could help me with that was Erick. But I had been avoiding him since Carlota's punishment.

I tried forgetting about him, but he, too, was part of my soul. I longed for him; my heart craved his company. Although my love for him grew every day, it was a forbidden feeling that I had to hide within myself. Anyway, the whole point was moot; I was invisible to him. I had to keep him in my dreams, a safe place I escaped to when things went wrong. *The heart is as the heart does, even if it is a lost dream.*

A cold and rainy afternoon greeted me at the end of school in December. The air seemed laden with dreariness and gloom. I donned my raincoat and rushed to the bike stand, water falling off my hat. I was irritated when the dampness seeped into my clothes; the raindrops made my skin itch. Unlocking the bike wasn't easy in this downpour, especially when I couldn't see much.

Quiet footsteps approached, and the rain ceased its stormy outburst. I looked up in wonder and saw the face of my dreams, not yet my reality. Erick.

"You're avoiding me."

123

He was holding an umbrella large enough for both of us. I could only stare at his beautiful gray eyes and remain silent.

"Was it something I said? Or did?" he persisted.

I sighed. How I wished things were that simple. "No, it wasn't, really."

"Ah, she speaks!"

I had to smile at his teasing. Trying to ignore him again, I turned to unlock my bike, but my trembling fingers dropped the key.

"Allow me to help." Erick gave me his umbrella and bent down to pick up the key. After a short conflict with the lock, he got my bike released. Instead of handing it to me, he walked it toward his car. I could do nothing but follow him.

He looked at me from the corner of his eye. "So, we good?" He grinned. My heart melted at his smile.

The walk to the car was short but relaxing. We were sheltered from the rain, a cozy bubble away from the world under one umbrella. I totally forgot about the itchy sensation as the warmth of his company blossomed inside me. As we stood in front of the car, words poured from my mouth in a rush to break the silence. "Francine must be waiting for you."

Erick flinched as if I had slapped him. His smile disappeared; his face became a stony mask. "I see." He gave me the bike and feigned a smile. "Well, I'm glad I saw you today." He turned to walk to the driver's seat.

"Wait!" I grabbed his arm and pulled him to a halt. I realized I had given him the wrong impression—that I didn't want to spend more time with him. "I'm sorry. I didn't mean it in that sense." I let go of his arm. My ears got hotter as I realized how foolish I sounded. I didn't want to push him away, yet I couldn't seem to come closer to him. All these feelings were so disturbing.

He waited for me to continue, giving me all the time I needed to gather my thoughts.

"Sometimes, I don't think before talking. I say what I feel. It may come across as foolish."

His smile returned like the sun peeking from behind gloomy clouds.

"That's a noble quality, Leen. You're honest." He stared at me for a few seconds. "How about starting over?"

"All right. I'm Leen, a proud non-crosser juvenile." I joked.

He laughed and bent down to look into my eyes. "Erick, a man who would be honored if the proud non-crosser accepted my invitation to the cinema tomorrow night."

My heart skipped a beat, and I felt that the Earth had stopped moving. For a moment, I wanted to launch into a happy dance, but I forced myself to stand still, responding to him with the dignity his invitation deserved.

I nodded.

"I'll pick you up at six. I should speak to your mother for permission. Would you give me her number?"

"Not needed. I'll talk to her, and I'll be waiting at the cinema hall."

A flicker of uncertainty passed over his face at the prospect of skipping such an important rule. "She wouldn't mind," I assured him, remembering that Mom already approved of him. But if she ever asked why I'd changed my mind about wanting to spend time with him, my face would probably flush with embarrassment, exposing my secret feelings for him. Although it might never cross her mind to ask that, I couldn't risk it.

"Well, if that's the way you want it—"

"So be it!"

He laughed, without taking his focus from my eyes. I could feel my face flushing from his attention.

"Well, see you later!" I called over my shoulder as I rode my bike.

Soon after I reached home, Mom got a call, and she rushed to her room upon hearing the caller's voice. I thought it might be work-related, so I didn't bother to enquire. I was more worried about how to get her permission for the movies. Once she returned, I had to lie and tell her that Francine wanted me to come to the cinema with her. Mom gave a big smile and welcomed it. *What's wrong with her? She hardly ever smiles so brightly about anything.*

What to wear confused me. I was seventeen, almost grown-up . . . yet a juvenile. *What do I wear that will make me look good?* A quick text to Mary sorted that out. White shirt and jeans with a short black jacket. I applied light makeup and black eyeliner to make my eyes look bigger. Once I was done, I sent a message to Jason. He was going to drop me off.

When I got into Jason's car, he welcomed me with a whistle. "You look stunning!" His gaze swept up my body, his focus lingering on my eyes.

"Shut up. You're making me nervous."

He chuckled and started driving. I looked out the window, smiling to myself, spinning my dreams about how tonight would be extraordinary with Erick sitting next to me.

"Jason. This is my first time at the cinema. Any special rules or advice?"

He smiled with the corner of his mouth. "Just be careful and watch your actions in front of the public. You're still a juvenile, and pretty much everyone knows you!" He parked the car at Aquarius Street in front of the cinema and looked at me. "I'll be back at nine. If he tries any funny stuff, call me right away. I'll be around."

I didn't know what he was implying. I liked his protectiveness about me, but at the same time, I had to say a few words in Erick's defense. "He's an honorable man!"

"An immoral man won't warn you in advance."

I got out of the car with widened eyes, looking at the crowded street. I'd never seen Zoiterra in the evening before. Even in this cold weather, people walked around loudly chatting and laughing. I stood in front of the cinema hall, restless with excitement, looking at the movies' showtimes. I noticed that they all started at 7:00 p.m. and none played on the weekends; that was for the Curfew days. I looked down the street again, waiting until Erick's car showed up. I was about to call out to him in joy when she stepped out of his car.

Francine was with him.

I could feel my heart being crushed by a tidal wave of disappointment. What was she doing here? It was supposed to be my time with Erick! Tears welled up in my eyes; I was hardly able to control them.

126

She came closer with an enormous smile. "Hey, Leen. Have you been waiting long?"

I sniffed. "No."

She tugged my sleeve. "Are you crying?"

"It's the cold breeze." I held her hand. "Where is Erick?"

"He will join us after he parks the car. Let's go inside."

I walked with her in a state of numbness, a husk of dying expectations. I couldn't even force a smile onto my face. I thought I would get to see a movie with just Erick. When did I agree to Francine too?

We stood in front of one of the money-deposit machines inside the foyer. Francine talked about school stuff that I didn't care about. My sadness was swallowing me into a bottomless well. I kept shaking and nodding my head without actually listening to her. My mind was swirling with questions. Why had Erick invited his sister? What did he want from me? Just friendship?

Erick walked in with a grin on his face. "Hey, Leen. How are you?" His fingers reached up to his hair.

"All good," I replied in a hushed tone.

His eyes narrowed at my reaction, and he looked confused. I walked ahead and scanned my ID. When I was about to pay for my ticket, Erick pushed my arm away with a big resounding "No!" and paid for all of us. That annoyed me. I refused to be indebted to anyone, and I decided I would pay him back later.

Erick hesitated a bit before handing me a round metal piece with a seat number inscribed on it. I sighed and walked inside the cinema hall with them.

I couldn't believe how huge it was, with a wide aisle dividing the seats into two sections. People rushed to their seats according to their number. I looked at my ticket: number 6, next to Erick's.

"Give me your ticket," said Erick before I took my seat without further explanation. I did, and my eyes followed him as he talked to one of the employees in the hall. He came back with a different seat number. I stared at the new ticket without understanding. Why did he change my seat?

Erick smiled and waved me ahead. "After you."

Right at that moment, I wanted to call Jason to take me home. But I had to behave and not make a scene in front of all these strangers. I took my seat between a juvenile boy and Francine.

"Put your ticket in this opening," said Francine, pointing to a small gap in the seat's arm. I did, and the arm glowed with a faint green light, like Francine's did. Erick's was orange.

The lights dimmed, and the movie started on the Ológramma. We had to put on large eyeglasses to feel like we were "inside" the movie. Each scene was associated with a smell that pumped through the theater, and our seats moved along with the characters' actions. But the loud voices annoyed me; it appeared they were snooping on my thoughts.

The entire movie was a blur. All I could feel was the pain in my chest and the keening disappointment in my heart. How terrible this feeling was: the love for a man who hardly saw me. I was living in one world and him in another, and our realms would never converge.

When the movie ended after two hours of bitterness, I jumped from my seat and headed to the door to escape any further agony, but a grip pulled me back.

"Not so fast!"

I turned to Erick. He let go of my arm at once, and a tense smile showed on his face. "Leen, I want to tell you something." He swallowed, and was about to speak, but Jason had arrived already. I could see his car in front of the cinema from the corner of my eye.

I was so upset that I couldn't hear a word from Erick. I didn't want any explanation; I just wanted to go home, to leave at once before my tears started dropping before him. "I've got to go."

I didn't give him a chance to reply. I went outside, got into Jason's car, and burst out crying.

"Leen!" exclaimed Jason. "What's wrong?"

"Just drive," I whispered, hiding my face in my hands.

Jason looked at Erick through the dark window, his eyes burning with anger. "Buckle up," he snapped, and his foot pressed hard on the pedal. I held onto my seat, scared that we might crash into the other cars.

"Could you slow down?"

He handed me a silk handkerchief bearing the initials J.V. "I knew it!" he yelled, racing down the road. "He's hurt you. God! I'll make him regret it."

"Slow down!" I yelled.

He punched the steering wheel. "What did he do?"

"I'll not talk before you slow down. Or at least switch the damn driving system."

He darted a look at me and slowed down, though his face remained red. "What happened?"

"He invited his sister." I wiped my tears. "I thought this outing was for us to get to know each other," I sighed, staring at the dashboard. "I thought he felt something for me that made him ask me out. I thought I was important."

Jason's face became thoughtful. "Maybe his sister was bored and asked to come along. Now, wipe your tears and don't make me kill him."

My eyes widened.

He peered at me. "I'm not joking, Leen. Not at all."

I gulped. I knew he wasn't joking. *Nobody dares to mess with the wealthy.* This statement was completely, 100% true. Especially when it came to Mr. William, his father. He owned half of the city through his investments, and he was the royals' favorite. I had heard rumors about Mr. William before; anyone who dared to stand against him would be terminated.

But I didn't know for sure, not yet.

PART III

"THE CROSSING"

All you need to live a normal life is a full third line . . . not two.
Are you ready for it?

CHAPTER 16

THE RAIN SHOWERED AGAINST THE floor-to-ceiling windows, obscuring the view from inside the house. I sat down to study after I'd made my finishing touches on the day's portraits. A pile of mathematical equations were waiting for me to solve them, along with a lot of other assignments. But trying to study amongst the chaos of thoughts and feelings was like sinking into quicksand—not that I had ever actually been in one. But for sure, it felt like I would imagine quicksand to be.

I looked out the window; the raindrops seemed to match the number of tears I cried over Erick last night. I focused again on the equations. Last night, I was determined to forget all about Erick. I knew that my love had to endure a natural end. Although it was so overwhelming, I had no choice. *He doesn't return my feelings.*

A car's honk, along with the screeching of brakes in front of my home, pulled me from my focus. The doorbell rang in a quick burst of music, as if the visitor had hesitated or had a second thought.

"Lenora!" Mom yelled from the kitchen. "Open the door."

That was unusual. Mom never asked me to stop my studies midway to open the door. I ran and opened it with a slam, expecting Danira or her mother.

The Earth tilted in that fraction of a second when sunlight splintered into the house. My heart woke up like a flower bud that had been hibernating throughout the long winter months, now looking up at the sky, happy to be in the sunshine.

"My God," I mumbled, hardly willing to believe what my eyes were seeing.

"Can I come in?" Erick's smile shone forth.

My body and mind could no longer communicate with each other. I was tongue-tied, and the best I could do was wave him in. He stepped inside, looking at our humble abode. I stood close to the door, hoping that my brain would reboot soon, or else it would surely move to embarrass me again. I hadn't expected this visit at all.

"Who is it?" Mom called out, pulling me from my frozen state.

"It's Erick," I yelled back, looking at him. "Francine's brother."

Mom rushed over with a smile and shook his hand. "Glory. Please take a seat."

I narrowed my eyes in response to her bizarrely warm greeting.

"Thank you, Mrs. Karakas." He glanced at me. "I was told that Lenora is a talented artist, and I would be fortunate if she would do me the honor of drawing my picture."

"Of course. You can sit in her room."

What? Why was Mom agreeing? She'd hardly allowed me to hang out with Jason since he'd crossed. And now she was all smiles about Erick wanting me to draw him! No questions. No stern looks. Just an *of course*. God! The world had gone mad! It seemed that the Earth was moving in the opposite direction today.

Mom turned to me. Her smile brought me back to reality. I was still mad about the night spent crying, so I spoke fast. "You can send your picture to Mom's Iméfono, and she'll inform you when it's done."

"Lenora!" Mom scolded, her eyes widening. "Don't be rude to your client." She turned to Erick, who blushed. "After you." She pointed at my room, totally ignoring me.

That wasn't my mom! It was like she was possessed by another woman I knew nothing about. I stood still as she ushered Erick into my room. She soon came back and whispered, "Will it kill you to show some kindness? He came all this way to see you."

I pursed my lips. Mom was getting crazy! After a deep breath, I raised my toes so I could whisper in her ear. "Just don't expect a wedding!"

I wandered into my room, keeping the door ajar. Erick was standing by the window, hands in his pockets. He turned to me once I got in, and a flash of the dream I had about him appeared before my eyes for a second. I shook my head, sliding the image away.

"So, how does this go?" he asked with a wide smile.

I jutted my chin toward the chair in front of my desk. He passed by me to sit on it without a word. I smiled to myself. Maybe he thought I would welcome him with a grin. Hell no! Not after all those tears.

I placed my easel in front of him and sat on my bed, holding my charcoal pencil, determined to remain professional. "Could you . . . sit on the edge of the chair?"

He sat, and raised his eyes to me, waiting for further instructions.

"Put your right leg on the spindle. Arms around the knee. Turn your chest more in my direction. Chin up. Relax your lips, and don't smile!"

He frowned.

"Don't frown, either!" I turned my favorite music on.

Erick leaned forward; his face turned thoughtful. "This is beautiful. Who is the musician?"

"Sit still," I ordered.

His cheeks plumped, desperately trying to choke a smile. "Yes, Your Honor."

I tried to remain as serious as possible. "Is that how you address the judge when you work on a case?"

"Aha."

As soon as my charcoal pencil started to move across the smooth canvas, I knew this was a terrible idea. Capturing the primary lines of his face without melting was challenging. His fine chin that I was longing to touch, the smooth hair that I wished to run my fingers through, the eyes I hoped to stare at for the rest of my life. My pulse sped up. *Leen, focus! He just tore your heart apart less than twenty-four hours ago, and now you're all into him!*

I decided to leave the eyes for later and began sketching.

Erick was relaxed, yet each part of his body looked tense. He wanted to talk, and I ignored his desire. I needed time to gather some wise words. Perhaps I wanted to torture him a bit, too.

After setting the baselines, I whispered, "Are you here to be judged?"

"A good marksman may miss," he teased. I peered at him from behind the easel, and his gorgeous gray eyes were staring at me. The sun's rays that broke through the heavy clouds glittered over his hazel hair.

"He that commits a fault believes everyone speaks of it," I replied.

"Innocent until proven guilty."

I narrowed my eyes at his lawyer's smartness. *Is that so? You want to play this game, Erick? Let's play, then.*

"It's no use crying over spilled milk." I sent my first message.

"Don't judge a book by its cover."

I lifted my eyes toward his solemn face. What was he trying to say? "Strike while the iron is hot, Erick."

He stared at me. "Walls have ears, Leen."

I couldn't agree more with the last one, but I wouldn't give up. "A word is enough to the wise."

"You're right." He got up. I gulped as he came closer and leaned his elbow on my easel. "After *us*, the deluge."

Us! My poor heart sped up. What the hell was he trying to say? *Does he have feelings for me?*

"Leen, I want us to get to know each other, if you don't mind."

136

I rolled my eyes. "You didn't seem to want to spend time with me at the cinema."

"I did! I was about to invite you to dinner, but you left without a word."

"Then why did Francine come with you?" It was difficult to keep the hurt away from my voice.

He frowned. "You know that you and I can't go to the cinema alone without a first-class juvenile relative. I can't even sit next to you. The rules are clearly listed inside the hall."

How had I missed reading the rules? And Jason! Why he didn't tell me about them?

I shook my head.

Erick explained further. "Your ticket number was nine, in the juvenile's area. I didn't want you to sit alone, so I changed it for you to sit between Francine and another juvenile."

Was I so upset that I'd held my ticket upside down and didn't notice?

"That's why you were so upset the entire time?" Erick's eyes glittered, and his smile clearly said, *I got you!*

He confused me. How on earth did he know about my feelings? Or maybe he didn't. Perhaps he thought I was upset because he ignored me, not because I was jealous and wanted him to be mine.

Erick sat on the bed beside me. Our shoulders touched, and I shivered a little before he moved a few centimeters away from me. His hand took the charcoal pencil I was holding in my left hand, and he leaned forward to write on the canvas:

Is there room for me among your friends?

I stared at the words, thinking. I might go with the *friend* term for now. But was that what he really wanted? I turned to him. His eyes became tender, searching mine for an answer.

My smile widened as I teased him. "Everything comes to he who waits."

We both laughed.

Nothing could precede the speed of light. Well, that was what Ole Rømer insisted. But that half-hour that I spent with Erick went much faster than light. We talked about many things, and we seemed to get along, agreeing to meet every Saturday at five.

Erick had just left when a siren pierced the air. A random Law Corps sin-spots searching team had stopped in front of Danira's place. Ms. Iris and her team headed inside, and minutes later, they came out with Danira's mother handcuffed, her face wan.

Danira ran into the street after the team's car, screaming her mom's name, her face wet with tears. I hurried to soothe her before they could arrest her too. Anger simmered in me at the injustice meted out to women in my country. Mere minutes had changed several people's lives again. Neither Danira nor her mother would survive this ordeal without help. I knew that I would do anything to become the first female lawyer in this kingdom.

While the Law Corps drove away, the neighbors cried out in support. "Glory to Elpax! Glory! Glory!"

I turned my back to them.

Danira's mom getting taken away cast a somber mood over the entire neighborhood. Each of us realized how fragile our life was and how easily we could lose our freedom with a single strike. As Hermes announced on the news, Danira's mom was accused of hiding a kitten. I wondered how that kitten escaped the animal sanctuary in our province, and why they punished Danira's mom for her humane attitude and good deeds.

Things at my home looked chirpier than before. Mom appeared to approve of my friendship with Erick, and the smile returned to her face more frequently. I was thankful to Erick for that. It was delightful to see

138

my mother's smile, which my father had stolen years ago. But I had a feeling that Erick's visit wasn't a coincidence—Mom had a hand in it. That was confusing—I didn't know how she'd found out about my feelings. Not that I was complaining.

I called Jason to help me tie up some loose ends and clear my doubts about the cinema. I could sense the honesty in his voice when he replied that he'd had no idea about the juvenile-adult seat rule, because he already had a cinema in his house. However, he was hopping mad about Erick's visit. Now I started to doubt my friend's actions. He was always so protective. But this recent attitude, the extreme care, was . . . bizarre.

At night, I spent my time finishing my usual tasks. First, I washed the floor-to-ceiling windows—Mom hated to see any spots on them, and they were supposed to glitter all the time. Next, I squeezed out the oranges for the morning juice, harvested sage from our little garden, and, at last, I made dinner. There weren't many dinner choices: egg sandwiches for the twins and Mom, cheese with tomato for me.

Moria picked up her sandwich, and after taking a big bite, she said, "Prince Thaddeus is in the news again."

"King Alexei looks nice, don't you think?" Sarah remarked.

Moria's eyes widened. "It's weird how they don't look alike."

I looked up, staring at Prince Thaddeus, who stood next to King Alexei on their official visit to Rome. The brothers looked as different as day and night. Alexei's fair skin and blond hair shone against his unremarkable features. His green eyes weren't as sharp as his mother's or brother's, but he looked more approachable, with his broad smile and pleasant demeanor.

Prince Thaddeus's handsome, slim face looked menacing. He didn't wear the same teal and silver uniform as the king, but tight pants with long knee boots and a tailcoat. The golden sword on his back enhanced his foreboding look—even more so with his black clothes and silver-mint hair.

"Because they aren't brothers from the same mother," Mom answered as she sipped her tea. "King Stavros's first wife, Queen . . ." She paused as she remembered something that seemed to disturb her.

"Which one?" asked Moria. I turned to her, sending a silent message to stop talking about this subject, but Mom soon continued.

"Rhea."

I didn't miss the shudder in her voice.

Mom blinked several times before clarifying. "Queen Rhea died on the day of Prince Thaddeus's birth. Ten years later, King Stavros married Queen Arianna, who gave birth to King Alexei."

"Oh, that explains their differences," said Moria.

I smiled at the accuracy of the twins' observation and turned back to the Ológramma. I could see Prince Thaddeus's disinterest. It was as if he had come to Rome against his will. He seemed to be restless and irritable.

"Queen Arianna isn't originally from the royal family," stated Mom out of nowhere.

"For real?" Moria shouted, her blue eyes glittering.

Mom nodded. "She isn't Elpaxian. She was a Greek journalist who met King Stavros when he was on an official trip to Rome. He returned home to surprise the people with his marriage."

"It must have saddened the princesses of the kingdom."

We laughed at Moria's utterance.

"As a matter of fact," Mom continued in the next breath, "King Stavros was seventy years old, while she was only a few years older than Lenora." And she winked at me.

My face flushed. She'd reminded me that I could marry soon if I crossed, even in a simple family gathering. How embarrassing!

I excused myself to my bedroom, and so did the twins. I sat on my bed, holding the notebook that Mary had gifted me on my birthday. An elegant one, composed of two wooden panels covered by dark purple fabric with gold feathers, and a side slot to hold a charcoal pencil.

It was an expensive and rare gift because papers were almost extinct in our kingdom. The desertification had crept from Alphatoli to the other provinces. Therefore, the late King Stavros forbade manufacturing papers except for passports—with exceptions for the wealthy, of course.

140

I got up to drink water, and when I came back to my room, I found Sarah sleeping on the other end of my bed.

"What happened? Did Moria start singing?"

She giggled. It was the sweetest sound. "Leen, there's something you should know."

My eyebrows lifted in a silent question.

"I was in the garden the other day, and I saw Mom in your room."

"What was she doing?"

"She was reading your notebook."

My blood ran cold. Mom had found out about my feelings!

CHAPTER 17

ERICK STARTED COMING OVER TO my place every Saturday. Not every one of them, to be honest. Sometimes he skipped his visits without an explanation. And each time, it left me with a profound disappointment until the next Saturday perked me up with anticipation. It felt as if my life was measured from one Saturday to the next. So many questions ran through my brain from Sunday to Friday, but none of them could be answered.

I couldn't see him at school, either, as Francine's father had started picking her up after he lost his job. Erick had to work all hours to make ends meet. I hated to push him, as I was sure that he had a principled reason for not meeting me. I hoped he wasn't playing me for a fool. He seemed so nice, and we gelled well together. I'd found a deeper connection with him—more than I'd ever felt with anyone. We could talk about anything—within the juvenile limits, of course.

Yet, somehow, I still felt unsettled . . .

Maybe it was the fact that the next Crossing Day was approaching.

Or that Mom knew all my secrets. Had she asked him to push me to cross? Though neither of them ever spoke about the crossing. Did Erick feel something real for me? How strong were those feelings?

I could see it in his eyes. He preferred my company most times. But occasionally, it felt like his focus was elsewhere. Sometimes, I would have to prod him to get him back to reality. Did he have too many problems? Or doubts? Jason kept warning me about trusting him so soon. Yet, Mary encouraged our relationship, often hinting that he would be a good husband.

The backfire of a car pulled me away from my doubtful musings. I rushed to the window to check. It was Erick.

I opened the front door, and my heart pounded at the sight of him. I should have been used to it by now. My heart had never worked so much in all my years. It had been lying dormant for eternity, as if in wait for Erick, and now it seemed to beat only for him. Every time my eyes captured a snapshot of his visage, my heart galloped. Blue jeans and a white shirt with rolled-up sleeves looked gorgeous on him—like the actor in that movie I saw on my first cinema outing.

"How are you doing, Leen?" His smile widened.

"All good." I wanted to ask him about last Saturday, when he'd missed our meeting and not bothered to call for the rest of the week. But I didn't want anything to mar our time today.

"Apologies, Leen. I've been busy at work, so . . ."

"I understand. It happens. Erick, I want to ask you something."

He could see the seriousness on my face, and gave me his complete attention, keeping his Iméfono inside the pocket.

"How can a student from the working class attend law school?" I asked.

"The subjects in high school aren't important for acceptance to law school." He sat on the front steps. "They simply help improve brain capacity and knowledge. The main requirement is that a student has to pass an entrance exam at the University, which is held in October every

143

year. That gives newly crossed adults enough time to prepare for it."

I sat next to him. "Are there any pre-requisites to study law?"

Erick narrowed his eyes, trying to remember the rules. "They scan the student's body every week for sin-spots. The exams have three sections: ethics, the rules and regulations of the kingdom, and an IQ test. Why? Do you know someone who wants to become a lawyer?"

Despite my misgivings and doubts about our relationship, I trusted Erick as a person. Hence, I confessed. "Yes. Me!"

His eyebrows rose in amazement, and an expression of delight crossed his face. But then he whispered, "Leen, a woman can't study law. It's against the rules."

I knew that. So far, a woman couldn't work in political or legal affairs. Her only option was the Law Corps. "Is it a divine law?"

Erick shook his head.

"So that means it's changeable. Will you help me?"

I looked at him with hope and eagerness, knowing he was the only man who would understand. I might not know what he was thinking at that moment, but I knew he was honest. I felt it deep within me. Only he could help me find a way out.

"I'll help you." His gaze turned to the horizon. "We may have to present a petition to the queen mother."

"A petition?"

"Yes. All change needs to start somewhere. Years ago, the government didn't allow women to attend college. It limited their roles to housework and motherhood. But now, anything is possible."

I grinned, hoping he would understand the gift he had given me. Erick turned toward me, his fingers grazing mine. "You know, Leen, this is one of the things that I li . . . let's say, caught my attention about you."

My heart pumped fast. I knew Erick was about to say *like about you* before he remembered the damn word-catchers and the fact that I was still a juvenile. So he couldn't profess his feelings for me and end this farce. Ugh! These absurd laws.

"Since the first day I saw you, I knew you were special," he stated while gazing into my eyes. "I saw a girl who did the right thing even when she was scared. Someone who tried to keep everyone happy but stood up for herself. A girl who was loyal and kind. Someone I could . . ."

Oh, my heart! Will he propose? Is he going to stop this torment that has overtaken both of us?

An interminable silence reigned between us. He opened his mouth to say the words, then thought better of it. His eyes stared into mine, and time disappeared. The entire world narrowed to just our gazes. The past and future melted into this one moment; our emotions were unspoken, yet felt by both of us.

Erick was the first to break the connection. He shifted his gaze, looking at the street, and we lost the moment. His eyes became shuttered once again, not revealing what was in his mind. It piqued me, wondering if he would ever propose . . . he was too damn enigmatic and mysterious.

"By the way, happy birthday," Erick said, his smile slowly coming back.

"You remembered!" I grinned widely. The truth was, with all my anxiety about the Crossing Day approaching, I had totally forgotten about my birthday. And he remembered! That had to mean something, right?

"How could I forget?" He eyed me. "Today, you'll turn eighteen, and we must do something special. How about a drive?"

"Where to?"

"I'll tell you on the way. Get your mom's permission while I wait for you in the car."

Ten minutes later, we arrived at Charites Park in town. It was a peaceful sunny day in May. Families were picnicking, and children were enjoying the playground. Erick grabbed something from the trunk and waved for me to follow him.

"A special gift for a special girl on her birthday," said Erick. As I approached, I saw that he was holding a pair of pink boots with wheels.

He opened the backseat door and gestured for me to sit down. "These are skates. You told me once that you couldn't run much because of asthma and nosebleeds. These will help you enjoy your freedom, to move with the wind in your hair, without affecting your health."

I was speechless. I'd told him about my asthma six months ago, and yet he remembered. "Thank you!" I found my lost voice. "This is so nice of you." I was touched by his solicitude and his need to make me happy, until he uttered his next words.

"This is the least I can do for my friend."

Friend! He'd said *friend*. Wasn't that the wrong label? Or was I imagining the connection between us and I really was just a friend to him?

I buried my thoughts—there was no point in spoiling this moment—and put on the skates. Erick started giving me instructions about how to walk in those boots, holding my hands while keeping a distance between us. The beginning was tenuous, and we laughed a lot until his Iméfono rang. He looked at the name, and his face shadowed.

"A moment, Leen. Excuse me."

He moved a scant distance away and started speaking. The person's voice on the other side was loud. I looked up, my eyes sparkling with fire.

"Helena, I'm with my sister. We'll talk later." His face hardened at whatever Helena had told him, and he hung up.

"Your sister?" I hissed.

He forced a smile. "Don't I respect you like my sister? Come on."

I love him, and he only respects me?

I couldn't believe how much coldness there was in his soul. He looked like a solid wall of indifference—a slab of distasteful intransigence that didn't care about my suffering.

As much as I wanted to forget about what had just happened, I couldn't. It was amazing that such disparate feelings could exist in my heart: passionate love and violent hatred. Still, one word or smile wouldn't be able to erase this disappointment like it had before. It seemed he was playing me, pulling me toward him while casting me aside. But hell no. No more. I couldn't take it.

"I'm not your sister!" I yelled, trying to run away in those ridiculous shoes.

It took his long legs two steps to follow me and grab my wrist. "I know. Let's talk about it." His tone was firm.

"I don't want to!"

His eyes grew tender. "Leen, calm down."

"I'm already calmer than I should be. Just . . . leave me alone." I sped away, driven by the pain, longing, and anger that filled my heart. He tried to persuade me to listen to him, but I couldn't see or hear anything beyond the crashing waves of emotion. There was no patience left in my soul for his explanations. My heart was tired, like a violin string that had played the same song for months.

Tears and emotional turmoil made me misstep; the skates didn't help, either. I overlooked a few stairs in my haste to escape, tripped, and fell to the ground. A sharp shooting pain ran up my ankle, and a scream escaped my throat. The roaring in my mind escalated to insurmountable wavelengths. As if that weren't enough, the processing alarm echoed all over the kingdom, and people started rushing to get their juveniles and children to the nearest Safe Cell.

We had only twenty minutes before the Law Corps came for us.

CHAPTER 18

I WAS ON THE GROUND, barely able to get to a sitting position, when I heard footsteps behind me. "Are you all right?" Erick's worried face met my eyes.

"My leg hurts."

He leaned over to examine it. Even though he barely brushed his fingers against my leg, his touch felt like a wave of thousand knives grating against it. I screamed in pain.

"It looks like you broke your leg or severely sprained it." He swiped a hand over his face. "We have little time to get you to the hospital. I'll drive the car closer to you."

I nodded, biting my lips to prevent myself from screaming again.

While on the ground, I wondered why the government didn't announce the processing time early enough for everyone to get ready. Twenty minutes was too short to get to the Safe Cell. Living in fear was what we did over the weekend when the alarm sounded. It was so frustrating—the kingdom didn't make intelligent rules. I didn't care for the safety rules;

I cared more for my sanity!

I heard Erick's car approaching. He stepped out and tried to help me stand up by holding onto my hands. I couldn't put weight on my injured leg, and it was challenging to find leverage with the other.

"Crawl on the ground, Leen."

"What?" My eyes popped out.

"Trust me, please."

I sighed, looking at him, then crawled through the mud and dirt of the park, screaming at the friction on my leg.

"That's enough." He kneeled. "Now, promise not to scream. Can I lift you?"

"What about the—"

"Well, all I can reveal is that you'll not catch a disease if I did."

I balanced the situation in my head for a few seconds, then nodded. Erick checked out the surroundings, and when he could find no one around, he placed one arm under my thighs and the other around my shoulders and lifted me up close to his chest. He was so near that my breath stopped. I never thought such a thing would be possible.

Erick placed me with great care in the passenger seat and started the car, rushing to the nearest Safe Cell. He sent a voice message to Mom, telling her not to worry. A few minutes later, he pulled over in front of the Safe Cell, opened the door, and yelled at the female soldiers that I had broken my leg. One of them pushed a wheelchair over, and the other looked into the car and turned a thoughtful gaze toward me.

"How did you get into the car?" she asked in a firm tone.

I wet my lips in sudden nervousness. "I crawled," I said, not looking up at Erick.

The soldier looked at my dirty clothes and nodded. She helped me sit in the wheelchair, and the national anthem started the second I got inside the Safe Cell.

An entire hour of torture. That was how long it took for the process of ten Eliminations. Each picture that came up made me realize that entire

149

families were getting destroyed at this moment. The tears that sprang in my eyes surprised me. After Carlota, I realized that the person on the screen could have committed a minor infraction, but the kingdom wouldn't grant justice or pardon for anything. It ruled with an iron fist.

Is it the same in other lands? What is it like in the terrifying Modern Roman Empire?

This question distracted me enough from my own pain. I could feel my ankle swelling. When I asked for pain relief, the soldier responded coolly, "You don't have medical insurance."

Would the kingdom's economy collapse if free medical aid were provided?

When it was over, they opened the doors, and a soldier pushed my wheelchair to where Erick stood. He seemed worried, face withdrawn and hair tousled. His clothes had too many creases on them. The soldier helped me into the car, and the first Curfew alarm reverberated across the entire land.

I calmly took off my skates. Erick looked at my ankle and decided I would require a visit to the hospital. A half an hour wasn't enough time for him to get me medical help, drop me off at home, and go home to Zoiterra. His hesitant eyes met mine.

"I know," I whispered, "We don't have much time. We can go home."

Erick took a deep breath and reached over to squeeze my hand. "Don't worry."

He pulled the car over and stepped out, making a call. I wondered why he had to get out of the car to speak on the Iméfono. He could have done it from inside the car itself. I shrugged, putting this thought out of my mind for the time being.

He got back in and started the car without looking at me. "Dalia will help. She is a nurse I worked with years ago."

I nodded and sat back with a sigh. "Who's Helena?"

He gave me a surprised glance. "My secretary."

Oh!

"What did you think?" A smile lurked on his face.

Now it was my turn to be surprised. He was teasing me, and he knew it.

We reached the hospital, which saved me from answering that question. Erick stopped in front of the emergency room and ran inside. I knew what would happen. They would tell him to come back after the Curfew, since my case wasn't an emergency. You had to be dying to stay in the hospital during Curfew.

And they called our kingdom the land of peace and hope!

Erick came back with a plump silver-mint-haired nurse, who carried a medical bag with her. She was warm-hearted and checked my ankle with a gentle touch. She injected a painkiller into my arm and declared that no bones were out of place. But I would require an X-ray to confirm it, which could be done in the next few days.

"Keep your weight off the leg and apply ice," she said, waving for Erick to hurry up.

Erick started the car again. We could barely reach my home in time. How would Erick make it to his? Ten minutes later, the second Curfew alarm sounded. Soon, the countdown would start. We were a few meters away from my home, but Erick parked the car at once and turned to me.

"I'm sorry," I said, my voice shaking with fear.

"We both will be very sorry if I don't get you home now." He turned around to open my door. "Put your arm around my neck."

He swept both his arms under my body to carry me, and he ran down the empty street, keeping to the shadows, risking his life to save mine. It was dark, but we could hear movements in the distance behind us—the Law Corps on their rounds. Erick ran faster to reach my home before they did. For a few minutes, all I could hear was his feet pounding the pavement and his gasping breaths in the silence, before the sound of bullets and a scream pierced the darkness.

"Erick!" I shuddered.

He couldn't answer me. He just kept running, faster and faster. The gunshots seemed to get closer with each step. It felt like we wouldn't be

151

able to outrun them however hard we tried. I had heard bullet sounds after some Elimination processes, and I was aware of the term "armed clashes." It might have been the Law Corps and rebels shooting at each other as usual, or the Law Corps firing upon anyone who wasn't a wealthy walking in the street or driving a car. Just like us.

We had almost reached home when the Law Corps armored car showed up at the other end of the neighborhood. This was a disaster. Now, Mom wouldn't be able to open the door—she couldn't silence the door music, and the government jammed the Iméfonos during Curfew so I couldn't call her. We were in a complete fix.

Erick extended his leg, carefully crossed the garden's low fence to the side of the kitchen, and placed me on the ground. We were partially hidden from the Law Corps at this end. But they were doing a door-to-door check. My entire body shook as I thought about the punishment and the repercussions. I shifted my head to see how far away the Corps were. Just one door. So close to home, and yet so far.

"Erick, they're around," I whispered in a rush, my words all jumbling together. We could hear the Law Corps talking to the next-door neighbor.

"How good is your mom's hearing?"

"I wish it was worse."

Erick gave a faint smile and threw a small stone at the kitchen window. No response.

Erick threw another stone.

"Mama, someone is at the kitchen window!" It was Moria's scared voice.

"In my room, both of you." That was Mom, and a few seconds later, her face appeared in the window. "Hurry up!"

Erick supported me and boosted me through the window. Mom's eyes widened at the sight of his hands on my body. But she understood the gravity of the situation, and she helped me in from the other side. I looked back. Erick was still outside. *Why is he not coming in?*

"Mom, you can't leave Erick outside during the ID scanning. They'll think he is a rebel and shoot him at once!"

Mom looked back and forth between us with hesitation. The Law Corps had nearly reached our home.

"Mom, he saved my life!"

"What about the twins, Lenora? He isn't a relative, and they can't lie. They don't know how to."

"I don't care, Mom!" I yelled-whispered. "We'll hide in the bathroom."

She sighed and waved Erick in. He climbed in through the window and picked me up again.

"Quickly, in here!" Mom hissed as he carried me to the bathroom. She closed the door and called out to the twins. I stood behind the door while Erick hid behind me, holding my waist, supporting me, as I couldn't stand on my leg.

"Sarah. Moria. Lenora is in the bathroom."

"But how, Mama? When did she come home?" asked Moria.

"Hush, now. I'll tell you later. I don't want you saying anything to the soldiers. Is that clear, Moria? Sarah?"

"At your command," both of the girls agreed.

"Sarah, go ask your sister why she is in the bathroom."

I liked how Mom had thought this plan out so quickly. She couldn't lie, as a sin-spot would appear on her body. What if a spot appeared right on her face at that very moment? And the twins couldn't lie, as they were still in their childhood. They didn't know how to.

I didn't wait for Sarah to ask me. I heard the Law Corps marching down our driveway, and they knocked on the door.

"My stomach hurts!" I yelled so that the twins could hear me. I looked back at Erick; he gave me a tense smile at my quick thinking.

Mom opened the door to the soldiers, and their heavy boots clomped on the floors. The sound of the ID scanners rang thrice. Each noise seemed to lance my heart with fear.

"Where is your third daughter?" asked the stern voice of a man.

"In the bathroom. Her stomach hurts," replied my clever Sarah.

I nodded to Erick, who moved further back, well hidden. I opened the door and kept it ajar, extending my left wrist to the soldier. He scanned my ID and nodded. He turned around just in time to see Moria's eyes widening and her jaw dropping open.

She'd seen Erick.

I closed my eyes, and a sinking feeling dropped into the pit of my stomach. *That's it! Our game is up!*

CHAPTER 19

THE SOLDIER KNEELED, DIRECTING HIS question at Moria. "Why do you seem surprised?"

"Mom said Leen was in the bathroom. But it is . . . odd."

God! This girl will get me killed; I know it! She can't lie, and she talks too much—a bad combination, especially with a soldier. But at least she didn't see Erick, like I thought she did! That is a relief.

"Why is it odd?" His solemn eyes stared at me. The other soldiers stood in anticipation, ready to act once he gave the order to arrest any of us.

"Because . . . well . . . we didn't hear a sound from her when we got back from the Safe Cell."

The soldier stood at once and looked at me with a newfound sharpness. I swallowed hard. My heart lost its rhythm, and my legs started to shake. Mom was no better, paling at once. Sarah widened her eyes. She looked terrified as she started to understand the severity of the situation.

"Where were you?" the soldier asked me firmly.

I had two options: tell the truth or tell a lie. But both would lead to imprisonment if he didn't believe me. Erick's warm hand on my back gave me the strength to gather myself. Shoving the dark thoughts aside, I spoke fast, trying to soften my tone as much as possible. "I had a fight with my friend over the Iméfono and wanted to hide until I calmed down."

I hoped neither of the twins would explain that they had used the bathroom earlier and I was nowhere to be found then. Lo and behold, Moria's words exploded through the air, stopping my breathing at once. "But I just used the bathroom!"

Sarah hurried to say, "Maybe she was in her room at that moment."

I nodded quickly. "I went to the kitchen to grab a napkin." My eyes sent sharp daggers toward Moria. *For God's sake, girl! Shut up! Shut the hell up for once!*

She shrugged. The soldier took a few seconds to look at all of us, ultimately fixing his gaze on Mom. I felt Erick's fingers digging into my waist. It appeared we were all holding our breaths, waiting for the soldier to make his decision.

He held his wireless device, his finger pressing on the call button. My pulse skyrocketed of the thought of him calling for Ms. Iris to investigate Mom. I talked fast. "Sir, is it against the law to spend time in the bathroom crying?" I lowered my eyes as if I was still sad.

He turned to me. There was uncertainty in his eyes, as if he was trying to assess the situation.

"No. It's not." He straightened his uniform and clicked his heels together. "Glory to Elpax."

We repeated the words, and he walked out of our house, followed by the other soldiers. I slammed the bathroom door shut and leaned against it, inhaling as if I had just learned how to breathe. Erick's hands held my waist, and he twisted my body to face him. He dragged me with great care to his chest and encircled me with his strong arms.

My body trembled. "Erick, what are you doing?" I whispered, "Will this hurt me?" Though my heart screamed in joy at being in his arms, I couldn't forget about that deadly disease.

"I can never hurt you. I already assured you that nothing would happen if we got close to each other." His arms tightened once, then released me. Without a word, he picked up my palm and drew letters on it, one by one.

H U G

Erick knows better than me, so this "hug" must be harmless after all. I wet my lips with a sudden nervousness. "It felt nice and warm."

Erick grinned, breathing in my ear. "I'll show you something nicer later."

I blushed, hugging him once more.

It was heaven.

We couldn't get out of the bathroom. Where could he hide in a glass house? Not that I was complaining—I could remain in his arms forever.

Erick bent his head. "What are you thinking about?"

"If I knew breaking a bone would get you to," I mouthed the words *hug me* without giving voice to them, "then I would have done it a lot earlier," I joked.

He tittered, and I buried my head in his chest out of shyness, hiding my smile. He held my left hand, caressing my ID lines.

"You're breaking a lot of rules, Mr. Mellas," I teased.

"For you, I'll do anything." My eyes lifted to meet his in wonder. "I want to make you happy. To buy you everything I can afford." His eyes became tender. "I want to make you feel things that you never knew existed. To help you realize your ambitions. I want to give wings to your dreams."

His words touched me deep in my soul, and I found a piece of myself that had always been missing.

"But I won't be able to do much while you're still a juvenile."

I stiffened. "If Mom has put you up to this, then she's living in a fantasy. I'll never cross over for a man."

Erick ran his fingers through my hair, tucking a lock behind my ear. "You've got it wrong. I called and asked her permission to get to know you."

"What?"

"After our cinema date, she told me, and I quote, 'I don't know how

157

this happened, but Lenora might feel something for you. If you ever hurt her, I'll make sure you never see her again.'"

How could Mom trust Erick with this secret about my adult emotions? She had acumen with people and never put her trust in those who didn't deserve it. And Erick could turn both of us over to the Law Corps.

She must have had a good reason to trust him. I was glad he proved that he was trustworthy today.

Erick continued. "I didn't believe it in the beginning, but after a while, I noticed the way you look at me."

"What way?"

"You tell me."

I blushed. *How do I tell him that he has made my innocent heart tremble in his presence? Even his absence has an effect on me. What if his feelings for me aren't as strong as mine for him?*

I opened my mouth, but my throat refused to verbalize my thoughts. How could I say all that in plain Greek? I did the next best thing. I accused him.

"But you didn't show up last weekend, and that wasn't the first time you let me down."

He bent his neck forward. "You think I am playing you, and my conscience has just woken up now?"

Heat flushed down my body. That was the exact thing I was trying to say.

Erick cupped my face, looking straight into my eyes. "You know the kingdom's laws. I can't see you as much as I want to."

Oh! I'd thought we could hang out any time because he was a lawyer. I totally forgot that this particular rule about adults and juveniles being forbidden to meet regularly applied to everyone in the kingdom—even the wealthy.

"But why did you want to get to know me so badly that you called Mom?" I asked, my heart trembling. Erick opened his lips to answer.

"Lenora!" Mom hissed from the other side of the door.

Oh, my goodness! Not now, Mom! She chose the worst time ever to interrupt.

I sighed, and Erick smiled at me before opening the door for Mom.

"The twins are sleeping," hissed Mom as she stepped inside the bathroom, shutting the door behind her. "Lenora, go to your room."

"What about Erick?"

She pointed at him. "You can't stay here. You have to leave."

"Mom!"

"I can't let him stay, Lenora. We've already risked a lot today. What if someone saw him?" She looked him up and down. "Don't you have to scan your ID at your home, like all middle-class citizens do?"

Erick nodded. "Yes. But it's too late, anyway. I can fix it up tomorrow, but I can't . . ." He left the rest of the line unsaid.

"He can't leave, Mom, or else the Corps will shoot him right away!"

Mom remained silent for a while, thinking.

"Can't he stay in the adult's room until the curfew ends tomorrow morning?" I asked Mom. Nobody ever slept on the bed inside that tiny space, but it looked comfortable enough when I snuck a glimpse that one time.

She exchanged looks with Erick. "That room has a sensor on the ground, Leen," explained Erick. "I can't get inside it without scanning my ID. Even if your mother scans her ID to let me in, I'll have to scan it again from inside to get out."

"I'll cover the windows with sheets," Mom eventually said. "Erick, you can take Leen's room. Leen, you are sleeping in mine."

Mom went out to cover the windows in my room. When she returned, Erick lifted me up. I winked at Mom, and her eyes popped out. Erick walked as quietly as possible into Mom's room and placed me in her bed, trying not to make any sound that would wake up the twins.

"I need to have a word with you," Mom whispered to Erick in a firm tone, and they left the room.

I could smell Erick's perfume on my clothes, feel his arms around me, and hear his breath in my ear. My heart felt as if it'd burst with joy. Erick was in my bedroom, and he would sleep on my bed. How I wished I could be with him.

Mom came back a few minutes later with my nightclothes. "Change and go to bed." She seemed worried. "We'll talk about it in the morning before the twins wake up."

Soon, Mom drifted off to sleep, but I was wide awake. How could I sleep with Erick a few meters away from me? I got up, keeping a watch on Mom's breathing. I slowly limped, hopped, and dragged myself to my bedroom, and then entered. Erick was sitting in my bed with my quilt around him.

"Hey, it's past your bedtime," he joked.

A light giggle escaped my lips as I walked over to him.

He sighed. "I promised your mother not to touch you again." Yet, he shifted to make space for me.

I sat beside him. "And why is that? You just told me that I won't catch any disease if you touch me."

He sighed. "Because you're underage."

I rolled my eyes. "So a fifteen-year-old who has crossed to adulthood is considered an adult, yet I, an eighteen-year-old, am still a juvenile because some stupid ID lines say so? This is ridiculous!"

He smiled. "Well, in Latina and in the Roman Empire, you would be an adult already. But things are different here."

"They are not," I huffed. "I already feel some adult feelings. And by the way, you haven't answered my question yet. Why did you want to get to know me so badly that you called Mom?"

His fingers reached out to mine. "I need to know first, how did you find out about these feelings?" There was fear on his face, along with other emotions that I couldn't be sure about.

I swallowed. "I kept seeing you in my dreams, and I searched for clarification about my feelings. Mary told me . . . I asked Jason about them, too."

160

"You asked Jason about it?" His eyes popped out. "Did you utter the word to him?"

"Erick, you're scaring me!"

"Do you have any idea how observant those word-catchers are?"

"I know about them." I recalled my library excursion. "And I know how to be careful." Tears filled my eyes.

"I'm sorry." Erick quietened his tone down and hugged me. "I didn't mean to upset you. I'm just worried about you." He wiped my tears with his fingers. "As a lawyer, I've seen some cases similar to this matter. All of them have ended badly for the woman."

I agreed. I had seen a woman being unfairly punished myself. *Selene Dukasi.* I could never forget the name of the civilian I saw being beaten up by the Corps last year.

He continued. "There are some politics at play as well. The Law Corps keep a watch on everybody in the kingdom. I'm sure that your Crossing Day has garnered some interest." He ducked his head for a moment. "Has anyone been watching you these past few months?"

"Other than the creepy crossing consultant?"

He nodded.

I thought hard, back to the days after my failed crossing. A chill spread down my body. "Yes! I remember it now. A strange white sedan kept following me everywhere until . . ." I just realized that the car had disappeared after Carlota's punishment. I hadn't seen it in the last few months. *Is it related to research I did at the library?*

"Until?"

I couldn't explain all that to Erick without revealing the trip to the library. So I shook my head.

"Why didn't you tell me?"

"It slipped my mind!"

He ducked his head again for a while. It was terrifying when a solemn man looked confused and desolate.

A moment later, he gazed into my eyes. "You said you saw me in a dream. What dream?"

I cleared my throat and told him everything about my dreams. He listened carefully, and his face looked worried and surprised. Perhaps he was concerned that I hadn't possessed the courage to tell him about my dreams until now.

"I've answered all of your questions. It's your turn now," I teased, and my gaze met his in the faint light. His pretty gray eyes glittered, and his face leaned over me. His warm breath was hot on my ear, smelling like mint leaves. His lips touched my cheek, and he made a soft sound that threw me into a sea of scattered colors.

Heat floated out of my body. I became weak as a marionette with its strings cut off. My lips curled into a tense smile, and he opened my palm to draw the letters.

K I S S

Erick swept one hand under my legs and the other behind my back, lifting me a little to lay me down in bed. His body came closer, and his eyes held a strange expression. It seemed like my body knew what it was feeling even when my mind couldn't compute it. I placed my palm on his chest; his heart was racing. His face moved closer till it blurred. His stubble rubbed against my cheeks. His gentle lips kissed their way across my chin and jaw, stopping at my ear.

"You want an answer?" he murmured. His breath in my ear gave me chill bumps. My skin tingled, and a shaky smile spread across my face. Erick lowered his lips to the corner of mine. I wasn't able to control my breaths anymore.

"Erick . . ." I was melting.

He pulled away enough to look into my eyes. His heart was beating as fast as mine, pounding against his ribs. I was so lost in his smell and warm kisses that I couldn't speak. But I knew there was something more to this kissing. Running my fingers through his hair, I pulled his head closer, taking charge and kissing the corner of his mouth, giving my silent approval to whatever he wanted to do with me.

His head lowered, and his lips touched mine with a short, delicate kiss that took my breath away. It was so soft, as if Erick was afraid that his lips would hurt mine. I kissed him back, and our kisses became longer and more profound.

This was actual heaven.

There was no Elpax anymore, no curfew, no broken leg. Just Erick and me, alone in our special place where our souls became one.

After a few minutes, Erick pulled back. His forehead touched mine as we waited for our pulses to calm down.

"Did that answer your question?"

I shook my head, teasing him, and he tittered. I couldn't tell him about my feelings before he told me about his. It would embarrass me if my feelings were stronger than his. I had to be sure about the entire thing.

"You're my other half," he whispered.

Oh, my heart! Was that a proposal?

Erick tucked a lock of my hair behind my ear. "Your mom might get up to check on you. You don't want her to throw me out of your house in the middle of the night."

It was challenging to pull myself out of bed. I nodded, resisting the urge to keep kissing him all night long.

"Goodnight, my proud non-crosser juvenile." He kissed me again on the forehead.

I smiled and hopped away, happier than ever. I looked back before closing the door, and my heart whispered, *goodnight, my everything*.

CHAPTER 20

THE SMELL OF SAGE TEA woke me up. I blinked, trying to remember last night. It felt like a dream where all my wishes had been answered.

With a loud yawn, I picked up my Iméfono to find a message from Jason waiting for me.

Hey, Leen. I am sorry I missed your birthday yesterday; I was in Theirna. You know . . . work. I want to make it up to you. How about we hang out today?

I told him I'd hurt my leg and couldn't walk, so he replied that he'd come over. Putting the Iméfono aside, I tried to move my leg, but the pain was excruciating.

"Mom!"

Her footsteps approached, and her face showed from the opening door.

"Where is he?" I whispered; in case the twins were in the living room.

"In the garden. Here, I'll help you get up." She came to help me walk to the bathroom.

"Mom. Where are the twins?"

"They got up early, so I took them to Karya's place to play with her sisters."

I peered out the house's floor-to-ceiling windows on the way to the bathroom. There were double the Law Corps cars outside compared to yesterday. The news from the Ológramma was about postponing the Crossing Day of Alphatoli province. Was it because of the armed clashes yesterday?

Mom helped me to my room. I sat on my bed and found that Erick's smell still lingered on the sheets—proof that he'd really slept there. My smile widened as I gathered part of my quilt into a ball, inhaling deeply. God! I would never wash this quilt.

"How's my proud non-crosser juvenile?" said Erick as he stood in the doorway. He looked tired, and there was a strange tension on his face. I wondered if he had problems that he hadn't shared with me yet.

I rolled my eyes and patted my bed, waiting for him to come and sit next to me. "So much better now that I've seen you."

It was his turn to roll his eyes, and I giggled. It was fun being silly with him. But instead of laughing along with me, Erick ran his fingers through his hair. His face lost its color for a second, looking different from yesterday. He was . . . cold.

"Erick, what is it?"

His expression smoothed out. Plastering a smile on his face, he sat and held my hand.

"I couldn't sleep last night because I was thinking about you . . . us . . . our future. I wondered why I couldn't translate my emotions into words." He opened my palm and pressed a soft kiss into it.

Excitement filled me as I understood the meaning of his words. *Is Erick going to proclaim his love for me?*

He pulled me toward him and pressed a soft kiss on my forehead. My heart burst with warmth and joy. I looked up at his face, and perceived his unwavering determination to do something significant for both of us. He took my palm and drew the letters one by one, my breath growing heavier with each stroke.

I LOVE YOU

He mouthed the words without giving voice to them. I froze in that moment of bliss, never wanting it to end. That was my home forever—in his eyes. Tears dropped down my cheeks. I tried to respond, but something stopped me. Was it because my father had done more mental harm than physical?

Erick smiled with complete understanding. "I'm not expecting an answer at the moment. I want to hear you say it out loud in front of everyone after you cross. Some words are worth waiting for."

I nodded. *Why are things so complicated in my country? What's wrong with showing love? Why can't we hug and kiss now? How can they ban something so incredible?*

I heard the sound of a car stopping in front of my home. Our front door opened, and I heard Jason saying hello to Mom. He entered my room, and his worried eyes greeted mine. His facial expressions tightened at once when he saw Erick.

"Did you hurt her?" Jason yelled. "I'm going to end you!"

"I dare you to try," provoked Erick, stepping forward.

"Jason! Erick! Enough! Keep your voices down. *No.* Erick saved my life. And Jason—you'll do nothing to him."

Mom stepped inside the room, looking at both of them. "Last time I checked, this was my home, and that's my daughter. So I decide who can do what. Both of you need to calm down and come with me."

Jason hesitated a bit, and then they all walked out of my room. He returned alone a few minutes later.

I tried to alleviate the tension. "Look at you!" I pointed to his well-built muscles that showed beneath his long-sleeved sweater. "Now I know why you disappeared for months."

He smiled and sat on the bed beside me. "I'm sorry I yelled. Your mom explained everything."

My smile widened as I touched his hand. "He feels the same. For me."

Jason pursed his lips and pressed my hand gently. "Leen, I don't want to sound . . . paranoid. But he's an older man, and I think these feelings need time to build . . . I beg you to think about your decision."

I cast a helpless look at him. "I can't. He's mine forever. He's my everything."

"How long have you known the man? Just a few months now. It isn't long enough to decide something that affects your entire life."

"The matters of the heart don't consider time, Jason. Fate etches them in stone."

He looked at the ceiling as if he was thinking of something. "I'm trying to find out more details about him, but it seems that the higher authorities have blocked it, which is highly suspicious. Do you want my father to look into it?"

"No. I trust Erick," I mumbled. *I trust him even though he's always on his Iméfono and doesn't show up every week. But again, he has strong reasons. He's probably busy with work.*

Jason exhaled. "Why him?" There was a wealth of hurt in his words. His sorrow shook my foundations for a moment. Jason was in obvious pain at the idea of me loving Erick. He'd known about my feelings from the beginning. He'd been my friend for so long, but now it appeared that every word I spoke was a lance that brought him harm.

Was it possible that Jason had feelings . . . for me?

That thought disturbed me. Nothing was worse than losing a best friend because of feelings.

But Jason had a point.

Was Erick an honorable man? Was he genuinely decent? Jason's words woke up old doubts that came from my past, and I thought back to eight years before. The day Mom's simple shoes knocked on the floor of the courtroom—a sound that didn't bring the peace we hoped it would. For after we arrived home, my father came along, knowing what Mom had told the judge, holding a glass bottle of clear liquid, staggering as usual.

The judge had been nice and understanding, but my father wasn't.

"You're filthy!" he yelled, and smashed the bottle on the kitchen wall over our heads. My small heart shivered when the glass scattered around us on the floor.

He reached out his hand for Mom, planning to leave more bruises on her skinny body. I stood between them to protect her, but he pushed me away with all his vigor. I fell face-first on the ground with my hand slamming into the floor. The force knocked out my three front teeth and broke my wrist.

The pain shot up my arm as if a car had just rolled over me. I screamed, and my teeth skittered across the floor as blood poured out of my mouth. Mom ran to check on me, but my father attacked her from behind, pulling her hair until a lock of it came out in his hand. He pummeled her to the ground and started kicking her with his heavy boots.

The twins started crying loudly. They were too little to understand what was happening—almost one year old—but they could hear our screams. I was in too much pain and couldn't remember any lullaby to calm them down. Mom crawled on the floor, reaching out for the knife she'd been cutting onions with, and thrust it into his thigh. Father screamed like a raging bull, staring at his grisly leg. "Damn! These pants are brand new."

I could never forget the determined look Mom had in her eyes at that moment. It came from her inner strength, her will to survive and save her babies. She didn't wait for him to retaliate—she lifted a chair and smashed it on his head. It felled him instantly. Mom hurried to pick up the twins, one in each arm, yelling at me to follow.

Father loomed in front of me, his fists ready to take me down. There was a murderous rage on his face. My lungs seized up. It was an asthma attack, but my father didn't care. He spat on me and dragged me by the hair, pushing me out the main door. "Get out of my house, all of you!"

"Wake up, Santos. Your daughter is dying!" Mom screamed while I struggled to breathe. I would never forget how he looked at me.

Like I was a burden.

"Good riddance!" He picked up my inhaler and threw it in the dirt. "Don't ever come back here, never again." He slammed the door hard.

Mom held Moria with both hands, keeping a distance between them, and I carried Sarah despite my broken wrist. We walked all the way to the subway and got inside, looking miserable—tears in our eyes, blood on our clothes, barefoot and shaking. But no one dared to help. Even when they knew that my father was the abuser, no one in the village wanted to help us to avoid dealing with his temper.

Mom sold her only silver ring. When I asked her, "Where should we go?" she looked at the map and spoke the words that sealed our future.

"As far as we can go. To the opposite end. To Zetikas."

When I remembered how people stared at us on the train, I could almost still feel the pain in my teeth. I recalled how children in school used to stare at me because of my missing teeth and how I used to mispronounce letters.

The only one who talked to me back then was Mary.

Mom didn't have any money when we arrived at Roses Hill. We had to sleep in the government-provided transparent capsules, where everyone walking in the streets could see us. We stayed there until she got a job at the only hospital in town and could rent a decent house. It took her a few months to pay for my expensive new teeth, and life smiled again.

But abusers were everywhere. They weren't just in Própodas village. One year after we arrived at Roses Hill, Mom had a fight with the hospital manager after he perpetrated a shameful action toward her. She had to push him away to defend herself, which left him with an ugly scar on his face.

Ms. Iris scanned her body and didn't find any sin-spots. So the government allowed Mom to continue her job, but fired the manager. He took his revenge in another manner. He planted illegal medicines at her clinic and informed the health ministry. Ms. Iris scanned Mom's body again to make sure that Mom didn't sell any illegal drugs and lie about it. Although Ms. Iris found no sin-spots, the judge refused to be lenient, and thought Mom had enough money and time to redeem her sins. He asked the government to withdraw her medical license.

They did.

To live a life of dignity, Mom had to work two jobs. When I turned fifteen, she pushed me to cross, as she couldn't manage the financial burden alone, even with the money I earned from drawing portraits.

I stopped trusting people after what happened to us. The only two who swooped into my circle of trust were Mary and Jason. So a fundamental question buzzed in my mind: could I trust Erick enough to cross for him?

"So, Miss Evgenís. Tell me more about your childhood."

I stirred from my contemplation to focus on the creepy crossing consultant. "I told you, I'm a worker, coming from a working family."

"Not working per se, I presume?" He smirked. God only knew why!

I pointed to his smartboard. "I think you already know that."

"Tell me, then. Is it marriage that you're afraid of? That's why you don't want to cross?"

I rolled my eyes.

"Miss Evgenís?"

"You know what?" I held my bag and got up from the seat. "I have a final exam tomorrow."

His eyebrows snapped together. "We're not done yet."

"*We* are wasting valuable time here," I replied, holding the door handle. "I've told you everything about my family and me, and I've answered your question a million times, and yet you don't want to listen! I'm sorry, but I need to go."

As I opened the door to leave, his calm words stopped me. "You can't cross without my approval."

I sighed and stood before the door, thinking. That was the first time he had brought this subject up. I turned to see his smirk. "Why?"

"They're my orders, right from His Royal Highness Prince Thaddeus."

"Why does he even care?" I asked, my fingers still on the door handle.

He crossed his legs and clasped his hands in front of him. "Do you know what happens to those who refuse to cross before their twentieth birthday?"

I gulped, remembering Karya. "Fine." I sat down on the chair again, waiting for his questions.

"You have two identical twin aunts," he began, looking at the smartboard. "Irida and Lotos."

I nodded, not knowing where he was going with this.

"Lotos worked in the royal palace, and she died a few months after she was fired. Do you know why?"

"She was sick."

"Oh! I see they didn't tell you everything." He raised his eyes to meet my confused ones. "I see that your second crossing was after you moved to Zetikas. Over the past years, your mother's call list doesn't show any contact with your father's family in Betis. They never called you to wish you a successful crossing."

By now, I was getting bored, and my feet started tapping on the floor. "And?" The question escaped my lips along with a yawn.

He fixed his stern gaze on me. "Did you know that your aunt Irida was a rebel?"

My eyes widened in shock.

"She died during an armed clash with the Law Corps after she tried to attack the late Queen Rhea at the royal palace."

The moment he uttered his words, I felt like my heart slipped down to my toes. His smirk had disappeared by now, and I battled not to show my fear.

He was talking about Prince Thaddeus's mother.

171

CHAPTER 21

NOW I UNDERSTOOD WHY MY failure to cross was so important to Prince Thaddeus that he sent this creepy consultant to my place. He must have assumed that I was starting a rebellion like my aunt. I couldn't blame her for what she did; she must have had a strong reason to rebel. But I highly doubted the attempted regicide thing. I knew by now that the government could falsify facts for its own benefit.

The consultant got up from the chair. "This is our last session. If you want to cross this year, then make up your mind now." He walked out of the room without another word, leaving me mired in confusion.

Was my aunt's rebellion the reason why my maternal grandfather refused to support my parents' marriage? Was that why no one helped us in the metro station? And why Mom never brought my aunt up?

What the consultant told me changed the way I saw things. I understood more about what Mom had to go through, how much she'd sacrificed for our family, and how much she needed me to grow up.

Right at that moment, I made my choice.

Yes, I'd do it. I wanted to help women. I wanted to be the daughter Mom had always longed for, and the one my sisters wanted me to be. I needed to be with the man I loved in public. I realized that Erick and I had known each other for nine months now, but each day my faith became stronger. He was the one—my soulmate. The issue was never to love or not to love; it was the need to say it. To proclaim it to the world. I didn't just love the man. I adored him.

I remembered the day when I swore that I wouldn't cross for any man. But matters of the heart didn't consider old promises.

I was so ready for it now.

When Mr. Kosmos came back, I stood and faced him. "Sir, I am not starting a rebellion like my aunt. I just can't cross with all the surrounding cameras and the loud noises. They make me dizzy."

His lips pressed with a slight frown. "Are you asking for VIP crossing permission?"

"Yes."

"That will be impossible."

"Why?"

"Your family history. You can't get special treatment for that particular reason."

I knew that Jason had offered to help me set up a quiet Crossing Day, but with this new information about my aunt, I wasn't sure if the government would approve his request. Still, I wasn't ready to give up.

"Sir, as you can see, I had no idea what my aunt did. I was raised by an honorable woman who has always respected the law. I'm politely asking for a chance to cross on a quiet day."

He sat behind the desk and tapped on his smartboard for a while, then waved for me to come. He pointed at the "sign here" line on the form he'd pulled up. My smile widened as I signed my name.

"Don't expect approval."

I shrugged.

Time is relative—or so said Albert Einstein. Love made me understand Einstein when the teachers in school couldn't. Days passed, feeling longer than eons. Moments away from Erick were like years. Every second with him made me long for more.

A few weeks later, I woke up to the sound of a governmental text message. I stared for several seconds before I could understand the written words.

Congratulations, Lenora Santos Evgenís! Your VIP request to cross to your third phase (Adulthood) was approved by Her Majesty Queen Arianna Vasilas. Please visit the Governmental Crossing Authority to set up a date for your Crossing Day and to choose your crossing guide. Glory to Elpax.

"I will cross!" I exclaimed with joy from the bottom of my heart. I jumped up and down on the bed. "I will cross! I will cross!"

The twins opened the door, their eyes wide at the sight of my smile and excitement. "I will cross over!" I laughed, my eyes shedding happy tears.

"You go, Leen!" chanted the twins as they joined me on the bed. We held each other's hands and laughed and jumped until we heard a cracking sound from the bed. Mom entered the room, crossing her arms.

"What is all this noise about?"

I'd never asked Mom about my aunt or the reasons behind hiding such a huge matter. I trusted my mother and I knew that she'd tell me at the right time. So I told her the happy news right away. "Mom, I'll cross. Queen Mother Arianna herself approved my petition."

"Lenora . . ." she whispered, and sat on the bed.

I kneeled on the ground, holding her hands. "You don't need to work so hard, Mom. I'll help us get back to the middle class. You'll have your own car, delicious food on the table, and nice furniture in one of those fancy apartments in Zoiterra. Or maybe Theirna."

There was a sheen in Mom's eyes, and her smile was as brilliant as the

174

rising sun. It had taken her more than nine years to smile with all her heart. I could see the relief in her eyes—the happiness and peace that my words brought her. Mom cupped my cheek gently. "Congratulations," she said, wiping away a tear.

I was glad that, for once, I'd made the right choice and made Mom happy. And now, I had to discuss the right time to apply to study at the Law School with Erick.

The evening brought its own air of eagerness. I tuned my ears to the sound of Erick's car, and my heart thudded when he got out of the driver's seat. Erick could make the air shimmer with his mere presence. I rushed to open the front door. His first glance. His slow smile. I knew it all. Every expression was dear to me.

"Leen, it thrills you to see Mama's friend," noticed Moria, my ever-observant sister.

"Isn't he friendly with you too?"

She nodded and went to play with Sarah. I looked out the door again. Erick was talking on his Iméfono in an indistinct voice and pacing back and forth. He clenched his fist, veins bulging from his arm. Frustration was so subtle in his body language that I'd have missed it if I weren't so familiar with his every mannerism. He seemed tense—more so than usual.

I caught his words faintly. "Not now. I don't want to talk about it. We'll talk later." He turned and saw me watching. His face blanked out for a second, and an expression of forced gaiety came over him. Then, he hung up on the caller without so much as a goodbye.

"What's happening, Erick? Everything okay?"

"Just work pressure." He made his smile wider and sat on the steps.

There was an awkwardness in his movements, as if he wanted to flee from this moment. I started talking about our daily routine, trying to calm him down. The moment soon passed, and his expressions were back to normal. He was my Erick now, someone I could depend on. Someone I was to live my entire life with.

"Lenora, come in to take the drinks."

"Coming, Mom."

"You sit, Leen. I'll get them."

Erick rushed inside, and I enjoyed the beauty of my garden as dusk settled in. There was a feeling of everything being well on my side of town. Erick's Iméfono lay on the step, and I saw it light up for a second. *A message*, I thought. *This man never stops working*. A second text soon popped up.

Are you done with her? Meet me. You know the place.

Shock rippled through my body. Who had sent such a text? Was Erick seeing someone else? Was he not loyal to me? Did he not love me? Why the need for pretense, then? Did he have some ulterior motive? Was Jason right? Did I trust Erick too soon?

My anger grew as thoughts ravaged my mind. Something more was going on. I had to get to the bottom of it. When he came back with the drinks and sat down again, my nervous words rushed out of my dry lips. "Who is she, Erick? If you don't have feelings for me, then why are you here?"

He scowled. "What are you talking about?"

"Don't you try to hide it! I just saw the text."

"What text?"

"This one." I thrust the Iméfono right under his nose, daring him to deny it.

"What about this text? It's from my secretary, Helena. We're supposed to meet after dinner at the office, as I have a court hearing on Monday."

"Why would she ask if you were done with me?" The corners of my eyes crinkled in confusion.

He shook his head. "It's just Helena's way of talking. She's quite brash when she is tense. It's a big case, and we have to prepare all the arguments for it. The royal family wants perfection in the legal affairs here."

A muscle in my jaw twitched. I couldn't help but study his face and his arms, looking for sin-spots. I didn't buy it. He was lying to me.

As if he understood my thoughts, Erick got up and stood before me. "Should I take off my shirt?"

Heat filled my body. I realized how my scrutiny had offended him. It was tantamount to accusing him of lying.

I shook my head. "No need." But I still wasn't convinced by his explanation.

Erick sat next to me again. He looked at the horizon and took a deep breath. "Leen, if I didn't want to be here, I wouldn't be. I came today because the next few weeks will be hectic, and I wanted to spend a quiet evening with you before my days in court began. Was I wrong to do that?"

His woebegone expression twisted my heart. Oh, God! What had I done? Doubted my love based on a text message?

"I'm sorry, Erick. I just . . . I couldn't help. . . I'm sorry. I couldn't help thinking the worst. I don't want to lose you."

"I understand, Leen. Next time, just ask me instead of turning into a volcano."

I had to laugh at that. Only Erick could make me laugh when I wanted to cry. Of course, I didn't doubt his love anymore, did I?

The dreams came back the night before my crossing. The fog that surrounded me appeared to be malevolent. It made me move away from my love, hissing and pushing at my being. The words coming from the fog weren't vociferous, but the emotions indeed were. It warned me: *be vigilant.*

I woke up with a start, and it was dawn. The dream had lasted through the darkness of the night. The fears plaguing my mind must have led my subconscious to envision such things. Erick had been supportive, but there were moments when he seemed lost in his own world. And those Iméfono calls of his . . . I didn't understand why anyone would want him so desperately on the weekend.

I stood at the windows. The sun's rays drove away the last vestiges of my nightmare and filled me with a buoyant hope. Today was going to be a good day. I could, at last, hear Erick tell me those three little words loudly in front of everyone.

CHAPTER 22

"LEEN! I MADE THIS FOR YOU," said Jason, handing me a colorful wreath made of pink roses. It was particularly touching because there'd been so much awkwardness between us over the past months. It overjoyed me to see him there on my Crossing Day.

"You came!"

"Duh! It's your day." He rolled his eyes.

Tears filled my eyes at the devotion of his friendship. He kept looking at my face as if he was memorizing my features. There was a hint of moisture in his eyes.

"Jason?"

"I'm pleased for you, Leen. I hope you'll always be happy."

"Stop the emotional nonsense, you two!" Mary exclaimed while walking toward us. "Isn't that your usual line, Jason?"

"Shut up, Mary. This is different." He smirked, and she giggled loudly. I smiled at them.

Jason nodded at us and walked away to the other side of the Crossing

Gate. He looked back once. There were definitely tears in his eyes. Oh, Jason . . .

"Forget it, Leen. He's a big boy and he'll get over his feelings for you."

"So, it's true?"

"Even a blind man can see it. Don't spoil your day thinking about it." She bent down to look me in the eyes. "Today is an historic event. The fifth of September: the day my best friend, Lenora Santos Evgenís, crosses over."

"It took three months for the governmental approval, though!"

"Stop complaining!" She giggled and took the wreath, pinning it to my hair. "By the way, should we call for Hermes? Seems like the experience will be incomplete without him."

Both of us looked at each other and burst out laughing. As if!

"Where's Erick?" she asked once we got over our giggling fit. "I thought he would be the first person to show."

"I have no idea," I said nervously. "He was supposed to be here. Mom tried to call him, but his Iméfono couldn't be reached. I won't cross until he is here."

"Don't worry, Leen. Keep your cool." Her gaze moved to someone behind me. "And here he comes—Prince Charming!"

I turned around and saw Erick approaching us. His gaze perused me from head to toe.

Mary whispered, "I'll make sure he doesn't run off!"

"Shut up." I poked her shoulder as she stepped away. I turned to Erick. "And you're late."

His eyes lost their sheen, yet he tried to control his emotions. I could see the tension in his face before it went blank. "Sorry. Just got stuck at work."

"I'll be keeping my eyes on you," said Mary, and whispered something in his ear. He shook his head at her words, and Mary winked at me before walking to the other side of the Crossing Gate.

"What was that about?"

"She said you look like a bride."

I rolled my eyes.

"But something is missing. This beautiful bride should wear something special." Erick pulled a small fabric bag from his pocket and untied it. A golden chain dropped into his palm. A pendant in the shape of a lambda, the first letter of my name in the Greek alphabet, hung from it. In its corner was a carved jasmine flower with a shiny bead centered in its petals.

He bought something this valuable for *me!* I was speechless, overwhelmed with love for him. He bent down to clasp the chain around my neck. I knew he wanted to hug me, and I desperately wanted him to do so. At that moment, all my feelings came gushing out of my heart, and I couldn't hold myself back.

"I love you," I mouthed for the first time.

Erick widened his eyes. "One more time, please. I don't think I caught that."

I giggled and mouthed it again. He tilted his head, looking at the sky with a big, gorgeous smile plastered on his handsome face.

"FINALLY!" he cried out loud. His cheerful reaction made me blush. Erick held both of my hands, and his eyes twinkled in mischief. "Lady Evgenís, would you do me the honor of saying those words to me after you walk out of that stupid passageway?"

I laughed. "At your command."

He squeezed my hands. "I will never command my girl. Ever."

We stared at each other for a while. How far we had come from the first day I bumped into him.

"I have something for you too, but don't look now. Look at it when you're alone." I gave him a rolled-up canvas. "It's your picture with a letter. Oh, keep my Iméfono with you too."

The guide's car arrived, and Erick let go of my hand as Mr. Barros stepped out from it. I'd asked for him, as he'd been nice to me last time. Sarah and Moria hurried to hold Erick's hands. They had become close to him in the past few months. He spoiled them with cakes and gifts. Erick

180

walked away with them, throwing an encouraging smile at me.

Mom came along, wearing a black scarf around her neck. "Are you ready, Leen?"

It was one of the few times she had ever called me by this nickname.

She held my hands and squeezed them. "You know, there are decent men in the world, and Erick is one of them. My experience with your father should not affect you or your choices in life."

I nodded.

"Go make me proud."

She turned around, but I called out to her. "Mom!"

She looked at me.

I continued. "I know things haven't always been easy for us, but you have always been there for me. I'll forever be grateful. You've been my rock. Now, I want to be *your* support."

Happiness suffused her face. Since Erick had become a part of our family, Mom had changed a lot. She was . . . happier.

"Leen, when you have children, you'll know how precious they are. They mean the world to a mother, even if she has to yell at them sometimes."

I smiled as she walked away to the other end of the Crossing Gate, where everyone was waiting. Mr. Barros gestured for me to keep up with him as he walked toward the gate to open it. I shuffled alongside him. *That's it! I will do it. I'm crossing over to the adult phase.*

"Identification successful."

So said Mr. Barros's scanner. I looked at the light that gleamed at the other end of the passageway and sighed.

"Are you sure you don't want the automatic wheelchair?"

"Positive," I said. I'd challenge everything and walk through the damn gate.

"All right, then. Listen to the instructions carefully. The procedure is different when you cross alone. Your journey starts now. Good luck."

Mr. Barros waited for me to step inside the gate. I took a shuddering breath and I placed my wrist on the scanner.

"Lenora Santos Evgenís," said a monotonous female voice. "You wish to cross to the third phase of your life. Please confirm this fact."

"Yes, I do."

"Voice recognized successfully. The rules are as follows. The crossing will take up to one minute. You cannot walk back, stop, or run. Such actions could put your life at risk. The ID lines on your left wrist must be visible at all times. After you step over the red line, you cannot go back. Do you agree to these rules?"

I looked down at the flashing red light. The dry voice and the smell of the wet wood annoyed me. Fear crawled over my skin, and I felt dizzy again. But the nausea wasn't as bad as it had been before. For a moment, I faltered. I looked up toward the shining sun. It seemed to encourage me.

"I do."

"The royal family wishes you a successful crossing."

Taking a deep breath, I closed my eyes to ignore my dizziness and stepped over the red line into the passageway's entrance. *I'm crossing for you, Erick. For our love, even if sometimes I don't feel completely ready. I'll uphold all the rules as long as you are with me. I won't mind if the Law Corps examine my naked body, as long as we share the same house. I'll do anything for our relationship, as long as you are good to me. And as long as you'll help me become the first female lawyer in this country. As you promised.*

The branches at once twisted behind me to close the entrance. I turned in surprise at the way they knitted back together as if they were locking me in. There was something ominous about them. The branches seemed to want to slither toward me—to suffocate me—and the dizziness overpowered me at the thought. My sweaty palm reached for Erick's chain. It was the only thing that comforted me and kept me rooted. I started to walk down the passageway, my body chilling from the inside out. A wave of warm energy seemed to spread in the opposite direction. I could feel the blood rushing down my veins.

I was growing up!

The passageway was so pretty, with pink flowers all over its domed roof and on the walls. I knew they weren't natural; there was something ethereal about them. They were sending a message—the hope that my life would become as pretty as they were.

I looked down at my left wrist. Half of the third line had already been etched. I kept walking until I got to the mid-section of the passage. The light at the end shone brighter with each step. I could see my family standing there with big smiles on their faces. I looked at each one of them from left to right. Mr. Barros. Mom. Sarah. Moria. Mary. Jason. My gaze moved back. I counted again. Where was Erick? He wasn't there. He was supposed to wait with everyone. What had happened?

I didn't know if they could hear me, but I cried out anyway. "Where's Erick?"

"Oh, he left," shouted Moria casually.

Her words were like a thunderbolt. I froze—children didn't lie. Why did he leave me? Did he read the love letter I included with his picture and hate it? Did he play with my feelings just to make me cross? *No, no. He loves me.* He must have had work to do. He must have had work.

A frightful female voice echoed around me. "The crosser must continue. The crosser must continue . . ."

Mom ran to Moria. Mary yelled something to me, but it was too late. Darkness overpowered me, and the light faded away. The sounds of my family quietened.

I was in a dark vacuum.

The world around me started revolving in slow motion, quickly gathering speed. Visions ravaged my brain. They came at me so fast, like zaps of electricity, each singeing my mind. I saw strange creatures, an evil dark mist, and a gigantic dog mauling a Roman soldier. An old king and the parchment he'd written on. A sword gleamed like sunlight, burning the back of my eyes. A cave, and a scream from the corner . . . *push . . . push . . .* and a baby cried out. A blanket with a crest wavered before me. Fire burned up a crystal throne, and a voice kept saying the word *OukSali.*

The visions whirled around me until I could see nothing else. Harsh winds formed a barrier around my body. I couldn't see or hear anything, and my head felt as if it were splitting in halves.

A vaguely familiar voice penetrated the cacophony in my mind. "Walk forward. Cross, my child."

Mom's voice echoed somewhere around me. I rushed around, trying to find my way out of the gate, but I didn't know which way to go. The path became as big as a ballroom, and I couldn't tell where everyone was. I stopped to take a breath, bent down, trying to fight the suffocating feeling caused by the surrounding light.

"But she's pale!" Jason yelled. His voice echoed all over the place, directing me to the exit. I could see them in the bright light. Mr. Barros waved for me to walk forward. Jason hurried to the gate; his face was redder than usual. Mary's lips moved as she yelled at me. I wasn't able to hear any more of their words.

Blood dripped out of my nose, coating my white dress in red dots. My lungs stopped working. I couldn't breathe at all. My body shook, my limbs cramping. I was petrified. A wall formed around my heart and moved out to the rest of my body. My eyes widened with horror when I tried to move my fingers and couldn't. They had hardened.

I lifted my stunned, helpless eyes to my mother. The ground tore apart beneath my feet; I fell into the abyss. The darkness took over, and my vision tunneled. The last thing I saw was Mom's pale face.

And I was gone.

September 5, 6:00 a.m.

Erick,

You live inside my every cell; my heart whispers your name in between every beat.

You own my mind and body, as I do yours. I measure my life from one glance of your gray eyes to the next. You can swear on it. I walk unconsciously behind you, following your path, trying to learn from it. Wherever you take a step, I take my own, hoping that your aura will comfort my soul. I wait for a smile from your lips, even if it happens accidentally when you are busy on the Iméfono. My eyes find their peace when they rest on your face. I imagine you when I'm awake and dream of you when I sleep. I see you in every passerby's face—my heart trembles when someone utters your name.

I may not know the minute details of your life. But I know every freckle on your cheeks, and every golden fleck in your eyes. I count every breath you take and keep pace with my own. I can feel every drop of blood running in your veins, and I can recall all of your thoughts, because you live inside me.

Your words and your actions shape me every day. Our love is legendary and immortal. The closer we are, the more it binds us together. The further you go, the more it calls out to me—the delightful pain of your absence increases.

My love can be selfish and fierce. And I don't promise to behave. But I give you my word: my heart is yours, always and forever. I'll look into your eyes as if it's the first and the last glance of my life. For in them is my eternal abode.

They are my everlasting homeland.

Yours,

Leen

P.S. I hope you'll like your picture. I told you not to frown! ;)

PART IV

"THE PROPHECY"

All you need to live a normal life is a full third line . . . not two.
But what if life gives you half a line?

CHAPTER 23

A SOUND PIERCED THE DARKNESS, loud and haunting, like the call of a siren before death. I didn't know where I was, but my consciousness followed the noise. My ears soon picked up a vibration coming from afar. It was a bird, soaring on the horizon, rippling the air with every flap of its strong, broad wings.

Where am I?

A dense fog surrounded me, with the thrum of the bird getting much closer. Its wings beat a strange rhythm against the air current, and its cries echoed in the void, sending a shiver of fear coursing down my spine. The creature loomed quite a distance above me, wheeling around in wide circles, enclosing me in its gloomy persistence.

I have to run away. I must go now.

My feet wanted to run—to escape the death that was certain to come—but they were heavy, and I couldn't lift them. A sharp pain tore at my shoulders. My eyes widened in horror at the sight. I was suspended between two mountains. A chain on my right arm stretched to the mountain on my right, and a chain on my left arm stretched to the mountain on my left. I hung in that abyss, and the clouds were drifting down. I couldn't comprehend what I was seeing.

In all of its urgency, the bird didn't give me time to think. The chains binding me vibrated with the thundering sound of its screech. My heart almost stopped when I saw how huge it was, like a flying giant.

An eagle.

Blood dried in my veins as I scrambled to understand. The only eagle that enormous was *Aetos Kaukasios*, from the Prometheus myth.

I cried out in panic. *"I'm not Prometheus. I didn't steal the fire!"* But not a whisper left my throat. My words were trapped in my mind.

The eagle swooped down, flying toward me with a dignity that could never be described in words. Fear ravaged me. The mighty avian was going to tear my body apart as a means of inevitable punishment.

"Lenora!"

I turned toward the deep voice calling my name. A tall man, well-built and tanned, ran toward me, traversing the void in easy steps, carrying a long glass stick in his hand with fire dancing on its end.

A torch.

"Restore the lost peace to your homeland," he chanted.

The eagle shifted its gaze in his direction, swooping toward him with its beak open.

The man threw the torch at me, screaming, *"TAKE IT!"*

As I stretched out to catch the stick, the chains disappeared, and my hands became free. I held the burning torch in victory. But everything disappeared, and I fell to the ground, surrounded by darkness.

"NO!" I screamed as I tried to move my paralyzed body. Bright light danced under my closed eyelids, and a pleasant warmth burned the darkness I was in. A sound cut through my peaceful silence, monotonous and rhythmic.

Beep . . . beep . . . beep . . .

I tried to open my eyes, but they felt too heavy to move. The beeping

190

noise echoed in my mind, causing my headache to escalate. I couldn't bear the mystery this noise presented. I forced myself to lift my eyelids one millimeter at a time, and a blurry vision welcomed me. I had to blink several times to focus on my surroundings. A compact room, cold and teal in color. Curtains covered the floor-to-ceiling window on my right, and a large screen hung on the wall in front of my bed with an Ológramma.

Where am I? Where is Mom?

I lifted my head, but my neck muscles spasmed, making my head throb. Every movement felt like spreading ripples in a lake, increasing my pain still further. I lay back on my pillow and tried to move my hands, but something was holding them in place.

"What the . . . ?" My voice came out hoarse. I shook my arms, again and again, trying to pull them out of the long chains that tied me to the bed. There was a needle in my right palm with fluids dripping into my veins. A small instrument was clipped to my thumb, connected to a machine with green hills rolling across its screen.

"She's awake!"

I turned my head to the woman who'd announced the obvious, causing the bongo in my head to beat even faster. She was looking at me through the glass panel in the door.

A slim-built, dark-haired man entered my room, along with four women. Each of them wore a green cap on their head and a mask on their face. All I could see were eyes gazing at me with suspicion.

"How do you feel, Ms. Evgenís?" The man checked a smartboard hanging at the end of my bed.

My fearful eyes lifted to meet his, hoping that his answer would save me from the panic rising in me. "Where am I? Where is Mama?"

"Well, you look fine, and your vital parameters are normal now." He pulled down his mask and nodded at the women to do the same.

One of the women silenced the machine's infernal beeping noise, while the other lowered the room's lighting.

"I'm Dr. Angelus," said the man as he checked my eyes with a flashlight.

"You are in a hospital in Zoiterra. Your coma lasted for two days."

Coma?

I fluttered my eyes all around the room, hoping that the doctor was joking, and my gaze came back to him with a question. He stared at me for a second, as if he was deciding what to do next, and walked to the screen facing my bed.

"You see . . ." He switched on the screen, which produced colored images of a skull. "Your brain scan showed unusual activity that we haven't yet figured out. We need to run more tests." He tapped on the smartboard, swiping up and down. "But first, let's make sure you have grown up, shall we?"

A weird gleam crossed his face, which sent a wave of apprehension through me. *What is he talking about?* I knew I was in for something that I wouldn't like. Why else would I be in a hospital? I blinked several times, trying to read between the lines. "Forgive me, but why am I here again?"

He nodded to the women. They all walked outside except for one, who held a small, round black device. Dr. Angelus said, "You fainted at the Crossing Gate. Don't you remember?"

I gasped in shock. I didn't remember anything he was talking about. The last thing I recalled was the disturbing dream about the eagle and the torch, and before that . . . not much. When did I agree to cross?

"Do you remember what year it is?" he asked.

I nodded. "127 post war."

"And according to the Gregorian calendar?"

"2147 . . . I think."

"Perfect! You remember your name, and the year, and your mother. It's only a matter of time before you remember everything else. Now, let's see how you fare in these tests. Relax your body and mind, and let the words flow around you. Love is a deep affection between two people."

My heartbeat sped up, and a green light flashed from the black device, followed by a voice. "Angelus Karos. Adults. Speaking to. Adults. Kathrine James. And . . . ."

The device never finished the sentence. The doctor frowned. "Would you repeat my sentence, Lenora? 'Love is a deep affection between two people.'"

I swallowed hard and repeated his words with my eyes fixed on the device. After a silent moment, it said, "Speaking to. Adults. Angelus Karos. Adults. Kathrine James."

The doctor's brow furrowed. He made me repeat several unfamiliar phrases to the device. The result was the same every time—the device never identified me in any of the statements it made.

What does that even mean?

A faint memory hit me. When I was standing in front of the Crossing Gate with Erick, he gave me a necklace. Now, my hand found it still hanging around my neck. *But where is he now? And my Mom and the twins? And my friends? Where is everybody?*

"Doctor, where is my family? Why aren't they here? And why am I chained to the bed?"

"I'm not authorized to talk to you about that. Let's move on to the Virginity Test."

"Excuse me? The what?"

Before I could understand anything, the nurses came back into the room and pulled the sheets around my bed, which formed a screen separating me from the doctor. The first nurse swept my covers aside with a rough hand; the other pulled my hospital gown up. The side barriers on the bed raised to the level of my thighs. The nurses bent my legs and forced me to move them apart, then tied them to the bed. I was completely naked from the waist down; they didn't even bother to keep me covered. My lower body bucked and tried to break free. One nurse held my thighs in a tight vise, and the other pressed on my stomach. I was in absolute mental agony.

What are they doing to me?

I started screaming at the top of my lungs. I wanted someone to come and set me free—to stop this inhumane treatment. The last time I was awake, I was an innocent juvenile, and now they were treating me like a toy that didn't deserve basic human respect.

The nurse slapped her hand over my mouth and pressed it hard to muffle my screams. "Shut up, or we'll tie your mouth too."

My eyes widened, and I realized that I was a thing they could use for their tests however they wanted. I didn't have rights in this hospital. I could never say no to them. These were women who should have been my support and who should have understood my predicament, because in Elpax, we women had no right to do anything. Instead, they debased and humiliated me for no reason. I didn't know what they would do, or how much pain to expect. But the shame I felt could have choked and killed me.

I could see a light being switched on, directed at my private parts, and something rough prodded me. It wasn't painful, but I knew that someone was touching me improperly.

The nurse finished in a few seconds. They were the worst moments of my life. I always thought the random check-up for sin-spots was the worst that could happen to a woman, but that didn't even come close to what I'd just experienced.

My tears wouldn't stop flowing while the nurse whispered a threat in my ear. "If you promise to be quiet, we'll untie you. Else we'll keep you as you are and tell the doctor that you're not a virgin. Do we have a deal?"

I could only nod my head at this threat, not knowing what a virgin even was. They un-cuffed my hands and covered me, pulled the screen from around the bed, and nodded to the doctor, who grinned with malice.

"Doctor, I didn't agree to that," I said.

"We don't need your agreement. This is the law. You're lucky you got me as your doctor. Others aren't as kind as I am."

What kind of law is this? Forcing me to expose my private parts, examining my body without explaining anything to me?

A nurse brought out a small device that looked like a flashlight, pulled my hair away from my shoulder, and placed the tip of the device on my upper arm. A sharp burning pain made me cry out.

"All done."

I touched my arm and twisted it to look at the black Π symbol—the first letter of the word virgin in Greek. I had no idea what that word even meant!

"Congratulations. You passed your first test. We have now confirmed your purity for your first partner, man or woman. It'll disappear on your first intimacy, although I doubt that you will ever have one."

"Excuse me?"

He ignored me and walked out with his team of nurses, leaving me alone in my misery. I doubled over in bed, and my tears didn't stop flowing for a long time after that.

A short, overweight nurse with a kind brown face stepped into the room and approached me. "Are you okay? I need to remove the tubes. May I?"

I nodded. She had a gentle touch, which was a relief. While she was removing them, she spoke without moving her lips much. "Girl, you're being charged with multiple serious crimes. If you want to survive, don't say a word to the Corps."

"But I don't remember—"

"Good," she interrupted. "I hope your memory stays lost a good while longer."

As she was about to leave, I had to speak up. "Nurse, please, where is my family?"

"Child, if I tell you that, they'll punish me." She walked out, taking my last ray of hope with her.

I wanted my family. Erick and my friends. I sat up, wondering what fate had in store for me. As I was about to encircle my knees with my arms, I saw something that squeezed the air from my lungs. Shock flooded me. I'd never heard of it happening to anyone in the kingdom, ever.

My ID was two-and-a-half lines.

This sealed my fate. I was aberrant. My Crossing Day was largely a mystery—I mostly just remembered falling in the passageway while the line was being formed. But nothing after or before that, except for Erick giving me the necklace. My memory had huge gaps in it.

What will happen to me?

The door swung open, and a flood of Law Corps troops entered my room, their heavy boots knocking on my small heart with every step. My palms became clammy with sweat. They surrounded me with stern demeanors and stiff backs. There were only three women among them. Panic made its way up my chest, and I had to force myself to breathe. A tall, blond general marched in, wearing a teal uniform replete with silver military medals attached to its lapel.

This was it. They would never release me.

CHAPTER 24

THE SOLDIERS YELLED, "GLORY TO Elpax!" and hit the floor with their boots at one pace. All eleven pairs of eyes turned to me, waiting for my reply with accusations in them.

"Glory," I murmured.

The leader sat on a chair, facing me, and stared at my face for a while. It was disconcerting to feel his eyes on me like that. There was no kindness written in the angular planes of his white face. I knew that telling him the truth would get me nowhere. There was a constant smirk on his lips, and his blue eyes had an iciness to them that would never melt.

"We meet at last, Miss Evgenís. I am General Obelius Alexopoulos, and I would like to ask you a few questions about your journey through the Crossing Gate. First, what happened to you in the passageway?"

I gulped. "I fainted."

"Why?"

"I honestly don't remember."

"Think twice, Miss Evgenís. Lying to me isn't an option. Unless you like punishment; we have plenty of those lined up, and each one will be harsher than the last. Make the right choice. Help the kingdom, and we will try to reduce your charges."

"I swear I don't remember. Believe me, I really don't!"

He raised an eyebrow. "Ah. You are one of those. You like to make life difficult, don't you? Maybe this will change your mind." He nodded at one of the female soldiers, who approached and slapped me hard.

My face jerked to one side with the force of her hand, and I could feel the burning sensation on my cheek. Tears sprang to my eyes as shock ran through me, and my body became taut in disbelief.

"Yes, Miss Evgenís. Perhaps now you would like to tell the truth. What happened in the passage?"

I wrapped my arms around myself. "I told you. I don't remember."

"We'll see about that." The general shook his finger toward my face, promising me fierce retribution.

At once, the blonde soldier next to me pulled the curtains closed around my bed and removed my covers. "Stand up, girl." Her tone was sharp enough to freeze water. I looked at her name tag. *Asta*.

Asta didn't wait for me to move. She pulled me up with force, and as soon as my feet touched the icy floor, she untied my gown, leaving me naked. My hands rushed to cover myself. Although I had seen the same thing happening to Mom and I knew that check-ups were routine for adults, I didn't think I would have to experience one so soon.

Tears filled my eyes. *How are they expecting me to expose my body already?* One moment couldn't be the separating line between adolescence and adulthood. It just couldn't.

Asta swiped my hands away and cuffed them behind my back. She curled my hair around her wrist, tilting my head more with each pull.

"All set," she called to the general.

"Well, Miss Evgenís," said the general from the other side of the sheets. "Now, we'll see how well you do in this interrogation. It's easy to detect lies through the sin-spots. Thanks to the late King Islabour, we're living in a

198

utopia."

A shiver ran down my body, and I couldn't stop trembling. Asta pulled on my hair harder.

"What happened in the Crossing Gate?" the general asked.

"I told you, sir. I. Don't. Remember."

Asta tilted my head toward her and slapped my face hard. The other female soldiers checked my body as I cursed the late King Islabour in my mind.

"All clear, sir. No sin-spots."

"Let's try another way, Miss Evgenís. Since you don't seem to remember anything from after you entered the Crossing Gate. Have you or your mother betrayed the covenant of trust and loyalty to the kingdom?"

"How dare you!"

Another slap. Asta instructed me in a frigid tone: "Answer in a complete sentence, traitor."

Traitor!

"No, we have never betrayed the kingdom."

"No spots, sir."

Complete silence reigned for a while before I whispered, "Where's my mom, sir?"

Asta slapped me again. "You don't speak unless spoken to!" she screamed in my ear. She looked at one of the other soldiers, who touched my shoulder with a device. Electricity coursed through me, sending me collapsing to the ground, screaming in pain. Only Asta's hold on my hair kept me from prostrating on the floor at their feet. She pulled me up to stand again.

"Enough," said the general, and Asta let go of my hair. He walked toward the curtain, and I could see his shadow bending wickedly. He spoke in a deceptively soft voice. "Your mother is in prison as we speak, and her life depends on you now. I suggest that you choose your words wisely."

I felt a visceral pain, and my trembling voice pleaded, "Please, don't hurt her!"

"We'll see. Are you or your mother spying for the Modern Roman Empire?"

"No!" I rushed out, pushing the sheets aside, forgetting that I had no clothes on. At once, the male Corps aimed their guns at me, stopping me in my tracks. The general looked down my body, his eyes slowly scanning every part from head to toe. My skin cringed at the dirty look that he gave me. I didn't care what would happen to me anymore. I just wanted my family to be safe.

"My family has always followed the law," I continued. "My mother's name has never appeared on the news among the sinners. She is a conscientious woman with respectful manners who is loyal to the kingdom, and she has always paid her taxes on time."

His jaw clenched. A tic appeared in his cheek, though his face remained stoic and stone hard. "Cover her," he ordered and turned away, only to stop at the door. "I'll be back, Miss Evgenís. My advice is for you to speak the truth next time."

I put my hospital gown back on and everyone exited behind him, leaving me shivering on the bed under the covers, with my jaw swollen and my scalp screaming in pain.

I didn't understand. I had spoken the truth every time. They had checked my body for sin-spots to see if I was lying, and there was nothing. *What the hell do they want from me?*

I stared at my two-and-a-half ID lines, wondering what I had gotten myself into. I needed to escape . . . to get to the truth. We weren't spies, yet I was being declared one. *I must call Erick, I thought. He's a lawyer. I must call Jason too, but how? Where is everyone?*

I got up from the bed and headed to the door, peeking through the glass panel. Soldiers were standing in the hallway with guns and other weapons. I checked the windows; they were sealed. I could see Zoiterra below. The main street seemed quiet, and there was nobody on the roads.

Was it the Curfew? But why? I remembered choosing to cross on a Tuesday, and I was in a coma for two days, so today wasn't the weekend.

I placed my palm on the cold window, and my memory flashed to the past. My breathing rushed, trying to keep up with the pace of the scenes. I had walked into the Crossing Gate, stepping into the shadows. Then, I ambled into the light. There stood Mom and the twins. Mary. Jason. Erick wasn't there. And what had Moria said? I had stopped for a second, and a strange energy froze my body. My limbs spasmed—then nothing. I couldn't remember how they got me out of the Crossing Gate or why they'd arrested Mom.

Wait a second. My eyes narrowed as I remembered something else. I saw a torch. The diviner's words echoed in my mind. *When you see the torch in your dreams, it will all start.* Or something like that. But what was the significance of it? The man in my dream had told me to restore the lost peace.

What was all of that supposed to mean?

I leaned my forehead on the windowpane just as the processing alarm sounded through the entire kingdom. *Oh, my God! What's wrong? Are they going to punish Mom?*

I rushed to the door, looking out into the hallway. "Open up!" I yelled at the nurses outside, thumping on the door, but they didn't even look at me. Only a soldier gave me a stern look. My trembling legs paced the room for almost half an hour as I prayed that Mom wouldn't show up on the Ológramma.

Suddenly, the Ológramma switched on automatically with the word *Urgent* written over the kingdom's flag. The view changed to show the Arch of Victory, with the word *LIVE* in the corner. The camera slowly panned to show the public square of the capital city, Theirna.

There was Hermes, standing behind a microphone. His smug smile was gone, and Law Corps were lined behind him.

"Glory to Elpax," he announced. "Fellow citizens, today we will start the punishments at once. These two men were found guilty of spying for the Modern Roman Empire."

My God! What? Who are they? Could it be Erick and Jason? Is it possible the government found out about the love letter I gave to Erick?

The national anthem started. My hands grew sweaty, and my pulse became erratic, waiting for Hermes to announce the men's identity.

"Following a royal decree by His Majesty King Alexei Vasilas, we will start with the Elimination process," said Hermes. Ten Law Corps officers escorted two handcuffed men with a black bag over each of their heads onto the stage. They forced them to kneel and attached their handcuffs to a hook on the ground. A masked man wearing teal overalls appeared with a point-less squared sword in his hand. Sunlight glittered on the blade, forcing me to close my eyes.

"These criminals," continued Hermes while two of the Law Corps removed the black bags, "Otis Barros and Kosmos Demos..."

"NO!" I screamed. My shaking hands covered my dry mouth, and I fought not to die of fear as I looked at my crossing consultant and Mr. Barros, my crossing guide. Fear seemed to rise behind their eyes as they knelt there, waiting for the process to start.

"Stop this! Stop it!" I rushed to the door and banged on the glass panel, hoping someone would come in and tell me that all of this was an illusion. I yelled at the Law Corps and the nurses, who were watching the process on the Ológramma in the hallway with eyes devoid of expression, ignoring my paroxysm.

It was stunning how indifferent they were.

I headed back to the Ológramma, defeated and lost. Hermes had stopped talking, and the masked man raised his sword. The very next second, the sharp edge fell on the neck of Mr. Barros, separating his head from his body. Blood gushed upon the ground.

I screamed in horror. My shuddering body fell down. My fists beat on the floor, and tears soaked my face as they carted his body away. His smashed eyeglasses remained on the ground—the only evidence that Mr. Barros had ever existed. An innocent man was murdered for no reason, all because I had asked him to be my guide and he was kind to me. I didn't understand how the kingdom could punish him for that.

Next, it was Kosmos's turn. I couldn't even watch it, as I was crying sorrowfully. I was sure he was innocent too, and his death was only because he was my consultant.

The door opened, and nurses carried me to the bed and handcuffed me to prevent me from hurting myself. Emptiness filled my heart. There was nothing left in me. The Law Corps, along with their general, entered my room again. I raised my eyes to him, and a faint, smug smile appeared on his stern face. "Miss Evgenís. I hope you enjoyed the show."

My hate-filled eyes were burning, but I didn't dare to speak a word.

"That was a confirmation of what I'm capable of. You don't want to see your mother on that screen going through the same thing or worse, do you?"

My soul shuddered at the thought of Mom being decapitated. What could be worse than that? Words rushed out of my mouth. "I've told you everything, yet you don't want to believe me. What else can I say?"

He nodded to the female Corps, who repeated the earlier process. Asta pulled the curtains around the bed and took off my gown. I couldn't fight anymore. They had filled my heart with sorrow.

"So, Miss Evgenís," said the general. The Curfew's first alarm echoed through the kingdom, interrupting him, and he waited until it died down before he continued. "Why did you ask Mr. Barros to be your guide?"

"Because he was nice to me when I tried to cross last year."

"Is this the only reason?"

I didn't answer.

"Miss Evgenís?"

"I just told you the reason, and yet you didn't believe me."

"Oh. I believe that you are keeping the truth from me. Let's play a little game. Tell me something that isn't true."

I remembered the doctor said the word love in front of me. "I'm so in love with you."

A loud laugh escaped him. "That's an excellent lie."

Asta and the other female Corps checked my body. I could sense a weird tension in their eyes; their silence spoke volumes. When Asta whispered in the general's ear from behind the curtain, I could see how worried she was after she turned back.

Something was wrong.

"I'm flattered, Miss Evgenís," said the general. His tone was quiet. "But I don't think you know anything about love yet. Tell me a lie about something you are familiar with."

I took a deep breath and looked at Asta. "Asta, I can't believe how beautiful you are."

Her eyes flared, staring at me. I heard some chuckles from behind the curtains. She swallowed and checked my body along with the other two. I could see the same fear in all three women's eyes. And when I looked down at my body, I realized the reason for the weird looks.

There were no sin-spots on my body.

"Cover her," the general ordered once Asta had reported back to him.

I put on my gown, and I heard his voice coming closer.

"There is a fine line between courage and foolery," he said, pulling the screen away and staring into my eyes. "I don't want to distort a pretty face like yours, but I will if I don't get the right answers."

I swallowed. "Please . . . I've answered all your questions, as you wanted."

The general straightened and nodded to the Corps, who held my arms in a firm grip. "Let's go."

My eyes widened. "Where are you taking me?"

"To Inferos."

CHAPTER 25

"YOU CAN'T DO THAT!" I yelled, struggling to free myself from the soldiers' strong grips.

"Watch us," one of the soldiers said. They began to drag my thrashing body out of the room.

"Sir, may I speak?" said Asta, not looking at me.

The general nodded at her.

"There are children and juveniles outside, and her gown shows more than what's acceptable."

He froze in his steps and signaled to Asta. "Take care of it."

The general strode out with the other soldiers. Asta spoke to a nurse, who fetched some folded scrubs and closed the room's door as she left. I looked at Asta, waiting for her next step. She stood with her back resting against the door, facing me.

"Change your clothes while I'm talking. Under no circumstances will you look at me. They are watching. Your family is safe. The general needs you alive. After you finish dressing, I will walk you to the door. My gun is loaded and safety's off. Take it out and use me as a shield to avoid the rubber bullets. There is an ambulance waiting for you downstairs. Make no mistakes, or you will be arrested."

I understood her plan. But I didn't know if she was helping or playing me to get me in more trouble. I spoke when my head was inside the scrubs' top. "How do I know you aren't lying?" I hissed from inside, and slid it down over my torso.

"You don't." She walked behind me and yelled, "Move, inmate!"

A nurse opened the door, and two soldiers entered the room to grab me. I knew I had to act fast. Adrenaline rushed into my veins. I turned to Asta, pulled her gun from her holster, and pointed it at her temple. "Don't move. Raise your hands."

Asta lifted her hands, and all the soldiers rushed toward us, their guns aimed at me. The sound of their hammers pulling back filled me with fear.

"I swear I'll kill her," I screamed. "I'll shoot her right in the head if anyone gets in my way."

Nurses outside screamed in panic and ran helter-skelter. For a moment, I wanted to do the same. I stepped closer to Asta, one hand pointing the gun at her and the other encircling her neck.

She was my human shield.

"All of you, out! Now!"

The general appeared in the open doorway, his eyes on fire. "Miss Evgenís, let's talk."

"I'm done talking. The first bullet will be in your head if they don't move."

We gazed at each other. I refused to blink or show any kind of expression. He was a cunning man and would take advantage of me if I showed the slightest hesitation. He nodded to his soldiers, and they moved aside and allowed us to pass.

"Move!" I yelled again, pushing Asta to send an obvious message. We walked out of the room, and once I was past the blockade of soldiers, I swiveled around to walk backward with her held in front of me. Nobody spoke a word; they needed me alive.

The soldiers tried to get closer, but the general cleared his throat and shook his head. I knew I was relatively safe in the hospital because other children were around, but the soldiers would try again once we were outside.

I backed around the corner, and I caught a glimpse of the new empty hallway behind me. "Asta, where to?"

"Stairs, to the left."

We went down six floors, and no one dared to rescue Asta. I found more Law Corps waiting for us at the ground level—they did nothing but stare at us as we passed. Asta and I stepped out of the hospital. The ambulance was in front of the gate with its doors open, and a tall, dark-skinned young man with corkscrew curls stood next to it. I didn't know if he was in this play or not, but I yelled at him anyway. "Drive!"

The general rushed out of the hospital. Within a split second, his arm shot out to Asta, trying to grab her and push her out of the way so his soldiers could overpower me. I shifted aside, raised the gun up, and fired the first bullet of my life into the air. "General, the next person who tries any funny stuff gets a bullet!"

The soldiers all backed up, and I dragged Asta into the ambulance. Before I closed the door, I raised my other hand to salute the stunned general.

I'd become an official enemy of the kingdom.

The driver took off at once. I sat next to Asta on the ground, trying to breathe.

"Asta, I apologize for what I said earlier," I mumbled, giving back her gun.

"Keep it," she advised. "The general will interrogate me and try to force some answers from me." She knocked on the window behind her, yelling to the driver. "Nizar, how's everything?"

"It's worse than you can imagine!" he shouted, racing down the road and trying to make himself heard over the noise of the Law Corps cars' siren. "They're behind us. I hope the helicopter doesn't get on our tail before we arrive."

"Where are we going?" I asked.

He took some swift turns on sharp bends to escape the Law Corps cars. I held on to the sidebar for my dear life and looked at Asta. "Where are we going? And why are you helping me?"

Asta sighed and didn't reply. Instead, she handed me an Iméfono. "This is a secure line. Hit number one."

I thought for several seconds. If I accepted the Iméfono, I would become part of something bigger. Since Asta was helping me, she was probably a rebel who might drag me into trouble with the government. But what choices did I have at the moment? I didn't know who to trust. Until I came to know the bigger game, I'd have to play along. I picked up the Iméfono.

Asta gave me a firm warning. "Just tell us the directions. Repeat nothing else he says in front of us. The less we know, the safer we'll all be."

Nothing he says . . . who was he?

I nodded and placed the Iméfono to my ear.

"Leen, don't utter my name. Just reply with a yes or no."

My heart leaped in relief. I could have cried with joy. It was Jason. "Yes!"

"Hear me well. Tell Nizar to go straight to the southern gate of the Maculosus neighborhood."

"Yes." I peered through the window and repeated his words to Nizar.

"Hold on!" Nizar shouted. The ambulance took some sharp turns, trying to evade our pursuers. Asta and I swayed with the momentum.

Jason continued, "All right. The ambulance can't get inside this neighborhood. You must drag Asta in front of the gate, using her to shield your body. Hold the gun to her temple and back up to the gate. Once the gate is about to close, push her and let her go. You slide through the gate. That way, nobody can follow you. You got that?"

"Yes." I had absolutely no idea what he was talking about. I'd never heard of such a gated neighborhood. The history lessons in school lacked for sure.

"We're almost there!" shouted Nizar. I looked out the window. We'd reached the gate, which had a stone wall along both sides and barbed wire on top. It was tall and thick and seemed like a fortress, keeping the world out. I couldn't see any of the neighborhood buildings beyond the walls.

Once Nizar stopped the ambulance, I pointed the gun at Asta. "I'm sorry. Let's go."

Opening the back door, I saw countless Law Corps with their guns trained on me. The general led the way with a smirk on his face. Although my heart jumped with trepidation, I had to stick with the plan. We got out of the ambulance and I moved backward toward the gate, holding Asta in front of me. Glancing over my shoulder, I saw the gate slide open a crack, and I caught a glimpse of masked men pointing their guns at the Law Corps.

Seeing the fortification, the general lost his smug smile. "Miss Evgenís, let's talk about this." He raised both hands.

Ignoring him, I stepped through the gate, which had started to close. Before I could get crushed, I pushed Asta out with a mouthed *sorry*, and the doors slammed shut between us. I stared at the closed gate and the masked men around me, trying to make sense of what had just happened.

Nizar was standing among them. Most likely, he had run inside before me. He shook hands with the guards, and one of them looked at me and pointed to a nearby guardhouse. "He's waiting for you there."

I ran to the place, and as soon as I saw Jason walking outside the guardhouse, I leaped into his arms.

"Wow, how do you know about hugging?" said Jason in a shocked voice, pulling back to look at me.

"Jason, what happened? Where are Mom and my sisters?"

His eyes meticulously scanned me from head to toe. His face hardened upon seeing my swollen jaw. "Did they hit you? Come here." He led me to sit down on a wooden bench. "Don't worry. The twins are at my place, and my mother is taking care of them."

"And Mom?"

"The Corps arrested your mom and sent her to Inferos. Asta had to lie to save you."

I jerked back. The news felt like a direct punch to my heart. Tears flooded my eyes at the thought of what they would do to her.

"Leen, don't cry. We'll try to help her escape."

"I don't understand. Why have they taken her?"

He looked down, thinking for a moment. "You were crossing at a normal pace, and I didn't understand why you fainted. The light in the tunnel became brighter after that, and energy started flowing into your body. Your mother got so worried that she rushed to the exit to carry you out. Mr. Barros tried to stop her from breaking the absolute law of the kingdom, but she pushed him away and threw herself inside the passageway, where a massive explosion of air rushed out like a ball of energy. The earth shook with a force that pushed us all down. It felt like an earthquake that lasted for a few seconds.

"Your mom crawled against the force, trying to reach you. At the same time, a loud alarm echoed in the passageway and spread across the entire kingdom. A beam of red light launched into the skies from the dome, and the voice in the passageway kept repeating the word *penetration* over and over. It was very scary, as if the sky itself was screaming in anger. Your mom reached you with a grand effort. She held you in her arms, and the gate's air pressure pushed both of you out."

He sighed. The events had occurred only two days ago, but they seemed to have exhausted him forever. "Mary was trying to soothe the twins, who were crying hysterically. I hurried to your mom, trying to help her with the CPR she was giving you. Before Mr. Barros could call for an ambulance, a helicopter arrived at the square, along with dozens of Law Corps cars, and soldiers charged toward us. All of them screamed madly, telling us to stay away from you and put our hands above our heads."

My hands flew to my mouth while Jason wiped his face with a

210

handkerchief.

"Your mom tried to explain your critical condition, but they weren't ready to listen. They hit her with their metal batons and handcuffed all of us. A general stepped out of the helicopter with a team of medics and took you with him.

"They released most of us half an hour later, but took your mom to Inferos. Dad couldn't even do what he usually does to get his way—threaten to stop paying taxes and get other members of the upper class to do the same. In this matter, nothing could sway Prince Thaddeus. He was obsessed and didn't allow anyone to interfere. So we planned your escape with help from a third party. I can't say who at the moment."

My heart wrenched with sorrow. I was suffocating, trying to take a single breath. I had to save Mom from those monsters. I tried not to imagine what they were doing to my proud and kind mother—what twisted, torturous methods they were using to force her to confess, all because she'd tried to save me. "Jason, they accused us of spying for the Empire. I don't understand why they would charge us with treason."

He inhaled a sharp breath, looking very serious. "Apparently, one of your aunts was a rebel. Prince Thaddeus believes that you and your mother are rebels too, and deliberately tried to break the gate, and all of it was a plot engineered by the Roman Empire."

"I swear, Jason, I didn't. We didn't." I moaned. He held my hand, trying to console me.

"I know that, but Thaddeus doesn't, and now he isn't willing to listen. I have one idea, though it's next to impossible. I'll try to take you to Theirna so you can seek asylum in the Latina Republic Embassy—your mom, too. But that would take some days to plan. In the meantime, you can hide here."

"I don't care about myself. Will my surrender get Mom released?"

"Hell no! You're not thinking straight. Father has a good connection with King Alexei, and we don't want to upset him in case he can help. This has become a national matter now, and Prince Thaddeus can't do anything

211

without King Alexei's approval."

My mind started making the connections, and questions quickly arose. If Prince Thaddeus couldn't do anything without King Alexei's permission, then how was Mr. Barros sacrificed? That made little sense. There was something more at play.

I raised my eyes and perused Jason's features. There was a bruise on his cheek and one close to his left eye, too. "I'm sorry the Corps hit you."

Jason's muscles tightened, and the color drained from his face. He tried to brush my concern aside. "Don't worry about it. Here, wear this." He took out a long, red cloak with a hood from a bag next to him.

"Red?" I hissed. "How can I wear red? It's forbidden. And what is this place we're in?"

"Leen, everything is allowed here. This neighborhood is a banned place for most people. They know it exists, but they don't know what happens inside it. It's a rough neighborhood where you'll see things that will shock you."

Hearing that filled me with dread. I wanted to run away and go back to my home and my room. *How did everything change so drastically and so quickly?*

I put the cloak on, and Jason pulled the hood up. There was a bridal cage attached to it, which went down over my face, hiding it. "An engaged virgin must wear this cloak here. It symbolizes that she belongs to her fiancé, and gangs won't molest her. That is, harm her. I can't explain what molestation is right now. We have no time."

"Mr. Jason!" Jason's driver, Nicholas, rushed inside. "We have to go."

Jason nodded and turned to me. "I can't escort you inside the neighborhood. Take the road straight ahead and go to Saturn Street. There is a nightclub called Pulchra. Knock on the red door next to it and ask for Alba. I have instructed her to take care of you. Don't stop walking for any reason. Don't talk to anyone on the way. Do you understand?"

I didn't know what was going on, but I nodded anyway. What other option did I have but to follow his instructions? Jason smiled faintly. There

212

was worry in his eyes. He hugged me close once and saw me out of the guardhouse.

"Jason, where is Erick?"

He shrugged. "I don't know. He left during your crossing and never showed up again."

I stared at him with an empty heart. How frightening were the disappointments of a broken dream that had been built on hope. If my heart could speak, it would cry with a scream so loud that the entire world would hear its anguish.

"Leen," said Jason before I left. "Look, I'm not sure how to say this . . . but Erick might be a Roman intelligence agent who used you emotionally to do this attack on the gate, and—"

"Are you for real, Jason?"

"Look, we all know the crossing's rules . . . he must have known that if you stopped walking—"

"Jason, stop," I snapped. "I don't think that Erick would do such a thing. He loves me. And how could he know that I would faint halfway through the gate?"

"But—"

I held his hands. "Please find him. I am afraid he's in trouble."

He nodded.

I turned and walked down the street, toward the Pulchra club and the unknown.

CHAPTER 26

WITH A DEEP SIGH, I walked down the street, keeping my head low. Even though I was wearing the red cloak, I didn't want to make myself conspicuous. The entire atmosphere of the neighborhood was quite different from what I was used to. There was an air of danger everywhere I went. Each step I took felt like a risk, warning me to move away. There were women wearing cloaks like mine, but they were very few. I noticed there were no children or juveniles. Most people on the street were men with sin-spots on their bodies, and they couldn't seem to walk straight. I remembered my father after he'd had the adult drink. He used to behave and walk in the same manner.

Only the wealthy's cars zipped down the roads. Two cars stood parked in front of buildings made up of scrap materials or wood left over from ancient times. The houses ran close together, dark and dank with a musty smell. No steel or glass anywhere in the entire neighborhood.

I walked faster, trying not to stumble, and soon reached Saturn Street. Here, the roads were narrow, and the houses were even more run down.

Men were sleeping on the road, or perhaps they were unconscious. Some were injecting themselves with needles in the corner of a building, and others were dropping liquid in their eyes. The way they smiled and walked suggested that they were seeing things I couldn't see.

I hurried ahead. A man in ragged clothes brushed past me while two other men ran after him. I looked back in time to see the man being stabbed by his pursuers. A shudder of dread coursed through my body. I rushed into an alley, hid in the alcove of a building, and looked out. The stabbed man was moaning on the road, blood pooling around him, his attackers disappearing down the street.

The entire place seemed to be filled with criminals. Now I knew why the neighborhood was called Maculosus. It was the Latin for the word spotted. All the men had spots on their bodies and spots in their hearts, too. I rested my forehead on the building's wall.

What would I give for my life to become normal as it had been two days ago?

I walked down Saturn Street and reached a stone and brick building with "Pulchra" on a sign above it. After I knocked on the red door, a slightly tanned girl with brown hair and big hazelnut eyes opened up. She looked askance at me.

"Excuse me. I'm looking for Alba."

She frowned with sudden anger, pulling me inside. "Jason, that man! Didn't he drive you here?"

I shook my head.

"All right. Come with me." She made her way through a dimly lit red corridor. I followed her up the spiral staircase at the end of the aisle.

"This is the second floor, where the living room is," explained Alba. "Your room will be on the third floor, where all the dancers sleep. But first, we have to change your appearance."

I nodded. We climbed up to the fourth floor and entered what must have been her bedroom. I stood by the door, trying to catch my breath, allowing my nerves to calm.

215

Her room had a golden-violet hue to it. The décor was classy without going over the top. The windows were tiny and covered with curtains. There were no floor-to-ceiling windows anywhere, and I noticed for the first time that there was no sign of the word-catchers.

Alba headed to her bathroom. "On this floor is my room, the manager's private quarters, the kitchen, and another gathering room."

"What is this place?" I enquired, setting my cloak on her bed.

"It's a dorm for the dancers of the nightclub next to it. If you are wondering what a nightclub is, you can see for yourself tonight."

Alba gestured for me to follow her to the bathroom. With a pair of scissors in her hand, she pointed to a chair in the middle of the floor.

"What do you think you're doing?"

"I'm sorry, but unless you grow a beard and mustache, I have to cut your hair and change its color."

I shook my head and backed away.

"Listen, girl. Your hair can grow again, but you have only one neck. Once that's gone, you can't get another."

I sighed and sat on the chair. She started cutting my hair, and I watched the strands falling on the ground—tears alongside them. Like my hair, my life had been cut in half. It seemed to have ended before it began. I tore apart my entire family. I wondered if the whole thing was because of my stupidity, my hesitation, or because Erick had left. Why couldn't I have just completed my crossing and then called him?

But I knew Erick. He would never leave me. Maybe he had to leave. I knew the feelings in his eyes, and they never lied to me. Or perhaps I thought I knew him, but I didn't . . .

"Your facial expressions will expose you."

I lifted my eyes to Alba, questioning her words.

"Wear a mask of ignorance and freeze your feelings. Else the girls will notice. They work from night until dawn," explained Alba. She started to color my hair with a cold mixture that smelled fishy.

"Who owns this place?"

216

"A wealthy. But Cordis is the manager. She used to work at the royal palace. You'll meet her soon."

She picked up a pen filled with black liquid. "This is a black henna. I can't tattoo your half-line, as there is no permanent black ink in the kingdom. So you must repaint it every day."

I nodded, and Alba drew the other half of my line. The first half of that line got Mom into prison and the twins separated from the only family they'd ever known. I couldn't hold back my tears, thinking about Mom. I couldn't handle the thought of how my foolish behavior had affected others. Carlota. Mr. Barros. Mr. Kosmos. Mom. Sarah. Moria. They were the real victims of my actions. *I have destroyed all of them.*

Alba looked at me with pity in her eyes. She handed me a handkerchief to wipe my tears. "I have to apply heavy makeup to hide your features. Pay attention. You must learn to apply it over your face every day."

I didn't know what Jason had told her about me, or why she was helping. Nevertheless, I was grateful for all her aid. I feared that she would come to hate me if she knew the harm I'd caused. I wouldn't blame her, for I despised myself already.

Alba finished applying the makeup and styling my blond hair. I looked in the mirror, and my reflection stared back at me in confusion. That wasn't me . . . or at least, it wasn't the old me.

"Come," said Alba, walking into her room. I followed while she searched through her cabinets. She handed me a short coppery backless dress. "We have to change your name, too. Do you have one in mind?"

"Yeah," I mumbled. "Sarah."

"It's supposed to be a Latin name, but I guess that's okay. Finish dressing up. You'll meet Cordis soon. She doesn't know about your story. No one else does. Just say you're my friend. If she asks when you crossed, just say two; don't add a year or day or month, as you may get sin-spots for lying. Oh, and don't talk unless she asks you a question. She detests talkative girls."

I nodded with resignation and went to the bathroom to dress up. I hated wearing such a dress, especially after what the Law Corps had done to me at the hospital, but I couldn't complain. Giving one last tug to the dress, I looked at myself in the mirror. I bent my head and closed my eyes, feeling overwhelmed by all that had happened today. When I opened them, the bathroom's gray floor had disappeared, and I found myself standing on pure white marble. I looked all around and couldn't believe my eyes.

What happened? Did I faint?

I was standing on a large white balcony with a beautifully engraved balustrade, supported by columns of white marble with teal gemstones sculpted into them. Lush green orchards spread out beyond the balcony's railing. A huge fire goblet carved out of a single white marble slab stood right in the balcony's center, bounded by a fence.

I recognized the place. I'd seen the goblet before on the news. The kingdom had used it to set up the eternal fire and keep it burning the whole year before fire itself was forbidden.

I pinched my hand, trying to wake myself up. Ouch! I tried counting in my mind. I could do that. My brain was working just fine. I curled my arms around my body. I could feel the warmth, so that meant I was awake, and everything was real.

I was in the royal palace!

CHAPTER 27

HOW THE HELL DID I get here?

I swallowed hard and walked closer to the fence around the goblet. The palace was built on Mount Gaia. Theirna's vast green orchards unfurled before me. The gloss of Poseidon Lake glittered like gold, reflecting the sun rays. A huge marble peacock fountain stood in the garden, water pouring from its beak and down the steps in front. Its tail feathers were spread out on the ground in its distinctive train, with flowerpots arranged to represent the eyes of the coverts. The whole construction was elaborate and magnificent. It completely awed me.

Slow footsteps from behind reached my ear. I turned around to see an old man walking toward me. His long hair's color matched the hue of my own natural hair, and his white beard hung down, hiding the top of his silver embellished robe. A chill ran down my body. I was sure he would have me arrested, and there was no place to hide. But the man didn't meet my eyes; he continued walking right up to me and through me, folding his elbows on the fence. I recognized him. It was the late King Stavros!

I stood there, confused, trying to make sense of it all. I moved to where he was standing, but there was no reaction from him.

I dared to whisper. "Can you see me, Your Majesty?" But the king continued looking down at the garden with a frown on his forehead. I turned my gaze down as well.

A small blond child played and giggled with a youthful woman on the grass lawn between the flowerpots. From between the shrubs rushed a young man dressed in black, lifting a golden sword toward the child's leg and pricked it. I gasped, putting a hand on my throat. The child screamed and started crying, while the young woman hurried to carry him away from danger and run into the palace.

There wasn't any reaction from King Stavros. I was sure the palace guards would take the young man in black to the dungeons, but he exploded with wicked laughter and ran away.

Looking sideways, I saw King Stavros standing still, his muscles taut with tension and his face getting redder by the second. Too many expressions crossed his face for me to get a read on them. Anger. Regret. Shock. He walked back inside with his head bowed down. There was a sense of defeat in the air surrounding him.

I followed him inside the huge room. It had a high domed crystal ceiling crafted in the royal colors. The walls held massive paintings of the past kings of Elpax dressed in their royal clothes: a teal tailcoat fully embroidered with silver threads and sparkling gems, and white lacy sleeves which burst from the vest, decorated with peacock feathers.

King Stavros sat on a high teal chair, dejected, deep in thought. Minutes later, he started coughing violently into his handkerchief.

There were blood spots.

I recalled that he'd died due to a lung cancer. It seemed that these were his last few days, which meant I hadn't been born yet. I wanted to console the disheartened man, but it seemed he couldn't hear me if I did.

Rushed footsteps from the hallway outside the room made me look up, and a door in the corner flew open. An enraged blonde woman sped to where King Stavros was sitting. The hem of her beige silk dress swung against her high-heeled shoes. It was the Queen Mother, Queen Arianna. Even in anger, her beauty was radiant.

"For how long will Thaddeus keep scaring my little Alexei?" yelled the queen, fury turning her face crimson. "For God's sake, Alexei isn't even five years old, and your son of seventeen brandishes a sharp sword in his face!"

King Stavros was quiet for a few moments before he slowly spoke, trying to placate his queen. "My dearest Arianna, Thaddeus lost his mother when he was a child. Spare my boy."

"Spare the boy? He keeps insulting me for not being royalty, and calls Alexei a mixed-blood in front of everyone. He bullies Alexei at every chance. He has no respect for me or for anyone else, and now you want him to rule the kingdom? He will destroy us all!"

King Stavros stood tall and strong. Even Arianna had to back up a step. *I know I did.* His commanding presence was enough to frighten me.

"Arianna, be careful with your words. That's a royal decree you're talking about, and Thaddeus is my heir. I have punished him for all his misdemeanors, and quite harshly, I might add. That's the reason for his behavior toward you and Alexei. He believes that I've changed and don't love him anymore. It's not entirely his fault."

"Dear King, I know that. But Thaddeus is a young man, not a juvenile anymore. If he is mean to Alexei, who is an innocent child, just think what he will do to the rest of the people once he becomes king! Who will control him then?"

King Stavros was furious, but still didn't justify himself.

"What if Thaddeus was the prince in the prophecy?" she continued. "We have already lost our first child. I don't want to lose another one." Tears rolled down her cheeks.

What the hell are they talking about? What prophecy? What first child?

King Stavros sat back on the chair and turned his face away from the queen. "Send Mandras over."

A series of knocks echoed in the surrounding space. Before I could react to them, the room swirled, and I was back in Alba's bathroom, staring at the mirror. I could hear Alba knocking on the door, yelling my name.

What had just happened? I couldn't understand. A vision? An illusion? Real or a mirage? It sure felt real, but I didn't know how I could possibly have seen that moment of royal history.

"Just a second," I responded, staring at my face to check for any changes. The heavy make-up couldn't counter my colorless features. I opened the door to see Alba's angry expression.

"I thought you'd fainted. I called your name many times. What took you so long?"

"I'm sorry. I lost track of the time."

"Well, hurry! Cordis wants to see you, and she doesn't like waiting."

She walked me out of the room to the door across the landing and knocked twice before opening it for me. I stepped into a luxurious room of gold and crimson. A pretty red-headed woman in her late forties sat on a golden couch, with a girl massaging her feet. The woman nodded, and the girl left the room. Cordis waved at me to take the chair across from her. She held a tube fitted to an electronic hubbly bubbly, and she puffed the smoke from the tube, all the while gazing at me with her electric blue eyes.

At last, she spoke. "Alba said that you're her friend."

I couldn't tell whether that was a question or a statement from her tone, so I nodded.

She peeked at my shoulder. "I see you are a virgin, so why did you come here?"

I swallowed. I didn't know what this place was, or why virgins couldn't work here. "I'm looking for a job."

She wrinkled her nose. "I can't hire you as a dancer; it's against the law. You can be my assistant. Can you cook?"

"Yes."

She nodded. "Make me strapatsada."

I hurried out of the room to find Alba waiting for me by the door, where she'd been listening to the conversation.

222

"Come on," she said. "Benita will help you in the kitchen."

We walked into a side room that had black couches along the walls and a thick red carpet in the center.

Girls lounged and chatted with each other. Silence fell in the room when Alba and I entered. They looked at me with curiosity.

"Girls, this is my friend Sarah," announced Alba.

No one said a word. A couple of them nodded. There was speculation in their glances as ten pairs of eyes scrutinized me from head to toe. Sweat dripped down my back as I waited for someone to say something.

A pretty, dark-skinned girl approached me, her long black hair tied in a straight ponytail. She extended her hand for a shake. "A new dancer?"

"No, Benita. She'll cook for Cordis."

Benita's eyes became frosty, and her mouth twisted into a scowl. "What's wrong with my food?"

Tension filled the atmosphere. The last thing I wanted was to get engaged in the internal politics of this place. I murmured, "I can do something else."

Benita looked back and forth between Alba and me, then gestured for me to follow her to the side door leading to the kitchen.

"So?" she looked at me searchingly once we were inside.

"Cordis wants strapatsada."

Benita bit her lip and gave me some tomatoes to wash. She instructed me in how to prepare Cordis's meal the way she liked it. She moved fast in the kitchen. It was obvious that it was her domain.

"Benita, I'm sorry . . ."

She turned to me. "It's not you. It's Alba who thinks she can do whatever she wants, just because she is one of the wealthy's concubines."

I couldn't ask her what a concubine was; that question could blow my cover instantly. I was supposed to be an adult who was familiar with all this world's terms. So I remained silent. When we finished up with the strapatsada, I was about to go out of the kitchen with the tray when I heard the kingdom's national anthem coming from the room the girls were in. *What's wrong?*

Benita rushed out, and I followed. All the girls were looking at the Ológramma. The word *Urgent* was written over the kingdom's flag in the void. Within seconds, the scene flashed with something that almost stopped my heart.

It was my picture on the news.

CHAPTER 28

"GLORY TO ELPAX AND ITS brave citizens," announced Hermes in a serious tone. "This girl, Lenora Santos Evgenís, penetrated and temporarily crashed the Crossing Gate, with the help of her mother, Yorra Karakas."

Mom's photo appeared next to mine. Fear petrified me to the spot. I couldn't have moved even if I wanted to; my shaky legs wouldn't carry me. My palms started sweating, and my heart pounded so fast that I was sure it would burn out and stop.

"These two were spying for the Modern Roman Empire. Karakas is under investigation, but Evgenís has escaped to the Maculosus neighborhood. A royal order from the Prince of Zetikas, His Royal Highness Thaddeus Vasilas the Second, states that anyone who informs the authorities about the escaped inmate will receive three hundred thousand paxins as a reward. Any cooperation to restore peace to our kingdom will be most appreciated. Glory to Elpax."

The girls gasped upon hearing how much my head would be worth. They all started chatting with obvious enthusiasm amongst themselves, wondering where I was, not knowing that I was right behind them, almost about to fall down on my quivering limbs.

Throughout her life, Mom had done everything right so that they never announced her name on the news. And now, thanks to me, she was on the Ológramma being labeled a traitor. My eyes filmed over as I glanced around, trying to control my tears. I saw Alba's speculative eyes watching me. There was annoyance in them. *Will she throw me out now and refuse to help me?*

I dragged myself to the kitchen again, moving with a mechanical motion. Behind me, Alba tried to diffuse the tension between the girls and changed the topic.

"New girl. Do you know anything about this?"

I turned to the tall brunette girl who had followed me into the kitchen. "Excuse me?" I mumbled.

She leaned on the kitchen table and took an apple from the fruit bowl. "Do you know anything about that spy?" She gazed at me with cold black eyes, making my throat go dry.

"N . . . why?"

"It's weird that you came here on the same day the spy escaped. You know, this is an ideal place for a fugitive, where the Corps have no say. Don't you think so?"

"I don't care." I wet my lips. "I'm spending a few days with Alba, since I don't know anyone else."

"If you say so. Where are you from?" She took a big bite from the apple, gazing at me.

"Isabella," interrupted Alba from behind, "Cordis needs you."

Isabella looked back and forth between us and walked out of the room, giving me a suspicious look.

Alba pointed at the kitchen door and whispered, "Go to my room and stay there. I'll deliver the food to Cordis. Don't come out until I say so."

I nodded and hurried to her room, pacing around for several minutes until her face showed at the door.

"I swear I'm not a spy," I whispered, shutting the door behind her.

Alba pursed her lips, trying to balance things in her head. She moved to the window and looked out for a moment. "Look, this has been a shock for you. Rest for some time in your room and I'll come to see you later. I'll bring you something to eat, too."

I agreed. The room she took me to was smaller than hers, with only basic furniture, but it was clean enough. I lay on the bed, thinking about everything that had happened. I missed Mom. I wanted to go back to the days when life was normal—going to school, playing with my sisters, spending time with my friends and with Erick.

Where are you, Erick? Why have you left me? Do you even know where I am?

Tears filled my eyes and fell upon the pillow, one by one, until sleep took me.

And I was transported.

I was standing in a spacious room with a vast oval table in the center and six old men sat around it. The décor of the hall was familiar. I saw the same marble walls with gemstones on them. Every stone in the place infused the air with royalty.

I'm in the Majestic Office in the royal palace! I'm dreaming, but it feels so real.

So real.

A young man whose hair color matched mine, wearing dark clothes and a golden sword on his back, entered the room. I recognized him right away. It was the youthful version of Prince Thaddeus, handsome and tall, with a regal presence about him. He took the head seat at the table without greeting the old men.

"That's the queen's chair," said one of them. His voice echoed through the room.

A mocking smile was all the man got in reply. After a few minutes of Thaddeus resting his thoughtful eyes on each one of them, he started talking. "You know, Uncle, I suggest you start packing. All of you, in fact.

227

I won't need your services anymore. I will run the kingdom alone—as I see fit."

Oh, they're the princes who used to rule the provinces.

The princes exchanged tense looks with each other, as though they hadn't expected such a declaration. The eldest among them spoke up. "What makes you so sure that our brother, the late King Stavros, has appointed you as the crown prince?"

Thaddeus's face was without expression. "The laws of succession give me the right." His voice was so cold that it spread a chill down my body. It dared anyone to impugn him.

A door at the room's corner opened, and a blond man with youthful features entered, along with Queen Mother Arianna in a black gown. She approached the table with anger infusing her face as she saw Thaddeus on her chair, announcing his insurgency over her. She held her tongue and took another seat while the young man stood before the table.

"Glory to Elpax, Your Royal Highnesses." He bowed. "I know that the kingdom is in mourning over the passing of His Majesty, King Stavros. But today, we must witness his will, which the king amended two weeks before his death."

Nervousness infiltrated the room. The princes glanced at each other. Even though I knew what had happened, to witness the historical moment was a big deal.

The blond man took a deep breath and turned on the Ológramma. King Stavros's face showed in the void. He looked tired, and it took him a while to start talking with a shaky voice.

"I, King Stavros Islabour Proximo Vasilas, the reigning king of the Great Elpax Kingdom, being of sound mind and memory, hereby make and declare this to be my last will and testament. The lawyer of the Elpax Kingdom and the official royal advisor, Mandras Argastos, witnessed and approved the will."

Ah, so this is Mandras who turned the Ológramma on. He seems so familiar. Where have I seen him?

228

King Stavros's voice pulled me out of my thoughts. "I command that, following my death, all the princes will remain in their exact positions, except for His Highness Zephyr Islabour Vasilas, who will be exempt from his position as the prince of Zetikas province. He will be confined to his duties as the Interior Minister."

Whispers arose between the princes. Tension hit Thaddeus's face, and a wave of icy fury grew in his eyes as he listened to his father's words.

"For several reasons, and after long deliberation, I have amended the first clause of the laws of succession. Thus, I declare as the legitimate heir of the Elpax Kingdom my son His Royal Highness Alexei—"

Thaddeus stood at once, knocking over his chair, thumping the table twice in a fury. He knocked an ornate vase to the floor as he stomped away.

"The heirdom comes with a mandate to his mother, Queen Arianna Vasilas, until Prince Alexei crosses over to adulthood. My son His Royal Highness Thaddeus Stavros Vasilas will be the prince of Zetikas province and the Minister of External Affairs and . . ."

The sarcastic words of the princes arose, and Queen Arianna looked at Mandras with wide eyes. "Can the king amend the laws of succession?"

"A king can do what he wants, Your Majesty. He is the ultimate law in the kingdom."

All thoughts flew from my brain when I understood the consequences of the will. I raced after Thaddeus, even though I had never been to the palace before. I entered his room, passing through the closed door like a ghost. He had smashed every article in the room until there was nothing left to turn his wrath upon. As I approached him, he stopped in front of a gigantic window, breathing violently.

"I will get my revenge," he whispered in a desperate voice. "I'm the oldest son. I am the one who carries the exclusive royal blood."

Tears of rage flowed down his cheeks as he stood in front of a large painting of an elegant woman with wise blue eyes. I knew her; it was his mother, the late Queen Rhea, the one my aunt had supposedly tried to kill.

"Did you see what happened, Mother?" said Thaddeus. "Arianna has orchestrated this injustice. She manipulated my father until he could think of nothing more than giving the throne to her mixed-blood son."

Regardless of what Thaddeus did to my family and me, I felt grim for the injustice done to him. He seemed to have lost everything. I could now understand why he was the way he was. Queen Arianna had shortchanged him with her constant advice to the king and subtle influence.

"I will get revenge, Mother, even if it's the last thing I do. I'll never forget or forgive."

His declaration jerked me out of my musings. A dense fog surrounded me until light penetrated through the swirling mist, and I found myself staring at my bedroom ceiling.

After sitting up straight in bed for a few minutes, my outlook changed. It was terribly strange. I never thought I would sympathize with Thaddeus, but Queen Arianna, too, had her own agenda. She wasn't as good as she had been portrayed.

But why am I being shown the royal family's past? I need answers, but where to find them?

My thoughts were all mixed up. Though I wasn't in a fit state of mind, I was curious enough about the nightclub and what the girls did there. I stepped out and saw two girls chatting and giggling in the room opposite me. As soon as they saw me, one of them hurried to bang the door closed. My eyes widened. I had no idea why the girls resented my presence here.

I headed to the red room on the second floor and heard loud music vibrating from a door in the corner. I stood there, wondering what was behind it, then opened it to quench my curiosity.

I stepped onto a metal balcony with stairs on one side, overlooking an enormous hall with a high ceiling. My eyes widened at the sight that lay before me. It was something I could never have imagined in my darkest dreams.

Couches and tables lined the outer edges of the room. Blue and purple lights broke through the cigarette smoke, giving the room an otherworldly look. The music was loud and so different from what I had ever heard.

And the girls were wearing . . . next to nothing! Long drapes of chiffon covered strategic parts of their body but revealed their curves. They were shaking their hips and twisting their waists as men clapped and threw money. Though it was beautiful to watch their clean legs and their waist movements, the excited men surprised me. Their predatory gazes toward the girls rolled my stomach. I was always upset when Mom had to show her naked body to the sin-spots searching team, and they were only women. Yet, these girls were stripping down voluntarily before men.

Or were the girls forced to do so? That idea was even more terrifying. Worse still, the men were mostly middle-aged, and even older; they reminded me of my abusive father. I could understand why a freshly-crossed man would be excited to come to such places out of curiosity. But these men—they were ordinary grown men, like my school principal and Mr. Barros. Was that how men saw women? Just a tool for their entertainment?

I stood there, shell-shocked at the world my adulthood had shown me.

Beneath me in the crowd, Alba spotted me. "Sarah, why didn't you wait for me?" she yelled. "Come on down."

My feet refused to move. Alba had to push through the girls and men to reach me. She tugged on my hand and rushed me down the stairs. "It's exciting, isn't it?"

I turned to her with my jaw hanging open. Was this what the adult world was all about? I didn't want to be a part of it, then. How did Jason know of this place? Did all adults know what nightclubs were? Did Mary? And Erick? Did he ever visit such a place? Was that why he had forgotten about me?

The men watching the nearly naked girls nauseated me. The expressions in their eyes disgusted me. The girls tried to pull them forward. Why would someone do that? Nothing seemed right. All the ideas I had about the adult world crashed in front of me. What I thought to be wrong felt right to others. The girls looked as if they were enjoying themselves. There were no boundaries here. No right or wrong. The line separating black and white seemed blurred.

Maybe my brain was still in the juvenile phase, not having grown up enough to accept the adult life.

"Alba, what kind of dancing is that?"

She gushed, "This is the Egyptian belly dance."

Egyptian! I recalled how the girls danced at Mary's wedding. They were only robots, but still, they didn't shake their lady parts like this! What else had the kingdom hidden from us?

"Who are these men?"

"Do you see the fat man there in the corner? He's a lawyer, and never misses a night here. The one there, he's a solicitor in the government and he's always drunk."

I gasped. "A worker in legal affairs?"

"Oh, they all are. And the wealthy. That old man over there with the white hair, he's a judge. One of our regulars who pays hundreds to the girl who gives him a lap dance."

"A what?" I'd never heard of such a dance before.

"Of course. We have back rooms for it. I bet his wife doesn't know what he does."

I looked around. Most of the men were drinking and moving the way my father did. Why were there no sin-spots on them? I directed my question to Alba.

"Oh, we sell Crepito too, for half the price on the black market. They can do what they want and apply it to hide their spots."

What is Crepito? Did she mean that there was a cream to hide sin-spots? Did all adults use it? Did Erick? Was his body filled with such spots that I couldn't see? Was that how he manipulated my feelings, hiding his sins under Crepito? My eyes met Alba's with bitterness.

"The Crepito," she explained, "is the sinful ticket to the world of virtue without real repentance. We can wash the cream off with water, yet it hides the spots from the naked eye. Of course, the blue-ray the searching team uses to scan sin-spots can capture it, but they don't ever test the men anyway unless the government suspects they are rebels."

232

Looking at the men and the girls swaying and hearing Alba's explanation broke the control in my mind. I had once thought that seeing Erick's body free of sin-spots would assure me of his honesty. Now, I knew that dishonesty could be concealed. Elpax wasn't a utopia, but a sin-spot of land, where anyone who had power and money could do whatever they wanted under the false cover of morality.

I backed away, wanting to hide from all the exposed truths, and ran into a well-dressed blond man who leaned in to greet Alba.

"My sweet Alba," he said with a heavy accent, kissing her on the cheek. He looked at me. "Who is this? A new dancer?" He scanned my body from head to toe, taking in my short, sleeveless dress. His eyes lingered on the tattoo on my shoulder. He touched it and exclaimed with joy, "A virgin!" He pulled me closer by the waist. His head moved in to smell my neck.

"Don't touch me!" I exclaimed, and pulled away.

"Oh, darling, I'll pay as much as you want."

"Leave me alone!" I screamed in utter panic, shoving him with trembling fingers. He looked at Alba with a demanding stare.

"Excuse me, Mr. Kirov. She's not for sale."

"Alba . . . Alba . . . don't disappoint me. You know the price you must pay if you disappoint me." He smirked at her. "Don't you know me at all? I didn't ask, darling. I'm saying it. I want her in my bed tonight. Make it happen." He gave me one last look before moving toward one of the dancers. Alba looked at me with helpless eyes.

"Alba?" My heart pounded. "What does he mean?"

Alba swallowed hard. "I . . . "

I trembled all over. Blood roared in my ears. "Alba. What is he going *to do to me?*"

CHAPTER 29

FEAR FOR MY SAFETY FILLED my body. I didn't understand what the man would do to me, but I was sure it was nothing decent. I looked at Alba, petrified, with goosebumps covering my arms. "Alba, call Jason!"

She sighed. "He can't come here. Just go to your room, and I'll tell Cordis. She'll deal with him. Go."

I backed away from the club, climbed the stairs, ran toward my dorm. Locking the door, I lay on the bed and pulled the covers over me. I couldn't stop crying. Huge sobs choked my throat, and my chest hurt as I tried to take a breath.

I don't want to be here. This is hell . . .

I want to go home . . .

I want Mama.

The following day, a knock on the door woke me up. I jumped from the bed, hoping it was Jason. But upon opening the door, my joy soon disappeared.

"Good morning," said Alba, smiling at me. "Did you sleep well?"

I couldn't smile. She sighed and leaned on the door. "I guess not. Well, freshen up and come to my room. I'll make breakfast."

Minutes later, after I'd washed my tired face and applied the heavy makeup, I accepted a plate of food from Alba in her room. "Alba, I want to find out more about the adult world. Where to start?"

She headed to the Ológramma and swiped her ID lines on the sensor. "I think last night was information overload for you. It's time to watch the educational film on the Adult Channel to understand all that you saw. I'll come back in half an hour."

I nodded and sat in front of the Ológramma while she went outside the room, shutting the door behind her. The film started, and my jaw dropped. I never thought such a bizarre thing could happen. My face blushed as I remembered when Erick and I had our first stolen kiss. His warm hands around me, his sweet lips touching mine, his tender gray eyes looking at me. I huffed and pushed my sleeves up. My forehead was sweating, and my ears were getting warmer. I felt like my body was about to explode; it was getting really hot in here. I got up to grab the A/C remote, used it to adjust the temperature, and sat back down to watch the whole film.

"Sarah, what's wrong?"

Alba's voice pulled me out of my stunned state. She must have returned without me noticing. I turned to her with vacuous eyes, and she laughed hysterically.

"Look at your face," she said in between her giggles. "We were all shocked when we learned about making love and sex, but the look on your face is priceless!"

I swallowed hard. "Is that what the man wanted from me yesterday?"

"Yes. Now you know why cats and dogs aren't hanging around the streets. The government doesn't want juveniles to see animals mating."

"So the story about Eros and the baby is a myth?"

Her smile widened. "Yes."

"Men can love men?"

"And women can love women. Anyway, it seems like you have experienced some adult feelings." Alba pointed at the A/C remote control that I was still holding in my hand. "Or is there a perfectly innocent explanation for why this room is so freezing?"

"Alba!" I exclaimed, covering my face with both hands to hide my embarrassment.

"You naughty girl!" she said, and we both laughed. Her jokes and her sense of humor came at just the right time to diffuse the tension in my body a little bit.

When our mirth died down, I bowed my head, considering for a while, and a thought struck me. "But how can juveniles have kids?"

Alba huffed in anger and bitterness. "We call it rape. Men force girls to do that. Then the government takes the girls to Inferos, so they don't tell the other juveniles about it."

I gasped. *This is so not fair! What injustice women face every day in the land of peace and hope.*

She continued. "That's why they told us when we were juveniles that getting close to others may result in catching a deadly disease. It was the government's way of protecting us from a danger we didn't know about. From being raped. It's the only thing they've done right in this fucked up kingdom."

"By fucked up, you mean . . . ?"

"Corrupted."

I couldn't agree more. "Alba, I've always wondered. Why do women have to deal with all this injustice?"

She sighed. "The government informed us that during the late King Stavros's rule, a woman started a rebellion for the women's rights in the royal palace."

I gulped. She was talking about my aunt.

"And King Alexei didn't want the same thing to happen again. He

236

believes that we—the women—are responsible for all the problems that have occurred since Pandora opened the box which contained evils and released them all into the universe."

We shared a sad look of commiseration and despair at the fate we had to deal with. Pandora, Icarus, Hera . . . none of them were real, and yet their stories controlled our society and the decisions that the government made about us.

"Alba, can I walk around this place? I need to find out more."

"I'm coming with you. I need some fresh air myself." She moved to the closet and handed me my red cloak. She wore a similar one in teal and put on a golden chain mask over her face, which showed off only her eyes while covering the rest. I had never seen anything like that before. It was hard to make out that it was her.

She must have seen me frowning at it, because she explained, "To show others I am a wealthy's concubine."

"What's that, exactly?"

"It means I'm his property until I give birth to a male child. He will free me once I give my son to him. Let's go."

A mother giving away her child? Is that really Alba's fate?

"Alba. Is that what you really want? Do you even love the guy?"

She sighed and stepped out of the room. I followed her as she considered her words. We remained silent until we reached the main street. A few women were walking around, and I shivered a little from the cold, light wind.

"My mom was late in dropping my brother and me to a Safe Cell," Alba explained after a while. "She wasn't well and slept right through the process alarm. The Law Corps arrested her and took her to Inferos, because we saw what only adults were allowed to see. They dragged us to Theirna as orphans under the protection of the State."

We were close to the market when Alba continued. "None of the wealthy adopted us. After our third crossing, I was fortunate enough to meet the criteria for becoming a wealthy's concubine." She indicated a store that had a signboard of a pink arrow. "Otherwise, I would have had to work in that brothel to pay my debt to the kingdom for taking care of me until my third crossing. A brothel is where men pay to have sex with women. André, my brother, wasn't that fortunate. He became a slave."

A slave in this time and era . . . so many things I didn't know about our esteemed land.

I turned my head toward a commotion I heard from the market. The sight shocked my soul out of my body. There was a high stand in the middle of the square, and many naked girls were standing on it. Men kept moving them ahead, yelling numbers. *Five hundred . . . six hundred . . . sold!*

"Those are the virgin orphan girls. Before the kingdom sends them to a brothel, they sell their virginity for the best price. Shops in Zoiterra with an apple with a chiffon tie around it symbol do that. Here, it's happening in the open."

I remembered this shop at once. Everything I'd heard so far led me to realize that there was a darker side to the kingdom, and almost everything was in favor of men.

Alba pointed at the shops, explaining each symbol. A rainbow flag was a nightclub for homosexuals. The blue storefront sold sex toys. The pink one with a lace ribbon carried women's lingerie, and a cherry was a nightclub—like ours.

We turned back to where we'd come from. I pointed to a store with the harem pants icon. "What's that?"

"A dorm for girls like me, but my master didn't want me to stay there. He likes his privacy and wanted me to stay in a decent place, like our nightclub. As to your question, yes. I love my master. He's only touched me once, though." She heaved a sigh. "He's in love with someone else. He can't have her, and it's killing me that he keeps coming to the club to have lap dances with other girls. He doesn't even like me as a consolation."

"I am so sorry," I whispered, remembering when I spent nights wondering if Erick could love me back, and the stabbing feeling when I saw the text on his Iméfono. "Do you know who is she?"

She turned her face sharply away and kept walking. I understood that she didn't want to say more, so I kept mum.

A little further along, I pointed to a shop I had never seen on the adult street in Zoiterra, or even in my own town. It had a handcuff symbol on its door. I turned to Alba, wondering.

Her eyes sank with sadness and fear. "This is a special brothel for legal affairs people only."

"I want to see." I wanted to check out this special place for people like Erick. The people who were *legally allowed to hang out with juveniles.*

"It's a gang rape club! Don't go!" But her stage whisper was too late. I had already walked a few meters into the place. I stopped abruptly, trying to understand anything, from the women's moaning to the men's deep grunts. It was one of the harshest scenes I had ever seen in my life.

Partitions of light curtains separated the long room every few meters. Naked girls were lying on beds, to which their hands and feet were handcuffed, keeping them from moving. Each had a tattoo on her neck with a number.

"What do you want?"

I turned to see a short, fat man with dirty clothes staring at me, blocking my way out.

"So, you want to know if your man is coming here. I can help you." He smirked, rubbing his thumb against his forefinger.

A girl screamed with pain, and something muffled her moaning as a blond man walked from behind a curtain, zipping his pants. He came closer and shouted to the manager, "This is the ninth girl I've slept with, and your smell was all over her like the others! I want a clean one."

The manager smirked again. "You know, it's hard to see all these open legs all the time, and I'm not a saint ... next time, I'll wash your choice." He winked at him, then gestured to another man who was sitting on a chair. "It's your turn now. Try not to kill her as you did with the last one."

I felt the acid boiling inside my stomach, ready to explode. I pushed the manager and hurried out of the place, his yells following me. I looked around frantically, trying to find the right direction, but tears blurred my vision. Alba followed me, and her arm took mine.

"This is so unfair," I hissed with resentment.

Alba remained silent until we reached the nightclub. She turned to look at me and whispered, "Look, I believe you're innocent of the crimes they said you committed. Even if you weren't, I would commend you for the steps taken. Someone has to teach King Alexei a lesson. We, the rebels, will support you!"

Leaning my head on my room's window, I thought about all that Alba told me when we returned from our excursion. She was a rebel, who was in touch with others, and they wanted to take King Alexei down. According to her, he made all the weird rules against women. He'd executed most of her relatives, even though they were innocent.

What shall I do with this information?

I looked across the street at a shadow next to a lamppost. I realized it was a tall man in dark clothes with a hood pulled low over his face. The silhouette looked like . . . Erick!

My heart sang at the chance to see him. I squinted to try and work out if it was really him, but he disappeared. *Was it a vision? Am I only seeing what I want to see?*

I went to the bathroom and looked hard in the mirror. "Show me," I whispered, but my reflection remained static. I sighed. Maybe I was losing my mind, and everything was a delusion.

Dusk fell in the neighborhood, and the club started coming alive. It was a Russian-themed night, and the girls were excited. Their constant chatter didn't stop while they were getting dressed. I felt so lonely and depressed, and Alba suggested coming down to the club. She told me that the odious man wouldn't bother me anymore, as Cordis had assured him I was with a wealthy. For extra safety, I asked her to cover my face and my tattoo with thicker makeup.

Going back to the narrow balcony above the dance floor, I stood in the deep shadows. Alba was there, mingling with the girls. I noticed a young man approach her from a side door. Was it the same nasty man who had asked about me? I peered into the darkness. I didn't think it was the same man. He reminded me of Jason. If it was Jason, I had never seen him in such dark clothes. The young man rushed to a back room, gesturing to one of the other girls to follow.

Was it Jason? Alba already told me that he couldn't come here. But if it was really him, then what was he going to do with the girl? *It can't be Jason. My Jason. My innocent Jason.*

I had to know the truth. I couldn't take any more of the lies. Climbing down the stairs, I kept to the shadows, slowly edged to the back room, and opened the door.

I could only stand there, stunned. My best friend, who I was told could never come to this place—the friend I trusted the most in my life—had his hands down the girl's thighs while she was swaying her hips and shaking her lady parts at him. Now I knew what a lap dance was.

I gasped. Jason turned his head, and the blood drained from his face.

I ran out of the club into the cold street without realizing I was in my short dress. I took the alleys and the narrow lanes. My feet didn't know where they were going. All I knew was that I wanted to escape. I couldn't bear to look at Jason. I wanted to forget that scene. I felt betrayed and lied to, and those feelings were suffocating me.

Even though I didn't return Jason's feelings, and I didn't have the right to prevent him from hanging around with other women, his feelings for me didn't stop him from behaving like other men in the club, exploiting girls as he pleased. I thought he was better than this. He was the one who always asked me to slow it down with Erick, because he was afraid that Erick might

241

harm me. Then he turned around and harmed other girls himself. Weren't we supposed to have a standard scale when it came to other people's rights?

And another thought terrified me—would Erick do the same as Jason? Was paying for a lap dance considered betrayal, or it was just some kind of entertainment that I, and other girls, had to accept from our men?

Tears rolled down my cheeks. My chest was tight, the deceit pulling me inside out. I felt disconnected from the world around me. An unprecedented, bitter alienation engulfed my being and surrounded my soul with a steel fist.

In all my anger and frustration, I didn't pay attention to where I was going. I was the lone presence on an almost-empty street. Soon, men came out like rats from the side lanes, surrounding me with their dazed strides and red eyes.

"What do we have here? Little raspberry in the garden!" said the one closest to me. He seemed younger than me—someone who had just crossed—but his silky shirt hung open, showing me the sin-spots on his chest.

I turned back, trying to find a way out. A trembling started deep in my body. I had fallen into even bigger trouble. I backed away from the men, but a hand grabbed my arm.

I yanked away. "Don't touch me!" My words came out scared, not the warning I wanted it to be. The young blond man who'd taken hold of me smiled, encouraged by the laughter of his friends. I tensed my body, ready to fight my way out. But before he touched me again, a fist punched him from behind, knocking him to the ground. A bottle smashed on another man's head, and the others retreated.

Looking up, I saw Jason. His eyes were blazing in a way I had never seen before. He grabbed my hand and pulled me down the roads. Up ahead, a door swung open, and Alba beckoned us inside. Once we stood in the small room, Jason nodded, and Alba left us alone.

Jason punched the door with his fist. "What the hell were you thinking?" he screamed. Fire leaped from his eyes.

242

I guessed I wasn't thinking at all. Only feeling all the terrible things that had been thrust on me. In the past two days, I had seen the dark side of humanity, and each truth of adulthood that I learned in this neighborhood had destroyed my innocence.

Words stuck in my throat. Anger and betrayal blazed through my veins. So I did the only thing I could think of.

I slapped him.

CHAPTER 30

THE SLAP SHOCKED BOTH OF us. I stared at my trembling hands, open-mouthed; I never thought I had violence in me. The red imprint of my hand showed up on Jason's fair face. His jaw tightened as his eyes met mine.

I wet my lips and ran up to my room. Jason followed, shutting the door behind him. We stared at each other for a while before I took a seat on my bed. Jason ran his fingers through his hair and came to sit beside me. "Leen, you weren't supposed to know about it."

I shook my head. "I'm not asking you for an explanation."

"You have no right to," he said with a crisp tone, making me flush with embarrassment. "There are things beyond your understanding."

"I'm sorry that I slapped you," I mumbled. "But you lied to me and brought me to this horrible place where everything is skewed."

"We had no choice. It's the only safe place for you at the moment."

I sighed. I wanted my mom, but she wasn't around. I needed to talk to someone who could understand me. When I asked Jason if I could call

Mary or the twins, his reply was, "Don't call anyone. For their safety and yours."

His mood was dark, so I felt it best not to ask about Erick.

I shifted to face him, and asked the question I had always wanted him to answer. "What makes the sin-spots appear?"

Jason's smile was bittersweet while he answered. "Sometimes, I think everything we do in this kingdom is a sin." After a moment of silence, he added, "The broad ones are: setting a fire, contempt of the royal family or any action against them, lying, stealing and killing. Telling anyone who isn't an adult about adult matters. Kissing, hugging, or raping a child or a juvenile. Those last ones scatter spots right on the face."

I had to blink several times to understand his words. I couldn't believe it at first, but then the truth came back at once to shock my body. We kissed, Erick and me. We kissed, and no sin-spots showed on his face. He must have been wearing the Crepito then!

I cupped my face and moaned. Jason put his arm around my shoulders. I leaned into his chest, and silent tears dropped from my eyes, wetting his shirt. My heart couldn't stop loving Erick, although he might have betrayed me, as Jason said earlier. And the pain of losing that love was cleaving me in half. I wished there was an on-off button so I could stop loving him, but there was none.

"I know it's difficult for you to reconcile everything at once. Just give it time. I promise I'll smuggle you and your mom out of the kingdom," Jason handed me his handkerchief, and I looked at him with empty and desperate eyes. He kissed my forehead. "I must go now. Please don't go out of the club. It's not safe for you. And if you must go, wear your red cloak."

Giving me one last encouraging smile, he walked out of the door with a backward glance. I dragged myself to the bathroom to wash my face. My thoughts were all over the place. My feelings felt ripped apart by my new understanding.

I looked at myself in the mirror, and the environment changed.

Again, I found myself in the royal palace. It took me a moment to realize that I was standing in Prince Thaddeus's room.

It was nighttime, and a storm was raging outside. Winds howled through the entire palace. Thaddeus stood in front of the window with a newborn baby screaming in his arms. The child was covered in a white royal silk blanket. Lightning illuminated the room with its intermittent flashes.

A man in a white coat spoke nearby. "My condolences at the tragic loss, Your Royal Highness."

I looked around to understand the scene before me. A woman lay still on the bed with open and empty eyes. A maid came and covered her face with a white sheet.

That must be Thaddeus's wife, Princess Dione, who died giving birth to his son.

Thaddeus turned around, looking at the doctor with no expression on his face. Both he and his son shared the same poor luck. Thaddeus had lost his mother and now his wife. Losses had taken a toll on him. It felt as if he had turned into stone.

A maid approached to take the child from him. He gave her the precious bundle, caressing the child's face with a gentle touch. The boy held on to his father's finger, not wanting to let go. A tear fell from Thaddeus's eyes before he wiped it away.

"His name is Thaddeus the Third," he boomed, scaring me. Even the nurses and maids were startled by his loud voice. "A *pure-blooded* child. The throne would be his birthright."

Thaddeus marched out of the room, each step making me quake in fear. I followed him, my breath leaving my body with a gasp. He walked down a long corridor and ascended a sweeping staircase. Determination permeated the very air he breathed. He shoved open a door, ignoring the guards who were standing there like stone. It was Queen Arianna's chamber. I was quite shocked at Thaddeus's audacity—he had entered without knocking while she was changing her clothes.

The queen startled at the unwelcome entry and dashed behind a folding screen. Her maids, who'd been helping her, stood aside, scared to move a step.

"Don't you ever knock?" she snapped.

With a mocking smile, Thaddeus answered her with another question. "What are you hiding?"

"What do you mean?" Arianna came from behind the screen, tucking a white robe around herself.

He moved toward her menacingly, his words dripping with hatred. "Mandras, for example."

What?!

Thaddeus tilted his head, observing Arianna's reaction carefully. Blood rose to her face, horror shining in her eyes. She lifted her eyebrows at the maids, who curtsied and left the room at once. She looked at Thaddeus and stumbled over her words. "How dare you accuse an honorable woman! Get out this instant."

"Not before you understand what I can do to you." He approached her and moved a lock of her hair away, whispering in her ear. "Hear me well before you threaten me. I have all the evidence, so don't you talk about honor. You were cheating on my father with Mandras, even when he was alive. You have been cheating since you entered my kingdom. I've filmed you both."

Oh, my goodness! The truth had been staring me and all of Elpax in the face for a long time. King Alexei looked just like Mandras. He was the father.

The queen's face blanched. She looked like death warmed over.

"So, honorable queen," Thaddeus continued with a smirk. "Starting from today, all the decisions of this kingdom are mine. You and your bastard son will sign any paper I present to you. If you ever have a thought—even the slightest one, to object to this deal—I will present the film to the public. Scandals will follow you and your son like a shadow wherever you go. I have no qualms about killing either of you and making it seem like an accident. And don't even think about hurting my son. The throne belongs to him.

It is his birthright."

He walked out with broad steps. Arianna slumped down on the floor, sobbing into her hands. Her breath became faster, her eyes filling with fear. She got up and picked up her Iméfono, texting someone.

A few minutes later, the door swung open, and it was her lover, Mandras. Queen Arianna jumped up to hug him. She was crying so hard that he kept soothing her to understand her words. She told him about Thaddeus and his threat to kill her.

Mandras kissed her hand passionately. "Don't worry, my love. I'll take care of him."

The room rotated around me. When I opened my eyes, I was back in my bathroom, looking at the mirror in horror, trying to gather all the pieces of the puzzle. I needed a paper or a smartboard on which to write my thoughts. I turned on the hot water and drew the royal family tree in the steam on the mirror.

If King Alexei was Mandras's son, then the throne had to go to Thaddeus. Queen Arianna had manipulated King Stavros to get the throne for her son. If Thaddeus knew all that, and he had proof, then why wasn't he exposing her? Why was Alexei the king today? *I must be missing something.* Moreover, Queen Arianna wasn't pure or ethical, and Thaddeus wasn't the only villain in the royal family. They were all the same, two sides of the same paxin.

What has all of this got to do with me? Why am I getting these visions?

Some of my visions were showing Arianna as a good person and some were showing the opposite. It was like my mind was receiving two different sources of information, where both sides were trying to win me over.

I needed more information before I could decide what my next step would be. I washed my face and had just wiped the drawing off the mirror when someone knocked on my door.

I answered, and frowned when I saw the visitor. It was Isabella.

A knowing smile spread across her face. She looked me over from top to bottom, taking in the color of my eyes and my non-made-up face.

There was some meanness in her gaze, as if she had seen through me and discovered all my secrets.

"Cordis wants you to make tea for two," she announced, chewing her gum and blowing a bubble in my face. She turned and walked down the corridor. "Leave the tray on the ground after knocking twice on her door." She looked back at me with a taunting smile and added, "Lenora."

The blood drained from my veins at her threatening stare. It wouldn't take long for her to tell the Law Corps. She would hold the knowledge over me from now on.

I pushed down my fears and headed to the kitchen. I made the tea and took the tray to Cordis's room, all the while thinking about my options. I had to tell Alba to call Jason. He had to hide me elsewhere as soon as possible.

I knocked on Cordis's door twice, my mind still troubled. When Cordis opened the door, my eyes widened to see her in a short transparent nightgown. I forgot to leave after knocking! She abruptly shut the door in my face without taking the tray, but not before I caught a glimpse of the man in her bedroom. He was wearing nothing more than scanty underwear.

I gasped, and the tray dropped from my hands. It was Mr. William Valemont.

Jason's father.

I'd once heard a proverb: two strokes make the head ache. And my head ached with all that I had seen! At once, I bent over and started picking up the glass pieces when the door opened again and Mr. William exclaimed, "Sarah, stop!"

I lifted my eyes to him. He had called me by my fake name, so he was willing to help me stay hidden. That meant Cordis didn't know who I really was. *What a relief.*

"Leave us," he demanded.

For a moment, I didn't know who he had given the order to. Cordis curtsied and answered in a formal tone, "Yes, sir." She walked out of the room without turning her back to him. That was the weirdest thing I had seen so far!

I could only gaze at her retreating form, completely stunned.

Mr. William waved at me to come in. I shut the door behind me and stood still. He turned to me after pulling on a robe. "I don't have to remind you to keep quiet about this."

"Sir, it is your business. I care for Lady Valemont, but I'm more concerned about my sisters now."

"I'm not cheating on my wife, Lenora," he said while pulling on his pants. "Cordis is my concubine."

I looked at him with inquiring eyes. It was ironic to see both the father and son in the same place with strange women. But it wasn't my place to question Mr. William.

He continued, "She's mine. She has given birth to my son. I asked her if she wanted to be free. But she didn't want that, and neither did I. We love each other."

I only caught one word of his speech. "A . . . son?"

"Yes," he clarified, wearing his shirt now. "Jason. Cordis is Jason's mother."

CHAPTER 31

I FROZE LIKE A STATUE upon hearing the news. What kind of games did the wealthy play? I couldn't even imagine the twisted life they lived.

"I will appreciate your discretion in this matter. It would kill Jason to find out that Margaret isn't his birth mother."

I swallowed hard. What else could I do in my position?

"Your mother will soon get out of prison, and your sisters are happy at my home," he said while tying his shoes. "Are you comfortable here?"

"Yes. But there's a girl," I blurted out.

"What about her?"

"I think she suspects me. I was going to call Jason to hide me in another place."

"No, he can't. This is the only place I own in this neighborhood. What's her name?"

Oh my God! He owns this place in this horrible neighborhood!

"Isabella," I replied after some hesitation.

"I'll take care of her."

As he was about to step outside the room, I gathered my courage and whispered, "Sir, there's a man. I want some information about him. Can you investigate?"

He frowned. "What's his name?"

"Erick Mellas—a lawyer. I want to know everything about him and where he is now. But please keep Jason away from it."

"Got it." He smiled and proceeded to walk downstairs. I cleaned up the mess I'd made, then walked to my room, trying to fit the pieces of information together.

I looked out of my room's window, and a deep sigh escaped me. Everyone in my life had shocked me so far. Just uttering Erick's name to Mr. William had caused an ache to spread in my heart. I missed him. I longed to be close to him. I loved him, even though he may have betrayed me. How badly I wished to hug him, to feel his breath in my ears and his kisses on my neck. I longed to look into his gray eyes.

I looked up at the skies, hoping to receive an answer from the heavens. The streets were so different here; a dangerous stillness filled the entire neighborhood. There was no scent of the twilight or flowers. I remembered our garden, with the smell of jasmine and Mom's morning sage tea. I missed the chirpy voices of my sisters telling me about their day. I missed everything about my old life. I missed *me*. I missed the Leen I knew.

A giant hole formed where my heart used to be. My entire life had changed, and danger dogged my steps. People surrounded me, but they were all strangers hunting for a bounty. Any mistake would cost me my life and my freedom—if I forgot to draw my third ID line with henna, or if a girl scrutinized me too hard, or if I turned my head by accident when someone called out my actual name.

I knew very little about the adult world—I hadn't received any courses after my half-walk through the Crossing Gate. I could stumble over the rules without realizing it. Dread filled both my waking hours and dreams, which put me in danger as well—there was no guarantee that I wouldn't call out my mom's name during sleep, or start speaking about my old life.

My life was shattered and scattered in the wind. Whose fault was it but my own? My follies and overconfidence that I could do anything for Erick were to blame. Or was it fate playing a game with me? Falling unconscious in the middle of the pathway had destroyed my family violently. Was there any way to fix all that without making sacrifices?

I felt as if my head would burst. It was past midnight. I slept, but my restless mind went searching for answers. A ballroom was where I ended up this time. It had the same décor as the rest of the royal palace. Women dressed in large puffed-up gowns embellished with feathers were dancing the Elpaxian waltz. It was quite different from what I had seen at Mary's wedding. The dancing couples were very close, arms encircled around one another.

Queen Arianna sat next to King Alexei at a long silver table in the middle of the hall. He was wearing the royal crown. So that meant he was the king by now. I had just ambled over to the table when an announcement echoed through the room.

"His Royal Highness, Prince Thaddeus Vasilas."

I turned to see Thaddeus entering the room with a majestic presence. The throng of people stopped dancing. They parted into a path for him, with the men bowing their heads and the women curtsying. Thaddeus ignored them all. Once he reached the royal chair on Alexei's other side, he threw himself on it without saying a word to Alexei or Arianna.

Alexei looked at him but said nothing. The thunderous expression on Thaddeus's face forbade all conversation, and nobody wished to risk their life. The party's noise picked up again after the awkward entry. People began to dance, talk, and laugh. Servants circulated with food and drinks. Thaddeus began to drink a massive amount of red liquid out of boredom; I knew by now that it was called wine. He looked at all the people with a perpetual smirk until his eyes rested on one particular person.

Following his gaze, I laid eyes upon a woman in a gorgeous turquoise dress, who was swaying among the dancers. His sharp eyes noticed each of her movements and became tender as he continued to look at her. A gentleness appeared on his stern face.

I knew that expression. It was the same way I had looked at Erick. Prince Thaddeus was feeling the first flickers of love.

The woman who'd caught his attention was quite far away, so I didn't recognize her. But from what I knew from the news and current politics, he had never remarried.

Thaddeus nodded to a butler, who moved closer to him. "Who's that?"

"Princess Olympia—grandchild of the late prince of Alphatoli province; His Royal Highness Achilles Vasilas."

Why is Thaddeus asking about Olympia?

"How old is she?"

"Twenty years, Your Royal Highness."

"Go."

The butler bowed low and walked away. My heart was about to stop as Thaddeus headed to the center of the ballroom, toward the woman who'd stolen his heart. As Olympia watched him approaching her, she froze, as if she were facing a loaded gun.

My heart went out to her. Thaddeus could cut an impenetrable figure with his royal demeanor. His reputation preceded him, too. Olympia acted fast, realizing that his attention would lead to her devastation. She curtsied and greeted him. Her dance companion backed up a few steps without a word.

Thaddeus picked up Olympia's trembling hand. "Let's dance."

Having no choice in the matter, she placed her other hand on his shoulder and started swaying to the music. Whispers circulated around the room, eyes glancing at the couple. Everyone knew that misfortune was bequeathed on the girl whom Thaddeus chose for himself.

Thaddeus danced with Olympia, his attention was only on her. His eyes were wholly possessive. Hers held apprehension and fear.

I turned to Queen Arianna. Her eyes followed the scene with a thoughtful expression on her face. As I approached the table again, I heard her whisper to King Alexei. "He likes her."

"I wanted to tell you earlier, Mother," Alexei sighed in sorrow. "I forged a new relationship of mutual approval with Olympia a few months ago. I was planning to propose to her. And I know she'll accept. But now Thaddeus will make things difficult for us."

"On the contrary, son. This coincidence is a gift that will be in our interest. It's time to take down that silver-haired fool."

"What do you have in mind?"

Her smile widened as she drank her wine. "You'll see."

My mind reeled, considering the implications of this manipulation. Light spread around me, and I woke up with a start. I sat on my bed and tried to get it all together. I knew by now how devious they all were, but I still had no idea why I saw these visions.

I dressed and went to Alba's room. She was sitting on the floor with a plate of sandwiches in front of her.

"I made a sandwich for you." She gestured for me to come. Her face was sulky.

"What's wrong?"

"I'm fine. Just a disagreement with my master."

"Oh. I'm sorry." I sat on the ground. After taking a big bite of my sandwich, I spoke again. "Alba, do you recall the princes who used to rule the provinces during King Stavros's reign?"

Her eyes narrowed in deep thought. "Yes. I think they all died soon after the late king's funeral."

"All of them?" My eyes popped out.

She nodded. "Don't you remember history class? They became ill due to a strange disease."

"And who replaced them? Who ruled instead of them?"

"Prince Thaddeus, of course. He took over all the provinces. What's with these questions today? What bee got caught in your bonnet?"

"Some random thoughts. Alba, does your Iméfono have a private web browser?"

She nodded and handed me her Iméfono, showing me where to type. My research through the internet encyclopedia, Grigopaideia, took me to a page about Queen Arianna. I remembered that in one of my visions, the one with King Stavros, she mentioned the loss of their first child. I clicked on the link to the article about that son. There was a tomb for him in Lutetia, which used to be Paris long ago.

Upon the arrival of the Queen of Elpax, Arianna Vasilas, to Lutetia, she gave premature birth to her first son. He died a day later due to a complicated heart condition. May his soul rest in peace.

That was quite a surprise—I had never heard or learned about him in school. The comment below the picture read:

Here lies Prince Philip Stavros Vasilas
Son of King Stavros Islabour Vasilas, King of The Kingdom of Elpax
Born: July 22, 101 P.B.
Died: July 23, 101 P.B.

101 Post-Bellum was the Latin phrase for "after the war." The Modern Roman Empire didn't use the Gregorian calendar like us.

So the first prince, Philip, was born one year before his brother, King Alexei. *I wonder why she buried him in Lutetia instead of Elpax.*

Moving on . . .

I searched for all the princes: Achilles, Boreas, Vidar, Ganymedes, Deimos, and Zephyr. The result was always the same. All of them died two years after the death of the late King Stavros. Then, I searched for Mandras, and the result sent a chill down my spine. He'd died a few days after Prince Thaddeus III was born.

So Thaddeus killed Mandras before Mandras could get rid of him, and he probably killed the princes, too. How come no one stopped Thaddeus or caught him?

I needed to know more. But how could I get more information from a page that was written by the government?

My mind made a wicked plan, and I turned to Alba. "Tonight, I want to get down to the club."

"After what happened to you last night? No way! Jason would kill me."

"Don't worry, I got your back. Just hide this stupid virginity symbol with makeup, and we're good to go."

She sighed and shook her head. But after half an hour of begging, she agreed.

The club's music was louder than ever, and the dancers were performing the Charleston on stage. I stood in the corner with Alba, wearing a drop-waist silk dress like the dancers, scrutinizing all the patrons as they entered the club.

"So, what are you looking for, Miss Sarah?" Alba asked.

"A man of top rank. Someone close to the royal family."

Alba frowned, but didn't question further. "Let me think." She looked around at the drunk men and leaned in to whisper, "That one! Mr. Roussallis, the National Security Advisor."

I nodded, and we sashayed toward him with drinks in our hands. Alba had taught me how to move my hips like the other girls. He was an old gentleman with white hair and a red face that was probably caused by the drinks. A girl sat on his lap, and he was busy kissing and fondling her.

"Rose," said Alba. "Find another one. This one is ours."

She gave us a hateful look, apparently calculating the loss of her tips, but she moved away.

"Ah . . . today is my lucky day . . . two beautiful girls. One for each of my thighs."

Disgusting man, I thought. Alba smiled and perched on his lap, taking up all the space there. She nodded at me to sit in the chair next to him.

He leaned in to kiss Alba, but she pulled back and exclaimed, "My dear Mr. Roussallis! Let's drink first." Alba winked at him, and he laughed gleefully. I offered him the drink in my hand, and we spent half an hour plying him with alcohol until he started to stutter.

I leaned closer to him with a question on my lips. "I overheard that the spy is hiding near us in the neighborhood. I hope we can turn her in to please His Majesty, King Alexei."

"I suspect that he would care if he knew," he guffawed. "Alexei has . . . no idea what's going on."

"I hope our beloved king is well and safe."

"Severely ill . . . he is."

My pulse quickened. There was nothing in the news about King Alexei falling ill, nor had my visions told me he was in poor health. I spoke the next words carefully. "The same disease the late princes died from?"

"Hush." He put his thick finger to my lips. "You never heard it from me."

I nodded with a nervous smile, frightened by the idea that Thaddeus was trying to kill Alexei as well.

His fingers crept down, touching my long pearl necklace. "That girl . . . Lenora something. She was . . . always . . . trouble. Right from the very beginning."

What beginning? Why did he say *always*?

Alba and I exchanged looks. "What do you mean?" I asked again in my sweetest voice, offering him another drink.

"She . . . she came to the library with a wealthy," he said with a hiccup. "As if we wouldn't notice. Stupid girl . . . Arianna said not to follow her . . . stupid queen."

My eyes widened at that revelation. Queen Arianna knew it was me in the library. I hadn't scanned my ID and I was in disguise, yet she found out. But she did nothing. Why?

I asked, "And who else knew?"

"Stupid Thaddeus. I had to bribe some of his men . . . and kill the

258

others on Arianna's orders. Don't let Thaddeus know about her . . . do that, Roussallis . . . kill that person, Roussallis . . . I'm sick of them all," he growled. Then, as if something had woken him up from his drunken stupor, he looked into my eyes. "Why do you ask?"

Alba and I shared a nervous glance. She turned his face and kissed him hard, caressing his body down below until he forgot I was there.

Leaning my head back, I thought about what he'd said. Queen Arianna knew I was in the library, and she didn't want Thaddeus to figure out I'd gone there . . . but why? Why would he care? And why didn't Arianna punish me, rather than Carlota? *Is it because I was with Mary? But that still makes no sense! Arianna's had plenty of opportunities to capture me when I wasn't with a wealthy.*

A girl approached me and leaned over to whisper in my ear, "Cordis wants to see you."

I swallowed, wondering if Cordis had discovered my secret. Or maybe she just wanted to ask about my foolish behavior in front of Mr. William.

I walked out of the club and went up to her room. Once I entered, Cordis looked at me with a chilly gaze. "Why are you dressed like a dancer?" As if she couldn't be bothered to hear my answer, she handed me her Iméfono. "Mr. William wants to speak to you."

I didn't ask her if the line was secure; such a question could blow my cover. An ordinary girl wouldn't care for such a matter. Only a wanted criminal would ask for untraceable Iméfono.

I picked up the Iméfono and said, "Yes, sir?"

"Sarah, about the girl—Isabella, or whatever. I took care of her."

"What do you mean?"

"Let's just say she won't bother you anymore. Now, the man you asked about . . ."

My pulse sped up. "What about him?"

"His father was working in one of my companies, but he was fired months ago. I'm sure about the information my men collected on him."

What? Did Erick's father work for Jason's father? Neither of the boys

259

told me that earlier.

"And?" My heart pumped furiously in my ears.

"Erick Mellas has immigrated to the Roman Empire permanently. Along with his family."

CHAPTER 32

I COULD ONLY STAND THERE as the words penetrated deep into my heart. Nothing could have prepared me for the pain of that moment. It felt like I was being torn apart. My last remaining shred of hope shriveled up with a silent scream and died. I was in a vacuum, and the world was moving far away.

"Sarah, are you still there?" asked Mr. William through the Iméfono. His voice sounded faint. I couldn't bear to deal with the bearer of the grievous news anymore.

"Are you sure?" Agony coated my faint words, making them tremble.

"My men are the best," said Jason's father.

I mumbled a quiet *thank you* and handed the Iméfono back to Cordis.

Girls were walking around the hallways as my feet drove me to Alba's room. Closing the door behind me, I dropped to the ground. Numbness overtook me from the inside out. All the noise in the universe became so loud, and everything sounded unreal. My vision blurred, and warm tears felt like acid dropped onto my cheeks, burning me with the fumes of betrayal.

"This isn't true," I whispered, but the knot in my chest told me the truth. I'd been lied to.

I couldn't stop the tears from falling like a waterfall; the drops fell even before I could wipe them away. My eyes cried for the one person I considered home. My body shivered with the pain of being separated from my soul. I cried for him. I cried for me. I cried for us, or what *could* have been us.

The memories of our love story ran in my mind, the images imprinting themselves under my eyelids. Each word he'd spoken to me carved itself deep into my being, laughing at me, mocking me for having trusted him without conditions. I couldn't understand how Erick fooled me so easily. I thought I'd seen love in his eyes. How could I have been so wrong about him?

I started shaking like a leaf in the swirling winds of deception. Alba came into the room and rushed to my side. Her eyes were full of fear, but I didn't care. Her lips were moving, but I couldn't hear a thing. I was no more than a void. Betrayal was suffocating me. I couldn't breathe between my loud sobs. My heart was splintered and crushed, my whole spirit shattered.

I was dying.

"Get up, Sarah. Wash your face. Come on," said Alba in a firm tone. She helped my weakened body to the bathroom, washed my face with gentle fingers, and clasped my shoulders. "I have no idea what's wrong, but it will get better."

I didn't respond. My throat was sore after the bout of crying. I stood still, barely aware of where I was.

Her voice echoed beside me again. "It'll be all right. Come. Let's go to the gathering room to divert your mind."

"No. I just . . . just want to be alone."

"Hell no! Look at your face. I can't leave you alone."

"Alba, please. The girls already hate me, and I don't have the strength to deal with being around them right now."

She held my shoulders. "They don't hate you, silly girl. They envy you. They were all raped and escaped the brothels to work here. Your virginity symbol reminds them of what they've lost. It's not your fault, and it isn't their fault either. The whole system in the kingdom is fucked up. Just give it time."

She took my arm, dragging me to the living room, and offered me some Ouzo. Throwing myself on the couch, I looked at my picture in the corner of the Ológramma's news program. I ran my fingers through my short hair and sighed. That was another thing I'd lost. Since my crossing, I had only half of a life, half of a line, and half of my hair. The result of half of everything was probably . . . nothing.

As I sipped my drink, a group of girls, still in their dancing costumes, dashed into the room with unfathomable expressions.

Alba's eyes widened. "What's wrong?"

A slender, brown-skinned girl answered while increasing the sound of the Ológramma. "A client just told me that the Crossing Gate will no longer work. Damn that Lenora Evgenís; she ruined it. If I ever find that bitch, I'll kill her."

Her hateful announcement made my spirits plummet even further. A strange quivering overtook me, and I hugged a pillow in a desperate attempt to hide my tension. The girl flung herself on the couch next to me, just as Benita shouted from across the room. "The news mentioned nothing about the Crossing Gate being broken!"

"Girl, my client is of the highest rank, and he revealed this information only after the drink addled his brain. I'm telling you, he wasn't making it up."

"That's right," said the other brunette girl. "I heard a wealthy tell his friend that the Law Corps prevented his daughter from crossing. He also said that troops enveloped the area and forbade anyone from approaching."

Oh my God!

Silence reigned in the room for a few moments. Then, one of them exclaimed, "Has anyone seen Isabella?"

"Not since this morning, no," said Benita. "A wealthy came in earlier asking for her, and she didn't return."

Her words horrified me. Was it possible that something terrible happened to Isabella?

Rose rushed into the room with a pale face. "Girls," she announced in a breathless voice. "Prince Thaddeus has negotiated with the neighborhood guards to search the area, and they've agreed to let him for the first time ever."

"What?" the girls shouted in unison. Some of them froze, and others placed their hands over their mouths.

"The Law Corps' Special Weapons Team will search the club in a few minutes."

My heart pounded, its beat rising with the increased tempo of the girls' angry exclamations. Cordis stepped in, and they all fell silent, looking at her with hope.

"I don't have the authority to prevent the team from searching the nightclub and verifying everyone's identity," she said as she looked at the pale faces surrounding her. "They're coming because that spy Evgenís is working with the rebels and they hid her in our neighborhood. I know you all have run away from paying your debt to the government through the brothels and come to work here instead. The club owner has promised that they won't arrest any of you. So I'm expecting your full cooperation."

She gazed at me before walking away. I knew that the Law Corps had found me out. The girls started exiting the room in twos and threes, their voices raised, insulting my mother and me. The hatred in their tone tore at my self-respect.

The room began to spin. The lights grew dim, and I seemed to be slipping into a murky world when a familiar voice shouted at me: "Leen, get up!"

My mind regained its balance with Alba's sharp tone. She poked me and tugged at my arms. "To the Church, hurry!"

I seemed to be in a daze. My limbs weren't strong enough to carry

264

my body. I looked at her in confusion, my mind unable to compute my impending recapture. Everything seemed to be in slow motion. I was about to tell Alba all of that when a sharp slap resounded on my cheek. My head jerked back, and I was awake at once.

"Sorry. I had to wake you up fast."

I held her hand, and together we hurried to the stairs leading to the second floor. The music stopped, and the Special Weapons Team's heavy boots invaded the club, pouring in on the first floor.

Alba peeked into the living room, which was filled with girls. She pointed to the upper floors, since it was now impossible to get me out of the club. I rushed up the stairs behind her, right to the roof. As she opened its metal door, the icy air slapped our faces, and the winds raged strongly along with the heavy rain.

Alba looked around and pointed at the large water tanks. "You're tiny enough to fit between them. They won't search there." She rushed back downstairs as I stepped up to the tanks and slid into the narrow space between them, barely able to breathe. I heard the heavy boots as the Corps climbed to the roof.

"Search every corner."

My limbs trembled at the rough voice of my nightmares. It was the same general who had interrogated me in the hospital. I held my breath as someone approached the tanks, climbing over the very spot I was hiding in. Then, finally, I gathered my courage and bent backward, shifting close to the tank mounted on the roof's edge. The chilly air rushed around me and caused me to shake savagely, the raindrops soaking my dress. I curled up, trying to make myself smaller so I could conserve body heat.

Don't look down, don't look down. Please don't look down.

That was my mantra. A stream of light from the handheld flashlight reflected on the tank next to me for a few seconds, followed by a sharp voice. "Nothing here." Heavy steps descended the stairs as all of the soldiers left the roof. I remained in the same spot, trying to guess if the general was playing games with me. They didn't return. Eventually, I came out of my

265

hiding place and collapsed on the roof, my tears falling in silence.

I couldn't believe what my life had come to—trying desperately to save myself. I never knew my actions could have such destructive repercussions. Just the thought that the Crossing Gate would never work again suffocated me with guilt. The twins would never grow up. All the other children and juveniles would remain the same.

I couldn't stand the idea of looking into Moria's accusatory eyes. She'd been so excited to cross, and now she would stay a child forever. I couldn't bear the thought of my sisters never growing up, marrying, having kids, and securing a better life. They would never perceive an emotion called love, and they would never understand how much I loved them. *Will they blame me too when they come to know?* I shuddered with misery. I had destroyed my family and millions of others' too. My mom was being tortured by the Law Corps in Inferos. I couldn't even begin to think about that.

My silent sobs rose deep in my heart as I stood again on the edge of the rooftop. I had lost everything today.

How much I hate myself now. And you, Erick.

You destroyed every dream I had and broke every promise you uttered. You scorched my insides with confusion when you silently vanished. I was no more than an entertaining game for you to play. I foolishly trusted you, and with your cold contempt and thorough calculation, you messed up my life, turned your back on me, and you didn't care. You made me what I've become today: the most hated girl in the whole of Elpax.

I still don't know who gave you the right to break a heart beating with love for you. I wish you a thousand-year damnation in hell for the man that you are, who even humanity has disowned. I curse you from every part of my broken being.

I hope you'll perish for what you've done to me.

How I once hoped that you'd be mine. I thought that I would wait for you until the end of time. Even if you were a window that brought dust to my life. Even if you'd rolled my heart between your hands indifferently—I would have loved you. How I wished you could be mine, even if you didn't want me back. But I never, ever wanted to spoil others' lives for us.

As I stand on the edge of this roof, my soul soaked in despair and sadness, I want you to know that I loved you more than I wished. Perhaps a bit too much . . . and certainly more than you deserve.

And now you, my life, Mom, and my family are all gone.

I can't find you in this vast world to get my revenge, so let me kill myself and pay the penance. Perhaps then I can escape from the aches that I've caused.

Just don't forget, Erick, you are the reason I lost my soul.

May my soul rest in peace.

I looked down, closed my eyes, and let myself go. Ready to end it all.

CHAPTER 33

A STRONG HAND PULLED ME back, and I fell to the hard ground. Alba threw herself over me. She pressed a hand over my mouth to keep me from screaming. I tried to push her away, but she was strong against my slim body.

"It's fine. They've gone," she whispered.

I looked at her through my tears, silently pleading her to let me end my life. Her gaze was panicked, but she embraced me. I only managed to shake my head repeatedly so she would leave me. But she didn't budge. Soon, my body gave up, and I rested my head on the floor, my eyes frozen with an empty look and my soul petrified in desperate silence.

"Do you promise not to throw yourself over if I let you go?"

Even with her firm voice, I couldn't answer. *What could I say?*

Alba sighed and moved away from me. "Damn! It's cold." She reached out to help me up, but I didn't respond. "Please, Leen. Just sit up."

I didn't look at her; it was difficult to move.

She pulled my head into her lap and caressed my hair with a deep sigh.

"Do you want me to call Jason?"

My mind was empty, and my eyes saw nothing. I kept them directed toward the horizon.

"Damn it, Leen. You almost killed yourself. From now on, you'll sleep in my room."

I had nothing to say. I'd almost ended my life for an unworthy man. I realized that, so far, all my decisions had been emotional and unbalanced. As a result, they'd all proved futile and foolhardy. Maybe it was time to grow up, but I didn't know how to grow up. I didn't know any other way to think.

"Alba," I whispered. "How do you endure the troubles of life?"

She inhaled. "Believe in yourself and trust your decisions even when others don't. Make a goal and strive to achieve it."

"What happens if I fail?"

"Oh, you'll fail. Trust me. You'll fail a lot in the beginning. But failing for something you believe in is better than regretting not doing it." She wiped her face. "In life, there's no painless path. Maybe that's the only rule."

I knew exactly what I'd wanted: to cross for Erick and for me. I'd failed in that, or perhaps not. Who knew? Did that half-line mean I'd succeeded or not? I didn't know what I would do in life, but I realized one thing now.

"Erick," I whispered. *Oh, Erick, know this now. My heart repents for ever loving you. It's as forbidden as the fire in my homeland. Damn me if I ever become delirious in your name again. I don't want revenge, but I order you to stay away from me forever.*

I took a deep breath while looking at the street. No more backups, no more foolish behavior, no more nonsense about love.

Let the day announce a new me—the new Leen.

We climbed down to Alba's room. The girls were busy elsewhere in the club, and nobody saw how wet we were. Alba turned to remove her soaked clothes. As she was taking off her dress, I looked up to ask her about Isabella when I saw the full name of her master tattooed on her back.

It was Jason.

I blinked. This crap was getting seriously annoying. Jason said that lap dancing was something beyond my understanding. Okay, I got that. But owning another person? That was disgusting, and even inhuman. How could he approve of doing such a thing? Couldn't he refuse such a *luxury* at all? Did he really believe that women were just sex tools for men?

I recalled that Alba said her master touched her only once. I didn't know if she meant he made love to her only once, or he just kissed her once. Either way, the idea was so frustrating to me. Would Jason leave her hanging like this, not freeing her and not being with her?

And who was the girl he loved? He never told me anything about this. She couldn't be me. Seriously, he might like me, but loving me? I didn't think so.

At that moment, I wasn't sure of anything anymore. He and I would have one hell of a conversation when we next spoke.

"Good morning, Leen."

At first, it had shocked me to see Jason's name on Alba's back two days ago. When I thought it over, though, I realized that Alba deserved a kind man like Jason. But not as a concubine, never a concubine. A girlfriend or a wife. Someone who shared his life with respect and care. I'd make sure to tell him to free the girl and be her equal partner, or just let her go her own way. It was her right to find a good husband. And I, too, needed a confirmation that Jason, my best friend, was the same decent man that I'd always known, and that he wasn't complicit in this systemic issue.

However, as soon as I called him, he answered with a harsh "Hello." When I asked what was wrong, he said, "Never mind."

I knew when he talked like that, he was in his *dark mood*. I couldn't discuss anything about Alba with him at that moment; I had to do it face to face later on if I wanted to have a productive conversation about it.

Anyway, he brusquely assured me that the Crossing Gate would start functioning again soon. He was working with his dad to get Mom out of prison, too. And we'd all seek asylum in the Latina Republic.

Isabella didn't come back to the club. I couldn't ask Mr. William about her, but I hoped she was all right. I prayed he hadn't taken care of her by killing her. After all, *taking care means solving the problem correctly without harming anyone, right?*

"Good afternoon, you mean?" I yawned. "I have my doubts." Isabella might not be having a good *anything*. I turned my mind away from that dark thought and asked the first idle question that came into my head. "What's with the Latin names for everyone?"

"The wealthy like it that way." Alba rolled her eyes at me while changing her sleepwear; we even had to work on the weekends.

"So what's your given name?"

"I'm not that girl anymore. I have a master now, although he . . ." She sounded sad, and didn't clarify more. Maybe she and Jason had some disagreement and she didn't want to talk about it, so I didn't push her. I freshened up and went to the kitchen to make our brunch.

As I prepared some sandwiches for Cordis, I heard Benita's voice piercing the girl's usual clamor. "Girls, come quick! An announcement on the Regular Channel about Yorra Karakas."

I was close to giving in to the darkness, but the need to know what happened to Mom kept me anchored. On shaky legs, I stood behind the gathering room's door, looking at the Ológramma's image in the void.

"Glory to Elpax and its brave citizens," said Hermes. "Under legal liability, all adults must switch to the Adult Channel at once in the private adult's room."

The national anthem started, and I gulped. *If Mom is getting out of prison, why can't children see the cheerful announcement?*

"In half an hour," he said once the anthem was done, "you will witness the recorded trial of the spy Yorra Karakas, who has confessed by her own free will to deliberately disrupting the Crossing Gate."

My body quivered in fear. *How is that possible? Jason promised*

271

everything was going to be all right!

"This morning, His Majesty King Alexei Stavros Vasilas issued a royal decree to Exclude the traitor and spy Yorra Karakas. You, the people of the great Kingdom of Elpax, will execute the judgment."

Dizziness coursed through me. "This is the punishment..." his words got louder. "Of all who tamper with the sanctities..." the room spun, and Hermes's voice echoed as if in a tunnel. "Of our great kingdom ..." the voices of the girls and Hermes got mixed up. "Glory to Elpax and its brave citizens ..." *How is that possible?* Mom, my pure Mom! Jason had assured me he would get her out. How did this happen? How ... how ... how ... ?

The processing alarm echoed, and my body froze in horror. Alba rushed to the kitchen and closed the door, blocking the Ológramma from my view.

"Leen, get ahold of yourself. Wipe that look off your face and come with me."

I stared at her with lost eyes, still in a state of denial. She grabbed my hand and walked me to Cordis's room.

"Shut the door, Alba," ordered Cordis. "Leen, look at me." She slapped my cheek to wake me up.

Cordis calling me by my actual name brought me to reality fast. There was no need to pretend anymore.

"What are you doing?" I jerked back. "Turn on the Ológramma. Hand me an Iméfono." I waved my hand, trying to get her to hurry. I needed an Iméfono now.

"Leen, listen ..." Alba tried to calm me down.

"No! You listen."

Cordis turned me toward her. "Lee—"

"Hand me the Iméfono!" I yelled at her. "I must confess now. I must . . ." A wave of numbness spread over me. I couldn't feel my fingers.

"I will ... Leen, I will," said Cordis. "Sit beside me, and I'll give you the Iméfono."

I sat next to her, and she put an arm around me to soothe my quivering body. She handed me her Iméfono. A short video from the Crossing Gate's security camera was playing on it, showing Mom rescuing me.

"Someone hacked this recording and broadcasted the film to the public," explained Cordis.

"What . . . what do you mean?"

She took the Iméfono from my hand. "Most of the citizens had seen the film before the government wiped it off the National Network. The rebels wanted to show the citizens how corrupt the kingdom was for holding an innocent woman in Inferos who simply wanted to save her daughter from the harmful energy of the Crossing Gate. She wasn't a spy, as the news announced. Your mother will be fine."

I shook my head. "No one can stop the royal order. Give me the Iméfono."

She sighed. "I will. But wait. There's something else I have to show you." She handed me a giant headset, which was something I'd never seen before. "After you see this, we'll talk."

I stared at the device without understanding. Cordis placed it on my head, and she touched a button to turn it on.

I was watching a scene through someone else's eyes, standing in a lush ballroom. It seemed that every corner had been decorated for a royal event. There were vases of white lilies everywhere. In the middle of the room sat Queen Olympia in an elegant white dress. Beside her was King Alexei, wearing his crown and royal military uniform, holding her hand.

Oh, it's their wedding day.

A young woman ambled toward the couple, escorted by the royal guards and well-built men. Her face was covered with tattoos that extended to her neck. That would have to be a diviner from the Alphatoli province. She began by reading Alexei's and Olympia's palms. She predicted the total nonsense of their happily ever after. *As if there's such a thing!* Then, she reached for Thaddeus, who sat in the corner. I could see the pain in his eyes. I could feel his suffering. He was heartbroken. Losing one's love hurts like a thousand knives tearing the rest of you into shadow.

The diviner was intense; she looked at his palm for a long time. The air around her changed. I felt it was her way of building up suspense for her impending prophecy.

"I see nothing," she announced, and looked away.

The whole ballroom reverberated with sarcastic laughter. Thaddeus stared at her with hatred. I couldn't blame him. She had mocked him with her prediction, and I knew there would be devastating repercussions for that.

"Reading the *greats* is impossible for the commons!" Thaddeus shouted. Silence reigned in the ballroom, leaving only the sound of his footsteps cracking on the floor as he rushed out, desperately trying to mute his anger.

What a cruel game that Olympia or Arianna had played to embarrass him in front of everyone. I understood why Thaddeus had turned villainous. If I had such a family, I probably would also become such a person. Yet, that didn't give him the right to kill innocent people.

My vision jumped to another place. I was watching a scene through a keyhole. An empty room lit by an orange searchlight in the corner. In the middle of the room, Prince Thaddeus sat on a stone chair, one leg above the other. His eyes burned with anger and frustration. The viewer pulled away from the keyhole and looked to the left, at the same diviner who had insulted Thaddeus in front of the others earlier. A hand stretched out to knock on the door, then opened it. "The diviner Nuri, Your Royal Highness."

I recognized the voice at once. It was Cordis. A very young Cordis.

The air turned ominous when Thaddeus laid his eyes on the diviner. I was sure something dreadful was about to happen. I watched through Cordis's eyes as she left the room, closing the door behind her. She ran to a gloomy side room and looked through a small hole in the wall.

The diviner bowed in silence and kept her head down. Thaddeus's voice boomed around the corners of the room with the force of his fury. "What are you hiding?"

The diviner looked up and approached him, treading slow. She took his palm and studied it carefully. "A waltz of sin and fire."

He waved his other hand for her to continue.

She gulped. "The Zetikas girl . . . a juvenile . . . an adult. She is living between the lines. She will raise the flame of love between the two worlds. The evil sinner will burn up, never to return. From its ashes, a wave of peace will be born to last all eternity."

I didn't understand the prophecy, but I noticed a stillness in Thaddeus. "Juveniles can't feel love in Elpax." The corner of his lips lifted along with his arrogant declaration.

My eyes went wide. I was the only juvenile I knew of who had felt love before her crossing!

"What was written in the book of Elpax is an inevitable reality. You cannot escape your destiny."

"So you're saying that destiny will happen. And you have seen it. But have you seen your own?" He swiftly arose, and with a slash of his sword, he ran the sharp blade into her neck. A horrified scream escaped me. He killed her; he had no conscience. All the empathy I'd felt for him disappeared as he wiped the sword on her black cloak. Two guards entered to take care of the body. Cordis rushed into the room again to help them.

I took off the headset, jumping away from Cordis, pointing at her with an accusing finger. My shaking words came out fast. "H . . . how did that happen? How could I see through your eyes?"

She moved away a lock of hair to show me a tiny black dot behind her ear. "Queen Arianna implanted a device called a *sitirá* in my head. She ordered me to follow Thaddeus and record everything he did. With this headset, I can play back my memories and show them to anyone I want, according to her orders."

Icy waves took over my body. *What is my life coming to?* I'd seen murders after becoming an adult. First Mr. Barros and Kosmos, then a man being killed on the road in this neighborhood. But that was the first time I'd seen so much hatred and darkness in a human being.

"You helped him!" I yelled. "He killed her in cold blood. And you . . . you helped him to hide her body. You were a part of her murder."

Cordis closed her eyes in defeat. "I had no choice, Leen. No choice at all. He killed the two guards, and he was about to kill me too. But Queen Arianna smuggled me out of the palace to Zetikas."

Alba got me a glass of water, and Cordis continued with her explanation.

"Please calm down, Leen. I have seen a lot of horrible things in the palace that I can show you. Thaddeus is truly evil, and everyone wants to get rid of him."

"Why did you show me this?"

She stared hard at me. "You heard the prophecy. You're the only juvenile who is stuck between two ID lines."

My eyes popped out. "What the hell are you talking about?"

She walked closer to me. "The adult-juvenile who doesn't have sin-spots on her body is the one who can light the fire and burn the evil prince." She looked pointedly at me.

"I won't!" I paced the room with shaky legs. Her words made sense, but my brain was still denying it. "Have you lost your mind?"

"Haven't you seen the royal family in your dreams?"

I stopped my pacing. How did she know that?

At my silence, she added. "Oshina told me she sent you those dreams so you would understand the reason behind your mission."

I narrowed my eyes, trying to remember where I heard that name before.

"The diviner who read your palm at your friend's wedding," she explained.

I recalled what Oshina predicted at Mary's wedding: *Mark my words, you might carry a red color that will generate a lost peace.* I realized that Oshina told me about the torch that I saw in my dream—the one Prometheus gave me. Now I understood why I saw the royal family in my dreams. It all seemed to lead to a common goal. Thaddeus.

276

A bittersweet smile spread on my face. "You knew I was the one, and you never told me. You waited until they sentenced my mother to death. I wasted precious time in your club, hiding like a rat instead of helping my mother escape. How could you?"

Cordis jerked back at my words, and her face hardened. "If I'd told you from the start, would you have believed me?"

"So you waited until I had a motive to kill Prince Thaddeus?"

"I only follow orders. I don't decide."

"Orders from who?"

"The queen mother."

CHAPTER 34

MY THOUGHTS SCATTERED. WHENEVER I tied a thread to another idea, I lost my comprehension again. My breaths quickened with apprehension. I couldn't think straight. Logical reasoning escaped me.

"As soon as you fell in the Crossing Gate," explained Cordis, "Oshina went to Queen Arianna and told her what she saw in your palm. Queen Arianna planned your escape with your friend Jason."

My limbs started shaking, and I had to sit on the ground while misery drowned me. Arianna was the third party Jason had told me about.

I finally understood why Thaddeus always attended the juvenile's Crossing Day in Zetikas. He wanted to make sure that he would get rid of the half adult-juvenile once she failed to cross. And that was why he Eliminated my crossing consultant, because Mr. Kosmos probably told Thaddeus that I was harmless. It turned out that I wasn't.

I frowned as I tried to put all the events together. "Cordis, the diviner had said that I *may* hold a torch. That means I have a choice. But you're making it sound like I am the chosen one who must do this extreme act.

Can't King Alexei do something?"

"The king is suffering from a severe illness. Besides, he doesn't make any decisions. He doesn't even know what's happening in the kingdom. Thaddeus controls everything. He's responsible for all the unjust rules against women, and even men. Thaddeus wants people to rebel against his brother so he will be the king."

I exchanged a quick look with Alba. *Do the rebels know they're focusing on the wrong royals?*

Cordis continued. "Queen Arianna's men are on their way to drive you to Alphatoli. There, you will meet with Oshina, who will instruct you about your mission. Queen Arianna has promised to rescue your mother in return for doing this."

This can't be true. This is a nightmare. I must kill the prince to save Mom. How come I was being offered a reward for a sin that would usually get me punished?

"Cordis, I'm not an assassin, and I don't have the right to do that."

Her sarcastic smile showed up. "Neither does the government, but they do it all the time, darling. They're about to kill your innocent mother. Consider it self-defense."

Tense silence prevailed among us as Cordis turned on the Ológramma. I kept pacing the room until the device lit up with the flickering flash of orange color. The sound of the anthem blared from its stereos.

"Warning: adult viewing only. Viewing under guidance is advised for newly crossed adults."

Under guidance? Were we about to see something so unusual and shocking that even adults would be disturbed by it?

Minutes later, Hermes appeared with a grim face and tension radiating across his visage. I realized that something catastrophic was about to occur.

Hermes was standing in the public yard of Theirna. The camera panned over the Arch of Victory behind him as he moved toward the mic. The stone arch had a peacock logo in the middle and the words *Justice is the Basis of Governance* written below it.

"Glory to Elpax and its honorable citizens," he said. "The Exclusion of Yorra Karakas will begin now."

The Earth stopped spinning with his words. The camera moved to include the wide square surrounded by armed Law Corps, and my mother in the center with her feet bound in chains.

"MAMA!" I screamed, tears falling from my horrified eyes.

"Hush, Leen. Alba, go and make sure the other girls stay in the gathering room," Cordis whispered. "Don't worry. Queen Arianna will act."

I prayed that her words would come true. Mom stood straight with dignity, her body draped in a red cloak, while many other men in teal cloaks formed a wide circle around her with stones in their hands. The royal guards separated them from an enormous crowd of citizens, who surrounded the square and shouted slogans.

Looking closely, I could see Mom's pale face had lost its shine, and her eyes were wrapped in misery. The smile that had found its way to her face after years of suffering was gone. I gulped, and my pain threatened to choke me. How much injustice and torture had she gone through despite being pure of soul? Oh, Mom!

One of the soldiers approached Mom and removed the cloak covering her body. I gasped, my hand flying to my mouth. Mom stood naked in front of everyone. Sin-spots filled her body, glittering in the sun's rays. *How did she get those spots? What happened to her in that interrogation?*

"The Exclusion of Yorra Karakas will be carried out by way of stoning!" announced Hermes.

It felt like a freezing wind went through my body. I turned to Cordis in horror. *Stoning?*

"Let the one among you who is without sin be the first to cast the stone!" yelled Hermes. "For the sake of justice, the king has carefully chosen some of the most honorable men in the kingdom—most of whom work in legal affairs—to start the process."

The men, too, took off their cloaks, and showed that their half-naked

280

bodies were clean of sin-spots. I went close to the image and pointed out a man to Cordis. "That one. Isn't he the despicable judge who betrayed his wife in your club?"

Cordis bit her lip with sorrow and nodded. I couldn't believe Thaddeus's insolence. They had painted the men with Crepito to hide their sin-spots and drawn them on Mom's body instead. How ethical was that?

"An honorable worker has volunteered to begin the process," stated Hermes. "Please step forward, honorable Santos Evgenís. You may throw the first stone."

A thunderbolt struck me upon hearing that name. My lips trembled, my eyes widening in fear as I watched my father's face. That despicable man deserved to be Excluded, not my mother. Never my mother.

"I know that silver-haired man!" exclaimed Cordis. "He is Lotos's brother. She used to work in the palace as King Stavros's concubine."

Her words stunned me. So that was why my aunt had rebelled against Thaddeus's mother, Queen Rhea?

My father's voice brought me back. He raised his hand and shouted, "Glory to Elpax and its honorable ones!"

The crowd, too, screamed the slogan, repeating his words over and over.

There were no words in the Greek dictionary, or in any book in the universe, to describe the emotions I felt in my heart. *When inhumanity joins hands with filth and injustice, then you are sure to be in the land of vermin—the land of Elpax.*

Silence spread across the square when my father stepped closer to Mom. I could read his lips. "I'm sorry, Yorra."

Why was my father apologizing to Mom? He never did that after hitting her. Mom lifted her sad eyes, and I wailed in pain. I could feel her wound in my heart. I could hear the howling of her soul, crying out for justice.

Father lifted the stone and shouted, "Long live the Republic!" He turned around and threw the stone at Hermes, hitting him right in the head. The Law Corps shot my father at once, and he dropped dead on the ground.

My mind could hardly analyze what he'd done. The events that happened next were utter chaos. Many men in the crowd threw stones at those surrounding my mother, and some of the punishers reciprocated. The Law Corps drew their weapons, shooting randomly at everyone. All we could see and hear were people shouting and getting shot. It was a complete bloodbath. Bodies of men lay on the ground with blood oozing from their wounds. Many tried to run away. A stampede ensued. The massacre was indescribable until the live broadcast was cut off. In the melee, I didn't know what happened to Mom.

I stood with my jaw dropped next to Cordis, gazing at the empty wall where the broadcast had been shown. Meanwhile, a long and ominous alarm echoed through the kingdom. I'd never heard it before. I turned to Cordis, who whispered a line that caused the floor to slide under my feet.

"A state of emergency has been declared in the kingdom."

CHAPTER 35

THE NOISE IN THE STREET picked up swiftly. I looked through the window. Everyone was running to the grocery stores, while the owners tried to push them out to shut their shops and run home. The wealthy's cars hurried through the neighborhood, and the girls were yelling from the gathering room.

Cordis rushed out to talk to the girls. Alba came along and stood before the window, watching the chaos in the street.

"Now we're all the same," she remarked, pointing to the wealthy's cars. "No one would survive the emergency state. Not even them."

But I knew better. They would find a way out of it.

Cordis came back and ordered Alba to leave us alone. As soon as she closed the door behind her, she turned to me. "Your mom is safe and was taken back to Inferos. Queen Arianna has ordered you to stay in the club. The neighborhood's gates are closed again, and no one is allowed to drive in the streets, so she'll send someone to pick you up in a few days. Don't look so worried."

But I was worried. Not only for Mom, but for what Father had done. What would happen to my sisters? They carried his name, and he'd called for a republic. How would the government deal with this situation?

"Cordis. I need to call Jason."

She handed me her Iméfono. I tried to call him many times, but he wasn't responding. I tried to calm down my heart. The twins were still in their childhood, and there was no way the government would harm them. Because that would cause a civil war. Children represented a red line . . . I hoped.

The next morning, we huddled in the gathering room, watching the news. Hermes appeared with the word *Urgent* flashing behind him. There was a bandage around his head, and he looked irritated.

"Glory to Elpax and its brave citizens. The terrorist acts carried out by vandals yesterday caused substantial damage to the State Electricity company. His Majesty King Alexei wants to inform the citizens that electricity will be cut off at 6:00 p.m. until further notice. Fellow citizens, be sure to charge your cars, heating devices, emergency lights, and anything else that runs on batteries. Starting from now, you are allowed to shop for two hours to buy your essentials. Glory to Elpax."

He ended his speech abruptly. The girls got up in resentment and anger. Obscene insults about me and my mother flew around the room. I left for the kitchen with the tea tray, trying to hold myself together. Anger overwhelmed me, and I threw the tray into the sink, smashing the teacups with a loud noise. Cordis's voice sounded behind me.

"Enough is enough. We have a lot of work to do. Where's Sarah?"

I rushed into the gathering room as she began her instructions. "I'll allow each of you a five-minute shower today. Get your blankets. All of us will sleep in the living room. Benita, cook all the food that's in the fridge today. Don't open the freezer; let that food remain cold for as long as possible."

Tensions rose in the air as Cordis continued. "Alba, charge the heater, radio, and searchlights. Rose, you will buy food."

Rose shook her head, refusing this dangerous mission. Cordis's eyes widened, and she was about to yell at the scared girl when I stepped forward.

"I'll go," I said, and glanced at Rose. "If you don't mind." I needed a distraction from this suffocating atmosphere.

Rose agreed at once. Cordis didn't speak for a while. Her eyes moved back and forth between us.

"Fine," she said. "Come."

Cordis stepped out of the room, and I followed. Once we reached her chamber, she headed to the closet and gave me some money. "Buy oatmeal, corn, and dates. I'll call the nearby church guard, Emilio, to help you with that. Wait for him outside the Church—don't go inside."

I nodded. I knew that all the holy places had an ID scanner on their doors, even in this neighborhood. The government banned all knowledge about religions from children and juveniles because all of them called for love. We only learned that there was a merciful creator, and we called him God.

"Queen Arianna didn't plan what happened to your mom," said Cordis, "but your father acted under the orders of a secret party of workers who have been planning a coup against the royal family for a long time. Your mom's trial was the right moment to act."

"The same party who damaged the elec—"

"The party did nothing to the electricity." She slammed the closet door shut. "The government turned it off themselves as a way to force the rebellion into submission."

"Do you mean the Electric company is still working?"

"You can bet that nothing harmed the company. But Thaddeus will not allow the rebels to appear as martyrs. Instead, he'll force the people to get rid of the rebels themselves by making us desperate for basic needs."

I nodded. She gave me a black scarf. "From now on, hide most of your face with this. Just say you are feeling cold if anyone asks you about it. I don't know if we can buy makeup anymore."

"Thank you." I hurriedly pulled on my cloak, climbed down the stairs, and pushed through the main door.

Cordis was right. We were all being held hostage to subdue the rebels.

We gathered in the living room on the second floor with just an emergency light guiding us, shivering from the cold. It had been thirteen weeks since the government gave us electricity for more than an hour a day. The streets appeared deserted and cold, and tension was infused everywhere. Soon, the intermittent roar of planes terrorized us. I turned on the radio, our only contact with the outside world, and looked out the window. The news was all about the people who had died of cold and hunger because of the rebels.

In the middle of September, right after the government announced the state of emergency, the rebels tried to persuade people to join their cause. Each party had its own agenda until the Law Corps gunned them down. Some called for a new government—a republic instead of a monarchy. Others called for monarchy and a parliament elected by the people. Until Thaddeus played his cards one month later. He issued a royal statement that he'd isolated King Alexei due to his mental illness, along with his wife and Queen Arianna. He set up a new constitution that would cancel all the rules and regulations that King Alexei had supposedly issued, from the word-catchers to the brothel work, as if those things had been the king's orders in the first place.

All the provinces, except Zetikas, accepted the deal, and electricity came back into their homes. The rebels here knew the truth about Thaddeus, most probably because Alba had told them. They wanted him out of the entire game of thrones. Still, Thaddeus was baying for blood. This conflict turned our quiet province into a burning land of war, filled with divisions between parties, each wanting the royals to fulfill their own demands.

In response to the uprising, Thaddeus set a curfew in Zetikas in early November, but that didn't curb the instability. The Law Corps bombed

Zetikas with a massive amount of Photoflash—sound and tear gas bombs. Then came the warplanes. Though they were directed at the rebels' offices, their devastating bombs also landed on the homes of civilians from small towns like Vetamosi, Argayosa, and Bafakios. The wealthy moved to the capital city of Theirna with their middle-class workers, leaving only the working-class to fight it out.

The tremors from the Law Corps' heavy artillery shook our nightclub, and bullet-ridden buildings were all that was left in Maculosus. Violence didn't spare the children either. People started disappearing. Nobody knew if they were kidnapped or dead.

Nevertheless, the Law Corps were eager to broadcast the hideous destruction of our province across the sky. They wanted to make sure that we would stop the rebels, which was what the people did. Moreover, no one was safe from Thaddeus's spies. No one was safe from anyone.

We got snippets of news from Emilio and the radio. There were no other means of communication. Iméfonos were dead as usual, and I'd heard no order from Queen Arianna since all of this started. Although her last orders were clear—that I should stay put—I couldn't stand it anymore. I had to do something. I had to go to Alphatoli, or Thaddeus would kill the million citizens living in Zetikas while I stood idly by.

A code of knocks on the door pierced our silence. Holding the flashlight, I headed downstairs. I opened the three locks on the door and saw Emilio's pale face.

"Here. This is all I could get," he said, giving me a bag that held three cans of tuna, two cans of beans, and some dried carrots.

I looked at him. "This will not suffice. We are too many here."

"This is all I could get. A gentleman spared some of his rations for you. There's no food in the district. Looters have robbed all the shops dry."

I sighed. "Emilio, can you find me a ride to get out of the neighborhood?"

He ducked his head, thinking for a while. "I know someone. But I have to warn you, this is very dangerous."

"I can manage it."

He sighed. "All right. Get dressed, and I'll be back in ten minutes."

I smiled and closed the door behind him. My plan was to go home to Roses Hill, collect my savings, and pay for a ride to Alphatoli so I could at last meet with Oshina. *First, I should ask Cordis how to find her.*

As I walked upstairs, an alarm sounded, causing the windows of the club to rattle. As I reached the second floor, my heart quivered at the sight beyond the window. A warplane flew over us, firing upon the church's towers, and the heavy bell on its steeple fell to the ground. The earth shook under my feet. I screamed in panic along with the girls.

"Girls, it's not safe here!" yelled Cordis. "We have to find a shelter. Scoot!"

I could hear the bullet sounds outside the nightclub's door. A grenade shattered the windows and doors. The girls ran everywhere, trying to escape. I sprinted to Alba's room for my bronchodilators; my asthma was acting up in the dust. I called out to Alba in a hushed tone as men crashed into the club and climbed up to the dorm. Alba got in and shut the door fast, and we rammed the dresser against it.

"Under my bed—chop chop," she whispered.

Heavy treads reached the door, and someone slammed against it with all their weight over and over. The dresser started sliding a little. Alba pushed me under the bed. Just as she was about to hide beside me, the door fell open. I held my breath; I could see the man's feet approaching her.

Alba resisted as he tried to get her on the bed. She fought him with great effort, kicking his knees and scratching. He punched her hard, and she fell on the mattress. I heard her clothes being torn; the bed shook from their combined weight as she screamed.

I have to do something. I must save her.

Gathering my strength, I crawled out from under the bed, took the heavy brass vase from the corner of the room, and crept toward the man pawing Alba. Anger rose in me like a wave of lava. All the hurt and injustice in the kingdom came crashing down on me. The days that I had spent in near darkness, starving, not knowing if I would live or die, lent their strength to me.

With a heavy swing, I smashed the vase on the back of his head. He stopped moving, and his body slumped over her. Alba quickly pushed him off, and I helped her off the bed. Her clothes were torn, and her body was covered with bruises. We looked at the man; he was down for the moment. We could hear the girls' screeches from the other rooms.

I pulled a jacket over Alba's shoulders. "Let's hide behind the water tanks."

We had just turned to leave the room when the man caught hold of my hair from behind. He dragged me back with one hand and slammed Alba's head against the wall with the other.

"You bitch!" He slapped me hard. "Now it's your turn." His fist punched me in the stomach. I fell down, gasping in pain. He pulled his gun out. I knew it was my last moment on this Earth as ruthless determination glittered in his eyes.

A shot rang through the room, and a warm spray of blood washed over my face as his body dropped to the ground. I turned to see Cordis with a gun in her hand.

"Both of you, get a move on to the roof."

I helped Alba up, and the three of us headed to the roof. As I shut the metal door behind me, my shaking words came out. "What about the other girls?"

Cordis headed toward the laundry room. "I can't help them all."

She returned with some sheets, waving for me to help her. We knotted them together as the men pushed against the heavy metal door. Cordis tied one end of the sheet rope to a water pipe and sent the rest of it down, making a pathway for us to escape. She looked at me.

The men pushed against the door, their voices getting angrier with each effort.

I shook my head. "Let Alba go first. Give me your gun."

She handed me the weapon and instructed Alba to slid down the

289

knotted sheets with her feet walking down the wall. Cordis followed her. "Come on, Leen!" yelled Cordis from the street.

As I grabbed the sheet, the door gave way.

Looking at the men's leering faces, I knew they would rape and kill me. I didn't think twice about my actions. I could only feel the adrenaline pumping into me. I just wanted to survive this ordeal. As they rushed toward me, I shot all the bullets before I could stop myself. All three of them dropped on the ground. They didn't die, but I managed to stall them.

I hid the gun in my pocket and slid down the sheet, trying to reach the ground fast when someone screamed from above. "That bitch shot them!"

I looked up. And bullets rained down on me.

CHAPTER 36

I STARTLED, AND MY HANDS let go of the sheets. My body fell into a garbage tank. Cordis pulled on my arm to help me escape before the man and his companions followed us.

We held each other's hands as we raced through the suffocating fog and the dim glimmer of the emergency lights. When we reached the crossroads, we found it blocked by heavy bags and seething with masked young men. They were shooting heavily from behind the sacks at the Law Corps patrolling the road. Scared people ran in all directions, trying to survive. Before we could decide where to go, a loud roar approached us, and the ground trembled violently.

A piece of heavy artillery emerged from the fog, only a few meters from where we were standing. It was the first time I'd seen weaponry this large at this proximity. My heart pounded as it approached, and the tiny hairs at the base of my neck rose in warning. The artillery stopped and released a flood of water, which indiscriminately hit the masked men.

For the first time in my life, I saw flesh melting and falling off bones, and the acrid smell of burning bodies rose in the air. I would never forget that smell or the men's screaming for the rest of my life. It was pure agony. Bile rose in my throat. Alba bent down and vomited. A masked woman pulled us behind a car and shouted, "Don't stand near the *firewater!*" She looked around and pointed to a broken door opposite us. "There. Hide there."

I held Alba's palm tightly, and we set off at lightning speed with Cordis. Rocks and shards of glass scattered everywhere. We stumbled around with strangers; people ran in a blind panic, trying to find shelter. I heard the whistle of an aircraft over our heads. It dropped a gas bomb in the middle of the deadly fog. I let go of Alba's hand and started coughing violently. My heartbeat rose as I hyperventilated, trying to breathe a tiny cascade of clean air that was nowhere to be found. The chemicals burned my lungs and caused my eyes to water. I couldn't see anything. Two puffs of my inhaler, and I could breathe a bit.

With such cloudy vision, I lost all sense of direction. The fog and dust were claustrophobic. I turned around, looking for Alba and Cordis, screaming their names hysterically until a firm hand grabbed me.

"To the church. Hurry!" yelled Cordis.

"Where's Alba?"

"I lost her." She pulled me onward. I wanted to search for Alba, but Cordis said she couldn't be far away, and we would search for her once the situation settled down.

My feet pounded the pavement while my heart stung with sorrow. We ran toward the church, expecting a bullet to hit us at any time. We entered the crowded chapel, and the nuns closed the door behind us. My eyes widened at the giant cross in the middle of the hall. It was the first time I had seen the inside of a church.

"We have no time." Cordis pulled me to one of the long chairs and handed me a penknife. "Cut your hair."

I stilled, thinking about the friend I'd just lost. Cordis didn't wait for me—she held my locks and started cutting them erratically.

"You have to look like a boy," was her only comment.

I looked around the high-ceilinged place. Women were sobbing and howling, their clothes bloody and tattered. The war had ravaged their faces; they looked terrified. It would take years for my province to come out of the repercussions of this war. It had stamped its effects on all of us.

"We have to find an Iméfono that works to call Queen Arianna," said Cordis after she finished cutting my hair. She handed me her penknife, and just then, the church's door was slammed hard.

Silence reigned. All eyes were fixed on the entrance.

"Open up, bitches!" yelled a Law Corps soldier from outside. The door rattled again as they tried to push it open.

"Get back!" yelled the old nun. "Try to find a place to hide."

I stood up, my eyes widening in horror. This was one enormous hall. *Where should we hide?* Women moved backward with every push on the door. Cordis and I ran to the far-left corner, where there were stairs behind a red curtain. Just as we were about to climb them, the main door crashed open with a singular joint force. Law Corps ran in, firing random bullets everywhere.

Cordis pushed me into the stairwell and screamed. I turned around. A Law Corps soldier was holding her hair. He didn't hesitate to shoot her right in her stomach. Her body dropped on the ground, blood oozing from the bullet wounds.

Before he could make another move, I screamed and jumped toward him in a rage, kicking him between his legs. He bent down, and I stabbed the penknife into his body wherever I could reach, over and over, until I was bathed in his blood. His body dropped dead on the ground.

I heard the Law Corps leaving the church, and I rushed to kneel next to Cordis, holding her shaking hand. Her mouth was full of blood, and she was trying to take her last breath.

"Hang on," I said in between sobs. "I'll get help."

She squeezed my hand with all the remaining strength in her body. "It was an honor to help you," she whispered, and coughed up some more

293

blood. I looked on helplessly as blood gushed out of her stomach wounds. "Remember me, Leen. Don't let our blood have drained for nothing."

"Stay with me, Cordis. I need you," I begged her. I looked around the quiet place. "HELP! Somebody, help me!"

I screamed until I had no voice left. This couldn't be happening to me. It seemed like a bloody nightmare.

Cordis whispered, looking straight into my eyes. "Kill . . . that . . . bastard . . . Thaddeus." She coughed again and added a few words while taking her last breath. "Tell my boy the truth . . . tell Jason I love him. Promise me."

Trying to stop my tears from falling, I replied, "I promise you, Cordis. Just stay with me, and you can tell him yourself."

She gave me a faint smile and stopped breathing. Her eyes lost their shine.

"No . . . Cordis . . . get up." I shook her. "Don't leave me. Get up! Cordis, get up!"

I slapped her and screamed her name. Her eyes remained open and lifeless, and a single tear trickled down her cheek. Just one tear for the precious life that was killed so brutally. A wail of agony split the air. I realized that it had come from me as I embraced her body. It was the first time I'd seen death that close. I had lost another person, this time while holding her hand. My heart felt empty once again. The sounds of the universe disappeared, and everything became quiet.

A nearby light bomb pulled me out of the vacuous moment. Another followed, causing dust to spread everywhere. After a while, I heard a man's voice from outside. "Corps are gone, everybody."

I let go of Cordis's hand, walked to the dead soldier, and grabbed his gun. Now I was determined to get to Alphatoli at any cost. The war had to end; Thaddeus had crossed a line.

Dead bodies were scattered all over the streets. Some honorable people were trying to help the injured. I walked among the blood and bodies, trying to find a way out of this neighborhood when a familiar voice called out my name.

"Leen . . . Leen!"

I turned around. Alba was getting down from a truck. I hurried to hug her, pleased to see her alive and well. "I thought I'd lost you!"

"I thought so too." She pulled back, scanning my appearance. "Are you hurt?"

"It's not my blood."

"Where's Cordis?" she asked, looking around for her.

I shook my head at that question.

She placed a hand over her mouth. "She's all I've got." Tears fell down her cheeks. Loud sobs tore from her throat for a long time as I embraced her.

"I'll honor her memory," I said, pulling back. "I promise you. But we need to get out of here. How did you get on the truck?"

"That gentleman helped me." She pointed to a red-haired man about my size standing in front of the truck. "His name is Noah."

I patted her shoulder and made my way to him. "Excuse me, where is this truck going?"

Noah replied as he wrapped a bandage around a girl's head. "To a Safe Cell in Zoiterra."

"Can you drop me off in Alphatoli, then?"

"Impossible, Miss. They will shoot any car trying to cross the border." He turned to me. "Are you getting in the truck? Corps will soon come back. You can try to find other aid from Zoiterra."

I looked at Alba and waved for her to get in the truck. Turning to Noah, I said, "Since you are here to help, I suggest you follow me."

"Where to?"

I was already moving toward a nearby brothel; the one I visited so many weeks earlier. "To free those girls."

Noah and I gathered some men and women, all with knives and weapons. We were all driven by anger and the desire for revenge. Slamming the door open, I found the dirty manager trying to escape, but the men caught him immediately. He started screaming, telling them that he was only following the king's orders, and all the money was going right to the government.

I looked right into his eyes. "And your orders were to rape them whenever you wanted, too?"

His eyes widened, and the men spat on him. With the other women's help, I started un-cuffing the girls and tearing the curtains to cover their bodies up. Many of them were dead, broken by hunger and abuse. The survivors were severely injured, but that didn't stop them from running to the manager and beating him until blood covered his body. Together, they carried him to the main door, where they tied a rope to hang him.

I turned to Noah after we finished releasing the last girl. "We should bury the dead girls decently."

"Let's find a priest."

And we did. It took a few hours, but we did. We also buried Cordis.

After we finished, I climbed into the truck with the other women and girls. As we set off on our way to Zoiterra, I swore that I would get revenge. For all the Elpaxians, I would do it.

I am coming for you, Thaddeus.

PART V

"ENILINI"

Would you fight to earn the other half?

CHAPTER 37

"LEEN, WAKE UP."

A voice penetrated my deep slumber, and my blurred vision cleared. I sat up straight, my eyes taking in the rough stone around me. Last night, the Law Corps closed the borders of Zoiterra, and we had to find another place to hide, which ending up being a cave in Mount Maroon. The darkness had stopped me from exploring it when we arrived. In the daylight, I could see that it was big, packed with women and children gathered in circles. There was an odd putrefying moldy smell, and the number of unwashed bodies didn't help. A medium-sized battery-powered fireplace sat in the middle, and searchlights occupied the corners.

"You want to sit closer to the fireplace?" hissed Alba.

I turned to her and shook my head. "You go; I have something else on my mind. Keep my gun with you." I got up, dusting off my clothes, and walked toward the cave's entrance. I looked around for Noah, but he was nowhere to be seen. Another taller man with a thick orange beard stood just outside, smoking.

"Excuse me, do you have a working Iméfono?" I said.

He looked at me, blowing away the smoke. "Iméfonos are dead."

I couldn't give up now. I had to call Jason or Mary and find Oshina. I couldn't sit in the cave for days, doing nothing until the borders opened again. Time was something I didn't have much of.

"Then I need to go to Roses Hill. Can you help me with that?"

"Listen, lady, if you want to leave alone, then fine. But all the borders between the provinces are closed."

"Until when?"

"Until things cool down. Then you can go to Roses Hill or across the borders."

I stared at him for a while, then took off the necklace Erick had given me. I looked at it with sorrow, remembering the innocence and joy, the love and the stolen kisses. Then, I recalled the war and the destruction—the people I'd killed—and my heart steeled over. I gave the chain to the man. "That should be enough to pay for the trip."

"We don't take payment."

"I insist."

He looked at it carefully, then scratched the pendant against his teeth. He returned it to me with a laugh. "That would not pay for a few steps out of this place. It's not original—just a simple accessory."

I gazed at him as if he were a fool. "Impossible. It's pure gold."

"Where's the stamp?"

"Huh?"

He sighed impatiently. "Every gold article is stamped with a universal symbol to signify its purity." He gave it back to me. "But this necklace doesn't have one, and even scratching it removes the gold plating. Who fooled you and told you it was real?"

I looked at the chain with astonishment. Erick's gift had turned out to be fake—just like him. Everything in our relationship had been a mirage. Lies. Lies. Lies. He'd lied to me in the most brutal manner. I thought I had no tears left in my eyes anymore, but a warm one ran down on my cheek.

Noah approached us with a skinny girl. She'd styled her silver-mint hair into crochet braids which fell over her shoulders, reflecting the beauty of her dark-brown skin. Her voice reached us first. "We have to recharge the battery of the heater, and the recharging panel is too heavy for me to spread alone. Come." She looked at me, and her eyes widened. "Derek, why is the girl crying?"

He whispered something in her ear. The girl looked at me with pity. "Don't cry, please." She shook my hand. "I am Evelyn."

"Sarah." I wiped my tear away. "Please take me home to Roses Hill. I have money there. I can pay you then."

"We don't take money," said Evelyn. She glanced at Derek, who shrugged and pointed at Noah. "Noah will drive you to the highway, but you have to manage it on your own from there. I must warn you, Roses Hill is very dangerous right now."

I nodded and went back to Alba, who was sitting with a group of women. I leaned over and whispered, "I must leave. Promise me you'll take care of yourself."

She shook her head. "I'm coming with you."

"No. I can't allow that. It's too dangerous. You'll be safe here with the group."

She tried to argue, but I stopped her. This was my fight now, and I couldn't be the reason for her being raped or killed. We hugged, but a mother screamed at us to stop while putting her hand in front of her kid's eyes.

Pulling back, I rolled my eyes at the woman and took my gun from Alba. I headed outside the cave and halted, watching the snow, which had started to come down heavily.

"Sarah, we can't drive in this blizzard," said Noah. "We have to wait for it to pass."

Amid the heavy, cruel snow, I collapsed at the cave's entrance, struggling to breathe, battling to stay alive. In . . . out . . . in . . . out. As I lay on the ground, my warm breath made clouds of condensation, blurring my vision. Through half-open eyes, I saw a stark and unforgiving world as the wind whistled through the trees.

The cave was crowded inside, and we had no room to lie down except a space near the mouth of the cave. Alba sat close to me, and I hoped our body warmth would prevent us from freezing. The snow covered the ground like a bright white garment. The clouds gathered like a lid, locking us under its mercy. The wind's sounds had risen. It echoed through the crevices in the cave, like a siren warning us of our frozen death.

Looking at so much snow was hypnotic. Its presence filled my soul with despair and misery. My mind raced, barely touching the reality of our lives. The bright white color, which should have symbolized peace, brought desperation and helplessness.

In the past nine days, all we'd had was a bowl of cold water. And the blizzard had intensified. The world outside the cave had darkened. As time passed, death was more a known certainty than life. Evelyn, Noah, and Derek couldn't do anything until it stopped snowing, as they needed the solar power to recharge their truck.

The old woman next to me moaned. It was horrible to see the elderly shed tears. Those who thought that all their life battles were over; instead found themselves confronting calamity.

I put my jacket on Alba's tenuous feeble body. A blue color covered her lips, and her chest moved fast as she breathed. I shook her, slapped her cheeks, pinched her. She barely flinched. I could discern a slight flick of her finger, but no other reaction. I had to be satisfied with that. I couldn't do much now. I spoke into her ear, praying she'd hear me. "Alba, hold on . . . just a few more days. Please."

The women and children sank into silence. This was a forced stillness, where the freezing bodies and the lack of food left them lethargic. Their faces looked as if there was nothing worth fighting for in this world—not

302

even their own lives. There, at that moment, the women hugged their children close.

"Lily," Alba whispered. "My name is Lily."

I held her cold palm closer to my heart. We huddled together, hoping for more body warmth. The weather raged hard as our bodies slowed down. I drifted off. The constricting band around my chest intensified—a hollow sense of loss from deep within me. My eyelids lowered, and unconsciousness overtook me.

My foggy mind slipped into darkness, recalling some events of the past. Puzzle pieces clicked together in my head. It was suddenly clear that Queen Arianna and Thaddeus both knew about the juvenile who would fail in her third crossing from the very beginning.

Arianna knew about the prophecy way before I was born, because Cordis would have showed her the memory of Nuri telling Thaddeus the prophecy. Arianna wanted to find the adult-juvenile from the prophecy before Thaddeus did, so she started the psychological school reports program. And those reports were sent to her every year. That program was established before I even crossed to adolescence. Arianna was looking for a juvenile who had problems crossing to adulthood.

And then, after years of Arianna waiting, my name came up. Of course. Arianna knew that a juvenile from Zetikas who hesitated to cross twice would likely fail to cross over a third time. And she would be the one to kill Thaddeus.

Then, I thought of that night in the nightclub, when Alba and I tried to get some answers from Mr. Roussallis, the National Security Advisor. He said that Arianna ordered him to kill Thaddeus's men. They were most likely the same men who followed me in the white sedan after the library chase. Thaddeus, too, somehow knew that I had tried to cross twice before, and he sent the crossing consultant over to find out if I was a danger to him.

How weird that my mind couldn't connect everything together until it started to shut down. Both Arianna and Thaddeus had been watching me from the very beginning.

I woke up to the pitiful cry of a child. His mother had wandered out of the cave, trying to find anything to feed him. I closed my eyes, listening to the child whining in hunger. *I'm so sorry, my child. I wish I could turn back time so none of this happened. I wish I hadn't crossed or attended Mary's wedding. How I wish all of this was a dream and not the nightmare it turned out to be.*

I looked at the child's mother. She picked an olive from a dry branch. With a lingering awareness in my foggy mind, I had a single thought: *If a person picked a fruit before its full maturity, what would be its destiny?*

A single tear ran down my face for the child who'd been lost. Her innocence was stolen—I was an adult who had no time to grow up. Trust was precious and sparingly given. I had none left.

I was a pawn in a cruel game of opposing combatants—like a young fruit, naïve and hidden, yet ripe for picking.

How awful it was. Early maturity.

Still, the most frightening reality was my inability to mature when the time arrived.

If only I had known the powers at play. If only I had understood the others involved in the game before it was too late. I cried for myself and for the lives lost. I cried enough to fill the whole of Elpax with the innocence of my tears. A young fruit, hiding in a cave . . . dying.

304

CHAPTER 38

"YOUR ROYAL HIGHNESS, REMUS CAESAR, Emperor of the Modern Roman Empire, is waiting online."

I looked at the royal guard who spoke these words at the same time Thaddeus did. He raised one eyebrow and waved approvingly. The guard knocked his shoes on the floor and turned on the Ológramma before leaving the room.

I was standing in a study room, where Thaddeus sat behind a desk. He touched the remote control, and Caesar's image appeared in the void.

"My dearest Thaddeus," said Caesar. "It's been ages since the last time we spoke."

Thaddeus responded with a slow nod.

Caesar's blond eyebrows came together. "I miss our short, delightful conversations." His smug smile filled his handsome face. His blue eyes were so sharp that they forced me to step backward.

"I wish I could say the same." Thaddeus's tone was colder than a block of ice.

Caesar burst out laughing. "Well, it was a sure thing that your foul mood brought war into your country."

Oh! This is a vision of something that's happening right now. How weird is that?

Thaddeus stared at Caesar with his intense eyes. Ignoring his furious look, Caesar continued. "His Royal Highness knows that we have eyes and ears in every corner of his precious kingdom."

Thaddeus held the tip of his sharp sword, gazing at it for a while before uttering his next slow words. "Just a few insects that we have to crush."

Caesar got up off his chair and rambled around the room. I backed away from him.

"The prophecy said the war starts from Gaul," said Caesar. "I—"

"France," snapped Thaddeus coldly, interrupting Caesar.

The emperor gave a half-smile and continued with his speech. "I can't possibly tell you, my dear Thaddeus, how my great grandfather felt for this prophecy of Nostradamus. It was the spark that led him to restore the glories of our forefathers."

Thaddeus got up from his chair and ambled toward Caesar.

"One can't help being fond of prophecies. They give you a glimpse of the future." Caesar stepped closer, facing Thaddeus. "Do you believe in prophecies, Your Highness?"

My spine tingled. The hate in their looks was unmistakably evident.

"No."

"Then open the borders."

"Prove me wrong. I assume that the great Caesar of Rome doesn't have the time to be concerned about things that don't *belong* to his empire."

Caesar smirked. "Speak to your own benefit, Your Highness." He waved his hand. "Your valuable wealthy couldn't survive without our goods. Or could it be that the prince is *afraid* the rich will emigrate from his kingdom?" He raised one eyebrow.

Thaddeus gathered his hands behind his back and stood tall with pride. His eyes were pure ice. "I am quite surprised that Caesar dares to mention the word *afraid*, considering the history of our lands."

Caesar's eyes remained calm as a peaceful river, yet his breath crowded into his chest. The two rivals were still staring at each other when the scene faded, and I found myself gazing up at the cave's ceiling.

"The borders are open," I whispered, looking at the cave's entrance. *The borders are open, or will be open soon. Why else would I have seen this scene?*

I turned to check on Lily. I was barely able to move my hand to touch her forehead. Her skin felt as cold as frozen meat.

"Lily!" Her lips were blue. "Wake up." I pinched her, and she opened her eyes a slit. I breathed with relief. "Here you are. I'll get you some water."

I couldn't stand on my feet. Gathering all the energy and strength that remained in me, I placed one elbow in front of the other until I could pull my body forward, crawling slowly outside the cave. The snow wasn't falling anymore, and a few light clouds allowed the sun's rays to pass. I only needed to crawl for more few meters to lie underneath the rays. I looked around. Derek and Evelyn were trying to spread a large solar panel metal sheet on the ground.

"At last, some power," I said to them.

Evelyn let go of the panel and hurried to help me stand up. I couldn't.

"I just need the sun," I hissed.

She nodded. "It looks like there is something common between us." She pointed at my hair. "I see your hair's roots are silver-mint." I nodded. She turned to Derek. "Hey, Derek. Carry this girl into the sun." She turned to me. "I hope you don't mind?"

"I don't."

Darek carried me a few meters, and he placed me on the wet grass.

"Do you think we can heat some snow to produce water?" I said to him. "My friend needs water very badly."

He nodded. "That's what we were doing. Which one is your friend?"

I pointed at Lily, and he left to collect clean snow in a container for her and the others.

I smiled as my bones' pain started to wear off, and my body got warmer. I remained there for almost half an hour until I could stand on my feet again. I walked into the cave, where Derek was giving Lily some water.

"Thank you, Derek," I said, kneeling beside Lily. "I will take it from here."

He gave me the cup. "She is having some difficulty swallowing. You need to be patient."

I nodded.

Lily opened her eye a slit, and she smiled weakly. "You are still here."

"Always," I said. I carefully helped her sip the water until she finished the cup and went back to sleep.

I looked at the other women. Some of them were walking outside the cave, enjoying the sun. Others were still sleeping inside the cave, and they looked as bad as Lily. I walked outside. "Evelyn." I came closer to her. "Allow me to help."

Evelyn gave me a small emergency kit bag. Remembering how Mom used to examine us, I took temperatures, cleaned wounds, and gave painkillers to the women and children.

"Some of our men just arrived from Delvoris province," said Evelyn as I was checking on Lily. "The borders are open for a few hours. It looks like Prince Thaddeus wants to transport some goods from the Zetikas borders to the capital. Our men will drive your friend to the nearest hospital in Delvoris, so get her ready."

I knew it! Even with Thaddeus's arrogance, he couldn't cut off a major resource for the kingdom. I grinned. "Thank you."

She smiled and walked over to check on the other children.

I turned to Lily. "Listen, you'll be fine. I need you to stay in the hospital until I find a way to call Jason. He'll take care of you."

She nodded with a faint smile. I helped her to the nearby truck, along with other children who were injured too. When the truck started moving, my tears fell. *I will miss her. But she will be safe in the hospital.*

Noah got in the truck, and Evelyn gestured for me to follow. "Sarah, we're going to Zoiterra. Are you coming?"

I nodded, almost not believing that I could do something after being stuck here for days. Noah dropped Evelyn and the women off at a Safe Cell in Zoiterra. Apparently, the rebels had taken over some of the Safe Cells in the province. Then, he offered to drive me to Roses Hill.

As we entered my town, I surveyed the damaged and empty security checkpoint, trying to comfort myself. I was determined to believe that the rest of my beloved town had been spared.

God, how wrong I was.

My eyes swam with tears as Noah drove through the streets. I couldn't recognize the place at first, for everything was destroyed.

Everything.

The bombs had shattered the sidewalks and broken the streets. Raw sewage was flooding from utility holes. Buildings that had stood for hundreds of years had been reduced to rubble. The glasshouses' walls were scattered in every direction, mixed with a sea of blood and melted human flesh.

My heart pounded as we reached my neighborhood. A few houses were still there, and mine was amongst them. The oak tree in our front garden—the one I'd climbed hundreds of times—had turned to ash, and Mom's favorite daisies were now black dust, scattered across the yard. The fence was broken, but the house itself was standing.

"Is this the right place?" asked Noah. My eyes met his with silent sorrow. He stopped the engine. "Watch your steps; the glass might cut through your shoes."

I stepped out of the truck, closing the door behind me. My trembling feet carried me to the main door. I tried to open it with my ID lines, but it didn't respond. Only when I hid the third half-line, the door clicked open. The door's music frightened the nearby crows away.

The sound brought back so many memories that I couldn't handle. I stood in the doorway, not daring to face the life I had lost.

"Sarah, is there a problem?" asked Noah. I shook my head, and with a deep breath, I took my first step inside the empty house.

Everything was as we'd left it a few months ago. Mom's perfume still floated in the air, and her voice echoed, calling for us. I could imagine the twins scampering around. I reached out to them, but they evaporated, and I was left alone in the cold, empty place. I couldn't fight the desire to cry. Tears rolled down my cheeks.

"Sarah, are you all right?"

I turned to Noah and wiped my face. "Yes. Please wait here."

I walked to my room, shut the door behind me, and sighed. Here on this bed, I'd dreamt about Erick. Here, we'd kissed and planned for the future.

Now it was all gone.

I hurried to change into clean clothes. Then, I swept my hand under my bedsheet. The money I saved was still there in my notebook. I shoved it into my pocket and stood up.

It's time to go to Alphatoli.

As I was walking out of my room, the loud noise of cars approaching caused my heart to race.

From the doorway, Noah's eyes popped out. "Sarah! These are Law Corps! Are you wanted?"

Blood drained from my veins. I had been stupid enough to open the door with my ID lines. It seemed the government hadn't disabled the security system even after causing this massive destruction. Or maybe a spy had heard the door's music and informed the authorities. Either way, I had to run, now.

"Follow me!" I yelled to Noah, sprinting to the kitchen. As we opened the window to jump outside, I saw the Law Corps cars surrounding the house.

The Law Corps' bullets pierced our front door, their heavy boots stomping into the living room. I hurried toward the cabinet underneath the sink and slipped inside the tight place. Noah followed, and he shut the door a split second before the heavy footsteps entered the kitchen.

CHAPTER 39

"SIR, IT LOOKS LIKE THE spy escaped through the window."

I swallowed, hoping this trick would fool them.

"Search the house and the garden."

My heart leaped into my throat. It was that general again, the one who'd investigated me in the hospital. I felt Noah's hand touching mine in the dark to calm me down.

One set of footsteps rushed out of the kitchen, and another came closer. The smell of cigarettes filled the air. Someone turned on the faucet, and I put my hand over my mouth, trying to hold my breath. The water kept running for a few seconds before the first man's voice came closer again.

"The spy is nowhere to be seen, sir. But we found these bloody clothes."

A few moments of silence passed before the general spoke. "She can't have gone that far. Close the area." Their footsteps walked out of the kitchen.

"Lenora Evgenís," Noah whispered a few minutes later, and I shivered. He squeezed my hand. "I will see if they're gone."

I sensed honesty in his voice. "Too dangerous," was my only response. But he let go of my hand and opened the cabinet door as quietly as possible. Noah crept forward until he reached the kitchen door. He tilted his head with great care, checking the living room, then stood up. I wasn't able to see him as he walked outside the kitchen. A few minutes passed before he came back. He put his finger in front of his lips, and I rolled out of the cabinet and stood on my feet.

"The Corps are gone, but I'm sure they'll come back." He looked through the window at the dark street. "We have to distract them."

"Noah, thank you for the ride. I can manage it from here."

"You can't get out of the neighborhood alone! Let me walk you to the nearest Safe Cell in Zoiterra."

I thought about it for a minute. "Is it dangerous for you?"

"We'll take the sewers—otherwise we'll be stuck in here until the Corps come back, and you don't want that, do you?"

I shook my head.

"Do you have a flashlight?"

"Yes." I hurried to the kitchen and grabbed a small one. When I returned, Noah was texting on his Iméfono and gestured me to come closer.

"I thought the Iméfonos were dead," I remarked.

"The safe ones aren't."

So he owned an Iméfono that was only available to the wealthy. Maybe that was why Derek told me all the Iméfonos were dead. Perhaps he thought that we wouldn't trust them if they had something that was obviously stolen from a wealthy.

Noah approached the main door. "Now, my people will get the Corps' attention so we can get out of here."

I nodded, and he started counting down from ten. Once he reached number one, a massive shooting sound broke the silence. Noah tilted his head and carefully peered out through the main door, checking the street.

312

Then he beckoned for me to follow.

We moved stealthily, hiding behind the burned trees until Noah waved for me to stop. Fishing a knife out of his pants pocket, he squatted on the floor and pulled up a manhole cover as quietly as possible.

"I'll go first." Noah held the flashlight between his teeth and he slid through the opening. A few seconds later, he waved the flashlight to invite me in. Taking a deep breath, I climbed down the stairs until I reached the moist ground. The heavy, humid air welcomed me, but the smell was unbearable; it caused my stomach to crunch in disgust. I barely stopped myself from screaming when a mouse ran over my shoes.

I touched my gun to feel the safety of the cold weapon. "It seems like you know where we're going."

"Sure. I lived here for most of my adult life."

What?

"I'm an orphan. A slave who ran away from his master and ended up with the rebels, fighting the Corps each time they'd kill one of us." He spat on the ground. "They call it a 'process'—a fantasy name for a cruel crime." His angry voice echoed in the closed place.

"So you were the people who . . ."

"The armed clashes? Yes, that was us. When the Corps were busy counting the people in their homes, we surprised them from these sewers." He turned to me, raising the flashlight to his face, and his eyes glittered. "Do you know what they do to prisoners in Inferos?"

I shook my head.

"They use them in secret experiments. You know that fire is banned from the kingdom, but have you ever tried to set a fire? Probably not, because even if you tried to, the fire can't be lit. Something puts out the fire at once. Not only that. Even if you ignite the fire from afar—even if you send a bullet through a bottle of alcohol, for example—you will still get sin-spots. And these particular sin-spots are not redeemable. They will invade the body at once, and they will start melting the flesh of the victims. It's like a curse the government is desperately trying to get around. They're trying

313

to find a way to set fire without melting themselves to use it against the Empire if they needed to, and whenever they find a chemical compound that causes a fire, they force a prisoner to try it. So that poor person will be melted alive . . . they melt us alive."

My brain couldn't comprehend the cruelty of this action. I was more than eager than ever to complete my mission now.

We kept walking until Noah broke the awkward silence. "Your dad was so brave."

I sighed with bitterness. A voice inside my chest screamed, *He's not my father!*

"Why did he agree?" I asked.

"Well, he was a drunk, broken man who hurt his family and knew he'd done awful things to his wife. He wanted to help her to try and make amends. I met him once. You have a lot of things in common."

"I have nothing in common with that man!" I exclaimed, halting.

Noah turned around. "You're both stubborn. That's for sure." He came to where I was standing. "Lenora, Santos looked everywhere for you. All of you. I know he—"

"You know nothing!" I hissed.

"Of course. I'm sorry. What I want to say is that he tried to redeem himself. Maybe his act will never fix what he already broke. Maybe it won't restore the past, but the man loved his family in the end. He died instead of your mother. Just give it some thought."

I wasn't comfortable discussing such a family dilemma with a stranger, especially with this suffocating smell around me. I kept on walking without a word. Noah followed me, and we kept silent for two hours until we reached a set of stairs going down.

"We're under a Safe Cell in Zoiterra," he said.

We climbed down the stairs until we reached a heavy metal door. Noah knocked on the door twice, and a girl with frizzy silver hair opened it. She smiled at him, but her eyebrows came together as she noticed me standing behind him. "Who the hell is she?"

"A surprise."

My face paled. Why did he say that? Was he going to turn me in? I stood there, unsure whether to follow or not.

Noah turned to me and smiled encouragingly. "There is someone you have to meet."

"Who is he?" I asked, my hand touching my gun.

"Lenora, we are your friends. I promise no one will hurt you here."

The girl's eyes widened as she heard my name. "It's really you!" A big smile drowned her face. "Sir will be so happy to meet you. Come on in."

What the hell? Who is Sir? I wiped the sweat off my forehead and glanced back. If I turned around and ran, I'd be stuck in these sewers for eternity. I squeezed the gun and nodded for them to go ahead.

I stepped into a vast windowless room filled with gigantic screens and offices, bustling with people who had sin-spots all over their arms. When I entered, they stopped their tasks, and many pairs of curious eyes turned to me.

A loud, familiar voice asked, "Why has everyone stopped working?" The speaker's face showed from behind a door in the corner.

It was Mr. Maximus Dorgalous!

CHAPTER 40

MR. DORGALOUS APPROACHED, HIS EYES checking my face carefully. He looked back and forth between Noah and me before he pointed at me with his electrical pipe. "Didn't I tell you, Noah, to stop bringing girls to this place?"

"Sir, she isn't just any girl," Noah rushed to explain. "It's Lenora Evgenís."

Mr. Dorgalous's face flushed with anger, and whispers scattered from all sides. "Do you think I'm a fool, boy?" he boomed, eyes squinting. "I know Lenora. I've eaten dinner with Lenora." He looked at the other men standing beside him. "She might be a spy. Take care of her." Then, he turned his back to me, walking away.

The men approached me, wanting to *take care* of me. Last time I heard that word—from Mr. William—the girl being *taken care* of, Isabella, never returned to the club.

I had to act fast.

"Hera!" I yelled. He didn't recognize me because of my short blond hair, but at least my voice had stayed the same.

Mr. Dorgalous turned again and frowned. "You told me once about Hera and her hundred-eyed companion at Mary's wedding."

Mr. Dorgalous lifted a hand to the men. They stepped back, and he came closer to me with measured steps, gazing at me with tightened lips. "Do you have any concrete proof that you're Lenora?"

"Is this enough?" I pushed up my jacket sleeve, revealing my identity lines. People around gasped, staring at my wrist.

"Damn me! It's really you." He held my wrist. "The heroine, the daughter of the heroes. We thought we'd lost you!"

"I'm no heroine, sir." I didn't feel that I deserved that title. I was only a stupid girl whose broken heart started a devastating war on the outskirts of her homeland.

Mr. Dorgalous put a large hand on my shoulder. A smile filled his face. "Come with me," he said, then shouted to everyone to return to work.

I walked with him to the small room he'd emerged from earlier. More screens were set up everywhere, complicated-looking equipment was piled in the corner, and a huge holographic map of Elpax covered one of the walls.

"What is this place?" I asked, looking at the screens.

He sat on a chair and gestured for me to sit beside him. "Welcome to the Hundredth Eye control room." He winked at me, and I smiled at the meaning of his words. "We're three floors below one of the Safe Cells in Zoiterra. As you can see, these screens are a live broadcast of the kingdom through small drones." He picked up a small blue bird from the pile of equipment in the corner and gave it to me. "This is an invention of one of our brilliant engineers. It's true that they're rudimentary . . . but they work."

"It's impressive!" The drone looked exactly like a real bird, moving and tilting its head like one. No one could possibly tell the difference. Even its feathers seemed natural.

"I hope the workers here didn't scare you with their sin-spots. They got them because they are rebels, and that's a sin, as you know." He rolled his eyes.

"I could never judge anyone for that sin, Mr. Dorgalous. I am a sinner too."

"Call me Maximus." He got up to pour a cup of hot tea for me. "This news will thrill Queen Arianna."

"What happened to her?"

He stretched his lips thin and handed me the cup. "Her order was to smuggle you from the nightclub, but we were surprised when Thaddeus dismissed her along with King Alexei and Queen Olympia. He confiscated all the Iméfonos from the royal family, and even those of the workers at the royal palace. That psychopath controls everything now. As you know, the war started, and it was total chaos. We couldn't enter the neighborhood again."

I nodded. "I need to go to Alphatoli," I said, putting the teacup on the table. "There is a woman I have to meet."

"Correct. The plan is to meet with that woman, then seek asylum in the Latina embassy."

I raised my eyebrows. "How do you know that?"

"Who do you think planned the whole damn thing?" His smile widened. "And you wanted to do all of this by yourself? How?"

I shook my head. "Well, I didn't give much thought as to how. I was going to call my friend for help."

"Which one?"

"Jason Valemont. You met him."

"Oh, that boy." He puffed the smoke from his pipe. "He's probably staying in Theirna with the other wealthy. His father won't allow him to help you."

"What do you mean?"

"William cannot involve himself in opposition to Thaddeus of any kind, as it runs against his own interests."

"But he helped me before . . . he hid me in the club, and—"

318

"He helped you when the queen mother was in a strong position, and of course after he had secured his own interests." He puffed his pipe again. "But not to worry. We'll help you."

The door opened, and a girl with short black hair rushed in, exclaiming with joy. "It's really you!" My neighbor Danira hugged me. I stood up and embraced her, so glad to see that she was safe.

"What are you doing here?" We both asked at the same time, then burst out laughing. She told me how the rebels had saved her at the last minute before her home was bombed. Since then, she'd joined the revolution. We spent a few minutes talking until an orange light flashed from the corner.

"Sir, you've got to see this!" exclaimed Noah, whose voice reached us before his worried face showed from the door. Another young man stood behind him, and I recognized the newcomer right away. He was the ambulance driver. *I think his name was Nizar.*

Noah rushed to a screen, tapping for a few minutes on a flat keyboard. The screen split, showing two video streams, which I presumed were live security camera broadcasts. The first was of the Safe Cell, which was packed with women and children. The other showed a wealthy's car parking in front of the Safe Cell's door. The driver stepped out of it, holding his Iméfono, looking back and forth between the screen and the building.

"That's Jason!" I exclaimed. What coincidence had brought him here?

"Damn that stupid boy!" yelled Sir Maximus. He turned to Noah. "Get out fast with Nizar. Tell the guards that he is one of us and that he stole that car. Hurry!"

Noah and Nizar rushed off, leaving me wondering what was wrong. The question popped up in my eyes as I looked at Sir Maximus. He struck the table with great force.

"How has he dared to drive his car in Zetikas? The rebels will smash it."

"I don't understand what—"

"When you rebel against the royal family, you fight against the wealthy by association. Most of the rebels here are workers who have suffered from the wealthy's oppression. His presence here is a threat to his life."

"But you're wealthy and—"

"Look," he interrupted, rolling up his sleeves. "This is bigger than you think. There are a lot of other wealthy in this game. But the guys here don't know that. They know I'm the one in charge and I'm leading the whole damn revolution. But if any other wealthy wanders into the area, my people will skin them alive. Or if they're lucky, they will be shot first."

My eyes followed the screens with anxiety. One of the guards left the Cell's front door, his rifle placed on his shoulder. He began talking to Jason, pointing at his ID lines. When Jason refused to show them, the man pushed him backward. Jason's Iméfono fell on the ground. He hurried to punch the man, who responded with a counterstrike and stepped backward. The man and three others who had joined him raised their rifles. Noah and Nizar shoved the door open at that moment and ran toward the men to talk some sense into them.

After a few seconds of discussion, the guards put their rifles on their shoulders again. The one who'd punched Jason reached his hand out to him, helping him stand up. It seemed that he was apologizing. Then, they all entered the Cell.

I rushed out of the room, running to the door in the big hall, and as soon as I saw Jason, I jumped to embrace him.

"Thank God you're safe!" Jason exclaimed as I pulled back. "I hardly recognized you." He touched my short blond hair.

"I'm so sorry they hit you."

Jason smiled. He let go of me and greeted Mr. Maximus, whose eyes were furious as he waved for us to follow him into the small room in the corner. Jason and I exchanged nervous looks on the way. When I closed the door, Mr. Maximus turned to Jason with sharp eyes and grabbed the collar of his jacket with both hands.

"Mr. Dorgalous!" I screamed, trying to get him off of Jason, whose face had turned red.

"Why did you come here? Who sent you?" yelled Mr. Maximus.

Jason's confused eyes glanced at me, his face deepening to crimson.

"Sir, please. You're killing him!" I pleaded, to no avail.

"I warn you," he growled to Jason, "I want the truth and only the truth. If I'm not convinced, I'll strip you in front of everyone here. I swear, if a sin-spot appears on your body . . ."

Mr. Maximus let go of Jason, who fell to the ground and started coughing violently, trying to breathe. I hurried toward him with a glass of water while Mr. Maximus stood there like a stone, waiting for an answer.

"I waited in the Evangelical Church for the curfew to end," said Jason after few gasps. "Then I went to the club, taking a tremendous risk, and discovered that the shelling destroyed it." His tired eyes turned to me. "I searched every shelter and hospital. I thought I lost you." A tear fell from his eyes.

I squeezed his hand and turned to Mr. Maximus angrily. "You almost killed him," I hissed.

"He will live." He gave a half-smile and asked Jason, "You drove around in your car?"

"This isn't my car; I actually stole it from a wealthy. You can ask the nuns in the church."

"And you're sure that no one followed you?"

"Positive."

"All right," said Mr. Maximus. "You both need to rest until we check his story out." He called for Noah to walk us into another room. I helped Jason get up, and we were led to a long room crowded with bunk beds. Noah pointed to a bed in the far-left corner.

"You both can take that one. Girls in the upper beds, guys in the lower ones. Sheets are clean. If you need to use the bathroom, there's one in here." He pointed toward a small door. "Try to spend a maximum of five minutes in the shower. Dinner is at seven."

I nodded and waited for him to leave before I turned to Jason and hugged him once more. "Jason, why didn't you ever tell me that Queen Arianna helped with planning my escape?"

He pulled back. "I had no choice. After the Corps released me when you failed to cross, her men kidnapped me, blindfolded me, and took me to a strange place, where the palace's spymaster was waiting for me. He made me swear that I wouldn't tell you anything, and he checked my body for sin-spots after I met with you."

I sighed. "So you have no idea what's going on, or why she helped me?

He shook his head.

"Then I've got to tell you something." I pulled on his hand, and we sat on a bed. I told him everything about the visions, trying my best to explain every detail. He listened carefully and never seemed to doubt a single word.

"I was never sure why she helped you. I was afraid that you would become a pawn in one of their games. Leen, this is very dangerous. Do you want to kill Thaddeus?"

"I don't have a choice."

Jason ducked his head, thinking for a moment. "I'll come with you."

"No way!"

"Yes, way. I have to make sure you're safe."

I got up and took a deep breath. "Jason William Valemont. Don't make this complicated. You're going back to Theirna."

I turned to leave, but he grabbed my arm right away. I turned to face him. His eyes showed pain, along with a little hope and desperation. "I said I'm coming. You mean the world to me. I . . . Leen, there's something I never told you, but it's what I've always felt."

"Jason . . . don't."

"Why not?" As he understood my hesitation, he took a deep breath. "Are you still thinking about him?"

I bit my lip. "I hate him, Jason. Okay? He is . . . he was my first love, and I . . . I don't know. But this isn't about Erick. It's about Alba."

He frowned in confusion. "What about her? What are you talking about?"

"I know she's your concubine. All she ever wanted was to be with you. She loves you. She's a wonderful and loyal girl."

322

"I know. But I never loved her."

I rolled my eyes. "Why didn't you free her, then? You were having all those lap dances. Do you know how that made her feel?"

He held my shoulders at arm's length, bending his head to look into my eyes. "I did. I freed her the night you slapped me, ignoring the 'giving birth to a boy' rule. I got a sin-spot for going against the law, but I didn't care. I paid the required money to redeem that sin and moved on." He blinked several times, as if he had a headache. "I never wanted a concubine, but my father forced me. He said that I should follow the law."

"Why did you agree?"

"Leen. No one can stand against my father, not even me. Look, there are some things that you don't know about. First, Alba was fifteen years old when I had to buy her last year. That was one of the reasons why I couldn't touch her. It didn't feel right. I told her that already, and offered to free her, but she didn't want to be freed." His fingers ran across his forehead. "I tried to make it up to her. I gave her a special room, in the club rather than the disgusting place she had been living in. I bought everything she wanted, but I couldn't touch her. I tried once . . ."

He sat on the bed, dunking his head between his knees. "I am sorry to disappoint you. I feel guilty about her all the time."

"I didn't know that. I am sorry." I sat beside him.

His eyes met mine. "I hate disappointing you, Leen. I have always only cared for one person, and I knew since my crossing that my heart belonged to you. I am in love with you, even if you don't love me back."

I froze. I thought that he only had a crush on me, and that his feelings would soon evaporate. I was sure Alba knew the truth all along. That hurt me the most; she was so nice to me, even knowing he loved me. She helped me because she loved him. The guilt was gnawing at me. She was now alone, heartbroken, without her family around her. Tears found their way into my eyes.

"Why are you crying?" Jason asked. "Please don't tell me she died!"

"She's fine. She's in the hospital."

He breathed a sigh. "I'll take care of her. You have my word. Now, let's eat some food."

CHAPTER 41

IT WAS NICE TO BATHE and eat a warm meal after all those days in the cave. I looked at the long tables around us, wondering how much money Mr. Maximus had put into this revolution. I didn't know if Mr. Maximus had learned about Arianna's intentions, or if he knew that my primary assignment was to kill Thaddeus. But his words about Mr. William were still in the back of my mind. 'William cannot involve himself in opposition of any kind, as it runs against his own interests.' So what exactly were those 'interests'? Or did Mr. Maximus merely not like Mr. William? However, if I asked him what he would gain from this revolution, he might think I was accusing him of something.

He'd told me before dinner that there were three revolutionary parties. The first was against the entire monarchy system, as my father had been. The second was Arianna's secret party, which included the women's liberation movement. They wanted to take down Thaddeus and reinstate king Alexei. The last party also wanted to keep King Alexei, but they wanted a parliament with him.

One thing wasn't clear: if Mr. Maximus was with Arianna's party, then why did the workers here accept him as their leader? Was Arianna planning to withdraw special privileges from the wealthy to placate the workers? Or maybe she was stringing the workers along with false promises until she got rid of Thaddeus, and then she would bribe everyone with money and high positions. From my visions about her, I had learned not to trust her, but I couldn't say a word to anyone when her agents were everywhere. Only time would tell if she was a good woman. Either way, Thaddeus had to be stopped.

I glanced at Jason, who sat next to me, eating his food. I remembered when Oshina told me, "If you lose him, he will come back to you." I smiled at the thought. At the same time, Jason turned to me.

"What are you smiling about?" He grinned at me, and I shrugged.

"Do you remember at Mary's wedding, when I couldn't tell which spoon to use?"

He chuckled. "Yes, it was that soup with . . ."

"A stupid blue dye," I completed the sentence with him, and we both giggled.

Jason leaned over to whisper, "Those were the days."

"Yes, they were, Jason." A deep hope rose inside me. I wished my heart had chosen him.

A moment passed before he peeked at my necklace, and his eyes became tender. "You know, Leen . . . love isn't always a crazy, obsessive emotion. Love is understanding and respecting each other, and giving space to grow and sacrifice and compromise. It's about being there for each other, not running away. And it certainly isn't *treason*."

The word *treason* annoyed me. I was sure by now that Erick's actions fell under that category, and Jason's words reminded me how foolish I was for trusting him so early. I didn't want to discuss this topic anymore. "Can I use your Iméfono to call my sisters?"

He was silent for a moment, sipping his soup. "I wish that was possible, but the men smashed it. And I think it's safer for you not to call them at the moment. Don't worry—they're happy. Mom is taking excellent care of them." His voice sounded sad as he added, "She always wanted girls."

Right, she did. She told me herself. I was worried about my mom, too, but at the moment, I couldn't do anything about it. I felt so helpless, But at least my sisters were okay.

We finished eating and went to bed. Lying there, I wondered why my heart wasn't able to return Jason's strong feelings. Maybe it was because wealthy-worker relationships were forbidden in Elpax. That was what had been burned into my brain since childhood.

Half of the rebels were sleeping in this room, and the others were guarding the Safe Cell. Jason lay in the lower bed beneath me. I didn't know if he was awake or asleep, but it wasn't polite to wake up the others by talking to him. I flipped over to sleep on my stomach, and left my arm dangling down. Jason caught my palm right away. I tilted my head to look at him. It wasn't that dark, and his blue eyes glittered in the faint light.

"A good boy," I whispered. "One who finds him becomes delighted."

"No symbols exist between you," Jason replied, giving me a soft kiss on the hand.

My smile widened.

Jason was familiar and safe.

Jason was home.

The next morning, Danira woke me up with a gentle touch. She placed fresh clothes for me on Jason's bed. "Wake up, lazy bones. We'll have breakfast in ten minutes."

I giggled, looking around the empty room, then slid down to the ground. "Where is everyone?"

"Working." She fidgeted with the hem of her shirt.

"What's wrong, Danira?"

She looked up at me. "Do you know how they burn inmates in

327

Inferos?"

I nodded. "Noah told me when the Law Corps ask an inmate to light the fire, he or she starts melting from the sin-spots."

She nodded too. "They just melt . . . they turn into ashes in a few hours. Not seconds, not minutes, but hours, Leen. They stay alive all that time, suffering, and no one helps them." A tear rolled down her cheek. "Mom is next in line."

"Oh God, no!" I held her palm. "I promise you, she will be fine."

"It was a kitten, Leen. A kitten." She wiped her tears. "I have lost everything because we took care of a damn kitten. She didn't damage the Crossing Gate. Yet, the entire country rose to defend your mom and not mine."

"Danira. They're all victims. Your mom . . . mine . . . women and kids, and even men. I'm trying to help all of them."

"Try to do it fast."

She walked out, leaving me with black thoughts. *Now I have another reason to stop Thaddeus.*

After breakfast, we gathered in the small room. Noah, Jason, Mr. Maximus, and I began to formulate a plan. Mr. Maximus had checked out Jason's story last night. Of course, he'd been telling the truth.

"We have a problem," said Nizar, entering the room with Danira. He pointed at the screen in front of us. "Our eyes on the inside just sent an encrypted message. It said that Prince Thaddeus won't open the borders of Zetikas again after the troops informed him that Lenora Evgenís entered her house last night. So we have to move fast through the sewers." He pointed to a line on the map. "We'll enter the sewers here in Zoiterra, walk through them to the nearest Safe Cell in Gamotos, and then make our way to the capital."

I gulped. "The capital?"

"Yes," said Sir Maximus. "I think if you go right to Theirna and seek asylum first, it'll be better than walking around the kingdom."

"And then?"

"Then the Latina embassy will send for Oshina. She can enter Theirna with their permission."

"And me? How am I going to get into the capital?" I asked, sitting up straight.

Noah glanced at Jason. "They don't search the cars of the wealthy, as you know. Therefore, they won't read your ID at the capital's gate if you arrive in one."

I turned to Jason. "You mean we will go together? In the same car?"

"Jason can provide protection for you," said Mr. Maximus.

I wasn't sure about his decision. It didn't feel wise. If I got caught, the last thing I wanted was to drag my best friend down with me.

"No . . . no." I shook my head. "The Law Corps won't allow the wealthy to remain immune and secure in the arrogance of their power if they catch him helping me. He will be tried for treason."

"Don't worry. We'll watch your back," said Mr. Maximus.

Danira gave me a small round black device. "It's a wireless earbud," she said, handing Jason a similar one. "Put it in your ear. You'll be able to hear us, and everyone here will hear you too. These are way better than Iméfonos."

I nodded, and we started testing the devices to make sure they worked.

"Now," said Mr. Maximus. "Jason, we need a wealthy car other than the one we have here. Can you provide it?"

He nodded. "I'll call my driver right away."

Danira walked Jason to another room so he could call Nicholas. Mr. Maximus closed the door behind them and turned to me. "We have a surprise for you."

"What surprise?" My eyebrows snapped together.

He exchanged looks with Nizar, who smiled and started tapping on the flat keyboard while Mr. Maximus continued. "We couldn't pass an Iméfono to her, but this is the best we can do."

I couldn't understand what he was talking about. *Who's she?* Was it my mother? I desperately hoped so, but I was wary of getting my hopes up too high after all I had gone through.

He pointed to the screen, and I came closer. It was a live broadcast showing the backyard of a huge old building made of red bricks. People with orange clothing were walking around, monitored by others who wore silver uniforms and held weapons in their hands.

"Beta two, do you copy?" Nizar asked through a small device like mine.

"Zeta nine, we copy," replied a voice I could hear clearly in my ear.

"The bee needs honey. Is there a flower?"

I turned to Mr. Maximus, who explained, "It's a code between us. Watch."

I looked at the screen again. The view zoomed in, and I noticed that all the people in the yard were women. Some of them sat in circles on the ground.

"The flower is blooming in three, two, one. Over," the voice said.

At that moment, a siren echoed from the screen's speakers, and the women started moving toward the building in a line. Nizar zoomed in closer, and one of the women lifted her face upward. My heartbeat sped to the maximum.

It was my mother.

CHAPTER 42

I GULPED. MY FACE BECAME soaked with tears. I hurried to touch the screen, not believing that I was actually seeing her. She looked tired, and her face had lost its shine, but she was in good health. Mom smiled, as if she knew I was watching her.

"Beta two, thank you. The bee ate the honey. Over," said Nizar, and the screen went black.

"What's wrong?" I exclaimed. "Please, I want to see her again."

"That's not possible," said Mr. Maximus. He put a heavy hand on my shoulder. "The drone can't fly over Inferos for long. Otherwise, the Secret Intelligence will locate it, and our men in Betis may be caught. A guard told your mom to look at the sky when the gathering bell started, but she didn't explain further for your mother's safety—and for ours. I am sure your mom knew deep in her heart that you were watching."

"Thank you," I whispered, and hugged Mr. Maximus, unable to contain myself. For a moment, I felt alive again after a long era of desperation. Mr. Maximus respected my feelings. He patted my back, trying to comfort me. He and Nizar kept quiet and let me cry until the door opened and Jason entered.

His eyes widened at the view in front of him. "Is everything all right?"

I wiped my tears and nodded. "I just had a moment." I didn't explain further. Taking Jason out of the room earlier might have been for security reasons, so I kept the news of seeing my mother to myself, although I was dying to share it with him.

"Did you call your driver?" asked Mr. Maximus.

"Yes," Jason replied. His expression became sour, and he blinked several times, as if he was trying to erase some memory from his head. "Yes . . . Nicholas will wait with the family car in front of the Cell in Gamotos." He glanced at me.

"Great." Mr. Maximus strode out of the room, gesturing for me to follow. As soon as I walked out into the Cell's main hall, the rebels stood, looking at me. All of them raised their left hands. My jaw dropped open at the sight.

They'd painted half of their third lines with their skin tone's color, so it would match mine.

They all cried out in one voice, "Victory for Enilini!"

Sir Maximus rolled his eyes. "I tried to talk them out of it, but they insisted on combining the words for "adult" and "juvenile" to come up with this silly name."

"I don't mind. It's pretty," I replied with a grin.

"We all look up to you," he said. "I wish you all the luck with your mission."

I smiled, and we shook hands before I hugged Danira. Jason and Nizar went out the door, and I followed, surrounded by the loud cheerful chants that filled the air as everyone wished us luck and success.

As we moved out of the Cell into the sewers, Jason whispered, "What were you doing in his arms?"

I laughed awkwardly. Jason was so ridiculous sometimes.

332

After a long journey through the sewers, we reached Gamotos province. Nicholas was waiting there in the car when we emerged at the Safe Cell. Of course, he had no idea about our mission or where we would go after that. He delivered a new secured Iméfono to Jason and whispered something to him, and my friend scowled. He kept shaking his head over and over, as though refusing what Nicholas was saying. When Jason's Iméfono rang, they exchanged looks, and Jason hung up on the caller.

I came closer, trying to figure out what was wrong. Jason looked away from Nicholas and I heard one line of his speech. "Tell him I don't care." Then, he saw me and waved for me to get into the car.

Nicholas stood there, as though unable to decide what to do. His Iméfono rang, and he walked away to talk. I leaned on the car's window and looked at Jason. "I want to use the bathroom in the Cell. Be right back."

I walked after Nicholas and inclined my head to indicate he should follow me. Once we were both inside the Cell behind a pillar, I asked him what was wrong, my eyes gazing through the window at Jason sitting in the car.

"He's not talking to his father, and Sir William is angry."

I looked at Nicholas. "And that's because of . . . me?"

"Miss Lenora, they don't tell me anything about the family business, and I'm not allowed to ask."

"Understood." My eyes shifted back to the car, but Jason wasn't there. I stepped from behind the pillar to look for him and almost ran into his chest.

"Everything all right?" asked Jason, looking back and forth between Nicholas and me. I had no idea if he'd heard our conversation, but I gathered myself and acted fast.

"Yes. Come on." I looped my arm through his and walked him to the car, not giving him a chance to ask Nicholas about our conversation. I sat with Jason in the back seat, Nizar sat in the front, and Nicholas started

333

driving. It was a long journey to Theirna, and I was so exhausted that I fell asleep.

A gentle touch on my shoulder woke me up. Opening my eyes, I sat up straight, looking at the light fog around us. Jason pointed toward the high walls of Theirna, which became clearer under the lights of their tall towers as the mist thinned out. My stress level rose with each turn of the car's wheels. Nicholas slowed the vehicle as we approached the entrance gate. My heart shuddered when I saw a three-dimensional picture of me on the walls, with the heading *Wanted for Treason* written in shining letters.

"Jason!" I shouted in horror. Jason held my hand to calm me down. Nicholas joined a long line of cars in front of the capital's gate. I looked out the window, trying to get a glimpse of what was happening. The Law Corps soldiers were forcing everyone to step out of their cars and checking their IDs. It looked like passengers had to leave their cars outside the city for the dogs to sniff, and another government vehicle would drive them into the capital.

"Jason," said Mr. Maximus through the earbud. "Tell your driver to turn around before they notice you. Hurry!"

Jason and I shared a worried glance. As Nicholas turned the car and drove away fast, I heard Mr. Maximus's voice in my ear.

"Jason, put the damn partition between you and your driver."

Jason did as he was told, separating Nicholas and Nizar from our rear passenger compartment.

"Our man just informed us that someone told the troops about your arrival. We only knew about the dogs at the last minute," said Mr. Maximus. "Jason, can you tell me how the hell the troops knew?"

Oh, boy!

"Are you accusing me of—"

"Not you," interrupted Mr. Maximus. "How much do you trust Nicholas?"

Silence reigned before I spoke. "Sir, I know Nicholas. He wouldn't tell anyone about me. He's risking his own life with us."

"So we have a mole. God damn it!" Maximus yelled.

I almost said that I'd already known it was a bad idea from the beginning. I may not have been smart enough to set up a plan, but I could recognize a foolish one. I sighed. "Sir, let me go to Alphatoli, and then we'll think about how to get into Theirna."

He didn't reply. We sat in silence for a while, watching the roadside trees go by.

"Get rid of Nicholas first," Mr. Maximus answered. "A man will meet you up in the town Kalendis to switch cars. Nizar, travel south of Poseidon Lake after you drop Nicholas."

Nizar didn't answer—of course, he was sitting right next to Nicholas, who had no idea about this conversation. But he hummed with a faint *yes*.

We spent the next half hour in silence until we reached the town. Nicholas stopped the car in a motel parking lot, and Jason told him to wait for a few hours until someone else came to drive him back to Theirna. Nizar drove us in the new car to Poseidon Lake. Once there, he parked under a tree and stepped outside to talk on the Iméfono for a few minutes.

"How are you holding up?" Jason asked sweetly.

"Jason, you have to go back to Theirna."

He shook his head.

"It's too dangerous," I said.

"I can't leave you alone."

"Jason . . . Jason, I'm a grown-up. I can manage it by myself. I don't want you to be part of this now. Your dad—"

He interrupted sharply, "I don't care about him. Why should you?"

"Because he's your dad, and family comes first. This has to end here." I couldn't ask him about their disagreements, nor could I tell him about Cordis—not just because everyone in the Cell was listening to our conversation, but because it simply wasn't the right time. I promised myself that nothing would happen to him, and I wanted to keep that promise.

Before he could argue further, Nizar got into the car. He held up his Iméfono and pointed to the map of the kingdom displayed there.

"We're here," he said, indicating the lake. "We've informed Oshina, and her men will wait for us on the borders between Betis and Alphatoli. They'll take you to see her."

I nodded, just as a car approached us. The driver gave Nizar a gun, and he tucked it into the waistband of his trousers and covered it with his jacket.

"We have to switch cars now," said Nizar, and we stepped toward the long, black new arrival. My eyes widened, and I shook my head in horror.

"I'm sorry, Lenora. We have no other choice."

"Not a mortuary car . . . Nizar! Is there a coffin inside?"

He ignored me and opened the back door, gesturing for me to step inside. There was a black coffin in the back, as I expected. I felt as if I was suffocating already.

"Not in the coffin." I shook my head. "I won't lie down inside. This is terrifying!"

"It's just here in case we need it, don't worry," said Jason. He got inside the car and patted the long seat beside him. It looked like I had no option but to go along with the plan. I sat next to Jason, and Nizar drove as fast as possible.

Vitoli was the prettiest province in the kingdom. The landscape was peppered with pine trees. The Apollo River flowed into Poseidon Lake, which almost swallowed the entire southern part of the province. Nizar took the tiny roads winding through the Ourea Southern Mountains, which stretched up to Betis. The only building in the area was the Theia Electrical Glass Factory, where the kingdom manufactured our Iméfonos and the houses' walls with advanced technology.

The car moved for two hours, lulling me into a light doze. As soon as we reached the Alphatoli Desert, Mr. Maximus spoke in my ear.

"We can't see you due to the fog, but the drone sent signals of a strange movement close to you. Stay alert."

"Should we abort?" replied Nizar.

"Wait for the signal. Over."

"Copy that."

I thought it might not be a serious problem until I heard Nizar cursing. He stopped the car and lowered the partition window. "Hide! There are Law Corps."

I trembled in fear as Jason hurried to open the coffin for me. I heard a vehicle stopping behind us while Nizar stepped out of the car. I lay down in the coffin, and Jason covered my face with a thin muslin cloth. The last thing I saw was Jason's expression, filled with burgeoning tension.

"Breathe, kid. The tribal members are close," said Mr. Maximus, trying to comfort me. But I was suffocating as I heard the back door open.

"Do you have a burial permit?" demanded a stern male voice.

"We'll get it in Alphatoli," replied Jason.

"No way! If you don't have a permit, you must leave the coffin here."

What the hell is he talking about?

I heard Nizar's voice. "But the tribes have their own way of burial, and their rituals—"

"Who are you to argue with a royal decree?" the voice yelled. "Show me your ID."

I heard a peep, and the soldier spoke to someone on his comms handset. The reply that squeaked from the handset caused my heart to hammer. "Arrest him. Check the coffin."

"Send backup," the soldier replied. His footsteps sounded inside the hearse, and he cocked his gun. "Open the coffin."

I saw death in front of my eyes, knowing the end was before me. Only a miracle could save me now. Jason and Nizar did as he ordered—they had no choice. Light flooded in. With half-closed eyes through the thin muslin cloth, I could see the gun pointed against Nizar's temple. I hoped I could pretend to be dead, at least until I could find a way to fight, but the soldier didn't give me a chance. He picked up my left wrist, and my heart fell down as his joyous yelling washed over me.

"Prepare for a reward. Got the traitor here!"

CHAPTER 43

WHAM!

The soldier whacked the gun's butt against the side of my head, and stars appeared in front of my eyes. The pain was too much to ignore. I screamed, unable to play dead, as much as I wished I could.

"Get up, traitor, before you really need the coffin." He pulled my hair and dragged me out of the vehicle. I staggered, trying to find my balance. Jason stepped forward to help me, but the soldier kept his gun pointed at my head.

A bullet whizzed by, hitting the other soldier by the side of the car. It was Nizar!

The sudden death of his mate startled the man who'd grabbed me; now it was three against one. Jason took advantage of the situation. He grabbed the hand with the soldier's gun, twisted it back, and kicked him hard. The gun fell to the ground next to me. I picked it up and pointed it toward him, my hands shaking with the effort.

"Stop! Just one bullet!" The soldier lifted both his arms in surrender.

Just then, cars roared behind us. I glanced back to see two four-wheeled jeeps with soldiers hanging out of the windows, pistols in their hands, yelling at us to lie on the ground. They all aimed their guns at *me*.

How come the backup had arrived so fast?

Then, one soldier's head exploded, blood gushing in all directions. Heavy war cries reverberated over the sand dunes. The tribal members had arrived on horseback, most of their faces covered with a headscarf.

Heavy shooting from both sides broke the silence of the Alphatoli Desert. The entire scene resembled a battlefield. Jason pulled me down at once, and we crawled on the ground beside our car. With the hearse shielding us from the combat, we put our hands over our heads. Time stretched out. I had lost my earbud when the soldier pulled me out of the coffin, so I had no idea what the next move was.

Bullets pelted the car, smashing the window above my head.

I yelled, "Jason, what can we do?"

"Stay where you are!" he yelled back. "Keep your head down."

Nizar broke away from the battle with one of the tribesmen in tow. "Get in the car!" he yelled, opening the driver's side door.

I didn't hesitate to follow his order. Stepping inside the car with Jason, I could see that the sands were covered with blood. We slouched down in our seats to avoid stray bullets, and Nizar took off at once in the mayhem's midst.

"What about the other men?" I asked, my voice shaking.

"They can manage it," said the young tribesman. He gave directions to Nizar, who kept his foot heavy on the pedal.

"We're sorry, team. We never saw that coming," said Jason, relaying to me what Mr. Maximus told him. He also said that drones couldn't fly over Alphatoli; the tribes liked their privacy, and it was their one condition for helping us. Mr. Maximus said to stay safe until they came up with an alternative plan. It wouldn't take the Corps long to gather a team to intercept us on our way back. Or worse, they might follow us to Alphatoli.

Jason checked out my head injury, and I winced as he touched it. "That bast . . ." He gritted his teeth, nails biting into his palm. "I wish I'd broken his hand. There's a goose egg bump on your head."

"It's okay, Jason. I'm fine."

I rested my head on his shoulder, and in less than an hour, we reached Oshina's camp. It was an oasis in the middle of nowhere. I didn't think I could find this place a second time. The wide, flat ground hosted many orange cloth tents, which were pitched deep into the sand with ropes and stakes. Most of the tent openings flapped in the desert wind. There was a water well between the palm trees and desert plants. Given the general hustle-bustle, it seemed the people were busy with the work assigned to them. Children sprinted about, playing a game known only to them, screaming at each other in an unfamiliar language.

The hooded man with us led us to a group of five tents in yellow and black. In the middle of the arrangement was a medium-sized battery-operated heater for the chilly nights of the desert, along with an electricity generator.

The man looked at me and pointed to a large yellow tent. "You go there to clean yourself up, and the rest come with me."

I nodded and walked to the tent. A gorgeous dark-haired girl greeted me at the entrance and showed me a bowl of clean water. I washed up and went out, looking for Jason. I found him in a black tent, sitting next to Nizar. He smiled as I sat beside him.

A man offered me a cup of dark yellow liquid. I took a sip. It was coffee, as Nizar explained—and quite a bitter one. Not for me, yet the warmth soothed my parched throat. I finished it and was about to place the cup on the ground when the man surprised me by pouring more coffee into it.

I looked around; he was doing the same thing for Jason. I leaned to my friend and whispered, "Why did he pour coffee again? I don't want it anymore."

"Me too! I'm too embarrassed to tell him that. We shouldn't offend him."

I saw Nizar trying to control his laughter, but he gave in and burst into a chuckle. I looked at him curiously. "If you don't want the coffee, shake the cup," he explained. "If you keep it down, he'll pour you more."

Jason and I looked at each other and at the man. We shook our cups, and the man nodded, stepping out of the tent.

Jason turned to Nizar. "Yo, man, why didn't you tell us earlier?"

He chuckled, and so did the others in the tent. "I wanted to have a little fun!"

After a few minutes of sipping their coffee, the men left the tent with Nizar, and I stayed inside with Jason until the dark-haired girl came. She waved for me to follow her. "Oshina will see you now."

I looked at Jason, who was busy ogling the girl. I got up and stamped his foot hard on the pretense of adjusting my shoes. He yelped and looked at me.

I whispered sternly, "Lower your eyes."

"Do I smell jealousy?" He smirked at me.

I shrugged carelessly. "Nah . . . I'm just afraid the men will cut off your head and I'll be stuck here alone."

"Are you sure?"

"In fact, no. They might start with the parts in your pants."

His smile vanished at once, and I chuckled.

The girl escorted me to another tent. She had a whispered conversation with someone inside before allowing me to enter. "Do you have any Iméfonos or weapons?"

I shook my head, and she waved me into the tent. Taking a deep breath, I stepped inside, and there was Oshina, sitting on the ground.

CHAPTER 44

OSHINA GESTURED FOR ME TO come closer. I sat in front of her. We remained in silence until I ended it.

"Why me?" I whispered with bitterness.

"Why not you?" Her reply was quiet. "Fate imposes nothing on you. We all have free will. You have the choice to do what you want in your life. Perhaps if you had completed your crossing normally, someone else would have been assigned the mission."

Despondency enveloped me. *How much of my life is really my choice?*

I didn't choose to love Erick; fate and the dreams made me. I didn't choose to faint at the Crossing Gate; destiny made me. But was I wrong about that? Was everything really a choice? Did women have the right to choose in this kingdom? Societal expectations, my mother, my abusive father, my unhappy childhood—how much did they really affect my free will? Could I have made different decisions if I hadn't been so weak?

So Oshina is saying I'm not a victim of circumstances, but the victim of my stupid choices.

"What if I refuse the mission?"

"You can. But think about the consequences of doing so. Remember, not only you but many other people will suffer."

The consequences of doing so. I smiled sarcastically. Two choices; both were bitter and dangerous. If I said no to the mission, Mom would spend her life in prison, and I would spend mine fleeing from the law.

"So, do you accept the mission to save your country from the evil, unjust prince?"

He might be evil. But was he unjust? Wasn't injustice done to him from his childhood? Didn't the queen mother do the same to him? Still, none of that excused the injustices he'd committed against others. I looked at Oshina, thinking.

If the prophecies are real, yours and Nuri's, then how did she not see her own death? And even if they are real, why should I kill Thaddeus just because a prophecy said so? I am not an assassin, and I can't imagine myself burning someone in cold blood. The prophecy may simply be a wrong assumption.

But the damage has already been done. Thaddeus is already searching for me because of that prophecy. Not accepting the mission means death to a lot of my countrymen, who are already feeling the effects of war and injustice—especially the women. Elpax will never have peace while Thaddeus is in control. I wanted to help people by becoming a lawyer, which I can't do now with the Law Corps chasing me, but I can help the citizens another way. The way that I might have been fated to help them all along.

"I need more details about it."

She nodded once. "Fair enough. This is going to be a lot to take in, so you must listen carefully. Are you familiar with the term *parallel universe*?"

I nodded.

She poured coffee and handed me the cup. "There is a gap in Malum forest. A place where our universe meets with another one. From that gap, good folks traveled to our planet. Their name was *Takasha*."

Takasha! I remembered that word from the tome in the library that Mary and I read.

"After their planet was destroyed, the late King Giannis welcomed them. They found the comfort and peace they wanted in Elpax. They considered it their home, living amongst us until the Roman Empire started its attack against the kingdom. The Takasha fought hard alongside the Elpaxian army, but they had one problem; they lost their power when it rained, and the Empire started attacking Elpax in winter."

"Hold on a minute, Oshina." I put my cup on the ground. Her words reminded me of something familiar. *I, too, feel very weak whenever the rain touches my skin.* "The Takasha lost their power in the rain?"

She nodded, sipping her coffee. "On their planet, it never rained. Their bodies didn't adjust to rain on Earth. The three suns on their planet had always given their bodies strength and power, so overcast days that weakened the light from Earth's single sun affected them especially badly. Their hair color matched your original one, too."

My jaw dropped open like a boy who had just learned about making love. I always thought there was something wrong with my genes. Never in a million years did I think that other silver-haired people and I had other creature's genetics! *That's crazy!*

Oshina offered me some raisins and continued while chewing one, "Elpax was about to fall, and King Islabour had no choice but to make a secret agreement with Lord Xacuns to save the kingdom."

"Lord Xacuns?" I grabbed a piece of raisin.

"He was the lord of darkness and evil that brought destruction to the Takasha's world."

My eyes widened. How could King Islabour do that to the Takasha?

Oshina took a deep breath. "Lord Xacuns had one condition for helping king Islabour: the Takasha had to be expelled from the kingdom. But King Islabour knew better. The Takasha had become part of the community, so kicking them out would only generate a coup against him. He told Lord Xacuns that the only way he could agree was if he had the power to control feelings. Love and all noble emotions had to be forbidden from the kingdom, because in love, Elpaxians would stick together and get

344

rid of the King if he expelled the Takasha. However, King Islabour's wife, Queen Hera, told him that it would be a better choice if he forbade noble feelings from children and juveniles only."

"Why?" My eyes widened in curiosity.

"Child, if you don't plant the seeds of love in children, the tree of kindness and loyalty won't grow. Besides, no one who has tasted love can stand a feeling-less life, and Hera loved her husband. They married after a great love story. She didn't want to lose the ability to feel love."

So people in other lands grow up with emotions. Kids there can feel love for their parents, their friends . . . what a blessing King Islabour and Queen Hera took from us.

"Lord Xacuns agreed. He covered our land with a shield that prevented the warplanes and bombs from falling on our heads. The bombs bounced off course and hit the warplanes. But Caesar of the Roman Empire didn't give up. His spies advised him to attack the island from the lowest point at sea level, in Malum Forest. When the Empire's ships arrived, Lord Xacuns and his monsters attacked the Roman soldiers, killing every one that tried to set foot in Elpax. After Caesar lost thousands of his men, he signed the peace treaty with Elpax. Lord Xacuns established the Crossing Gate with his unknown high technology, and his shield remains over the kingdom to this day. The Takasha were thrown to another dimension, and the people who were alive when Takasha dwelled in Elpax had their memory wiped the first time they entered the Crossing Gate."

Wiped! That's why Mary's grandma didn't remember anything before her crossing! I recalled everything I'd read in the old books. Takasha, the lord . . . a whole period of Elpax's history had been turned into a mere story.

"But Oshina, why did Elpax keep using the gate?"

"Because Takasha can use telepathy to communicate with the half-Takashan like you. The government needs everyone to cross through the Crossing Gate three times before the age of twenty for its energy to disable this communication. Otherwise, Lord Xacuns will pull off his protective shield, and the Empire will strike again." She took a deep breath.

"Furthermore, if the Crossing Gate is damaged, and if the Takasha return to Elpax, then Lord Xacuns will withdraw from his agreement with Elpax.

"Now, Queen Hera used to visit the Akashic records. It is a place where all universal events in the past, present, and future are recorded. On her last visit, she saw that one of her descendants would make people suffer. She read the prophecy that darkness would spread through the kingdom, and a prince would die if a juvenile-adult burned him. She found a way to talk to Takasha and ask for help in case the prophecy came true."

"Did they agree? After what her husband did to them?"

"Yes. She was half-Takashan herself. The Takasha told her how the juvenile-adult—you—could fulfill the prophecy and save Elpax. Takasha has an artifact called the peace torch with them. You must lead them with the torch from the other dimension so they can enter the kingdom and fight side by side with the rebels to free the kingdom from the injustice that has befallen it."

A bitter smile spread across my face. A battle between good and evil, she said, but I knew by now that nobody was completely good or completely evil. In a war between the spotted and the pure, Crepito would likely win the fight.

"But why the torch?" I asked.

"The shield Lord Xacuns established to cover our land will also prevent any spark from starting a fire. He knew about this prophecy, too. He made sure that sin-spots would turn anyone to ashes if he or she tried to light a fire and bring Takasha back. Only the half-adult who carries the blood of Elpaxian and Takasha can light a fire without getting burned. She can start the fire from where the Takasha are staying and break the gate between the two worlds. This is the only way for the shield to vanish. The torch represents the unity of both parties against Lord Xacuns."

My hands covered my eyes. This was too much for me to handle . . . too much.

Oshina blinked at me. "This is group work, Lenora. You, the rebels, and Takasha will work together to save the kingdom. Your part is to open the gate between the two worlds so the shield will vanish and the Takasha can come in. We need Takasha, child."

"Forgive me, but how do you know all of this?"

"King Islabour left an old parchment explaining everything for his son, King Stavros, who told his wife."

"Queen Arianna," I whispered, and she nodded.

I narrowed my eyes, thinking. Her words connected all the strange things I'd seen before I collapsed in the gate . . . almost everything.

"Do you accept the mission?"

My eyes scanned her old face. Should I trust her? Everything she told me seemed . . . unreal. I couldn't stop myself from asking her this question. "Why should I believe you?"

Oshina got up and walked out of the tent. She called out for Hakaan and returned to sit patiently on the floor. A few moments later, a dark-haired man with intense black eyes entered the tent with a scarf over the lower part of his face. He bowed low to Oshina, then looked at me. It was the same man who had guided us to this encampment.

"Lenora, this is Hakaan, Nuri's son. Child, tell her about your mother."

He removed his scarf and ran his fingers through his shoulder-length hair. He was soft-spoken, and there was pain palpable in his eyes. "I was a child when this happened, but I remember it just like yesterday. My mother went to the palace for the first time at King Alexei's wedding. She read Prince Thaddeus's palm, but refused to foretell it. When she came back home, she told my father that she saw how the prince would die. She didn't explain much, and said she was afraid of the future. She was sure Thaddeus wouldn't leave her alone. And the same occurred.

"The very next day, he called for her. And my mother couldn't refuse. She went to the palace, knowing she'd have to proclaim the truth, or else sin-spots would appear on her body. She hoped the prince would show mercy, but she didn't expect it. And she didn't come back. My father went to ask about her, but he was told that she had finished her job and left.

"Father searched for her high and low, but she'd vanished. We lost all hope of finding her body when Oshina had a vision of my mother's death. My father rushed to the palace again, this time to see Queen Arianna and demand justice, threatening to launch a coup over his missing wife. The queen mother tried to take care of it, but Thaddeus had grown too powerful. He had turned many of the officials and wealthy to his side using false promises. Arianna asked us to wait until the juvenile from the prophecy appeared in a few years. She would have the power to kill Thaddeus and restore the lost peace."

His eyes glittered. "We have been waiting for you for so many years. I'll do anything to help you, at any cost. I need to avenge my mother's death at Thaddeus's hands."

I heard his story in deep silence, my heart wrenching for the child he had been when he lost his loving mother. I didn't trust Oshina completely, but I trusted Hakaan's story. There were years of pain in it. I could understand his hurt. My mom, too, was far away from me, suffering at the hands of Thaddeus.

Hakaan left the tent, and Oshina turned to face me. Her eyes met mine, waiting for an answer.

My people, the Elpaxians, were depending on me now.

I could do this. For them.

I took a deep breath. "I accept."

Oshina nodded, smiling for the first time. "Excellent. Now listen carefully. You have to get out of the kingdom and travel to Rome. A man named Antonio will meet you there to give you an important device before he escorts you to the Latina Republic Embassy in Rome. From there, our people will arrange for you to travel to Bolivia, where a man named Miguel will take you to Guatemala to meet with Zormesi, the Takasha's leader. Zormesi will tell you what you need to do, and how to break the gate between the two worlds. He is the only one who knows the exact details of your mission."

Then, she removed a small blue spherical bead from her dress's pocket and handed it to me. "Queen Arianna found this bead in the palace. It dates back to the time of the Takasha. It has the power to help you when needed. Lenora, if you ever need to escape from any place, use it. But it will only work outside the kingdom. I am not sure how it works, but you can test it once you are outside the borders."

I rolled the bead between my fingers, trying to get a feel for its power. Nothing. It was just a bead.

"Now, do you have any more questions?"

Lots more. But I asked the first one I had in mind. "The Crossing Gate was established to affect human bodies only, right?"

"Most likely."

"So is that why those who have Takasha genes feel dizzy in front of the gate?"

"Do they?" She seemed surprised. "Have you?"

I nodded, thinking. If my genes were the cause, then why I had crossed just fine to my second phase? Did the Crossing Gate activate something in my body during my second crossing that made me feel dizzy when I stepped inside it a third time?

"My daughter is also a silver-hair," said Oshina. "She never mentioned such a thing. She crossed normally to adulthood."

Thaddeus was a silver-hair, too. So for my theory to be right, he must also have felt dizzy when he crossed to adulthood. Oshina's words confirmed that some of us could cross just fine. Maybe Thaddeus was one of unaffected ones. Otherwise, he would have issued a decree to make everyone with silver hair use the wheelchair to cross.

Now that I thought of it, why didn't he order that everyone should use the wheelchair? In that case, he would make sure that the prophecy wouldn't come true. He must have had a reason for not doing that. The only one who could answer such a question was Thaddeus himself.

"Do you have more questions?" said Oshina.

I shook myself from those confusing thoughts and nodded. "Yes. I've been having some strange visions about the royals . . ." I didn't know how to formulate the question correctly.

349

She smiled beatifically. "In the hospital, a doctor implanted a device called a sitirá in your head, allowing you to receive the late king's memories. They were saved on a nano-chip secured in a special safe in the royal palace. I sent you certain scenes through a cellular network during your sleep, so you could better understand your mission."

Her words annoyed me. I understood the necessity of the mission. But playing with my mind was something else. It was like my thoughts weren't mine anymore. How could I tell the difference between reality and someone else's feelings, thoughts, and memories? I got up as she did. "You were spying on me, Oshina?" My jaw clenched hard enough to ache.

"No. You are only a receiver."

"Oshina," I snapped under my breath. "Get this thing out of my head, right now."

"It can't be removed without a doctor."

We gazed at each other for a while. I came closer and hissed, "Then promise not to send me any other visions, about the royals or *Caesar*, at any cost. I need your word, now."

She scowled darkly. "I never sent you visions about Caesar!"

Yes, I expected that. She'd said memories, but I saw Thaddeus talking to Caesar in real time. Plus, no way had she sent me a memory about Queen Arianna cheating on her husband. There must be an explanation for this case. Maybe the Takasha were helping me. Until I found who was behind it, I had to play on.

I shook my head. "Never mind. Just promise me."

"I promise," she said, then asked, "How's the good boy?"

I shook my head regretfully, expressing my silent pain. "He is fine. But the five-letter boy hurt me and disappeared."

"But he is *not* gone," Oshina said.

CHAPTER 45

I HELD MY BREATH. *IS it possible?*

"He loves you, even though he's made a terrible mistake," added Oshina.

My heart leaped at her words, even though my brain kept cautioning me. What did she mean that he didn't leave? Was Erick here? In the kingdom and looking for me? Then why did he disappear? Besides, Mr. William said Erick moved to the Roman Empire.

Hope emerged in me like a lone flower in an arid land, searching for the rain. But I couldn't trust emotions anymore.

Whenever I try to forget you, Erick, something brings you back into my memory. And whenever I want to drive emotions away from me, they quickly return as thoughts or dreams . . . or the words of an old woman.

Perhaps loneliness has forced me to hang on to the faint spectrum of your memory—kept my heart longing in painstaking eagerness. But no . . . no more, and not again. How long can my heart withstand the seesaw of emotions?

If I had one wish, I would want you and me to be two parallel lines, either on flat or spherical earth . . . never to meet.

A noise came from outside, and Jason dashed into the tent, his expression filled with urgency and stress. "Leen, quick, we have to leave. The Law Corps are on their way!"

I thanked Oshina and took the earbud from Jason. "Mr. Maximus?"

"I'm here. We're listening."

"Oshina said I have to leave for Rome."

Nizar came closer. "Sir," he said to Mr. Maximus, "in this case, we'll return to Zetikas through Mount Maroon."

"You mean to escape the kingdom across the Zetikas border?" I asked Nizar.

"That's right, Lenora," said Mr. Maximus through the device. "Legally."

I told Jason what they had just suggested, wanting to hear his opinion. In my view, it wasn't a solid plan. How could I travel legally out of the kingdom? Jason directed the question to Nizar.

"That's my job. I can forge her ID lines."

"Why didn't you do so when we arrived at the capital?" I asked. "Is it because of the dogs?"

"No. There's a dog-spray we could use, but now the search is more complicated at the capital's gate than at the kingdom's borders," answered Mr. Maximus.

"Leen," said Nizar, "I can forge your ID information and add it to the system, but I can't hack the border control system for over thirty seconds. Otherwise, they'll find my location first, then get to you. The capital system now gets notified even more frequently—every twenty-five seconds—which won't be enough for you to get inside. Thirty seconds, I can handle."

"Okay," I said. "Mr. Maximus, the car noise will draw attention to us. May I suggest using horses instead of the car to leave the desert?"

He was silent for a few seconds. "Copy that."

I turned to Oshina. "I need to rent some horses. And where is the nearest subway station? I need to plan for how long we'll be riding."

She nodded, and gave some of her tribe members instructions. I paid for her services handsomely. Hakaan insisted on coming with us—I agreed, and Mr. Maximus approved as well. I turned, looking for Jason, who was speaking with Oshina, and gestured for him to hurry. We mounted horses that could run fast over the sand dunes, and two other members of the tribe came along with us for protection.

We moved quickly in the dark. None of us spoke, as we didn't want the wind to carry our words. We only used hand signals and gestures. We rode south for an hour until we reached the Ourea Southern Mountains, near the Theia Electrical Glass Factory.

There was an insignificant town there, Orakros. We left our horses with the two tribesmen, and Nizar left his gun with them as well; he couldn't possibly risk going to the station with a weapon. We kept to the darkness of the footpaths. The town was small, with few shops. The glass factory was probably the only place of employment for the working-class in the area. I put forth my theory to Jason.

"No idea, Leen. This is the first time I've been to this place."

Nizar moved on to ask someone about the subway station, and the local directed us to it. Hakaan rushed into the station, then returned a few minutes later, taking off his scarf.

"Cover your head," he said, "so that you look like a normal townsman going home after a day's work. Try not to halt, no matter what you see."

Whatever I see? What am I going to see?

My heart began to hammer painfully. The past few months of my life had been most exhausting, but I looked down and put one foot in front of the other. As we approached the building, I gave Hakaan some money, and we waited by the entrance while he deposited the money to his metro account to pay for all of us using his ID lines. That was the safest way for all of us to get on the train; Nizar was wanted now after the soldiers scanned his ID in the desert. When Hakaan was done transferring the money, we

353

walked through the door, and I understood what he'd warned me about.

The Law Corps were walking around and monitoring people in the station. Some of them were scanning people's ID lines randomly. My picture was everywhere, labeled as the Most Wanted Traitor.

Each breath seemed difficult; this was worse than when I had bronchitis. My legs couldn't seem to move; the tremble in them caused my entire body to shake. Jason stood beside me and squeezed my hand.

"Breathe, Leen. You can do it. Don't look at the soldiers. Try to count the steps in your head and concentrate on them."

I sprinted down the stairs behind Nizar and Hakaan until we reached the iron ticket barrier. Hakaan scanned his ID lines four times, and the barrier lifted up, allowing us to cross over. I scurried to the train and jumped inside, trying not to fall down. I threw my body onto the first seat without saying a word. The guys followed me with frigid faces. When the train left the station, moving toward Gamotos, I let out a deep breath.

Nizar spoke after carefully listening to the new instructions from Mr. Maximus. "A vegetable truck will be waiting at the Gamotos metro station, and it will take us to the Zetikas borders via Mount Maroon. We have time now to rest up and eat before the next leg of our journey."

Four hours later, the train entered the Gamotos province, and we stepped out of the station. A medium-sized truck was waiting for us. All of us crept in, and the driver gave Jason a gun. Nizar banged on the side to signal the driver to start moving.

The smooth movement of the vehicle, along with the fresh breeze, lulled us into silence. Soon, I could hear the flow of water over rocks. Finally, we were nearing the Apollo river. As the truck drove onto the bridge to Delvoris province, it slowed down and jerked once. Then, it jerked again.

"Driver, what's happening?" asked Nizar via the partly closed partition.

"There are dark shadows ahead. It seems to be jeeps."

"Mr. Maximus, do you copy?" asked Nizar, but there was no answer. "Damn! It looks like we lost connection with him." He turned to me. "Stay calm. If they're Law Corps, there's no reason for them to search the truck."

I was going to remind him that they searched the hearse we were in earlier, but the driver yelled, "They're blocking the way! I have kids . . . they'll stop the truck for sure. You have to jump out."

"You're kidding!" yelled Jason. The driver's scared eyes were blazing at Jason through the rear-view mirror.

Jason spoke to the driver again. "Can you reverse?"

"No, sir, they'll be suspicious. I've slowed down, and all of you can jump. I'll switch on the front headlights along with the booster ones. For a split second, they'll be blinded and won't be able to see you escape. I'll pick you up after the security checkpoint."

I listened to the conversation with wide eyes, trying to come up with a better plan. But I couldn't think of anything before the driver yelled, "Get out! Now!"

The truck jerked once again. Hakaan slid open the side door, and the chilly wind slapped our faces. Jason's Iméfono fell to the truck's floor as I dashed into him, but we had no time to search for it. The truck slowed to a crawl at the side of the bridge railing.

"Hakaan, can you swim?" I asked him, and he nodded.

A voice boomed through a speaker, asking the driver to stop his truck. I took a deep breath and we all jumped into the dark river.

I felt like I couldn't breathe or hear anything as the cold water blasted my senses. It squeezed my lungs and nearly froze them. I barely remembered how to swim. Scissoring my legs one after the other, I tried to reach the surface, but the pressure in my lungs built up, and the need to breathe became imminent. Air escaped through my nose and mouth. The cold soon zapped the strength from my legs, and I was suffocating; the surface seemed so far away. I wanted to breathe. My lungs demanded air. Just one breath. One tiny breath . . . .

I was ready to give in just as I reached the surface, gasping frantically. I heard a nearby splash, and Jason appeared beside me. He put his finger on his lips, and I nodded, my mouth trembling.

We swam to the nearest column of the bridge. Nizar and Hakaan had reached the neighboring column. We clung there as the Law Corps stopped the truck and questioned the driver.

Jason pointed to the other side of the river, which was dense with trees. As quietly as possible, we swam to the edge, crawled silently out of the water, and hid behind the trunk of a big pine tree to see what was happening on the bridge. The Law Corps had already started their search inside the truck when a thought struck me like a bolt of lightning.

"Your Iméfono!" I whispered to Jason.

He smacked his forehead in anger. "Damn!"

I sighed. If the Law Corps found Jason's Iméfono in the truck, it wouldn't take Thaddeus long to connect the dots. I had entered my home in Zetikas; Jason was a wealthy who was arrested after my crossing and wasn't staying in Theirna like the others. Soon, Thaddeus would figure out I was in Delvoris, and Jason was helping me.

I didn't want my friend to get in trouble because of me. I whispered my fears to Jason, and his response was, "Thaddeus has nothing against me!"

During our argument, Nizar approached us. His face was dark with unfathomable emotion. "Get rid of this," he said to Jason, and pointed to the earbud. Jason threw it into the water and turned to Nizar questioningly. Something was seriously wrong.

"I just received a message from Noah. A spy told the Corps about the control room. The rebels had a few minutes to escape before the troops attacked them."

"My God!" I gasped. "Did anyone die?"

"No idea. But we're on our own until they gather themselves."

I looked again at the truck. The troops had handcuffed the driver and were escorting him to their armored car. Soon, they would lock down the entire area.

356

It was impossible to walk through Mount Maroon to the border of Zetikas; the journey would take forever. Plus, the Corps had already secured the highway between our spot and the street leading to Mount Maroon.

We were trapped.

CHAPTER 46

NIZAR BACKED AWAY FROM THE riverside, waving for us to follow. The wind slapped our wet clothes. I was shaking, huddled close to Jason, who wasn't faring any better than me. Looking aside, I glimpsed a light behind the trees.

"Guys." I ambled toward the light. The trees parted to reveal a few glasshouses, and one of them had the flashing light of an Ológramma.

"It's a village," said Nizar. "Wait here." He walked to the nearest house and knocked on the main door. I heard the melodic notification when a bald, plump man opened the door.

"Excuse me, sir. I need some dry clothes," said Nizar to the owner. "My friends and I fell in the river, and now we're about to freeze. I will pay you back when I can."

"No," answered the owner, and he was about to shut the door when Jason pulled out his gun and rushed toward him.

"We need dry clothes!" yelled Jason at the man's face.

I followed him at once and tugged his hand to stop him from such a criminal act. "Jason. No!"

"Be quiet!" His eyes burned with fire, and he looked at the man again, gesturing to him with his gun. "Go on."

The man lifted his hands in surrender and glanced at his wife, who was standing behind the door, her kids around her. "Get some dry clothes, Hana."

"Four sets. Flashlights and some money, too," demanded Jason.

I understood that he was beyond reasoning, and that the river had sucked all the patience from him, but it wasn't right to start threatening civilians. I gave him a stern look. I didn't want to be part of abusing or stealing anything from anyone. That wasn't how Mom had raised me.

I looked at the man to apologize, and I swallowed. The expression in his eyes said that he recognized me, but he kept mum. His wife came out with clothes and a flashlight. She looked confused, and tears glittered in her eyes. I came closer to pick up the stuff, wanting to make her feel better, since we both were women.

"I'm very sorry. We'll pay you back." I retreated to the nearby trees. The guys followed me, and we ran into the forest before they could call the Law Corps on us.

The clothes were big, but there was no room for complaining. Jason held his jacket to cover me while I was changing my wet pants and blouse.

"Jason, you shouldn't have done that."

He sighed. "You know I'll pay them back right away, and more than these clothes are even worth. Now, are you done?"

I knew that he had entered one of his dark moods, and wasn't thinking straight. My Jason would understand my words. It wasn't about the money; I was talking about the attitude. But I kept silent. It wasn't the right time to reproach him.

"Yes," I said, and I emerged from behind his jacket. We threw our old clothes on the ground and covered them with tree leaves. I didn't forget to grab the bead that Oshina had given me from my old pants and put it inside a pocket in the new ones.

"That man gave us only one jacket," said Jason, giving it to me. "Wear it. We can handle the cold."

Well, that was the advantage of being the only girl among boys. "No. Please give it to Hakaan. The boy has lived his entire life in the desert. I can handle the cold." Jason and Hakaan started to argue with me, but I refused to listen. Eventually, Hakaan accepted the coat.

As we moved fast through the quiet town, the threat of Thaddeus loomed larger and larger over me. If the house's owner kept quiet, I would be safe. But if he spoke, his evidence—along with Jason's Iméfono in the truck—would tell Thaddeus that I was alive, and that Jason was helping me. But I couldn't think about it any further. We had reached the edge of an impenetrable border.

The Malum Forest stood in front of us, daring us to cross it.

"We have to go inside," said Nizar. "We have no other option."

I swallowed, looking around. The entire forest was like a fortress, with tall pine trees growing close together. The air held a sense of danger, further compounded by the electronic signboard which had words of warning written on it:

Enter at your own risk.
Don't trust your senses.

That was all we needed after our harrowing journey and jumping into the river. Although I was disappointed and scared, I knew we had no choice. The Law Corps would be upon us any minute.

"We'll walk through to Hera Falls. I'll tell Noah to meet us there, if he can." Nizar tapped on his Iméfono.

We looked at each other. "You realize that no one ever gets out of this forest alive, right?" I said.

"Leen, we don't have a choice," said Jason, holding my hand.

I didn't know how to tell the boys about the monsters that used to live in the forest. I wasn't sure if they were still there, but if they were, then the

360

chances that we would end up being their dinner were very high. I couldn't risk the boys' lives.

I looked at them. "Well, if that's the case, I'm afraid you can't come with me."

"What the hell are you talking about?" exclaimed Jason. "You can't go inside by yourself!"

"Maybe I can't, but I should. Your safety is more important."

"She's got a point," agreed Nizar. "You are wealthy, and still have a chance to save your ass. Don't worry. I'll take care of her."

His subtle impudence hit a nerve in Jason, and they started arguing. Their voices rose. It seemed like they would come to blows soon.

"Enough!" I yelled. "I will lead. Follow me." I held the flashlight and took my first step between the trees.

We walked in single file, each move feeling like bricks were being dropped on the ground. The acoustics of the forest amplified even the slightest sound. Looking around, I swallowed hard. The entire place was daunting.

The forest consisted of four hundred hectares of land, covered with tall pine trees and shrouded in mist. A light dusting of snow, interspersed with shrubs and plants that I'd never seen before, covered the ground. The moon only cast its light on the forest floor when the wind gave its permission by sweeping the branches aside.

We sprinted for a few minutes, but it felt like hours. Something was zapping the energy from our legs. My mind felt as if it were filled with cotton. I couldn't seem to think straight. Voices echoed in my mind. Soon, I heard whispers of children speaking to me.

Eat the apple . . . eat the apple . . .

I halted, turning my head in all directions. "What was that? Who's there?"

"Leen, what's wrong?" asked Jason.

"I thought I heard someone talking to me."

He nodded. "I hear them too, but don't worry about it. Remember,

361

don't trust your senses. Just keep walking."

The voices seemed to follow me, until it felt like they'd imprinted the words in my mind. I looked around wildly. I saw a small bonsai-sized plant growing from the base of a tree with gnarled branches drooping to the ground. Small blue apples the size of berries hung from its twig-like branches. It looked like the image I had seen in the old book in the library.

"What if they're right, Jason? Remember the time when we went to the library? I saw a picture of this plant in that old tome. I think we should eat the fruit."

"What if they're poisonous?"

I didn't have an answer to that, but my instincts kept telling me to eat the apple, though my brain sided with Jason. I called Nizar and Hakaan over as I picked one from the plant.

"We should eat this apple," I said, and dropped it in my mouth.

"Leen, no!" The boys screamed together, but it was too late.

"You should all have one too," I said, plucking three more.

Jason took one. "I trust you."

Nizar refused it outright, giving me a pointed look. "I'm not dumb enough to eat anything growing in this place!"

Hakaan took one and ate it. "The word "Malum" in the forest's name could simply mean an apple. You wouldn't be scared of an apple forest, would you?"

But Nizar had another opinion. "It could be an evil apple."

I didn't argue with him, and we continued walking. The entire forest became shrouded in darkness as we approached its depths. I looked up, trying to locate the stars and determine our direction, but that seemed futile. It was supposed to be a full moon night, but the gloomy clouds cast angry shadows across the sky, obscuring the light completely, save for fleeting moments of moonshine.

The first thing that struck me as we reached the heart of the wooded area was the absolute silence; no birds, no insects, no night sounds. The wind had stopped moving the leaves, and the surrounding air shuddered with every lungful. It seemed the forest was holding its breath, waiting for us to leave. We hurried onward, eager to escape such a claustrophobic atmosphere. The fog became thicker and swirled around me. Evil had pervaded this area, right down to the soil we walked on. I thought about the ghosts of the thousands of imperial troops living in the forest, and what they would do if we disturbed their rest.

Nizar halted. "Guys, did you see that?"

I looked around and shook my head. He closed his eyes, trying to center his focus, and resumed walking. I felt his fear in every step, and it reverberated through me.

After two hours of brisk walking, I heard sea waves crashing over the rocks. A rush of exhilaration went through me. The air became lighter as we reached the edge of the tree line bordering the cliff. I could see the sky after hours of darkness. The full moon shone, greeting us with its soothing light. Comfort swept over us, and Nizar and Hakaan walked to the cliff edge. I approached more sedately, with Jason supporting me when my tired legs couldn't seem to take the load anymore.

I let go of his arm, walked to the edge, and peered down. The cliffs were massive—maybe over one hundred meters tall. It was the first time I had seen the sea in real life, which was sad, given that I'd grown up on an island.

Angry waves beat on the rocks at the bottom of the cliff, seemingly trying to break them down. I remembered an old rumor that the island was connected to Greece before an earthquake separated them. Large parts of the old land bridge sank into the sea, leaving behind this enormous cliff, which formed a natural barrier around the island. The lowest part of the cliff was a few kilometers ahead, but it was surrounded by an electrical fence, preventing anyone from entering or leaving the island illegally.

I watched the waves for a few minutes, getting lost in their hypnotic rhythm until Jason's words broke it.

"Well, this is the northern border, and we have to head west." Jason looked at his watch, calculating the sunrise time. "We have five hours to reach Hera Falls."

We didn't have water or food to sustain us, and exhaustion peeled the skin off our bodies. Yet, I knew we had to continue. Jason nodded to the other guys, and they worked out which direction was west.

Something flickered in the corner of my eye. I turned around to the space between the trees. For a second, I saw ripples in the air. I walked a few steps toward them. They disappeared, then reappeared, shimmering in the surrounding air.

I grabbed Jason's hand. "Jason, there's something there."

He focused for a while before the flickering light formed a rainbow—a real rainbow—glittering in the dark between the trees.

"Oh my God! What a pretty rainbow!" said Jason. "Guys, come see it."

"Where is it?" Nizar sneered.

"It's right there," I said, pointing at the rainbow.

"Now you're all hallucinating. I told you, you shouldn't have eaten those apples." Nizar walked backward, still talking to himself.

His words annoyed me. I ignored him and walked with Hakaan and Jason toward the rainbow between the trees. As I reached my hand out, trying to touch it, Hakaan's eyes widened with horror, looking behind me.

"Aman ya Rabbi," he said in a tremulous voice—it seemed to be a prayer.

I turned around to see what had scared him so much. And there, slicing through the fog, was an enormous translucent gray dog, with green eyes sparkling like emeralds. It was over ten times our size, nearly reaching the top of the trees.

If it decided to attack, there was no way we could defend ourselves.

CHAPTER 47

MY LEGS SHOOK WITH FEAR. I knew it! Those damn monsters were still living in the forest. I stood there, transfixed. The dog advanced, one paw in front of the other. Each of its legs was thicker than the trunk of the biggest tree in the forest. Its claws made a scraping noise on the ground, and we all cringed, taking a collective step back. Only Nizar seemed unaffected.

"Guys, what is it? Why are you moving back?"

Jason murmured, "Shut up, Nizar. There's a huge wolf behind you."

A wolf? I thought it was a gigantic dog.

"Jason." I swallowed hard. "This monster killed the Roman soldiers."

He turned to me, his face paling at once.

I spoke to Nizar as quietly as possible. "Don't move. There's an actual wolf."

"Oh, not you joining them in this prank too." He turned around and taunted, "You big wolf, I'm not scared of you. If you want me, come and get me!"

"Don't be stupid!" My eyes widened. "It's right behind you!"

The wolf moved a step closer to Nizar, and it howled. Goosebumps spread across my limbs at the evil sound. We moved back further, and the hound of hell advanced, growling. It set its sights on Nizar only.

"Jason, it seems the wolf can't see us."

Jason and Hakaan exchanged glances in an unspoken agreement. Hakaan raised his dagger and ran to the wolf's side. The wolf flicked its paw when Hakaan took a stab at it. He flew back and crashed into the bark of a tree.

Nizar looked nonplussed at the sight unfolding in front of him. He whispered, "The wolf . . . it's really there?"

The beast howled again, and its green eyes glittered in the darkness, looking at the ground. It seemed to be searching for the source of its injury.

I nodded and looked at the beast, whose snout was about to touch Nizar's shoulder. It took a sniff and opened its mouth wide. Two layers of sharp teeth gleamed in the night. Its massive tongue rolled out, and drool splattered the ground. The powerful stench of fumes arose—perhaps some kind of acid. I was sure the wolf would burn Nizar alive.

With no other way to escape inevitable death, Jason removed his gun, took aim, and shot at the hairy beast. Nizar leaped aside at once, and the bullets found their target. The wolf scampered away with a growl. I sank down on the ground right where I was standing, my legs shaking too much to support my weight.

"Hakaan, you okay?" yelled Jason.

Hakaan waved his hand in response and got up, dusting himself off. Jason looked at the ground for a moment, then gestured for Nizar to come closer. "Come and see for yourself."

I got up, and so did Nizar. We approached Jason, who was pointing at a liquid spot on the ground that smelled of chemicals. The definitive evidence that we hadn't been hallucinating.

"I told you!" I yelled at Nizar. "Eat. The. Damn. Apple!"

Nizar looked as if he was about to lose consciousness. He took the apple from me and swallowed it at once.

As I examined the spot, I noticed a white fragment protruding from the ground. It looked so out of place in that world of greenery. I dug it out and looked at the guys with trepidatious eyes. "Jason, is this a bone?"

All the boys looked up at once. Hakaan was the first to identify it. "Yes."

"Is it from an animal?"

We all looked at Hakaan, and gasped when he shook his head.

"Human?" I whispered.

"Yes." Hakaan grabbed the flashlight from me, casting light everywhere on the ground. A chill ran down my spine. There were countless skulls and bones scattered all over. "The Roman soldiers."

I gulped and stood there, thinking for a minute. Oshina never told me to keep what she told me a secret, so I had to speak up. "Guys, I have to tell you something. You all know that the Roman soldiers died here, but you never knew how." I turned to Hakaan. "Did you hear voices telling you to eat apples?" He nodded, and so did Nizar. "And those who ate the apples were immune. I think the monster couldn't see us for that one reason. It's a protection for the Elpaxians, so the monster would only attack the Roman soldiers."

"Seems plausible," agreed Jason.

I wet my lips. "I think we're now immune, so let's continue. Stick together no matter what, and I'll lead."

The four of us moved ahead on shaky limbs. I stopped for a few seconds, thinking about the rainbow. *Could it be the gate where the wolves come from?*

Hakaan's loud scream pulled me from my thoughts. I ran to him, and so did the other guys.

"Are you okay? What happened?"

"I don't know!" he yelled, holding his bleeding nose. "I bumped into . . . something."

I pointed the searchlight forward, and at an angle. Nothing. Jason kept his gun at the ready. I stretched my hand out and touched the air in front of me. My fingers hit something solid. Looking closely, I saw a wide frosted glass wall touching the skies and stretching into the forest.

"How come it's not reflecting the flashlight? Who built it?" I wondered.

Hakaan shook his head. No answers were forthcoming. I turned to Jason, who was exploring the wall a little further.

"How far does it go, Jason?" I asked.

"No idea. But it cuts our path. Now we have to walk around it to reach our destination."

"I hope it doesn't go right up to the highway, or else the troops will find us," Nizar mumbled.

We exchanged nervous looks and pressed on, walking alongside the wall. I flicked on the searchlight intermittently, trying to conserve its battery. Out of nowhere, I saw a huge structure on the other side of the wall. It looked imposing in my feeble flashlight beam.

It was something from ancient times. A lengthy set of stairs rose to reach an enormous pyramidal structure. It seemed to be carved from a single piece of gold, solid and precise, and was surrounded by trees, which protected it from the ravages of time. I recalled at once that I had seen it when I bumped my head at Mary's wedding. I had been standing in a rain forest, and this pyramid was behind me. I was holding a stick, not a flashlight, and an old man had been chanting, accompanied by the sound of drums in the air.

"I know this," remarked Jason. "It looks like the Tikal Temple. A holy place in Guatemala."

"Guatemala?" I narrowed my eyes, remembering that Oshina told me a few hours ago that I would be going there. I also read the same name in the ancient library book.

"Yes, it's in the Latina Republic," agreed Hakaan.

"Oh, my goodness! This wall is the gate between the two worlds!" I whispered in astonishment.

"What gate?" asked Nizar.

Before I could answer his question, a face popped up on the other side of the wall—a menacing one, with dark eyes outlined with black eyeliner. A silver bullring hung from the man's nose, and thick lips stretched to reveal a set of pointed teeth. He was dark-skinned with blue tattoos all over his body. Only a white loincloth maintained his dignity. The thick spear he carried added to the aura of danger, and he pointed it toward us. I didn't know if the spear could penetrate the glass wall, but none of the boys stopped to test its durability.

"Run!" Nizar shouted.

"Wait!" I yelled, but he ran as fast as he could, panic giving him wings. I knew that we'd reached safety—Oshina had told me about the gate, so I thought this person was harmless, but Nizar didn't know about all of that.

I ran after him with Jason and Hakaan, trying to find him and talk some sense to him, but he had vanished. My heart pounded as fast as my legs raced. The trees rushed by me; thorny shrubs scratched my limbs as I brushed by them. The soles of my feet trampled over the grass and small plants. I didn't know which direction we were headed. All I knew was that I needed to find him before we got lost for all eternity.

I slowed down once I'd covered quite a distance, and there he was on the ground, exhausted. I stopped, my lungs pulling in as much oxygen as I could, and my heart rate came down to a manageable rhythm. "Why the hell did you run? He's harmless!" I yelled.

But Nizar didn't answer. He simply dusted off his clothes with a shameful look on his face.

"You stay here," I said. "I'll go back and talk to the man."

"You don't have to." Jason gulped, pointing forward.

I followed his gaze. The glass wall was still present, a silent spectator to our sprint through the forest. We were back to where we'd started. The Tikal Temple was gleaming, staring back at us, daring us to run again. We had lost; there was no way out of this forest.

How was that possible? I couldn't imagine what trickery it could have played on us. Did the Earth stop rotating, or did we go around in a circle? Did the forest move, or was there something else going on here?

369

"Can anyone tell me who that man was?" asked Nizar.

"See, that's a confusing thing," answered Jason. "It looks like he is one of the Mayans, but they don't dress like that nowadays."

My eyes popped out. I knew it! Oshina said that Lord Xacuns threw the Takasha into another dimension, and she directed me to go to Guatemala to bring them back.

A movement to my right caused me to shine the light in that direction. "Who's there?" I asked, retreating in the opposite direction.

Behind the wall, a young Mayan girl was attired in a light brown top and a long skirt. A thick chest-plate made of leather hung in the middle of her chest. Heavy bead necklaces adorned her neck, and her headgear was elaborate and decorated with the feathers of her clan. She gestured for me to come closer. A large group of men stood behind her in silence.

It felt like I was in a hypnotic state. An unknown force made me approach her, ignoring the boys' objections. She put her palm on the glass wall, smiling at me. When I placed my hand to line up with hers, lightning flashed in the sky, bringing with it memories of my dream of Erick. I realized that the stormy night and the trees behind the girl were like the ones I had seen in that dream.

"Don't go any closer to her!" yelled Nizar.

But I ignored him. The girl whispered, *"Sikya fi'an, mastale sot un lu kannta."*

My breath quickened. I understood what she said, as it was my mother language too.

"Ek ma?" I asked, and a group of men approached to stand behind her. They had the same hair color as mine; they were barefoot and wearing long, white robes. The same group of men I saw in the library book.

They were the Takasha!

"Leen," the boys whispered. I turned to them, raising one hand to assure them that it was totally okay, and looked back at the Takasha.

The tallest one among them was the man I had a vision about when I hit my head at Mary's wedding. He bowed, and all of the men bowed low with him.

"Mi ka sen satori," he said.

I wet my lips with a sudden nervousness and replied, "Mi ka sen satori ... yari." *I am glad that we met, too.*

I asked about his name. His silver eyes glittered as he answered, "Zormesi."

So this was Zormesi, their leader!

"Why . . . why can I understand you?"

His skin glowed as he smiled, switching to Greek. "You are one of us. The energy in the Crossing Gate activated a dormant part of your brain and gave you this knowledge. I tried to warn you before. You need to run; they are coming after you."

The howling of the beast shook the forest again, and a bolt of lightning struck the top of the temple. It cast light on the glass wall, spreading to the sides, transforming the trees behind it into those typically seen in a rainforest. As the glow receded, the trees, the Takasha, and the Mayan girl disappeared, along with the wall itself.

Jason grabbed my arm and pulled me into a run. I knew by then that the glass wall was the Takasha's entrance to Elpax, right from Guatemala. I wished I could stay longer to ask the girl about what she said to me. Her exact words were, "Find your lover. Get us into the kingdom."

I had responded by asking, "Who?" Still, I knew that she could only be referring to one person: Erick. But why? What did all of this have to do with him? I didn't want to see him again. I didn't want anything to do with him. I didn't love him anymore. Or did I?

The faint light of dawn crept between the leaves. I looked at Jason's watch. It was 6:20 a.m.

We kept moving until the rush of the water over rocks reached our ears.

We'd found Hera Falls.

Just as we were about to step out from the trees' cover, a whirring sound arose. The trees' branches swayed sharply in the rising gale, and a giant gray helicopter appeared, with a spotlight circling the falls.

"Lenora Santos Evgenís." The announcement rang through the forest. "We know you're inside. There's no way out. We have surrounded you from all sides."

CHAPTER 48

I JUMPED WITH HORROR UPON hearing my name. It was the voice of my nightmares; the general who had investigated me in the hospital! How did this happen? How did he find me?

Jason pulled my arm at once, hiding me behind a tree trunk. We were so close to escaping, yet so far.

"Breathe, Leen," whispered Jason, though he was obviously freaking out more than me.

"How . . . how did they find me?"

"Looks like they found my Iméfono," said Jason. "And that man from the village must have called the troops."

"And the sound of your bullets confirmed it," said Hakaan. "They must have been waiting until we got closer to the forest's edge to catch us."

"But this is an Elikopata," said Nizar. "Soldiers are too scared to enter the forest, so they use this instead. It's a helicopter with a trawl and thermal cameras."

"Thermal cameras?"

Nizar had to yell so we could hear him. "Yeah, Leen, they get switched on when anyone with a normal body temperature walks in front of them. Once they capture the images, they'll know exactly where we are, shoot us with rubber bullets, and pick us up with the trawl. That's the reason the helicopter is flying so low."

"How do we circumvent the cameras?" I asked, my tone hushed. Silence fell upon us until Nizar spoke up. "Look, I have a crude idea. Not sure if it would work. It is kind of extreme. Look at the waterfall."

I looked. Water descended steeply over the cliff and rocks, falling at least twenty meters. At the base, there was a pool where the water collected, before it gathered speed and fell another thirty meters to the bottom to form the river. Long blades of grass grew on either side of the lower falls, while mossy stones surrounded the pool. Some of them were large and sharp.

Nizar pointed to the right. "We used to hide in the rundown electric company's building. It's close by, and their tunnel leads right to the edge of the forest. There's a small cave behind the waterfall, linked to the tunnels. In terms of getting there unnoticed, a normal body temperature will trigger the camera, but only when the Elikopata flies low."

He pointed at the grass. "We'll move as quietly as possible in the grass, dip ourselves into the water until we're about to freeze, then crawl up the rocks, keeping to the side of the pool until we reach the cave. It's dangerous, but since it's not full daylight, I think we can make it. We need to hide in the rocks when we hear the Elikopata and take dips in the freezing water when our bodies get warm. Climbing is hard work."

We looked at each other. We had no other choice.

"One more thing. Be careful. The waterfall stream might be strong," he added.

The moment the spotlight disappeared, we started crawling through the grass on our elbows and knees. There was no sound other than the fall of the water. The spray drenched us slowly, and the water was freezing. I thought I would become a block of ice if I went into the pool. I had to find my courage to jump at a moment's notice. My insides turned to dust at the thought of it. I tuned in to the memories of my family, and what Mom might be going through for me. I remembered Cordis and the way she had sacrificed her life for me. And my insides turned numb.

We had almost moved on to the rocks when the sound of the engine reached us again.

"Jump!" yelled Nizar. We all took a deep breath and leaped into the pool, sinking ourselves into its depths. The Elikopata made a slow turn, with the general again calling out my name. But the whirring of the mechanical bird didn't stop, and soon it faded away.

We got out of the pool, shivering and trembling. The wind was like so many whips hitting our bodies relentlessly. We climbed to a higher level. The Elikopata was coming back. We jumped and sank again, hoping it wouldn't detect us. We got out and climbed higher. We had a few more rocks to ascend to reach the cave's mouth. I was the first to climb to it. When I reached the top, I turned back around and gasped. Jason had lost his balance and slid down, scraping his arms, knees, and the front of his body as he fell into the pool.

"JASON!" I screamed, and the Elikopata's noise came back.

Hakaan followed me. "Get into the cave!" He helped Nizar inside before the spotlight could expose them both.

"We can't leave Jason!" I cried, but Hakaan pushed me into the cave. I scrambled inside, while Nizar yelled down at Jason.

"Jason, take a deep breath!"

Knowing that Jason was too bruised and battered to swim, I was terrified he would drown. I ran to the entrance again, but Hakaan caught me with all his strength.

"Get your hands off me!" I yelled, trying to wiggle away.

"You'll get us all killed!" he yelled, and tried to talk some sense to me. He was right, but my fear for Jason blinded me.

The spotlight came closer, the general repeating the same line over and over. Once it faded away, Hakaan let go of me with an apology, and I rushed out of the cave, sliding down into the pool. Nizar followed. We swam to where Jason's body was lying, his head in the water. I gulped, flipping him over. His face was severely pale, and he wasn't breathing. *Oh, no. No, no, no . . . this can't be happening. This can't be happening.*

"Help me or we'll lose him!" Nizar yelled. His words brought me back to reality fast. We pulled Jason's body to a grassy spot, and at once Nizar gave chest compressions to Jason. "Lean over and give him a rescue breath. Blow into his mouth. Hurry!"

I leaned in to obey, pouring all my will to live into Jason.

"He's not responding!" I said, panicking. Nizar didn't answer; he kept pushing on Jason's chest.

"Come back . . . Jason . . . come back to me . . ." my shaky voice hissed. I breathed into his mouth again, repeating the process, trying to give him some air unmixed with salty tears.

At last, Jason opened his eyes, spat the water out of his lungs, and started gasping.

"Welcome back, mate!" said Nizar.

Jason's confused eyes looked back and forth between my weeping face and Nizar's worried one. "What happened?" he asked in a weak voice.

"You drowned," said Nizar, helping him to stand up. Jason looked at me. I got to my feet, wrapping my hands around my shaking body. Jason approached me, but I stepped backward.

"This is it, Jason." My tone came out harsh. "I can't afford to lose you . . . I can't . . ."

I couldn't complete my sentence; tears choked me. Jason's hand grabbed my arm as he pulled me in for an unexpected hug. I embraced him tightly, and couldn't help but groan, terrified by the idea of losing him.

"Hush . . . it's okay, my love . . . I'm okay." He rubbed my back, trying to calm me down, but I couldn't stop my body from trembling. "You love me," he stated, smelling my hair.

I could only nod.

He knew it before I did. It surprised me how I felt about him. I always

376

thought I had nothing for Jason beyond friendship, that my heart was unusable while I was healing from the last disappointment of the only man I ever loved—until the moment I thought Jason would die. The pain I felt in my heart was stabbing. It went far beyond the agony of losing Erick.

"Okay, love birds, we have to keep on going," remarked Nizar. The Elikopata's sound increased yet again.

We helped Jason to swim through the pool to the rocks. Nizar pushed Jason from below, while Hakaan pulled him out before the Elikopata swept by again. We all rushed through the cave as fast as we could and plunged into the tunnels.

Slowly, we saw the light at the end of the shaft, and then the electric company appeared before us. The Elikopata approached again, making even wider circles.

They had trapped us.

"Damn! They aren't giving up!" said Nizar. "If we go out now, they'll see us. One of us has to stay back and divert its attention."

"I'll do it," came Hakaan's quick decision.

"No, you'll not!" I yelled. "We'll take a chance and run fast. If you stay here, they'll arrest or kill you. Thaddeus won't pardon you."

"Look, none of us can outrun the Elikopata. You know that. They'll use rubber bullets because they need you alive. They won't kill me."

"They will Eliminate you after the investigation!"

"We have no other option. You're important for this mission—for our kingdom's freedom."

My face wrinkled in pain. I heard the truth in his voice. This mission had taken too much from all of us, and it was still taking. My soul shattered into pieces at all their sacrifices. Their trust in me brought me down to my knees. Hakaan had proved his loyalty so many times over. He was a beautiful human being, and I would never see him again. Ever. That was our goodbye.

How many more would I have to say goodbye to?

"Don't cry, Lenora. Let me do this. For our mothers. For us."

I wiped my tears and stood up. "Hakaan. No one will be arrested or die today. I'll not allow it. Do you hear me?"

He remained silent, and I turned to Nizar. "Do we even have a car waiting for us?"

"Noah is close, but the troops surrounded the whole forest. And now with the Elikopata . . . I don't know what to do."

"I have an idea. It might work. I know you have a secured Iméfono. But what if there's a way to make the troops locate it?"

Nizar snapped his fingers. "I see your point." His smile widened, and he called Noah right away, planning the next step for a few minutes before he handed me the Iméfono again. "It's all yours."

"What will you do, Leen?" asked Jason.

"You'll see." I took a deep breath and hit the Law Corps emergency number. "This is Lenora Evgenís. Connect me with Prince Thaddeus Vasilas."

CHAPTER 49

JASON'S JAW DROPPED OPEN. MY muscles tensed, and I was about to fall on the ground. I squeezed his arm, fixing my eyes on the nearby Elikopata.

The soldier's stern voice shouted from the Iméfono. "Do you think this is a joke?"

"Not at all. I think the voice detector just confirmed my identity."

He was silent for a while. "What do you want from His Royal Highness?"

I could imagine the chaos my call was causing in the Secret Intelligence Headquarters. A vast room filled with high-ranking people listening to our conversation, collecting data, asking the soldier to stall me so they could find my location and arrest me. That was exactly what I wanted.

"I just want to talk to him." The idea that the soldier would actually connect me with Thaddeus terrified me. But he was the best person to ask for if I wanted to grab attention.

The soldier guffawed. "His Royal Highness doesn't negotiate with traitors."

"I have the right to talk to him. Now, if you think this a bad idea, then fine. I'll hang up."

"Wait!" he said. "I'll connect you."

That was fast! My breath accelerated. The ringing tone seemed to knock on my heart rather than my ear. I never thought he would do it; I just wanted to give them time to hack the Iméfono and find our *wrong* location—the one Noah had added to the Iméfono location settings—so we could get out of the forest. I hoped Thaddeus was asleep, or the Corps would locate us before the prince picked up. A loud noise blustered in my head as a cold, stern voice answered.

"Yes?"

My throat felt like it had turned into a massive cotton ball. I almost fainted as I recalled his appearance, his cold eyes. But I had to stay strong— for Mom and everyone else. I had absolutely nothing in mind to tell him— just my ragged breaths.

"Did you call to stay silent?"

I gulped. "No." I closed my eyes, trying to think of some wise words. "Mom . . . and I . . . We're not spies."

"You will receive a fair trial."

"Just like that of Mr. Barros?"

The Elikopata flew away, and I heard tons of cars driving down the nearby highway, rushing to the other end of the forest as I wanted.

"There's no way out, Miss Evgenís." Thaddeus's voice echoed across the sky. "Surrender, and I might show mercy to the rebels."

I almost dropped the Iméfono; the troops had just broadcasted our call to all of Elpax to show the rebels I was in a weak position. I knew that I couldn't be rude to Thaddeus, because he would punish them, and they had faith in me.

I looked at Nizar with confused eyes, but he nodded approvingly. "Do it. He bombed us anyway. Send them *the* message," he hissed. "Send *him* one too."

Anger, anguish, and grief fluctuated in my body as I recalled all that had happened to the people in Zetikas because of him. To me, and to my family. I had to deliver a message for both Thaddeus and the rebels in one line before the troops got the chance to cut off my speech.

I wanted him to know that we both knew about the prophecy, and that I would do whatever it took to free my homeland. I wanted the rebels to know that I was there for them, too.

I took a deep breath and spoke the next words with determination. "Your Royal Highness. We *love* our homeland, and what was taken by *sins* can only be restored by *fire*."

The troops cut off my call, but not as fast as they wanted to. My words echoed across the skies over the entire kingdom.

"Now!" yelled Nizar. Jason had to drag me forward, as my feet were shaking. We sprinted out of the tunnels and crossed the dirt road to reach the back of the electric company's one-story building. It was a derelict property, and I couldn't see any open doors.

"Come around the corner," said Nizar, pointing to a top window. "This window is open. Jason, get in and pull Leen inside. I'll give her a leg-up. Let's go."

I got in with their help. We ran through the building with Nizar guiding us, then exited through another window and ran down the winding road to reach Noah's car, which was waiting on the roadside, hiding behind the trees. A whisper of movement, and we were in.

Noah exclaimed, "Guys, you should have seen them! They drove like crazy to the forest's eastern borders. Man. Those were good words."

He kept his foot on the pedal, driving away from the wretched forest. I exchanged looks with Jason. He smiled at me, yet his eyes were worried.

"What's wrong?" I leaned in to whisper.

"What if Thaddeus gets mad for this? He might punish your mom even harder."

"She is his bargaining chip. He can't hurt her because I will make sure to burn him alive if he does. She's relatively safe at this point."

381

He nodded and shifted to look at Nizar. "What happened to the truck driver?"

"They released him," answered Noah.

"My Iméfono is in that truck," said Jason with a deep breath.

"I don't think they found it," said Noah. "If they did, you would be wanted by now. I'll get it to you. Don't worry."

I rested my head on Jason's shoulder. We settled down for the journey along the harbor line to reach the Elpax International Port, where the ship to my freedom was docked. The car's gentle movement lulled us into a deep slumber, and I felt rested by the time we reached the port and the flea market around it.

Noah parked the car in an alley, and Nizar stepped outside. "Follow me."

Keeping my head down, I walked with Jason behind Hakaan and Nizar, who led us to an old bakery in the flea market. Nizar knocked on the inner door twice, then paused for two seconds and knocked twice again. I looked at Jason and found him smiling at me. Eons ago, Jason used to knock on my house's door using his own unique code.

An old, brown-skinned woman opened a small window in the door. "Do you need fresh bread?"

"Bread upsets my stomach. Do you have cakes?" Nizar answered.

She opened the door and guided us to the back room. Nizar asked for the money that the man gave us, so I passed it to him.

"Let me do a little recon," said Nizar, nodding to Hakaan. "We'll be back in half an hour."

After he left with Hakaan, Jason embraced me. "I'm proud of you," he whispered. We were so close that I felt his heartbeat racing. "Leen?"

"Hmmm?"

"Please don't tell me that Nizar gave me those rescue breaths!"

I burst out laughing. "Well, we couldn't leave you to die!" I teased in between my giggles.

"Seriously, Leen!" He wiped his forehead, and I reached out for his hand, crossing his fingers through mine.

"No, it was me."

His smile widened. "I wish I'd been awake."

I blushed and didn't comment.

His expression turned solemn. "Would it be a sin if I couldn't stop loving you?" Pain showed in his eyes.

I was silent for a moment. "Here's the thing, Jason. I don't know how long this mission will take . . . maybe days, maybe years. I don't know if it will cost me my life, and it won't be fair to keep you hanging. You deserve a good girl, and I need you to promise that if anything happens—"

He cupped my face. "Nothing will happen to you."

"We don't know that." My eyes swam with tears.

His fingers reached up to wipe them. "Don't worry about me. Just focus on your mission, and I'll be there for you at every step. I'm coming with you to Rome. It's a very dangerous place."

"But you promised!" I exclaimed. "I couldn't handle it if anything happened to you. Please! Stay here . . . at home."

He shook his head. "I need time away from home anyway."

"Because of . . . your dad?"

Jason sighed bitterly. After a long silence, he said, "I found out he was cheating on Mom. He broke her heart."

Oh no! He was talking about Cordis! *Should I tell him the truth? But no . . . this isn't the right time . . . shut up, Leen, just shut up!*

I tried to say the wisest words I had in mind without hinting at anything suspicious. "Just . . . talk to him. Perhaps he can explain the—" I stopped talking when Noah came along with Jason's Iméfono and asked to speak with him alone. They walked to another room opposite mine. I could see them arguing with each other, but couldn't make out the words. Minutes later, Jason came back to me with a pale face.

"What happened?"

"Noah just told me that Mr. Maximus and most of the rebels are safe. Your message thrilled them, and they found the spy."

"Who was it?"

He paused. "This will be hard, Leen. I—"

"Just tell me. Don't sugarcoat it."

He inhaled a sharp breath. "It was Danira."

I froze.

"She made an agreement with the troops," said Jason. "Her mother in return for you. She's been telling them where they can find you each time we move. But she had no access to the full details, like the car's color or plate number, so her information wasn't accurate. We still don't know how the Corps followed her calls and found out the Cell's location. Did she say anything that caught your attention?"

I stood there, holding my stomach. It felt like I was about to tear in half from the pain. "She . . . she said that her mom was next in line to be burned in Inferos."

"Why didn't you tell me?"

"I don't know, Jason. I thought she was just upset. It never occurred to me that she might be a spy."

Jason took a deep breath. "The Corps raided the headquarters. Many of the rebels died in this attack, and Danira confessed while she was taking her last breath, asking for forgiveness." He kissed me on the forehead. "I'll give you a moment."

A hot tear made its way down my cheek. Danira had set me up, even though she knew I was trying my best to free not only her mother but the entire kingdom. How was I ever going to trust anyone again after that? I turned to the heavy flour sacks and punched them over and over until my hand turned red and was about to bleed.

Jason rushed over and stopped me from harming my hands any further. I embraced him while moaning and shedding hot tears that soaked his shirt.

"It's okay, baby . . . it's okay . . ." He pulled back to wipe my tears and leaned down to look me in the eyes. "I know this is very hard on you, to find yourself in a huge mess, and everything around you is falling apart.

People are lying to you, betraying you, and doing awful things to you while you're fighting to save them."

"I'm tired, Jason," I confessed. *I'm so damn tired.*

"I know, baby. But you're stronger than you think. Don't stop believing in yourself just because a few people betrayed you. You're so powerful. God! You even conquered my sealed heart!"

His joke made me laugh away my tears.

Jason smiled at me. "That's the spirit. You're strong. Don't let anyone tell you otherwise." He kissed my palm. "Come on, let's check these hands out."

While we waited for Nizar to come back, the nice old woman took care of Jason's bruises and my hands, and fed us some cakes and tea. At last, Nizar came back with Hakaan, carrying two small bags. He grabbed a piece of cake and started talking.

"The borders are closed to everyone. Only the wealthy, the merchants, diplomats, and legal affairs workers can travel. Barbed wires and Law Corps are guarding the entire harbor. In front of the passenger terminal, they're only checking the women."

"What do we do now?" asked Jason.

"The ship to the Empire is leaving in half an hour." He pointed at the bags. "Leen, inside are your clothes, a beard, a wig, and a mustache. Before you put on your disguise, coat your entire body with the dog-spray. There are dogs everywhere."

I sighed. This was it—the last leg of my journey. I'd be leaving my country as a wanted traitor, dressed as someone else. Jason squeezed my shoulder, and the boys left the room to give me privacy.

I coated every centimeter of my body with the dog-spray. Then, I put on the big black clothes. I found the 'magical' bead in the pocket of the pants we stole earlier and tucked it into my fresh ones. I put the wig on my head and called Jason to help me attach the beard and the mustache. He was wearing fresh clothes too.

"Nobody will make out it's you!" said Jason after he finished attaching the beard. "By the way, I just called Nicholas and transferred some money to him. He'll drive to Delvoris after we leave the country to pay back the man in the village."

"That's the Jason I know!" My smile widened.

"And my assistant, Yves, found the hospital where Alba is recovering. I called her. She says hi, by the way. She'll be transferred to Theirna this afternoon to receive the best treatment money can buy."

"Are you doing these things to please me, Jason?"

He heaved a sigh. "I know I have disappointed you, considering all the foolish things I did in the past. But I am trying to change. I've been struggling with a lot of things lately, Leen. There are things I've never told you about, and I want to make it up to both of us." He took a deep breath. "I hope that you'll forgive me. I—"

"Jason," I interrupted, putting my hand on his cheek. "There is nothing to forgive. We all learn from our mistakes."

The door opened, and the other guys came back. I smiled encouragingly at Jason. Nizar pointed at a wall. "Please stand there." He took a picture of me and started tapping on his Iméfono. "Now, you're a pharmacist who works for Mr. William Valemont. Your job is to buy medicine for his family. Your name is George Kristos. Repeat it a few times so it feels familiar to you."

He pasted thin black lines over my original ones. I looked askance at him. "These are forged lines of silicon," he explained. "They have an ID number that corresponds to the fake information that I'll enter into the governmental system."

I peered at them. The lines seemed good to me—the same color as real ones, not like the clumsy henna that Alba had painted on my wrist . . . or my eyeliner disaster.

"Now," said Noah, "I want you to read this sentence. Change your voice. Try to thicken it, so that Nizar can attach it to your information."

After we were finished with this complicated process, Nizar gave me the money for the ticket.

"Never walk together," Nizar said. "Jason, you go out of the bakery first, then after a few minutes, Leen will follow. Don't even look at her when she boards the ship. Even though you're not wanted, we don't want Thaddeus to get any doubts."

He turned to me. "Noah will follow you to tell me if the guards at the gate intend to scan your ID, so that I can handle the situation. He can't follow you inside the building because only travelers are allowed to pass, and we don't have enough money for him or Hakaan to go with you.

"Inside the hall, Jason, I want you to count the exact number of passengers before Leen in the passport issue line, so I can enter the information into the system on time. Remember, I only get thirty seconds for each try, and ten minutes between each attempt."

I shook the guys' hands, gratitude in my eyes. "You all did a good job. In fact, all the rebels have done an incredible job. I wouldn't be here without your help."

Nizar shook my hand. "We'll be waiting for you. Don't . . . please don't forget my—"

"Homeland." I completed the line from a famous childhood song. "Never."

Jason squeezed my fingers and left. I followed a few minutes later. We moved in the shadows of the stalls and stayed within the crowd of people. As we approached the port, my heartbeat sped up like the metro train. The passenger building seethed with Law Corps. My picture hung above in the void everywhere. An innocent Leen looked down at me with a not-so-innocent caption: Wanted for Treason.

Jason turned around casually and gave me a slight nod before walking ahead and disappearing in the throng. I stood in the line in front of the gate. Two men were patrolling, pacing back and forth. They held the leashes of huge black dogs, who were panting hard, sniffing and growling at anyone who walked through the gate. The pair of soldiers scrutinized the wrist of every woman entering the gate, scanning their ID even if she was wealthy. It was a scary sight that they weren't sparing any woman.

When it was my turn, the dog barked once and growled at me, showing its sharp incisors. It came closer to sniff me. Color faded from my face as my panic rose. A sharp-faced soldier, tall and well-built with a glint of cruelty in his eyes, came over to me. My throat dried up. He looked at me from top to bottom and pointed to my left wrist.

I held myself together on shaky legs, even when I had to brush by the dog. I extended my wrist and hoped it wouldn't tremble too much, praying that Nizar was watching me. The soldier looked at it for a few seconds, tilting it at different angles in the sunlight, and scanned it with his device.

CHAPTER 50

MY HEART WAS ABOUT TO stop, thinking it was the end. But the soldier permitted me to enter the gate. The forgery had worked!

I rushed into the spacious hall before he could change his mind, thanking God that Nizar had acted fast and entered my false ID information into the system on time. Stopping in the middle of the room, I looked around. The typical tone of the conversation among people in public was lost; they spoke in hushed voices. The soldiers were checking women without any concern for their dignity. They not only monitored the camera feeds but constantly pulled people from the queue and checked them. The women who protested had the butt of a rifle thrust into their stomach or against their heads. It was a gruesome sight.

Despite all my preparations, my lungs seized up. I couldn't seem to take a deep breath. I thought I would fall at any moment. Jason ambled closer to me, pretending to check the line he was supposed to stand in.

"Jason, I will faint," I hissed.

He looked in the opposite direction and whispered, "Calm down. You can do it." He bent down, pretending to tie his shoes. "Walk to the line in front of the office issuing passports."

I swallowed hard. "My legs are stuck. I can't move."

"You can. And you will. Think of your mom."

The clock in front of the office told me there were exactly twelve minutes before the gates would close. I had a small window of opportunity to escape Elpax. Standing in line, I noticed that other people were also panicking. Somehow, that made me calm.

I tilted my head to one side and pretended to look around. I whispered to Jason, who was standing behind me: "Five."

He pulled out his Iméfono and sent a text to Nizar that there were five people ahead of me. We waited for the line to move. When the woman in front of me was done, Jason sent a text to Nizar that it was time to hack. But the lady turned to the employee and shouted in a screechy voice, "You didn't issue the baby's passport!"

My chest tightened with panic. *What baby?* Nizar said that only adults could cross the borders, and . . .

The woman turned for a second, and I saw the baby she was holding in her hands, wrapped in a blanket of feathers. I gulped. She was wealthy.

If the employee issued a passport for the child, that meant I'd given the wrong count to Nizar. There'd been six people ahead of me, not five. I felt like I might have a stroke. Nizar said that he only got thirty seconds for each try and ten minutes between each attempt. *Now they will close the gate in less than five minutes.*

"He's only days old; I added his name to your passport," said the employee.

"The royal orders are explicit. Issue a passport for all."

"Ma'am, your child didn't cross through the Crossing Gate. He isn't a citizen and won't be allowed to enter the country again. Now, it's your choice to immigrate to the Empire, but . . ."

"You dumb girl! I want a passport for my child."

As a wealthy, the woman was used to getting her own way. She kept

390

arguing with the employee. I looked at the clock. The minute hand was getting closer to the finish point. I knew there would be no time for my turn. Now the other employees had joined in the fray, and the debate escalated. Fear choked the air from my lungs. I couldn't seem to think. The imaginary timer in my brain was ticking.

Tick . . . tick . . . tick . . .

The timer was sliding to zero at the speed of a rocket. Soon, I wouldn't have enough time to escape. I couldn't abort the mission. We had no idea if Thaddeus would close the borders again. And Nizar had entered my fake data, which would disappear in fifteen seconds from now unless I did something. Anything.

I was about to screech when Jason yelled, "Madam, the ship is about to go!"

At last, the employee put up her hand and said, "If you have a problem, give me back your passport and talk to the Law Corps." She pointed to a well-built, burly man with a machine gun in his hand.

The woman gulped and moved on. I knew I had only seconds left, and a glance at the clock told me that I was right. The employee waved for me to come closer, and with no time left, I extended my wrist. The employee scanned my ID lines.

A loud siren screech came from the machine.

The guards all looked at me. My breathing hastened.

They'd found me. This was the end.

I. Am. Dead.

The Corps from across the room gathered around my counter. We didn't have a Plan B. This was my only shot at freedom.

The employee started typing again on the screen. A soldier approached her. "Something wrong?"

"Looks like the system froze again." She looked at me. "I have to re-take your information."

The color drained from my face, and the air whooshed out of my lungs. Fear coiled around my chest like a python. It seemed like I would have a stroke, but the printer beeped and a piece of paper eased out. The employee looked at it, checking it carefully.

"Never mind. I have your information." She gave it to the soldier, who stamped it.

"Mr. Kristos," the soldier began. "During your stay out of the kingdom, you must keep away from fire. The punishment for bringing an accelerant or anything that might light a fire back to Elpax is direct Elimination. No trial."

I nodded again, trying to prevent the fear from showing on my face. What if he knew that I would bring the fire itself?

With trembling hands, I picked up my passport. I couldn't believe I was touching it. Jason nudged my back, and I headed to the line for the ticket counter, where the terrifying golden-red flag of the Modern Roman Empire shone on the screen.

"Mr. Kristos, where do you plan to travel?"

"Leuca city." I handed her the money and put my bag on the carousel. She printed the ticket. "Have a pleasant trip, sir."

I gave a slight nod and turned around, searching for Jason. He was standing in the far corner, arguing with one of the Corps, sweat covering his forehead. I wanted to go to him, but he glanced at me and raised an eyebrow in warning.

An army man in a complete military suit approached him with a group of Law Corps. "Mr. Jason Valemont, please come with me."

My chest tightened with worry. *What the hell is happening?*

"Mr. Valemont, you are hereby detained from traveling by order of His Royal Highness Prince Thaddeus. Please come with me."

Oh, my goodness! No, no, no. My heart leaped in my chest. My tear-filled eyes followed him as the men took him away. I didn't know what to do. Abandon the mission and be with Jason? Or go to the Empire?

"This is the last boarding call for the ship Minerva, trip number 90063 to Leuca city. All passengers are requested to proceed to gate twenty-four immediately."

If I backed out now, I would betray everyone's trust. I sighed and rushed to the gate, hoping I was making the right choice, convincing myself that Jason knew what to do. As a wealthy whose his father had connections everywhere, he would survive. After all, Thaddeus had nothing against him.

I followed the arrows and stood in line in front of a metal entryway. Eight Law Corps surrounded the frame. The security guard soon waved for me to pass through.

I took a deep breath and put my foot through the frame, at which point it made a disturbing ringing noise.

"Sir, remove your belt and any metal objects," said the guard. "Put them in the plastic basket."

I stepped back and took off my necklace, then stepped again into the frame. The same ringing sound occurred.

"Sir, please keep your arms and legs apart for a detailed examination." *Detailed examination! What is that?*

It was another obstacle that I hadn't considered. I did what the guard ordered. He approached me, carrying a long iron device, and coursed it along my right arm. As soon as the wand touched my right trouser pocket, the wand beeped with a frighteningly loud noise.

All at once, the soldiers pointed their guns at me with fierce concentration, pulling the hammers back. If a stray fly happened to pass at the moment, they would have shot madly.

I was trapped yet again.

CHAPTER 51

"SIR, EMPTY YOUR POCKETS SLOWLY!" the guard shouted, taking a wary step back.

I looked at them with fearful eyes. I didn't understand why my pocket would beep so loudly. I slowly put my hand into it, and my fingers found the damn bead.

I pulled it out and showed them. "It's a stupid bead!" I said with a thickening voice.

The guard looked at me with suspicion. "Sir, place it on the heavy metal detector."

I did. I was terrified, wondered if the machine would find something strange that would force me into imprisonment. But the man behind the screen stared at the bead from all angles, and eventually allowed me to take it, along with my necklace.

I rushed to the outer gate, the last line between me and freedom. A cold sea breeze greeted me with a salty scent as I made my way to the ship's passenger bridge. Another guard standing at the opposite end took my ticket, split it into two sections, and handed one to me.

As soon as I stepped on the ship, it began sailing away from my homeland.

I stood on the ship's deck, looking at Elpax as it became smaller and smaller. As I spotted the Statue of Victory—a sculpture of late Queen Hera holding a peacock—my eyes blurred with tears. What a journey to freedom it had been. It came at a steep price, with sacrifices and lost lives. I sighed with sorrow. One moment had turned my life upside-down and destroyed my happiness. I was alone—without family, friends, or the man I madly loved.

But I'll be back soon. I'll come with help and save my family, and everyone else.

I looked at my wrist and removed my fake lines, throwing them into the ocean. Where I was going, I wouldn't need them, half or full.

Half a line had caused so much chaos in the kingdom, including an outbreak of war. Was the other half line all I needed to live a normal life? But what was normal anymore? None of my problems were limited to halves. They came full-on.

I wasn't a juvenile anymore, though not yet an adult woman. Still, the rebels understood the significance of the half-line. I didn't get it until now.

I had always thought that missing half-line was problematic. But what about the advantages of the remaining one?

I exhaled. Maybe I would fail. Perhaps I would win. But that was life. Gray. Volatile. Unfair. Whatever had happened in the past, it wasn't too late to take responsibility.

Just like my five fingers weren't matched in size, adult people weren't all sinners or fully awful, wonderful in their own ways. I saw courage in a young brunette girl who never missed a chance to prove her loyalty. I saw the love of a mother who died instead of me, believing that the loss of her own soul could save millions of her homeland's people. I saw honest determination to fight for the right thing in the rebels, generosity in Hakaan, and respect in Jason.

I was lost in my thoughts when I heard the shuffling of feet next to me, and a tall woman stood by my side, wearing a black cloak with a hood.

"Leen, don't look at me. Look straight," she hissed.

I trained my eyes forward, absolutely stunned, trying to keep my head steady despite the emotions coursing through me.

"Mary!" I whispered her name like a prayer.

"Cabin thirty in one minute." With that, she walked away, toward the central part of the ship where the cabins were.

After counting to sixty, I looked around and sashayed down the same path as Mary. Nobody paid me the slightest attention.

I rushed to the aisle where all the cabins lay, searching for number thirty. I didn't know if I should knock or wait. I did neither. I pushed the door open and stepped inside. My eyes scanned the empty room, wondering where Mary had gone.

The door shut behind me. I turned around, and there she was. We hugged each other tightly, and tears flowed down both our faces.

"Mary, I've missed you so freaking much!"

She held my hand and walked me to the bed. "I missed you more." She looked at my wrist and smiled. "Sometimes, imperfection is perfection."

I smiled at her compliment. Her hand reached to my face, taking off my beard and mustache.

"Don't you like my new style?" I joked.

She giggled. "I'm so happy you're still the quirky Leen I know and love."

I shrugged. "I've lost everything else. What could be worse than what happened to me? Might as well keep my sense of humor."

Her face grew tense in an instant, and I understood that there was something more. "Leen, this will be hard on you. Promise me you'll handle it with wisdom."

I clasped my hands to my chest. "What are you talking about?"

"Just a few truths. First, Erick never left on your Crossing Day. He was standing with us when you went into the Crossing Gate. He moved to the side because he received a call from his sister telling him about a break-in at their home. He walked away from us while talking. After all, he thought it was for only a minute. What harm could it do? But your sister said that he had left because he was out of her sight. It was all a misunderstanding."

My face crumpled in pain at the revelation. Mary continued. "I yelled at you, telling you the truth that he didn't leave, but you refused to listen."

"I didn't hear you!" I yelled. "Inside the Crossing Gate, I could barely hear anything."

"Oh! Anyway, Erick came back when you fell down, and he was about to go inside the gate to save you when Jason punched him. Jason was screaming that it was all Erick's fault. He even threatened that if Erick ever spoke to you or even came near you, he would use his influence as a wealthy to kill him. They got into a terrible fight, so your Mom demanded that Erick leave. What else could he do? He left."

"What? Jason never told me that!" I exclaimed. I remembered Jason had bruises on his face when we met in the Maculosus neighborhood. At the time, I thought the Corps had hit him during the investigation.

"Why would he tell you? Leen, he loves you, and Erick was standing in his way. It was the best way to get rid of him," explained Mary bitterly. "I told Jason many times that he should tell you the truth about what really happened that day. I even threatened to tell you myself, and we had a fight. He stopped returning my calls, then blocked me. I didn't even know where he'd hidden you." Tears of anger and frustration sparkled in her eyes.

The truths she was revealing stunned me. Jason helped me so much throughout the entire journey. He even risked his life for me. How could he do that to me? How could he lie to me about the most important thing? I finally realized why he'd continually refused to let me call Mary and the twins, using lame excuses.

I couldn't even cry out my pain.

"That's not everything. There's something worse."

My eyes widened. What could be worse?

"I kept searching for you until the war started. Then, we were deported to Theirna. Jason's family was staying next to mine. I spoke to his mother, and she told me that Jason had stayed back in Zoiterra despite the war. That's when I realized that he'd hidden you there."

Mary took a deep breath and continued. "You gave your Iméfono to Erick before you crossed. That's how he found my number and called me later. He said that the necklace he gave you had a GPS system, and he could find where you were at all times. Leen. You must have seen him in Zoiterra."

I scowled, thinking back. Then it hit me—that tall guy with a hood. I'd seen him many times standing in front of the club. God! It really *had* been Erick!

I nodded, tears flowing down my cheeks.

"You had told Erick about a white car that was following you, and he was so scared of losing you that he gifted you the GPS necklace. Anyway, he had to go to Rome because his mother needed better medical treatment than Elpax could offer. When you fell in with the rebels, he texted Jason, sending him the coordinates of your hiding place in the Safe Cell with an online tracking link. He couldn't come back on that day because of his mother's illness, but he signed his name on the text. I suppose Jason didn't tell you that either."

I shook my head as the significance of her words struck me. Was all this why Jason asked for my forgiveness an hour ago?

"I moved from Theirna to the port while you were in the forest. Erick was sure that you'd leave the kingdom through the port. Otherwise, why would you come back to Zetikas again? And he turned out to be correct. I was just behind Jason in the line. He saw us, but it was too late. He was already moving with the Corps."

"Us?"

Mary squeezed my shoulder and added, "He had the chance to come back yesterday."

For a few seconds, I couldn't follow her words. She shifted her gaze to someone behind me. I turned around, and there was Erick, standing by the bathroom door. He was the same as I remembered—handsome as always—but there was fatigue in his eyes, as if life's battles had taken a toll on his soul.

We looked at each other.

He stepped closer, but I lifted a hand to stop him in his tracks. I needed a few minutes to process the wealth of information that Mary had unloaded on me. The strength of Jason's betrayal was too much, and I began to sob.

Erick sighed. "I tried to talk to you many times. Once, Jason saw me standing in front of the club, we had a fight. On the same night, he sent a gang of goons into my house. They smashed everything and hit Francine. They left a parting gift to let me know that Jason was responsible." He came closer, holding a silk handkerchief with J.V. embroidered in the corner. "Doesn't this belong to Jason?"

I couldn't breathe. The cruelty of my so-called best friend, what he'd subjected Erick and Mary to—it was just too much.

"Forgive me, Leen. But no one messes with the wealthy," he added with bitterness.

Mary squeezed my fingers and got up. "I'll leave you two alone. You've got a lot to discuss." She passed by Erick, patted his shoulder, and closed the door behind her.

Tears flowed down my face—for the friend lost, the lives sacrificed, and the innocence destroyed. Deliberate was the hand that had caused all that destruction. I was a half-adult who'd grown up before her time. Trust was the spark lost along the way.

I lifted my head and turned to Erick. I always thought that when we met again, I would scream at him—slap him, perhaps. I'd thought he was one of the major reasons for everything bad that had happened to me and my mom. But that wasn't the truth at all.

How can I digest it all in a few seconds?

I wiped my tears with my palms. "Take off your shirt," I ordered sharply.

He didn't hesitate—he simply reached for the buttons, all the while looking at me.

"Your pants, too." I wouldn't allow anyone to fool me again. I would make sure he wasn't lying before I talked to him.

He stood with his strong, well-built body, wearing only his underwear, waiting for my next order.

I pointed. "To the bathroom."

He sighed and walked in while I followed. Once we got inside, he turned to me. "Leen . . ."

"Hit the shower," I ordered, trying hard to ignore his sweet smell. What if he'd applied Crepito before coming?

Erick stepped into the running water and stood with hope glittering in his eyes. The water flowed down his body, and once I made sure he was clean and had no sin-spots, I began with my questions. "Did you deliberately leave me in the gate alone?"

Pain entered his expression before he answered. "No."

"A full answer, please."

"No, I didn't leave you deliberately when you were inside the Crossing Gate. I got an Iméfono call."

"Did you have an agreement with my mother to encourage me to cross?"

"No, I didn't have any agreement with her."

I waited to see if any sin-spots appeared. There were none.

I swallowed hard. "Was everything that Mary said true? Were you there for me the entire time?"

"Yes. I never left you, and I never will." His eyes became tender. "You mean the world to me. I would never hurt you."

I looked into his face. There was honesty there. I recalled all of our moments together, and all that we'd gone through. I hated to be cruel—to treat him like a criminal—but life had taught me to be wary. Trust would not be easy this time.

400

"Turn around." I wanted to be sure I hadn't missed a spot on his body, though I wasn't enthusiastic about asking him to take off his underwear.

He turned around with his arms open wide for me to check, then stood facing me, his shoulders slumped. He wasn't lying. He was telling the truth.

But how am I ever going to know if there is a waterproof version of Crepito available? He kissed me when I was still a juvenile, after all, so he should have at least one sin-spot somewhere. Unless he paid enough money to have it removed. I stared at him. The voice of my heart grew louder, scared of another disappointment.

New beginnings needed a pure white paper, where fresh lines could be drawn with a different pencil of a unique color—lines that didn't mourn with sadness and didn't cry from oppression.

"I want you to know that I love you," said Erick.

I blinked with bitterness. My heart sank in sorrow. How I'd longed to hear those words. How I'd longed to say the same words to him. But now . . . I wasn't sure anymore.

Erick stepped out of the shower and held my hands. "I love you, and I will always stand next to you."

I was quiet for a moment, looking into his tender gray eyes, battling to think clearly despite my jumping heart.

"You know, Erick. I drew the trajectory of my life in a fantasy world, but the facts slapped me repeatedly to wake me up from my ignorance. I need time to think. Trust is difficult for me now."

His eyes glittered with sadness. "I see you've changed."

"No, Erick, I didn't." I walked toward the door. "I grew up."

I slammed the door behind me with determination. *Not only will I take revenge on those who played games with me and hurt my family, but also on those who manipulated the people of my homeland.*

I am no longer a pawn, caught up in the cruel game of friends and foes alike. I am not innocent—just a girl wanting justice. Vengeance is mine now.

And I am ready to fight.

ACKNOWLEDGMENTS

Hey, awesome readers! So, here is the fun part. Thank you for reading my book! I hope you enjoyed this long journey, Elpax, and its honorable citizens as much as I enjoyed writing them. I would much appreciate your honest review wherever you purchased this book.

To my husband, M.T., I can't find the words to thank you for your constant encouragement over the past three years. Your support in finishing this hell of a book gave wings to my dreams! Honey, from the bottom of my heart, I love you.

To my LO, Rakan. Although you were five years old when I started writing, you understood how important this book was to me, and you gave me the space and peace of mind to finish it. You often wanted to hear a bedtime story about Leen, and with your big, hazel eyes staring at me, you asked, "When will you print the book, Mamy?" Well, darling, it's finally done!

To the strongest woman, I've ever met, my mother. She read the first rough draft and thought it was a good book that must be shared with the world. I can't thank you enough for your constant encouragement. You have always stood by me, for me.

To Dad, who used to buy my favorite magazine every Wednesday and thought that I would make a good writer one day. Just skip over the intimate scenes, Daddy!

To my sister, who read the story on her flight to Ireland until she got a headache! Thank you, Koki! I hope that your upcoming baby girl will be a strong, kick-ass feminist like Lenora!

To my brilliant brother, who shared his thoughtful ideas on improving things! Dude, you are my strength, and you will always have a special place in my heart.

To my friends and their incurable support. Sarah—you kept pushing me forward over the past two years when I was about to give up. I am so proud of you, the same way you are proud of me, and even more. You rock, girl!

Fouad—although you live far, far away from me, you never missed an opportunity to encourage me, even when you don't agree with me sometimes. You patiently answered all of my questions regarding one of the characters here. I can't thank you enough for that. And I can't thank you and Sarah enough for a stunning 15 years of friendship! You guys are part of my family, and you always will have a chunk of my heart.

To the amazing Shalini Gopal. A big, huge thanks for your extraordinary, thoughtful ideas. You helped me to craft the plot in a way that won't distract the reader. The multitude of emails we sent over the past four months was so much fun, and I will always be grateful for your support. I couldn't have done it without you!

To my awesome editor, Ellie Firestone. It was a pleasure to work with you—you made this story really shine!

To Eleni G, Despoina Kemeridou, author of FATED TO MEET YOU and Maria Vrisanaki, author of Θεοί και δαίμονες series. Thank you so much for your great help with the Greek words.

To my beta readers: T. M. Kohl, author of THE WARRIORS OF BHREA, F. A. Eid, Eliza Hubbard, Maddie, Gabby D'Aloia, Taylor Knight, Mamta Menon and Mohammad Hamad. You guys are the best! Thank you so much.

To Sara Oliver, a HUGE thank you for the stunning book cover.

To Niha Abid, thank you for the awesome synopsis! Although I wrote around 400 pages of a complicated story, I couldn't summarize it the way you have done it.

And finally, to Panos Kiamos, a Greek singer, who has probably never heard of me! Your songs gave me the perfect atmosphere to keep on writing!

GLOSSARY

- **Aetos Kaukasios**: was a gigantic eagle sent by Zeus to eat Prometheus liver. It was his punishment for stealing fire from the gods.
- **Akashic records**: are a compendium of all universal events.
- **Aman ya Rabbi**: Oh my god. (Arabic/Turkish)
- **Anílikoi "Ανήλικοι"**: underage. (Greek)
- **Argus Panoptes "Argos"**: was a hundred-eyed giant in Greek mythology. He was a servant of Hera.
- **Bonum vesperum**: Good evening (Latin)
- **Crepito**: cream. (Latin). It is the cream that hides the sin-spots from the naked eye.
- **Elikopata**: a helicopter with a trawl and thermal cameras.
- **Enílikos "Ενήλικος"**: grownup (Greek)
- **Gaul**: France.
- **Grigopaideia**: the internet encyclopedia in Elpax.
- **Iméfono**: is similar to a smartphon.
- **Maculosus**: macular, stained, spotted. (Latin)
- **Malum**: 1- an evil. 2- an apple. (Latin)
- **Parthéna "Παρθένα"**: virgin (Greek)
- **Post-Bellum "P.B."**: after the war (Latin)
- **Pulchra**: beautiful. (Latin). A nightclub.
- **Se agapó "Σε αγαπώ"**: I love you. (Greek)
- **Sitirá "Σιτηρά"**: cereals/ grain (Greek). It is a fictional implantable device.
- **Ológramma**: the holographic television.
- **Zorba "Zorba's Dance"**: is an instrumental by Greek composer Mikis Theodorakis.

THE VASILAS FAMILY TREE

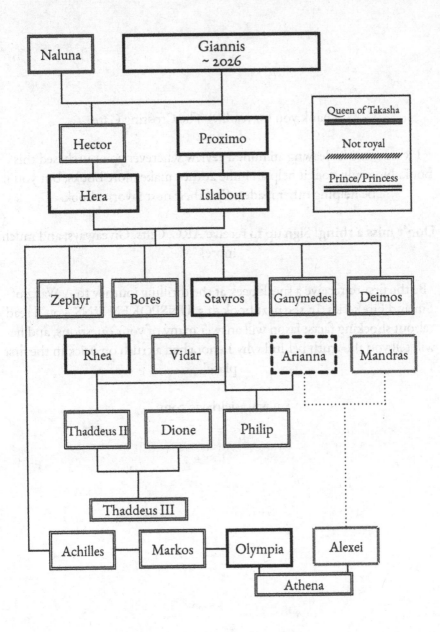

Naluna

Giannis
~ 2026

Queen of Takasha

Not royal

Prince/Princess

Hector

Proximo

Hera

Islabour

Zephyr

Bores

Stavros

Ganymedes

Deimos

Rhea

Vidar

Arianna

Mandras

Thaddeus II

Dione

Philip

Thaddeus III

Achilles

Markos

Olympia

Alexei

Athena

For you

Thank you for reading The Crossing Gate

Please consider leaving an honest review wherever you purchased this book. Not only does it help an indie author make more books, but you'll be helping other readers find their next favorite book.

Don't miss a thing! Sign up to receive ARC, Gifts, Giveaways, and much more!

Be the first to receive a sneak peek at the thrilling journey to A Waltz of Sin and Fire series. In the next book #1.5, UNSPOKEN SINS, you'll read about shocking facts; Jason will answer many of your questions, and he will tell you the truth behind why Lenora had a crush on Erick in the first place!

www.asielrlavie.com

About the author

Asiel R. Lavie holds a bachelor's degree in pharmacy, but writing stories was her passion since childhood. She's a book reviewer, a World Story Book contributor, co-admin, and an official Arabic translator for The World Story Book Young Adult Edition; a project was created by the Canadian author Edge O. Erne.

Aside from The Crossing Gate, Lavie is working hard to sign with an agent and bring her work to a larger audience and readers.

When she's not reading or writing, you might find her either in the garden playing with her kid or watching movies.

CPSIA information can be obtained
at www.ICGtesting.com
Printed in the USA
LVHW101053020122
707429LV00035B/471/J

9 781649 532664